THE GIRL IN THE SCRAPBOOK

Carolyn Ruffles

The Girl in the Scrapbook is an original work of fiction and, except in the case of historical fact, any resemblance to actual persons, living or dead, is purely coincidental.

To the amazing women in my family: my daughter, Alex; my mum, Sue; my sisters, Ros and Sara; finally, my grandmother, Nora, who was the inspiration for this novel.

'Man is a mystery. It needs to be unravelled, and if you spend your whole life unravelling it, don't say that you've wasted time.'   Fyodor Dostoyevsky.

'In every conceivable manner, the family is the link to our past, the bridge to our future.' Alex Haley.

'What greater thing is there for human souls than to find they are joined for life – to be with each other in silent, unspeakable memories.'   George Eliot.

PROLOGUE

I stand alone staring at the cold, starry sky. The night surrounds me and I can feel the silence humming, throbbing like a heartbeat. In this moment, I feel my smallness, my insignificance. I feel the world relentlessly spinning past as I watch, isolated, bereft, adrift.

I have always felt a sense of otherness, of not belonging; the person on the edge of the crowd; the gate crasher at the party. Maybe it stems from being an only child but I have never felt it more keenly than now, in this time of abandonment.

Overhead so many stars shine brightly, a glittering myriad, each in its place, each part of a greater pattern, the like of which is beyond human comprehension. Where is my place in life's pattern? I so want to be a part of it all but I cannot find my way. I am lost, disconnected, standing alone ...

Yet still I cling on, still I hope to become a piece in the puzzle, to fit in, to feel that comfort of belonging. I am like a loose thread hanging from an unknown tapestry, slowly unravelling...

CHAPTER ONE

Emily - November 2016

I t was quite a shock to see Molly again after such a long time. It had been five years; five years in which she had buried deep within her that yearning rootlessness, building up the surface layers, the perfect wife, the devoted mother. She had done a good job; she was content. This life, the present - it was enough, she told herself.

But it was not enough. She had sensed it for a while, a slow, insidious creeping, simmering, building, and now here was the proof. Molly was back.

Emily Conway sat staring into the fire on a grey November afternoon, a paperback book on her lap, struggling to subdue her restlessness. It seemed that, despite all the plans she had made with the confidence of youth, her life was not her own to act out as she wished after all. There were too many mysteries out there, waiting like dark intruders, waiting to send her tumbling down another, booby-trapped path and away from the route she had so carefully mapped out.

'Now what?' she had sighed, as Molly's face had shimmered into her consciousness. There was no answer. There were never any answers.

She knew her life was enviable. Upstairs, her beautiful, blond, blue-eyed cherub, her three-year-old son, Alex, was having his afternoon nap. Her husband Adam, a successful wine importer, was returning home after two days away this evening. When she had first met Adam, and described him to friends, they had laughed that he sounded far too good to be true, like an ad on a dating agency website. He was gorgeous; tall and athletic, blue-eyed, intelligent, great sense of humour. Tomorrow the two of them would be going to their favourite restaurant in the town of Bury St Edmunds where they lived to celebrate their fifth wedding anniversary. She had a lovely home on the outskirts of town – a four-bedroomed, modern brick house with a generous garden- and great friends who made her laugh on nights out and who didn't switch off when she proudly described Alex's latest achievement. So why did she feel that something was missing?

She exhaled heavily once more. 'I just feel that life is passing me by,' she said to Molly who sat silently beside her. 'I guess I need to do something or I'm going to go crazy.'

No reply. Molly never replied. Usually Emily spoke for her but today she could not think of a response and she lapsed back into a brooding silence. It was all about the secrets of the past, she knew. She had tried to unravel them before but with no success. Then she had tried to ignore them but that was not working either.

Of course, the first secret was her own. Emily knew it was not cool to have an imaginary friend. That was why she kept it to herself, strictly private and jealously guarded like a guilty pleasure. She never mentioned Molly to anyone- not even her husband.

It had not always been that way. Molly had been a presence in her life for as long as she could remember. One of her earliest memories was when she was lying in her new bed- she must have been about three or four years old- and she could not sleep. Her new duvet did not feel as worn and soft as her old one and the full moon was bathing her room in a ghostly glow. She had cried and cried to be allowed to go back downstairs with her parents but they would not be moved.

Her parents were like that. They were a couple in their forties who loved her dearly and believed the key to successful parenting was routine and consistency. Nothing could swerve them from the normal bedtime ritual- a cup of milk, a bedtime story and lights out at six o'clock. But it had not been dark at six o'clock and the excitement of her new bed had meant that she just could not settle. First her mum had come and spent some while reassuring her; then, when she started crying again, her dad had appeared, patient but a little stern to settle her once again. She remembered that by now it was getting dark and the light from the moon was casting scary shapes on her wall. She could not help it; she began to cry again, even more loudly than before. This time when her dad had stomped up the stairs he was cross but he did switch on the lamp on her bedside table for 'just a little while.'

That was when she first saw Molly- although she had not named her Molly then- sitting calmly at the foot of her bed, all dressed in black, watching her intently with sad, green eyes. Curiously, she had not been afraid; instead she felt strangely comforted, content to close her eyes and relax into sleep. When Emily awoke in the morning, the figure was gone but it reappeared regularly after that, so much so that Emily christened her Molly, after a character in one of her favourite stories.

Molly never spoke but Emily did not mind - she had always been a chatterbox and was happy to talk for both of them. Molly was a watchful, calming presence, with long, dark auburn hair and green eyes much like Emily's own. Always she was dressed the same, in an old-fashioned, plain, belted, black dress and sturdy black shoes. Mostly she sat with Emily in her bedroom but she had appeared once during a trip to the supermarket with her mum. Emily remembered it particularly because she had been trying to climb out of the trolley at the time to reach a very tempting display of chocolate bars while her mum had her back to her. Molly had stood in front of her, blocking the route and she had meekly sat back down. At least she had tried to but her leg had got stuck in the precariously rocking trolley and then a helpful shopper had alerted her mum. She had received a severe telling off, she remembered, and no sweets at all for a week. It was for her own good so she would know not to do it again, she was told.

Inevitably, she soon started mentioning Molly in the course of conversation at home, imbuing her with all sorts of wisdoms, completely fabricated by Emily herself, to help her get her own way. 'Molly said that you should take me to the park' or 'Molly said you should buy me some sweeties' were two of her favourites. Her mum and dad had looked at each other across the breakfast table when she had first tried it. There was no Molly, as far as they knew, at the nursery Emily attended every morning.

'Who is Molly, darling?' her mum had asked.

Emily had wrinkled her face into a frown. How could she describe Molly? 'She ... she's ... my ... friend,' she replied slowly and then with a bit more conviction. 'Friend.'

'Yes, I realise that, darling,' her mum had said patiently. 'But where from? Does Molly go to nursery?'

Emily pondered the question. No, she had never seen her at nursery. She shook her head.

'Then who is she? Where did you meet her?'

She thought it best to keep quiet about the supermarket. 'My room,' she had admitted cautiously.

Emily remembered that her parents had been understandably alarmed at this point and asked her all sorts of questions to which she really did not know the answers. Eventually they had given up but told her that she was to tell them whenever she next saw Molly.

It just so happened that it was the very same evening when Molly reappeared and Emily had eagerly called her parents. They had come charging up the stairs and switched on the light.

'Where? Where is she?' Dad had demanded as he searched the room, even peering behind the curtains.

Emily was frightened by their panic. She had pointed, wide-eyed, to where Molly was sitting, as usual, at the bottom of her bed.

'There's no one there, darling.' Her mum had instantly relaxed and smiled across at her husband who at this point was on all fours peering under the bed. 'It's just your imagination.'

'What's imag ... imag ...?' It was a difficult word for a four-year-old to get her tongue around.

'It means she's not real. She's someone you've made up,' Mum had replied, giving her a hug. 'It's nothing to worry about, sweetheart. Lots of children have imaginary friends, especially when they have no brothers and sisters of their own. It's good that you have Molly to play with.'

Emily was confused. Did that mean they could not see her? *Why* couldn't they see her when she was right there? 'Look, she's here,' she insisted, pointing again.

'We know,' Mum had reassured her. 'Now it's time for you to lie back down and go to sleep. Say goodnight to Molly.'

'Goodnight, Molly,' Emily had repeated obediently.

From that point on, Emily became used to hearing Molly referred to as 'Emily's imaginary friend' when her parents were talking to their own friends, her two aunts and, when she started school, her teachers. The other children were curious and Emily delighted in inventing a catalogue of tales recalling adventures she had undertaken with Molly. This afforded her a pleasing celebrity status amongst her peers and the stories became more and more far-fetched. One day, Molly had taken her for a ride on her broomstick to see the Queen, she was casually informing a crowd of open-mouthed, six-year-old girls in the playground, when her stardom had been shattered by supercool seven-year-old, Jordan Smith.

'You're a liar,' he accused with a sneer. 'No one likes liars.'

Emily was mortified. 'No, I'm not,' she had retorted angrily but the damage had been done. She had seen the scepticism provoked by Jordan's words and soon learnt how easy it was to fall from grace. Her friends had drifted away and she had later been forced to admit that, whilst Molly was real, the stories were made up. Sadly though, no one really believed in Molly herself anymore and Emily quickly realised it was best not to talk about her.

It was fine at home though, at least at the beginning. Her parents had googled 'childhood imaginary friends' and then avidly devoured all the advice written by psychologists on the subject. They learnt it was best to acknowledge Molly in all their dealings with their daughter but also to encourage Emily to take responsibility for her own actions. When she said that it was Molly who had made a mess in her bedroom, Emily was told that it was *her* bedroom and she would need to tidy it. When she had tried to claim that Molly had borrowed Mum's new nail varnish to paint her dolls' finger and toenails and spilt most of it on the carpet, it was Emily who was punished. 'You should have told Molly that it's wrong to touch Mummy's things without asking,' her dad had said. At this point, Emily had begun to wonder if there was any point in having an imaginary friend.

However, throughout her childhood, Molly had always appeared at difficult moments: when she had fallen out with her best friend Jade; when she had split up with her first boyfriend at the age of fourteen; when she was facing a physics exam (Emily just could not get her head around physics whereas all the other subjects came easily to her); her first night away from home at university when everyone else seemed to belong and she did not. She was always just there for Emily to talk to, listening but never speaking, an oasis of calm.

Of course, by now, Emily had realised that Molly could not be real - that she was just a figment of her imagination. She kept expecting to outgrow her, as all the experts said she would, but it had never happened. It was just as well because she did not know how she would have coped, without Molly, when her world fell apart.

Emily was nineteen and in her second year reading English literature at the University of Kent at Canterbury. Life was good. She was popular and had a great group of friends. People were drawn to her lively personality and mischievous sense of humour. She was also, unlike so many of her girlfriends, happy with her looks and confident in her own skin. She knew she was lucky, having been blessed with a slim build, strawberry blond curls which tumbled around her shoulders, unusual green eyes and a killer smile. Her friend Ellie had said that when Emily switched on her smile, boys swarmed around her like bees around a honeypot. Indeed, recently she had started going out with the best-looking boy on campus, a third-year social sciences student named Connor, much to the envy of her friends. What was more, she thrived on the academic side of university life. She loved her course – she had always been a passionate reader – and, at the moment, was on course for a first-class degree. As yet she had not completely decided upon a career but one of her friends was studying journalism and Emily was drawn to the idea of seeking out stories and writing them for a living. She had not told her parents but she had already been researching journalism courses. This was typical of Emily, her friends all agreed. She had always been a planner, someone who liked to be in control of things. In the meantime, she was studying conscientiously, partying when she felt like it and generally having a good time.

It was a bright, warm day in early May which saw Emily returning to campus after a reading week reluctantly spent back at home with her parents. She had been desperate to get back to Canterbury, mostly because she hated being apart from Connor, but also because the buzz of university life had made time at home seem staid and boring. All of her school friends were also away, studying assorted subjects in various educational establishments around the country, and her parents, now in their sixties and retired, were so pleased to see her it felt claustrophobic. Her mum kept trying to feed her massive portions of all her favourite meals whilst her dad had kept reminding her of different things she had said or done when she was younger. It was exhausting. On the train on her way back, she had texted Connor, 'Made my escape. Remind me not to get old. Cu later xx'.

Surprisingly, but to her delight, Connor was waiting for at the station. She did not immediately notice that he was not alone. He stood, white-faced and unsmiling, as she leapt off the train and flung herself into his arms. 'Wow. I didn't expect you to meet me. You must have missed me.'

He hugged her briefly, a little awkwardly and then stood back. 'Em ... there's been an accident ... I'm so sorry ... it's your parents.'

Time seemed to stand still. She stared at him in horror while the world as she knew it tilted away from her.

'What do you mean? Are they ok?'

Inside her brain was screaming; she felt as if she was falling, spinning out of control.

'I ...,' Connor turned helplessly to the two police officers who were standing beside him.

'Let's get you into the car,' a young policewoman said kindly, putting her arm around Emily.

She was ushered by the officer off the station platform and steered into the rear seat of a waiting panda car. Connor remained outside the vehicle as the full extent of the tragedy was divulged. Both her parents had been killed in a car accident which had occurred shortly after Emily had left home, probably on their return journey from having delivered her to the local station. The officers would drive her to the hospital morgue where, if she felt able, she would identify the bodies. They were very sorry for her loss.

The screaming in her head went on and on but Emily sat in silence, ashen-faced. Her first conscious feelings were of guilt. It was her fault. The accident would not have happened had they not driven her to the station. What was worse though was the fact that she had made no secret of her boredom during that last final week she had spent with them. She had sat for most of the time in her room, supposedly studying but actually spending a significant amount of time on social media, bemoaning the fact that she had let her parents talk her into spending the week at home. They had made such a fuss of her and she had acted like a spoilt child. When they hugged her goodbye, her only thoughts were for herself – relief that she was going away and embarrassment at their displays of affection in public.

She shook her head. It could not be true; this was not happening. It was a nightmare – a Kafkaesque imagining conjured up by her own insecurities. She began to shiver uncontrollably and the female police officer sent her male colleague after some sugary coffee. 'It's the shock,' she said. Her tone was sympathetic and grated on Emily's nerves like a knife scraping across a plate. Everything about this was just wrong. She should not be here, not in this car, not being told to drink coffee, which she detested, not listening to this, not while people were rushing past, on their phones, racing to catch the next train, going about their normal business. She should not be sitting there whilst her boyfriend of just a few weeks looked on with pitiful eyes, unsure of his role in this unfolding drama. She needed to get out, escape, go back to the way things were and she reached desperately for the door.

'NO!' she heard someone shout over and over. It was some time before she realised the voice was hers.

CHAPTER 2

Norah -June 1ˢᵗ 1922

It had been the best birthday ever! Norah stared out of the window at the fields of wheat, lush and green, as she reflected on the day's events so far.

Firstly, she had received her present - her very own box brownie camera and a beautiful scrapbook in which to stick all her photographs. Her friends would be so jealous when she told them at school on Monday.

Then, this year, it had just so happened that her twelfth birthday had coincided with the Great Chalkham horse and pony show. Rusty, her beautiful bay pony, had seemed to know that today was a special occasion and had not put a foot wrong. Daddy had taken lots of photographs of them in action and then of them both resplendent wearing four red rosettes for their four wins- every class they had entered. Mummy and Daddy had been so proud of her. Lots of people had praised her riding skills and even Arthur, the new stable lad who seemed a lot more impressed by the horses than their riders, had told her she had good hands.

Now she had changed out of her riding breeches and boots into her best cotton frock embroidered with green ribbon which Mummy said matched the unusual colour of her eyes and was waiting impatiently for her parents to join her for her birthday tea. She had already been to the kitchen to see what delights Mrs Morris the cook was preparing but had been immediately shooed out of the way.

'Out you go this instant!' Mrs Morris had exclaimed. 'You're not to see the cake until the candles are lit.' Then her face had softened and she had smiled. 'My, you do look lovely, dearie. Quite the young lady. You are growing up so fast.'

Norah had to admit that she was pleased with her appearance in the new dress. It suited her dark auburn hair, brushed and glowing in long tresses down her back, as well as her eyes. She had twirled in front of the mirror and admired the way it fitted her slim, boyish frame. She *had* hoped desperately that she would start developing breasts by her twelfth birthday, like her friend Sybil who had a pair that were the envy of all the young girls in the village, but so far they did not appear to be forthcoming. Thrusting her chest out at the mirror made no difference and she resolved to put that minor disappointment aside. She was looking her best and that was what mattered.

'Hello, young lady. What have you done with my daughter, scruffy, little Nolly?' She turned to see her father, tall and handsome in his dark suit, striding towards her, wearing a broad grin. 'Oh, my goodness!' He feigned surprise. 'It is Nolly ... but she's all grown up! You look lovely, darling.' He clasped her in a brief hug and then spun her around. 'Now let's have a proper look at you. Gorgeous- just like your mother.'

'Where is Mummy? I'm starving!'

Her father's face clouded for an instant. 'I'm sorry darling but Mummy isn't feeling too well. All that excitement at the show has taken it out of her. She's in bed resting.'

'What again?' Norah frowned. Her mother had been really quite poorly for the last few months and had taken to her bed on a number of occasions. 'But it's my birthday!'

'I know darling and she's very sorry but she's just not up to it. She wants me to take lots of pictures of you with your camera and said to be sure to go up and see her later so she can see you in your dress. Now I think it's time for a special someone to have her birthday tea.'

George Dunn escorted his daughter on his arm through to the dining room where Mrs Morris and the maid, Elsie, were just putting the final touches to the feast laid out on the immaculate, starched white tablecloth.

'Oh, it all looks lovely, Mrs Morris. Thank you,' exclaimed Norah, eagerly taking her seat and surveying the spread. There were ham, cheese and egg sandwiches, sausage rolls and meat pasties and a whole array of beautifully iced, dainty cakes.

Her father said grace as he always did and then made a fuss of her throughout the meal as they helped themselves to the food. Norah always had a good appetite and tucked in appreciatively. When they had sampled most of what was on offer, Mrs Morris and Elsie reappeared with an enormous white birthday cake, tied with a green ribbon to match the ribbon on her dress and alight with twelve candles. They all sang 'Happy birthday to you' and then Norah blew the candles out with gusto.

'I've made a wish that every birthday is as good as this one. It really has been the best ever,' she sighed happily as Mrs Morris handed her a piece of cake.

George smiled as he watched his daughter. He too had made a wish but it was not one he could share with her.

Later that evening Norah had gone upstairs to see her mother. The room was dark so she took a candle and placed it on the dresser beside the bed. Her mother was asleep and her face seemed so pale and drawn that Norah felt a jolt of anxiety. Then her eyelids fluttered and she smiled.

'Norah, darling,' she whispered. 'Help me up so I can look at you properly.' Norah put her right arm around her mother and helped lift her into an upright position. She noticed for the first time how frail she was, how she seemed to be just bones beneath her nightdress.

'Oh,' she breathed after a lengthy appraisal of her daughter. 'You look so beautiful.' Her eyes filled with tears.

'Why are you crying, Mummy?' Norah asked.

'They're happy tears, darling. Take no notice. It's a mummy thing. You'll understand one day when you have a daughter. It's because you look like an angel. Now give me a kiss before you go.'

Norah hugged her mother protectively as she kissed her pale cheek. 'Goodnight, Mummy. I hope you feel better in the morning.'

However, when morning dawned, clear, bright and golden, Norah's mother failed to appear at breakfast and remained in bed all day. This was to set the tone for the days and weeks to come. Sometimes, when it was neither too warm or too cold, she was helped into a chair to sit outside in her beloved rose garden and Norah would sit with her for a time until she became bored and restless. However, most days she was too ill to surface and the servants spoke of her condition in hushed tones. Norah herself firmly refused to believe anything other than this was a temporary illness and her mother would soon be back to normal. She prefaced many conversations with her father with the words, 'When Mummy's better,' and he started to do the same.

Meanwhile the thrum of village life continued its gentle sway. The mill continued to turn and grind; every day the miller's boy, Johnnie Mason, steered his pony and trap through the village, past the Dunn's farm and out to the village of Little Chalkham with his bread deliveries; Charles Mallon, the thatcher, took advantage of the fine summer weather and was to be seen on the roof of the Emersons' house which had been badly damaged by a fire in the spring; men and children were out in the fields, helping with the harvest. There was a solidity and a permanence in the sheer predictability of village life which Norah found comforting and reassuring.

Surely nothing bad could happen when everyone else was going about their business as normal.

Even in Great Chalkham, though, there was the occasional unexpected event or scandal for everyone to get excited about. In this case, that summer, it came in the form of a shy lad in his early twenties called Ralph Watson who, according to village gospel, had been a prominent member of the church choir when he was a boy and had led an otherwise blameless life. He had been visiting the wife of farmer George Coombes, in the marital bed no less, when George had arrived home unexpectedly in the middle of the day. Ralph had hastily struggled into his breeches and, in his terror of imminent discovery, jumped out of an upstairs window. Unluckily for him, he broke his leg and was unable to escape a further beating from the angry farmer. George's wife, a plain girl at least thirty years his junior, had not been seen out in public since. The village gossips were euphoric and talk of the scandal buzzed through shops, streets and the church congregation for several days.

Throughout the summer, Norah and Rusty had further success at local horse shows but, on these occasions, only Arthur the stable lad, a tall, dark, gangly boy, was there to witness their triumph. Mother was too ill and Father was too busy with harvest. On a show day, Arthur would be there to help her plait Rusty's mane and tail and to walk with her as she rode to whichever neighbouring village was hosting the event. His quiet support and encouragement gave her confidence and she enjoyed the time they spent together. He was only four years older than her and, throughout the course of their days out together, he divulged glimpses of his earlier life. He had previously lived in Yorkshire in a small mining village, the youngest of six children. His father had followed his own father down the mines at a young age and had married his childhood sweetheart, Arthur's mother, when he was just seventeen. Tragically, he had been killed in the Great War at the age of thirty-five when Arthur was just nine years old and then his mother had also died when he was fifteen. His three older brothers, true to the family tradition, were all miners and his two older sisters were both married with families of their own.

Arthur himself had thought of no other existence than remaining part of this community and working down the pit. However, for the duration of the one day he spent down the mine, he had suffered from the most appalling claustrophobia. He was unable to overcome his terror of being trapped underground and, despite the jibes from his brothers, had not returned. Instead he had headed south, seeking work on farms and often doing a day's labour in exchange for a bed and a decent meal until he ended up in Great Chalkham where he had been taken on as stable lad and farmworker.

'Don't you miss your brothers and sisters?' Norah, who was an only child, could not imagine living away from her family.

Arthur shrugged and nodded. 'Aye, but needs must,' he responded simply. 'Now, let's check your girth.' Norah obediently raised her knee as she sat on Rusty so that Arthur could tighten the girth which held the saddle in place. 'It's your turn in a minute.'

'Do you think you'll always work here?' she persisted.

'Who knows. I like the work and your father's a good man. But who knows what the future will bring.'

'What do you mean?' Norah, protected and cosseted as she was, was firmly of the belief that a man's destiny was in his own hands. 'If you like it here, then there's no reason for you to leave.'

'True enough, while things stay as they are, but things, especially good things, don't last for ever. I try not to make too many plans because then I will probably be disappointed.'

'But nothing's going to change here,' Norah persisted. 'I heard Daddy saying just the other day what a good worker you are. He was even talking about old Tom's cottage and saying that now he's died, you could move in there. I'm sure your job here is safe.'

'Maybe.' He turned his serious, brown eyes away from her intent gaze. 'You just never know. Things can change in an instant and I think it's best to remember that.'

Norah shivered suddenly. His words trickled a tingle of anxiety down her spine. 'Well I know what the future holds for me,' she said defiantly. 'I'm going to go to St Hilda's at Oxford like Lydia Turner.'

'Who's Lydia Turner?' Arthur asked.

'A girl who lived in the village and went to school there a few years back. She was the first girl from Chalkham to go to university. Now she's a doctor. That's what I'm going to do.'

'Well I'm glad you've got it all mapped out. Let's hope nothing happens to scupper your plans.'

'What do you mean?' Norah asked but there was no time for a response. Her name was being called and she turned her attention to the show ring.

When she returned home later that day, flushed with the triumph of another win and two seconds, the house was deathly quiet. Her father, solemn and grim-faced, greeted her at the door and Norah excitedly showed him her latest rosettes.

'Rusty was brilliant as usual,' she chattered happily, 'and I only made two mistakes, Arthur said. Oh, I wish you could have been there.'

He led her into the sitting room without speaking and Norah felt a prickle of fear as he sat her down beside him.

'Is something wrong? What is it, Daddy?'

Then she realised her father was fighting back tears. 'It's your mother.' The words came out in a sob of despair. 'She's gone, Nolly. She's left us.' He was crying openly now and clutching her tightly as if he would never let her go.

Norah did not understand. 'What do you mean?' she asked. 'Where's she gone? She was in bed when I left her this morning. Don't worry, Daddy, she can't have gone far. She was much too sick to ...' Her voice tailed off as her father shook his head.

'No,' he sobbed. 'I'm sorry, Nolly. I just couldn't bring myself to say the words. She's dead, Nolly ... She died this morning in her sleep. Elsie found her. Oh Nolly, what are we going to do?'

Norah hugged her father tightly. Confronted with his grief, her instinct was to think of nothing other than comforting him. 'Don't worry, Daddy. I'll look after you.'

She repeated the words over and over as she held her father in her arms, helpless in the face of his utter despair. 'Please don't cry, Daddy. I can take care of you.'

At last the sobbing subsided and George gently pulled away from her. 'I'm sorry, Nolly. I should be the one looking after you. Forgive me.'

'There's nothing to forgive.'

He looked into her eyes, filled with concern for him, and put his arms around her once more. 'You're such a brave girl. We'll be fine, won't we?' He gave her a squeeze. 'Now, shall we go upstairs and see her?'

Norah swallowed. Up until now, her own feelings had been completely suspended, pushed aside and she had felt strangely numb as she had comforted her father. Now, suddenly, the reality of the situation threatened to intrude and overwhelm her.

'No, I can't,' she exclaimed. 'I don't want to see ....' The burning lump in her throat was choking her but still she felt she could not let her father down. 'Not yet,' she finished quietly.

'Of course, Nolly. Will you be alright if I leave you just for a bit? I feel I need to be with her.'

She nodded, biting her lip to hold back the tears, and watched him as he walked, shoulders hunched, out of the room. Her tall, handsome father suddenly looked so old, so defeated.

Immediately following his departure, there was a gentle knock and Mrs Morris, her face full of concern, peered around the door. 'Are you alright, lovey? Can I get you anything?'

Norah could not bring herself to speak. She shook her head as Mrs Morris ventured further into the room. 'Oh, you poor, dear girl,' the well-meaning woman prattled on. 'Of course, you're not alright. Hark at me, making things worse. I just wanted you to know that if you need anything, anything at all, you can find me in the kitchen ... or would you like me to sit with you while your father is ... well, you know ...'

Again, Norah shook her head, not trusting herself to speak, willing Mrs Morris to leave her alone.

With a sigh and a comforting pat on Norah's shoulder, the cook bustled out of the room and at last the tears started to flow. Her poor, dear, gentle mother was dead – there was nothing anyone could do to make things better. The three of them had been such a close, tight-knit family. It had always felt to Norah that their love for one another was like a cocoon, protecting them from the outside world. Now that cocoon had been ripped apart and nothing would ever be the same again. In her head, she could hear herself screaming, 'NO, IT'S NOT TRUE, NO' over and over again but she made no sound. Her silent grief felt so painful she thought her chest would explode and she wondered if this was what a broken heart was like.

Arthur's words earlier, like a portent of doom, came back to her as she slumped, clutching a cushion, on the sofa. He was right. Good things do *not* last forever.

CHAPTER 3

Emily – November 2016

T he accident which had claimed the lives of both her parents had happened ten years earlier but Emily had relived that moment of revelation so often in her nightmares that the sharpness of it remained unblunted. The immediate aftermath was less clear, more of a fog of misery but those feelings of isolation had remained with her. Only the presence of Molly had kept her from feeling completely abandoned. However, there had been more shocks to come. She let her mind drift back...

Six weeks after the tragedy, Emily was still struggling to come to terms with the loss of her parents. It felt like she was living in a vacuum and she seemed to have become incapable of making any decisions about her future. She assumed that at some point she would return to university but her desire to do so seemed to have disappeared and for the moment she could only drift aimlessly through each day. Since the accident, she had been staying at her childhood home with her aunts, Jen and Liz, her dad's unmarried sisters and the only family she now had. The two sisters lived together in a modest house in nearby Sudbury and, throughout Emily's childhood, had always been a fixture at family celebrations. She loved them dearly and was very grateful for their company during these early, grief-filled days.

Jen was the elder of the two, large and buxom with frizzy, grey hair and a bustling, organising way about her. She had been a teacher and was used to being in charge while Liz, a retired office manager, thinner, quieter but physically very similar to her sister, was used to taking care of the details. Together, they submerged their own sadness at the loss of their much-loved younger brother and sister-in-law; instead, they busied themselves looking after Emily and protecting her from having to deal with all the things officialdom demanded. They dealt with the police, organised the death certificates and supported her when she met with the funeral directors. Meanwhile Emily was oblivious to it all, lost in a sea of grief and steered through the melee in the lifeboat they provided.

Her friends also rallied around her as friends do in situations like those. Ellie and Jo, her two best friends from university, had travelled up together and booked accommodation at a nearby B & B and many of her friends from school days had returned for the funeral. They had all done their best to support her and to make her feel loved and she had appreciated that, but they were not the two people who had loved her most and who had made her feel cherished her whole life. Eventually they had returned to their own lives with promises to keep in touch and left her to her aunts' care. Connor had phoned once but their relationship was too new and still too tentative for him to know what to say. He had tried - he sent lots of texts the first few days- but gradually these had dried up and Emily felt relieved. She really could not deal with a boyfriend at a time like this.

Aunt Jen and Aunt Liz were great but Emily found herself spending more and more time in her room with Molly, looking through the photo albums her parents had kept and trawling through images she had stored on their old laptop computer. She especially loved those early photographs before she was born. Her parents had really enjoyed travelling and each destination had its own set of photographs, all painstakingly captioned and dated. Her favourite was dated June 1984 and taken by a stranger. It depicted her parents laughing by the Trevi fountain in Rome. She remembered them telling her how they had each thrown a coin into the fountain and made a wish, promising only to tell each other what they had wished for if it came true. When she was born three years later, her dad had taken her into his arms and smiled at his wife.

'Remember the Trevi fountain in Rome?' he had asked. 'This is what I wished for.'

'Me too,' she had replied.

Emily had never tired of that story and tears filled her eyes as she looked at their faces in the photograph. They had been so happy together but they had always longed for a child and, as they reached their late thirties, had almost given up hope.

'You were our little miracle,' her mum had said.

It had made Emily feel so special growing up, like she was meant for great things, and the fact that she had an imaginary friend enhanced that sense of specialness. She had always felt that Molly was her guardian angel, keeping her safe so that she could fulfil her destiny. Instead here she was. The reality, she realised, was that she was just as ordinary as anyone else, facing terrible loss just the same as countless others before her.

She was interrupted in her thoughts by a gentle knock and then her bedroom door being hesitantly pushed open. It was Aunt Liz.

'Emily dear, the solicitor will be here any minute. Are you ready to come down?'

She nodded and, taking a deep breath, got to her feet. Life seemed to be a series of ordeals at the moment and this was the next thing to face. She assumed this would be the reading of the will. 'Thank you. Yes. I'll come down now.'

The doorbell sounded as she was coming down the stairs and, after introductions had been performed and tea had been made, they all assembled in the old-fashioned, sitting room. It had not been decorated for as long as Emily could remember, presumably since floral wallpaper had been fashionable, and was cluttered with heavy mahogany furniture and prints of gilt-framed oil paintings.

Mr Blake, the solicitor, was a short, portly man with thinning grey hair and large, black-framed glasses. As he withdrew a box file from his case, Aunt Jen, who was sitting next to Emily on the faded, worn sofa, grabbed her hand and held it tightly. Emily could feel her shaking and patted her arm reassuringly. Why was her aunt nervous? She had assumed the reading of the will would be routine, no surprises.

Mr Blake cleared his throat. 'I would have visited sooner,' he began, speaking directly to Emily. His voice felt loud and overpowering in the small room. 'But your aunts expressly asked me to wait until ... until ... well, they wanted to give you some time.'

Emily gave Aunt Jen's hand a squeeze and smiled across at Liz. She knew her aunts were looking out for her. They were both looking incredibly worried, she thought, but it was just a fleeting notion and she concentrated her attention on the solicitor who had withdrawn a white envelope from his file and was now tapping it lightly with his stubby fingers.

'I have something here for you that you need to read,' he said. 'It's from your parents.' He handed Emily the envelope. Sure enough, there was her name on the front, written in black ink in her mother's slightly spidery hand.

She looked up. 'Do you want me to read it now?' she asked. She wanted to take it upstairs; to be on her own.

Mr Blake nodded. 'I think that would be best.'

Emily took a deep breath and peeled open the envelope as carefully as she could. The atmosphere in the room was so heavy with expectation she could feel the weight of it bearing down on her. There was no sound apart from the relentless ticking of the grandfather clock in the hallway. Inside the envelope was a single sheet of folded, A4 paper. She opened it up and read.

Our darling Emily,

If you are reading this, then something has happened to your dad and I and we can no longer be with you.

We have something to tell you, something we should have told you long ago but the time never seemed to be quite right and it seemed easier to carry on in our little family bubble of love and happiness.

The truth is that when you asked questions, lots of questions- you were such a bright, inquisitive child- about your birth, your dad and I were not entirely honest. You were not born in Ipswich hospital as we told you and the reason there are no early baby photos of you (you kept asking!) is that we adopted you when you were six weeks old.

Emily gasped in shock and looked up. The words, so stark on the page, were like a punch to her stomach. 'Did you know?' she demanded. 'Do you know what's in this letter?'

'Yes, we did.' Aunt Jen tried to put her arm round her but she shrugged her off and went back to the letter.

I'm so sorry we never told you but your dad and I both agree that if we could have the time over again, we still wouldn't tell you. You were our daughter in every way except biologically and we couldn't have loved you more. We didn't want anything, or anyone, to come between us. That maybe sounds selfish but remember that we acted as we did because you were our whole world. You brought us such joy.

You have just started at university and we are so proud of you- our beautiful, talented, incredible daughter. Always know that you are amazing and capable of great things. Be happy, my darling, and try to forgive us.

All our love,

Mum and Dad xx

Emily let the letter fall on her lap and looked up with unseeing eyes. Adopted. Her whole life had been a lie. It *was* selfish of them not to tell her. She had a right to know. Anger flared, hot and painful and she swung round to her aunt.

'You knew.' Her tone was harsh, accusing. 'Who else knew?'

'No one else,' Aunt Jen was quick to try to placate her. 'Just us. We're so sorry Emily but we were sworn to secrecy. It wasn't our place to tell you.'

Her rage dissipated as quickly as it had sparked and she was left feeling flat and empty. They were right. It was not their fault. Her mum and dad were to blame but they were not here to rail against. She wanted to argue with them, to tell them they had been wrong, but those feelings were pointless and a fresh wave of guilt swept over her. Everything they had done, they had done because they loved her and now they were dead. They were beyond her self-centred indignation.

'Are you alright, sweetheart?' Aunt Liz had come to perch anxiously on the other side of her.

Emily shook her head. It might not have been their fault but she was not ready to reassure them, to let them off the hook. Instead she stood up abruptly, allowing the letter to flutter like a dead leaf to the floor. 'I'm going for a walk,' she said curtly. 'I need to be on my own.'

She felt three pairs of troubled eyes follow her out of the room but she ignored them and, grabbing her coat, she yanked open the front door and let it slam behind her.

It was several hours before she returned and she knew her aunts had been worried but she refused to acknowledge it. Her thoughts were still spinning through all the implications of this revelation and her emotions were likewise in turmoil. The whole fabric of her existence had shifted and she had no idea how she was going to cope with it.

A few more details about the adoption emerged in the days that followed. Mr Blake had left the box file for Emily to look through. Her parents had left this with him when they had given him their letter. Apparently, its contents had been given to the adoption agency by her real mother when she had given her up. However, to begin with, Emily refused to touch it. It sat like an unexploded bomb on the mahogany coffee table. What other secrets and shocks might she have to face?

Instead, as her natural curiosity about her past began to surface, she had questioned her aunts, attempting to cushion the possibility of further grief. They were only too happy to share what they knew but sadly that was very little. They were able to tell her that she had been born somewhere in London but they knew nothing else.

'I don't think your parents knew anything either. The adoption agency had very strict rules about information. They did say once that they would have liked to send your natural mother some photos of you so that she could see how happy you were but of course they couldn't,' Liz said.

There was nothing for it. She was going to have to look in the box. It felt quite light when she picked it up and took it upstairs to her room. As usual, Molly was waiting there, standing by her primrose-coloured curtains, her green eyes spilling over with sympathy. Emily placed the box carefully on the bed and, with trembling fingers, lifted the lid. Inside there were three items: a small, blue, velveteen jewellery box, an old, tattered, white envelope and a brown, leather-bound book.

Emily paused and took a deep breath. Could these three innocuous looking items hold information about her birth? Mr Blake's instructions had been only to give her the letter from her parents first and then let her have the box. She was struck afresh by rage towards them. All those years they had guarded their secret. They should have been here, with her, when she opened the box. She should not have had to face this alone.

The envelope was lying on the top of the book and she picked that up first. It was blank and unsealed and she could see a piece of paper folded inside. When she pulled it out, she could see that it was a crumpled piece of lined paper torn from a notepad. She unfolded it. The writing was small and neat and very brief.

My baby,
I hope with all my heart you have a happy life which I know, due to my present circumstances, I would be unable to give you. I love you and it breaks my heart to give you up but I have no choice.
Please forgive me.
With love from your Mum xx

Emily sat on her bed and read the words over and over again. There were no answers – only questions? Who was she? Why did she have no choice but to have her baby adopted? The picture she had in her head was of a young girl, frightened and alone, and Emily could feel her pain radiating through her words. Her eyes filled with tears. How terrible to have to give up your baby. Of course, she could forgive her. After all she had always felt safe, loved and protected. Her parents had always done their best, as her mother had wanted, to ensure she had a happy life.

Carefully, she refolded the note and returned it to its envelope. Next, she picked up the jewellery box. It was light and felt smooth and luxurious in her hands. Inside, nestled against the ivory, satin lining of the box was a silver locket. It was oval shaped and the front was artistically engraved with two, intertwined initials - ND. She felt a pulse of excitement. Were these the initials of her real mother? There was a tiny clip on the side and when she applied pressure to it, it snapped open. However, disappointingly, there was nothing inside.

The last item was the book and, having returned the locket to its case, Emily lifted it onto her lap. The leather cover was smooth and worn but of good quality. The front was plain except for the same two initials stamped into the leather- ND. With a growing sense of expectation, Emily turned the cover to look inside. Written on the flyleaf, in bold, childish hand, were the words *Norah's Scrapbook* and underneath a date - *June 1ˢᵗ, 1922*. The disappointment was instant; that was far too long ago to be her mother. So, who was Norah and why had her book and presumably her locket been given to her all these years later?

She turned the next page to find four grainy, black and white photographs of a young girl on a pony. There were two action shots of the pair jumping some small fences in what looked like a show jumping competition. Then there was a photo of the girl receiving a trophy from a man in a bowler hat. The last showed the girl in a blurry close up, beaming at the camera, with a man and woman standing, smiling, either side of her. She looked so happy, this young girl from 1923, so joyful that Emily could not help but smile. She also looked strangely familiar. Who was she?

Now, ten years later, she looked again at the photographs of the girl in Norah's scrapbook, as she had done so often, but she was still no closer to finding answers. Since her marriage and Alex's birth, it had lain untouched in a box and she had tried to get on with her life. However, over the course of this last year, she had become more and more restless and unsettled. Adam had been away from home a lot more on business and, left alone with a three-year-old, her thoughts had become more introspective.

Then, this morning, Molly's appearance in her bedroom, after a five-year absence, had shaken her. She had been convinced that she had at last outgrown her imaginary friend. Her presence had reawakened suppressed memories and made her wonder if her current listlessness was a symptom of unfinished business. As soon as she had put Alex down for his nap, she had emptied cupboards looking for the box and, on finding it, had turned once again to the first page of the scrapbook. If only she knew what the D in the initials stood for. It was a mystery which had always haunted her dreams. This girl on the pony was somehow linked to her real mother but her smiling face revealed no clues. It was as familiar to her as her own but she was no closer, all these years later, to knowing her identity, just as she was no closer to knowing her own identity.

Noises from the baby monitor snapped her out of her reverie. Alex was awake and moving about in his bedroom upstairs. As she stood, she laid the book, still open, on a side table – a reminder to look through the rest of the photographs and news clippings it contained later on. There must be something in there she had missed, she was convinced of it.

CHAPTER 4

Jennifer – November 2016

Everything had been going so well, Jennifer Thompson thought as she gave a final wave to the Fowlers, her guests for the past three days, but there always had to be a fly in the ointment. Her moment of triumph at a job well done was soon forgotten when she saw the unmistakeable, tall, muscular, dark-haired figure of David Brewer striding up the lane towards her. What did *he* want? She was sorely tempted to shut the door behind her and pretend she was not in but she knew she was too late for such tactics. He would have already seen her.

'Morning, Jen,' he bellowed cheerfully as he approached. Jen! No one ever called her Jen or Jenny. She had always been Jennifer; she had patiently pointed this out to him on more than one occasion but he had taken no notice. That was the problem. The man took absolutely no notice of anything she said.

'Morning,' she replied shortly. 'Sorry but I was just about to go in. It's cold out here.' She turned away dismissively, hoping he would say his piece quickly and be gone.

'Great. I'll join you. A nice cup of coffee will soon warm us both up.'

He followed her into her newly refurbished cottage and paused to take his boots off at the front door. 'I saw your first guests leaving,' he said. 'How did it go?'

'Very well thank you,' she replied stiffly and put the kettle on while he leaned comfortably against the marble kitchen worktop, his large frame overpowering in the small space. She smiled briefly as she recalled how effusive the Fowlers had been in their praise. They had been her first official 'bed and breakfast' guests and had been delighted with everything. It had been a great start to her new career.

'That's good. Two sugars please.' He looked around appreciatively. 'Of course, they couldn't fail to be impressed. We've done a great job here, you and I, if I say so myself. We make a great team.' He beamed at her as she handed him one of her huge collection of 'Best Teacher' mugs and took a gulp. 'Mm, that hits the spot.'

'Can I help you with anything, David?' she asked politely. The sooner he told her the reason for his visit, the sooner she could get rid of him.

He raised his eyebrows in the semblance of a leer. 'I'm sure a lovely lady like you could help me with lots of things.'

Ugh. The man was beyond belief, an anachronism from the dark ages of wolf whistles and Benny Hill. Jennifer folded her arms across her chest protectively and gave him her best, cold stare. 'The point of this visit?' she prompted again.

David Brewer took his time in answering, taking slow mouthfuls of coffee and silently appraising the woman in front of him. She was very attractive with her blond hair coiffed in a sleek bob, her clear, grey eyes and slim figure. She definitely had a hint of Helen Mirren about her. Such a shame that she did not seem to have much of a sense of humour. He knew she found his presence irksome and could not resist teasing her, trying to soften some of her sharp edges.

'I was wondering what you were doing next Saturday night? There's a charity race night on at the village hall and I thought, if you weren't busy, you might want to come along.'

'Er ... next Saturday ...' Completely flummoxed, Jennifer fumbled for an excuse. 'Er ... let me check my diary.' She turned away from him and leafed through the pages. Frustratingly, Saturday night was completely blank but there was no way she was going on a date with this man. She simply could not stand him. He was everything that irritated her in a man: brash, arrogant, opinionated and he was never ever wrong. 'Oh,' she feigned disappointment. 'I've got a visit from my friend, Heather, pencilled in. Sorry.'

'No problem. You could bring her along,' he replied smoothly.

'Yes ... well ... I'm not sure what time she will be arriving. It's probably best to leave it.' God, she hated lying. She was really bad at it too and was very conscious of the tell-tale flags of colour on her cheeks.

He shrugged. 'No problem. Jill from the pub asked me to ask you. She's organising a table and thought you might like an opportunity to meet some of Chalkham's finest. Still, if you're busy, she'll understand. Maybe next time.' He put down his mug. 'Right, I'll be off. Thanks for the coffee.'

'Ok.' She followed him to the door. 'Thanks for the thought. Bye.'

He gave her a friendly wave and took off with long-legged strides back up the lane.

Damn, she thought as she returned to her kitchen. Not a date at all, and it would have been good to meet some new people. She had always had an active social life in the past and was aware that she had not been out in Chalkham since she moved into the village a month ago. How infuriating that David had not made that clear from the start! Instead she had been forced into a lie to spare his feelings and she may well need to lie again when Heather, currently living in Australia, failed to show up.

She mentally chalked up another notch of irritation against David Brewer. He was her nearest neighbour and lived at the top of her lane in a converted barn. He was also the builder who had supervised the renovation of Horseshoes Cottage, as she had renamed it when she took possession. There was no doubt that he'd done an excellent job. His advice and ideas for refurbishment were very much in tune with her own and his team of workers had been unfailingly prompt, polite and tidy whenever she had made a site visit. The modern kitchen and new ensuite bathrooms had been installed with the minimum of fuss and without spoiling the rustic charm of the cottage with which she had fallen in love in the first place. It was just his manner that constantly set her teeth on edge. He was so high-handed and patronising! As a headteacher of a large village primary school for the past ten years, she was used to dealing with all sorts of people but never before had she been so often wrong-footed by someone. In school, even parents with a grievance who had angrily demanded redress for some imagined wrongdoing were soon soothed by her calm, professional manner and she always felt in charge of the situation. It was disconcerting now at the age of fifty-six, having taken early retirement and embarking on a new challenge, to find herself so frequently in the company of someone who always managed to put her on the back foot.

She had told everyone that buying a cottage in the country and running a B & B had been a dream for her retirement from teaching for some time. This statement was not entirely honest but it had enough truth in it to convince people when she said it. She had always loved cooking for people. Her food was a bit like her, she always thought, plain and straightforward, but her friends insisted that whatever she cooked always tasted amazing. Having sampled her breakfast on the first morning of their stay, the Fowlers had promptly requested dinner too, and then told her that they would recommend her to all their friends.

Jennifer also enjoyed meeting new people. She had a wide circle of friends but always had room for more. Certainly, she did not mind living alone and was happy in her own company but she also appreciated lively debate and interesting conversation. At different times in her life she had become romantically involved with a number of very charming men but these relationships had never lasted long enough to threaten her independent, single, career-minded lifestyle. She just wasn't the marrying type, she told herself ruefully.

Jennifer's other passion was the countryside. She loved nothing better than long walks or cycle rides, soaking up the beauty of the scenery and finding joy in the patterns of nature. As a busy headteacher, there had been so little spare time to indulge these simple pastimes and she felt fortunate that she was fit and healthy enough to enjoy them in her retirement. Earlier that year, her closest friend had died from cancer and it had hit her hard. It was a wakeup call, she finally decided. Life was too short to spend so much of it working and she needed to 'seize the day' while she had the chance. She spoke to a pensions advisor and realised that she could easily afford to retire so what was she waiting for? She was still debating the issue though when tragedy had struck her school and her future was determined. Overwhelmed with grief and guilt, she had handed in her resignation, sold her house in Norwich and, with the proceeds, bought her dream cottage in the picturesque, 'chocolate box' village of Great Chalkham.

So far so good. Now the cottage was up and running but there were, as yet, no more bookings on her online diary. Jennifer knew that she would need to advertise more widely to publicise it and to attract customers. The Fowlers had been friends of a friend but they had assured her that they would be returning and eventually she hoped that repeat business might be enough to keep her ticking along. In the meantime, she had set up a web page promoting the cottage and a freelance journalist friend from university days had brought a photographer to the cottage and done an interview with Jennifer two months ago. She was writing a series of articles on country retreats and Jennifer had managed to persuade her to include Horseshoes Cottage. The building work had not been completed but the photographer was able to angle his shots artfully to show the cottage to its best advantage. Hopefully it would be great publicity. She had also contacted some of the national companies who advertised holiday accommodation to request a listing on their websites and was awaiting inspections from two of them. Things were moving forward, she thought with quiet satisfaction.

The best thing of all was that she was now living in a gorgeous cottage in an idyllic location. The main living room especially boasted a fantastic view over the surrounding fields and had apparently been the original farmworker's cottage when it was built over two hundred years ago. The large brick fireplace and exposed oak beams were its best features but Jennifer privately liked the little nooks and crannies which gave the room its character. Various extensions had been added to the rear of the property by more recent occupants to add more bedrooms and Jennifer also had extended it further still, to provide ensuite facilities for the two guest bedrooms and a separate 'snug' for herself when she had visitors staying.

It had not all been plain sailing. When Jennifer had embarked on the project, she had obtained quotes from three different builders and had chosen Howlett and Son whose quote was the lowest. However, things had gone badly from the start when they were a week late in beginning the work. Then, one month in, when Jennifer had paid a surprise site visit, she found only one builder there, the other two having been 'called away on an urgent job.' Very little had been accomplished and Jennifer had been disappointed with the quality of the workmanship on display. She had phoned Tom Howlett immediately but his phone told her 'he was currently unavailable', as he was every time she tried to call him in the following week. It was another week on before he called her back and then it was to tell her that, because of his involvement in another, much larger project, they would be unable to continue with her cottage renovations for the immediate future. He would bill her for the work they had completed so far and would 'quite understand' if she wanted to employ a different builder. Jennifer had turned to the second builder on her list but he was no longer available so she finally contacted David Brewer who had tendered the highest quote. When she had questioned the cost, he told her that high quality materials and first-rate workmanship came at a cost. He had surveyed the work already completed and had been singularly unimpressed. 'You get what you pay for,' he told her coolly, 'and if you pay cowboy prices, that's what you get.' He gestured at some especially poor brickwork. Jennifer had no suitable retort and reluctantly agreed to retain his services. She then retreated back to Norwich, hating the disadvantaged position in which she found herself and seething at his arrogance.

At last, though, the work had begun in earnest and, when she visited the following weekend, she could not help but be impressed by what had been achieved. However, there was then another drawback. An inspection of the wiring had revealed some major failings and she had been forced to agree to having the whole property rewired, something which had eaten an even bigger hole into her budget. Fortunately, David Brewer's electrician had been able to do the job straight away and the resultant damage to plaster and paintwork had been easily fixed. He had been a very pleasant, young chap, she remembered – so helpful and eager to please. He had reminded her of a Labrador she had owned as a child. If only David Brewer himself had been a bit more like him but instead he had been forthright, full of himself and constantly behaved as if he was doing her a favour. When she had tried to win him over with her charm and had praised his men's work, he had raised his supercilious, dark eyebrows and said, 'I'm pleased that you can now see how the benefits of craftsmanship outweigh the expense.' His words had made her seethe. How pompous could you get! Clamping down her irritation, she bit her tongue and mumbled something under her breath. At least she would not have to put up with him for too much longer.

So, it had come as something of a shock when she had discovered he was also her nearest neighbour and lived in the beautiful, converted barn at the top of her lane. It was the day she'd moved in and she'd been following the removal lorry up the lane in her ancient, blue Peugeot when there he was, walking his dog, a lively, black and white collie. Reluctantly, she'd slowed to a halt and wound down her window; she just could not bring herself to be rude and ignore him.

'David, this is a surprise!' she exclaimed with false cheeriness. 'Do you live around here?'

'Just up the road.' He gestured towards the barn.

Her heart sank. 'Lovely. Then I expect we'll bump into each other from time to time.' But not if I see you first, she thought privately. What a nuisance! When his team had finished the work on the cottage, she had felt relieved that her dealings with him had come to an end. Hopefully, he would keep himself to himself and she would hardly be aware of his existence. At least, his house was a few hundred metres away and not right next door.

Sadly though, he seemed determined to make something of a nuisance of himself and turned up at the cottage on a regular basis. She was sure he was just being friendly and his heart was in the right place but he seemed to feel she needed guidance on all things connected to the cottage and her new business. As a strong, independent woman, she resented his unwanted advice but found it impossible, for some reason she had yet to fathom, to say so bluntly. Possibly it was because she was a conciliatory person herself and preferred to remain distantly polite. Certainly, he seemed to have the hide of a rhinoceros and, despite the negative vibes she sent his way, he continued to proffer his opinions. The worst of it was that his ideas were generally sound and useful. When she started tackling the overgrown garden, he offered her the use of his rotavator and brought over some old bricks to create some raised beds.

'They'll give the garden a more cottagey feel and also save you a lot of backache,' he advised.

Of course, David just *had* to be something of a plant expert. It was he who had informed her that most of the perennials in the garden had just needed cutting back when discovered her about to pull them all up, having mistaken them for weeds. Brilliant!

'What would I do without you here telling me how to do it properly?' she retorted acidly but he just grinned, obviously missing her sarcasm.

'I know. Glad you appreciate it.'

Now the garden, although not finished, was beginning to take shape. She had pruned, tidied and planted lots of bulbs in her new beds. At least, it was looking tidy for the winter and she could look forward to seeing what emerged in the spring.

There was just one other problem with the cottage though and it was one which Jennifer had no idea how to solve. It had first happened on her second morning in the cottage. She had been unloading the dishwasher when she became aware of another presence in the kitchen. It was like a prickling of the hairs on her neck and a sense that the air in the room had somehow shifted. She looked up to see a shadowy dark figure with long auburn hair and startling green eyes. There was a feeling of overwhelming sadness - and then the figure was gone.

Had she just seen a ghost? Jennifer had rubbed her eyes in disbelief and shaken her head. She was far too old and sensible for such supernatural nonsense! The girl had seemed incredibly real, though and she pondered the encounter at different times over the next few days. In the end, however, she could come up with no rational explanation and decided to dismiss it from her mind ... until it happened again.

A few weeks later, she was looking out of her kitchen window when she saw the figure, dressed in black, once more. This time, she seemed to be looking for something in the garden, frantically pacing back and forth, staring wildly and wringing her hands. Jennifer was just opening the window to call out to her when she disappeared – simply vanished. One moment she was there and the next she was gone. Jennifer stood for a long time, watching and waiting, but she did not return.

It was at that point she allowed herself to contemplate the possibility of a ghost, for surely that was what she was. Perhaps she was someone who had lived, and maybe died, in the cottage many years before. Her dress looked early twentieth century so she was probably from that era. Even as the thoughts crossed her mind, she berated herself for her fancifulness. How ridiculous! A ghost! There was no such thing! And yet ...

Since then, she had seen the woman several times and had come to the reluctant conclusion that either her cottage was haunted or she was losing her mind. This was a very uncomfortable thought and not one, she felt, she could possibly discuss with anyone else. They would think, probably quite correctly, that the trauma of that terrible incident earlier in the year had sent her over the edge. Maybe it had ...

CHAPTER 5

Emily - November 2016

E mily was upstairs with Alex reading him the Gruffalo, currently his favourite bedtime story, when she heard Adam return home.

'Daddy's back,' she announced and smiled at the instant joy on his face.

'Daddy!' he squealed, scrummaging to get out of bed.

'Stay there, darling. Daddy will come up and see you.' She went to the bedroom door and called down the stairs. 'We're up here.'

Adam was hanging up his coat and grinned up at her. 'Hi sweetheart. Sorry I'm late. I'll be right up.'

Emily turned back to her blond haired, blue eyed son, so like his father. 'Quick. Back under the covers. He's on his way.'

Giggling, Alex scrambled under his duvet so he was completely hidden as his dad appeared in the doorway.

'Where's Alex?' he asked in mock confusion.

'I'm here!' Alex burst out of the covers and launched himself into his father's arms. Adam hugged him tightly. His eyes met Emily's and his loving smile, as always, made her catch her breath. After five years of marriage, the spark between them was as strong as ever and she still could not quite believe her luck in having him as a husband. She reached across to join in the hug and to kiss him lightly on the lips, inhaling the musky scent of him. That smell and the deep, velvet tone of his voice, were the first things she had noticed about him.

It had been seven years ago and she had been at a friend's birthday party, talking with a group of girlfriends whom she had not seen recently when she became aware of a man's voice, politely greeting someone behind her. He was close enough for her to smell his after shave. It was an instant reaction. She felt a tingling down her spine and she found herself switching off from the group and tuning in to what he was saying. She almost didn't want to turn around to look at him in case it spoilt the moment.

Her friends, who had the benefit of a view, were also distracted.

'Who's he?' Annie, tall, dark-haired and currently single, had zeroed in and was now looking across at him with blatant invitation.

'Oh, that's Adam Conway. He's a friend of Paul's,' her married friend, Jenna, said carelessly.

Annie's eyes had widened. 'You know him? Quick – introduce me to him.'

'He might already have a girlfriend,' Emily pointed out. She was used to Annie's predatory antics.

'No, he's single,' Jenna confirmed. She sighed. 'He is gorgeous. If I wasn't married to Paul, I'd definitely be interested.'

At that point, Adam had joined their circle and grinned across at Jenna. 'Hey Jenna,' he said. 'How are you doing?'

Jenna took the opportunity to introduce him to each of her friends and Emily felt herself melting when he looked into her eyes. She could feel the heat from her body flushing her cheeks as she mumbled a self-consciously offhand greeting. Meanwhile Annie attached herself to his arm and began to steer him away.

'Let's head to the bar and I'll buy you a drink,' she was saying.

'Oh great. Thanks.' He allowed himself to be dragged off but made a point of turning to say, 'See you later.' Emily was sure he was looking at her when he said it and the thought gave her a warm glow as she watched him being politely attentive to Annie at the bar. In all her twenty-four years, she had never experienced such a strong attraction to a man and it left her feeling a little disorientated and confused. Her coping mechanism was to turn herself into the life and soul of the party, circulating the room, chatting enthusiastically with all the women she knew, flirting light-heartedly with the men and making a point of ignoring Adam. The effort was beginning to wear her out when he suddenly reappeared at her shoulder.

'Hey, Emily, isn't it?' he said.

'Oh, hello ... Adam.' Her heart was hammering, her mouth felt dry and she found herself smiling a bit too brightly.

'Do you fancy going to find somewhere a bit quieter for a drink? I've been wanting to talk to you all evening.'

It felt like one of those really important moments when the pattern of her life was about to change. Desperately, she searched her brain for a cool, witty response but instead found herself nodding dumbly. Then she remembered Annie.

'Hold on a sec. I need to tell Annie where I'm going. We came to the party together.'

She approached Annie with some trepidation, unwilling to cause her any upset, but she hadn't needed to worry. Annie had a philosophical attitude towards her love life and she shrugged when Emily expressed concerns that she was treading on her friend's toes.

'Don't be daft,' Annie had said. 'I knew he wasn't interested in me because all he did when we were talking was to quiz me about you. Go for it, girl.'

Emily returned to where she had left Adam standing, feeling slightly sick with anticipation. He took hold of her hand, led her from the room and they had been together ever since. As well as being a great friend and wonderful lover, Adam provided her with the stability which had been missing from her life for the past four years.

After her parents' death, she hadn't been able to face going back to university and, instead, with the support of her two aunts, had concentrated her energies in finding her real mother but to no avail. Having contacted the adoption agency, she had met with a counsellor who had been able to obtain a record of her birth - a promising start. She remembered how excited she had been at the time, how hopeful of instant success. Her birth certificate revealed that she had been born in Dulwich hospital on May 7th, 1987. Her mother was listed as Grace Smith, unemployed, of Heygate, London. Her father was named as John Smith, musician. There had been no other information about her parents and she'd been unable to find any record of their marriage. The surname Smith, she quickly discovered, was very unhelpful and every search she initiated had hundreds of hits. She had tried trawling through them and listing any possibilities but, after hundreds of futile phone calls, she had given it up as a hopeless task.

With her aunts, she had made a trip to London in November 2006 and visited the Heygate estate where her parents had lived. She found lots of homes already empty pending redevelopment and residents anxious about their future but no one knew anything about John and Grace Smith. The only thing she did find out was that the address she had for them had been occupied by squatters during the mid-eighties. Emily recalled her crushing disappointment that she had arrived at yet another dead end.

In early 2007, Emily decided to give up on her efforts to find her real parents. She resolved to sell her adoptive parents' house, which had been left to her in their will, and make a fresh start. Her aunts, tearful at parting from her, had moved back to their own home in Sudbury. After sending off a number of job applications, she secured a job working as a clerk for an insurance company in Ipswich and rented a flat. The work was dull and she did not stay there long.

Instead she got a job as an office junior for a large firm of solicitors in the town. That was where she had met Annie. The two had quickly become close friends and, when Annie split up from her boyfriend and asked Emily to share her flat with her, she'd jumped at the offer. Annie was very outgoing and had a large circle of friends who soon became Emily's friends and the two of them enjoyed a busy, social life together – until two and a half years later when they met Adam at a party.

Within six months, Emily had moved into his flat and nine months later, they were married and had bought their first home together. At the time, Adam had been working for a wine importer and, after they got married, he set up his own business. He was ambitious, worked hard, wine producers liked his genuine, easy going personality and the wholesalers he supplied respected his professionalism. The business had quickly grown and now commanded a small staff team but it had meant that Adam was now working harder than ever. He was frequently away on buying trips abroad and Emily found herself left at home with her young son. She had not returned to employment after Alex's birth. There had been lots of talk of it but somehow it had just never happened. It would have been difficult in terms of childcare with Adam away so much but that was an easy excuse. The truth was that she really had no enthusiasm for returning to office work which she'd always found tedious but she didn't know what else to do. Her dreams of being a journalist had long since died and any professional ambitions she'd previously held had stagnated. The 'planner' Emily of the past had morphed into someone far more indecisive and lacking confidence.

The trouble was that staying at home with Alex, whom she adored, had gradually left her feeling isolated and slightly useless. Many of her friends were also married or had partners but most did not have children and those who did seemed to juggle parenthood successfully with a career. They told her she was lucky she had the choice to stay at home and look after her son. For them, it was not a viable option financially. But she couldn't help feeling slightly envious when they talked enthusiastically about their work or quite disregard the feeling of underachievement in her own life. The sense of specialness she had experienced as a child now taunted her with a sense of failure – of settling for less than her best. Adam and Alex had helped her rebuild her life but she felt, deep down, there was something missing.

Then, this morning, Molly had returned to her life. She had looked just the same as she always had with her dark, auburn hair, sad, green eyes and dark clothing. Emily had been clearing away the breakfast things and, when she looked up, there she was, standing by the sink, watching her with doleful eyes. 'Have you forgotten?' those eyes seemed to be saying. Emily sighed. The past was still haunting the present.

'I know, I know,' Emily said. 'But I've been busy with other things.'

'Who are you talking to, Mummy?' Alex had asked, appearing in the kitchen doorway.

'Oh, no one. Just talking to myself,' she had replied, scooping him up and carrying him through to the room they had designated the playroom because it had been taken over by Alex's toys. 'Now, what shall we play with?'

It had been later, when Alex was having his afternoon nap, that Molly had reappeared and Emily could feel her reproach. She had immediately searched for the box containing the scrapbook but, by the time she had found it and sat down with it by the fire, Alex had woken up. She had been busy with him and with preparing food and then, in the evening, Adam had returned and had provided his own brand of distraction.

So, it was not until the following day that she had the opportunity to return to the book. Alex was sitting on the kitchen floor playing with his toy garage, cars, lorries and tractors and Emily sat at the kitchen table with a cup of coffee and the book in front of her. As she had done hundreds of times before, she started to turn the pages, working through slowly, trying to absorb every detail.

The first two pages contained the black and white photographs of the girl on the pony. She was perhaps eleven or twelve, Emily had always thought, as her smiling face still retained a childhood chubbiness. Some of the pictures also contained a man and a woman, presumably the girl's parents but the poor quality of the photos made it difficult to see any family resemblance.

The next page contained a newspaper clipping. It contained a brief story about someone called Lydia Turner, the twenty-one-year-old daughter of solicitor Felix Turner, who was one of the first women from Suffolk to be awarded a place at St Hilda's, Oxford. She was going to read medicine, the report said, and hoped one day to become a surgeon. There was also a photograph of the woman looking very serious and formidable as she stared from the page, her hair scraped back from her face in a tight bun. She was wearing a smart, light-coloured blouse buttoned to the neck with the hint of a frill around the collar and a dark skirt. Emily had googled Lydia Turner and also contacted St Hilda's but had been unable to find out any more about her. She wondered if she was a relative of Norah's or maybe a family friend.

The next page contained two photographs of a house, slightly blurry but quite large with a thatched roof and a number of windows. It looked a typical farmhouse with ploughed fields in the background. Emily had always thought that this was Norah's home. These were followed by two prints of the same woman who had appeared in the earlier photos. These showed her sitting in a garden surrounded by roses. The woman was smiling but looked very frail and was sitting with a blanket tucked around her knees.

Turning the page again, Emily smiled at a picture of the pony with its head over a stable door. It was holding its head at an angle and showing his teeth in a cheeky grimace. The next photograph was of a tall, thin, very serious young man holding a pitchfork and standing by another stable door. He was wearing a shirt with the sleeves rolled up, a waistcoat and dark trousers. Emily had always wondered who he was. At first, she had thought he might be Norah's brother but later photos had ruled that out and she decided he must have worked on the farm.

It was the following page which had contained the bombshell. Emily remembered her shock as she had stared at the photograph alone in her bedroom almost ten years ago. It was peculiar in the first instance because it was only half a picture. The long-jagged edge down one side made her think that someone had torn the photograph in two. It depicted a tall, older man and a young woman. Both looked serious and unsmiling as they stared out of the photograph. The man was an older version of the man in the first photographs whom Emily had always assumed to be Norah's father. He was wearing a suit, waistcoat, shirt and tie and his left arm was entwined with a plump, feminine arm which disappeared tantalisingly off the edge of the photograph. It seemed to bear no resemblance to the frail limbs of the woman who was probably Norah's mother. There was no other photograph on that page and no caption or dates written underneath.

Who had torn the photograph? Was it Norah? Where was the missing half? What did it contain? She had asked these questions over and over again but Molly had never replied. She had watched Emily with sorrowful eyes but remained stubbornly mute as Emily had looked up with a gasp that first time and stared at her in shock. The young woman in the photograph and Molly were the same person.

CHAPTER 6

Norah - October - December, 1925

Angrily, Norah ripped the photograph she was holding in half and let one side flutter to the floor. She was sitting upstairs in her bedroom on a rainy autumn day with her scrapbook open in front of her. Seeing the photographs of her at the horse show had brought the memories flooding back. It had been her birthday, she recalled - such a happy day. There she was, in her best riding breeches and tweed jacket, beaming atop Rusty while her mother, slim and elegant in a floral dress, stood proudly beside her, smiling at the camera. Norah struggled to remember the colours of the dress from the black and white image. Blue, she thought, with white and yellow flowers. The next photograph depicted her father, tall and handsome, grinning broadly as he was giving Rusty a pat. Then there was a photograph of the three of them together. Arthur had taken it, she remembered, and it was her favourite. All three of them were smiling and looking so happy. Norah wondered if she would ever be that happy again. At that moment, it seemed unlikely.

With a sigh, she traced a finger over her mother and then her father. The photo brought home to her just how much he had aged in the past four years and how he had changed. Previously, he had always liked a laugh and a joke and, although he worked hard, he had always made plenty of time for his family. Now he never smiled and seemed to be rarely at home. Despite her best efforts, she'd been unable to help him recover from his grief.

Then, over the past year, he'd started to seek other female company. Norah had thought this was a good sign, that he was ready to move on, but that hadn't been the case. He remained desperately unhappy and withdrawn.

She carefully stuck the torn half of the photograph in her scrapbook. Her own face, serious and unsmiling, looked back at her. She was wearing her best cotton frock and her hair hung in waves around her shoulders. Compared to the earlier pictures, she looked very grown up and, at sixteen, she supposed she was now considered a young woman. She didn't feel like one, though, and she certainly didn't behave like one. She was still a tomboy who liked nothing better than riding her horse Trojan – she had long outgrown Rusty who still lived a spoilt, pampered existence in his retirement.

Sighing again, she picked up the discarded half of the photograph. *That* had been the problem, she realised. George Dunn had listened to the ladies of the village telling him that she needed a civilising influence and decided that she needed a stepmother. Not only that - a stepsister too! Vehemently, she ripped the offending half of the picture into shreds and threw them onto the fire. It had been a wedding photograph, taken at the start of the summer, on the day that her life had suddenly become so much worse.

George's new wife, Adele Gatting, had flattered and simpered her way into their home and had managed what so many other village matrons had unsuccessfully tried to do – ensnared the most eligible widower in the district. She was a widow of two years herself, having previously been married to the Reverend Robert Gatting of the parish of Thaxford, a village six miles west of Great Chalkham, and lauded herself as a model of social propriety and Christian values. She was a slightly plump, attractive woman with dark, only slightly greying hair always worn in a neat bun. Her daughter, Hope, was a moon-faced girl of fourteen with blue eyes and silky, corn-coloured ringlets. She dressed in lace and frills and prided herself on her accomplishments - singing, playing the piano, embroidery and painting.

When Norah had first met Mrs Gatting, she'd considered her a definite improvement on the two women George had previously introduced to her. Adele had smiled, taken an interest in Norah and displayed a refreshing, self-deprecating sense of humour. However, as soon as she'd become George's fiancée, her attitude to Norah had become far more critical and Norah found herself unfavourably compared to the paragon, Hope.

Now they were married and Adele's true colours had been well and truly revealed. She was a nagging, whining woman. Her lips were constantly pursed in a disapproving pout whenever she spoke to Norah and, increasingly, when she spoke to George. Consequently, George was choosing to spend more and more of his time outside and many of his evenings down at The Fox and Hare. This in turn provoked many a sermon from his wife on the dangers of alcohol and eulogies for her abstemious late husband.

Whilst her new stepmother was bad enough, Norah also found it impossible to like her new stepsister. When Hope had first moved in, she complained every morning of the sleepless night she had spent in her bedroom, which was much smaller than Norah's and directly above the kitchen. She demanded that Norah should give up her own bedroom as an act of Christian charity. When Norah refused, she'd wept bitter tears to her mother and claimed she was becoming unwell through lack of sleep. Adele had spoken to George of the matter and berated him for the selfishness of his daughter but George refused to get involved.

'It's always been Norah's room,' he said quietly. 'She shouldn't have to swap with Hope unless she wants to.'

The women had been outraged but George had refused to budge on the subject and Norah refused to give up her bedroom so that was the end of the matter. At least, that was what Norah had thought. Unfortunately, though, Hope was not prepared to overlook this thwarting of her own desires and Norah found herself victim of a continual stream of spiteful acts.

First, she discovered that the final pages had been torn out of a book she was reading. Then, on the occasion of her sixteenth birthday, she went to put on her best dress only to find it had mysterious blotches all over it. Most recently, she found that her silver locket, given to her by her mother, had disappeared from her jewellery box. When she'd questioned Hope, the younger girl had rushed to her mother weeping that she had been wrongly accused and how could anyone believe such a thing of her. Even George, who by now was growing used to Hope's tirades, could not entertain the notion that she'd taken the locket out of spite. On this occasion, he'd sided against Norah and told her she needed to apologise. Norah did so and noticed the ill-concealed glint of triumph beneath Hope's false tears.

After that, she made sure she hid anything of value to her and nothing else had disappeared from her room. However, Hope would still make up tales about Norah in her attempts to turn others against her. Just that morning, Norah had overheard her telling the maid, Elsie, that Norah had said she was fat and looked like a meringue in her new dress. It had just enough of the ring of truth about it to convince Elsie and Norah heard her consoling the sobbing girl.

'You look beautiful in that dress, Miss Hope. She's probably jealous that she doesn't fill her dresses as well as you. Come now, don't fret so. Mrs Morris has been baking scones and they're still warm. Come down to the kitchen. One of them, with some butter and strawberry jam, will cheer you up.'

Hope had allowed herself to be led, like a martyr, to the kitchen where she'd then regaled Mrs Morris with the same story and Norah had since found herself on the receiving end of disapproving glances from both the servants, whom she'd always regarded as her friends.

Now it was almost time for dinner. Sighing heavily, Norah changed out of her riding breeches and into a skirt. Since her arrival, the new Mrs Dunn had insisted that they all change for dinner and then collect in the drawing room while they waited for the evening meal to be announced. Norah couldn't see the point of it when there was just the four of them but, apparently, ladies in decent society always dressed for dinner and she knew it wasn't worth arguing. She'd already learnt that, where Adele was concerned, she needed to choose her battles carefully.

She was last into the drawing room and crossed over to the window where her father was standing, morosely looking out over the rose garden. It had been a good year for the roses but now the bushes had received their autumn pruning and were looking sadly bare and forlorn.

'Have you seen Arthur today, Daddy?' she asked. 'He wasn't round the stables when I went down earlier and I wanted to ask him about Trojan's leg. There seemed to be a little heat in his near foreleg when I'd ridden him today and I wanted his opinion. He's not lame or anything,' she continued, 'but he always seems to know what to do for the best.'

'He's been out ploughing all day,' replied her father grimly. 'He's no time at the moment to be fussing about the horses unless they're pulling the plough.'

'I realise that. I know how busy it is this time of year. I just wanted his opinion, that's all.'

George did not reply and Norah turned away. He obviously had things on his mind, she thought, and it would not do to trouble him.

'Oh Norah, I do wish you would make more of an effort with your appearance!' Adele's shrill voice cut through the chilly evening air. 'I swear it looks as if you haven't even taken a brush to that hair of yours. Look at Hope. See how beautiful *she* looks this evening! Of course, she would look lovely, no matter what she was wearing, but that new dress is particularly becoming.'

Norah surveyed Hope's attire and remembered her stepsister's earlier meringue reference. Privately, she thought she looked more like a blancmange than a meringue. She was dressed in shiny, pink satin which quivered as she preened at her mother's praise.

'Very nice,' she said politely. 'I wonder what's for dinner. I'm famished.'

'Young ladies should never be *famished*. They keep their appetites to themselves,' Adele admonished.

Norah was saved from a reply by Elsie's arrival. 'Dinner is served. Would you like to come through?' she announced formally, as she'd been instructed by her new mistress.

Silently, they followed Elsie into the dining room and took their places at the beautifully laid table. The white linen tablecloth was covered by an impressive array of shining silverware and sparkling glassware. Although Adele did not approve of wine, or alcohol of any type for that matter, and a jug of water was all that was allowed, she insisted that three different wine glasses were displayed at every evening meal.

After the grace was said and, as Elsie served the roast lamb and vegetables, Adele chattered about her day. She'd been busily dispensing largesse to the poor of the village and liked to talk at length about how grateful everyone had been and how greatly she was admired. Today she'd visited Jack Fowler who had been unable to work since he'd fallen from a horse and broken his back. His wife Agnes had struggled to make ends meet and relied heavily on charity to feed her four young children.

'Poor little mites. They were glad to see me, I can tell you. First I instructed them from the bible so they knew how to be properly grateful and then we opened the basket. I have to say Mrs Morris had outdone herself. There was some freshly baked bread, raspberry jam, fruit cake, biscuits and some apple jelly. It made me feel quite peckish myself but, of course, I declined when I was offered some. Mrs Fowler called me a saint but I told her I was just doing the Lord's work. Apparently, none of the other ladies of the village do as much as I for the poor, not even Mrs Rogers. You would think, being the vicar's wife, she would make more of an effort. I have to say the people of Great Chalkham are very glad you married me, I can tell you.' This last remark was directed smugly at George who had been concentrating on his food more than his wife.

Norah, concerned that her father seemed very withdrawn and troubled, laid a hand on his arm. 'Is everything alright, Daddy?' she asked. 'You look as if you're worrying about something.'

George laid down his knife and fork and looked round at the three faces staring at him. 'I might as well tell you,' he said harshly. 'Corn prices are down again and today I've had to lay off three men. I hated to do it but I've got no choice. We haven't the money to pay their wages. This also means that we have to tighten our belts or we too will be in need of charity.'

'Oh no. Poor you. That must have been terrible!' Norah exclaimed. 'Er ... who did you lay off?' Her thoughts had immediately rushed to Arthur who had become a close friend over the past four years.

'Three chaps who should have long retired but haven't been able to afford to do so – Jack Nobbs, George Darkins and Arnold Crabtree,' George answered. 'Poor sods. They might not be the only ones to go either, if prices at the Corn Exchange continue to fall.'

'Language please George!' scolded Adele, frowning at her husband and then brightening as a thought occurred to her. 'Obviously, this means my work will be even more important. I'll speak to Mrs Morris about organising some food for me to take round to them all tomorrow.'

George sighed. 'Adele, I admire your concern for the poor but I don't think you understand the seriousness of the situation. We can't afford to keep feeding the village like this. And we can't afford to keep buying new dresses.' He looked pointedly across at Hope. 'We need to make some adjustments so that we don't go under ourselves.'

'My goodness, George. You're making it sound as if we're one step away from destitution!' Adele exclaimed shrilly. 'I'm quite sure things are not as bad as all that. You're all doom and gloom at the moment. In fact, you're quite scaring me!'

George sighed heavily. 'I'm just saying that farming is not at all profitable at the moment. In fact, it hasn't been since the corn price guarantees ended in 1921. Lots of farmland has already been sold up around here and I don't want that to happen to us. The situation is serious, Adele, but I'm sure we'll get through it. We just need to be more prudent, that's all. I'm sorry if I scared you.'

'Well, I'm sure we can all give up something to help, can't we girls?' Adele replied nobly, 'But George, I must insist on helping the poor where I can. They rely on me for so much, you see. I have to give them the spiritual guidance they don't receive from that idle vicar and his wife and they all look up to me. I couldn't possibly let them down.' She gave him her most sanctimonious smile.

George sighed again. 'I'm sure you're very good, Adele, and I wouldn't want to deprive the poor of anything but perhaps more spiritual than actual sustenance would be helpful. Just for a while'

Adele nodded sympathetically. 'I understand, George. I'll do what I can and so will Hope.'

At her mother's prompting, Hope nodded. 'I suppose I could manage without a new dress for my birthday next week,' she said with a martyred air.

'Oh darling, I don't think things are so bad that you can't have a new frock ... not when it's your fifteenth birthday!' Adele interrupted quickly. 'We'll think of something else ... but you're such a good girl for offering.' She patted her daughter's hand with approval before turning her attentions to her stepdaughter. 'Now, what about you, Norah? What are you going to give up? It's not just Hope and I who have to make sacrifices you know. I know ...' She smiled in triumph. 'You could give up your horse! It's high time you concentrated on more ladylike pursuits anyway!'

Norah looked up in shock and dismay. 'Not Trojan! I'd willingly forego any number of new dresses but not my horse.' She turned to her father. 'Daddy, please don't say I have to lose Trojan. I'll make sure that no one else has to look after him from now on so we would only be saving the cost of his feed. Please, Daddy!'

'Don't fret, Nolly,' her father replied. 'Of course, you can keep him. I know how much he means to you. And I would appreciate you looking after him and perhaps my horse too. Arthur really doesn't have the time for it these days. I need him on the farm – he's excellent with the plough horses.'

Norah was flooded with relief. 'Thanks Daddy. I really will try to be more of a help to you. And I mean it about the dresses.'

Adele snorted with disapproval. 'I think you're missing the whole point of sacrifice, Norah. It means being prepared to give up something you *want* to keep, not giving up essential items like dresses which you have no time for anyway. I don't know how we're ever going to find you a husband at this rate.'

Wisely, Norah bit back the retort which had sprung to her lips. She had no intention of getting married, at least not until she had been to university and perhaps pursued a career but, as yet, she had not shared this radical notion with her stepmother.

The rest of the mealtime passed uneventfully. After the plates had been cleared away, Adele and Hope withdrew to their sitting room and Norah was afforded a rare moment alone with her father. He had picked up the newspaper and she watched him reading, his face creased in a frown. She really wanted to question him further about his money worries but at the same time she didnt want to trouble him further. In the end, she settled for a topical item of conversation.

'Did you hear that Amelia Hodge has won a place at Cambridge? Do you remember her? She's Herbert Hodges' daughter, just three years older than me. She hopes to become a surgeon, just like Lydia Turner. Isn't that marvellous?'

'It certainly is.' George lifted his head from the newspaper and smiled at her. 'I'm all for clever women carving out a career for themselves. Ever since they won the vote, more and more are making a name for themselves in their own right, just like you will, my dear. The world is changing and I'm all for giving power to women of good sense.' Then he sighed. 'Talking of women of good sense, I realise now Norah that I may have rushed into things a bit too hastily with your stepmother. I think she has a good heart but she certainly doesn't seem to have much sense, especially where that simpleton daughter of hers is concerned. I thought I was doing the right thing for both of us in marrying her. You had been lacking female companionship but I'm sorry it hasn't worked out as I'd hoped.'

Norah privately disagreed with her father about Adele's good heart but, as she always did, sought to reassure him. 'Don't apologise, Daddy,' she said. 'I know you've always done what you thought best for me. Things have been difficult for us both since Mummy died and at least now I have another woman to turn to when I need help with female matters.' This last comment was not actually true as she had no intention of ever consulting her stepmother on anything. Instead, she'd always turned to Mrs Morris when she needed advice of a feminine nature. 'And at least I've still got you.' She walked over to him and gave him a hug. 'The best daddy in the world.'

He squeezed her in return. 'If only ...' he replied. 'Now I need to go out and haven't you some embroidery which requires your urgent attention?'

She rolled her eyes. 'Absolutely. Apparently, my stitching is nowhere near neat enough at the moment and I lack concentration. I can't think why.'

'Well, you'd best get on with it then.'

George watched his daughter give him a mock salute and leave the room. With her strong, confident stride and hair tumbling down her back, he realised how lovely she had become and his heart ached. Her mother would have been so proud of her and he felt desperately sad that she had missed their daughter's transition from a gangly child to a beautiful woman. For himself, he felt he had failed her as a father by saddling her with a narrow-minded, unloving stepmother. Already he knew that his recent marriage had been a big mistake and wished he knew how to resolve the situation. After just a few weeks of marriage, Adele had turfed him out of the marital bed, claiming that his snoring kept her awake, and she'd instructed the servants to move his things into the one remaining bedroom. It was a small, dark room facing east and the single bed was uncomfortable for his large frame but he had borne it without complaint. At least now he could return from the pub without the fear of waking her and receiving a sharp rebuke.

His new wife and stepdaughter, however, were the least of his worries. Earlier in the year he'd been forced to take out a loan to keep the farm afloat and pay the wages. He'd hoped corn prices would recover sufficiently to enable him to make good the loan once he had sold this year's crop but that hadn't been the case. Instead, he was going to have to ask the bank to increase his debt to tide things over and the future looked bleak.

Pushing such thoughts aside, he reached for his coat and headed out of the door. The temporary respite afforded by a few pints of beer and several whiskies had become a daily necessity and tonight was certainly no different.

The days shortened and autumn became winter. The people of Great Chalkham went about their business as usual but there was no denying that many were feeling the pinch of financial instability. It was common knowledge that farms, the lifeblood of the village, were impoverished. It was clear to see in the rusted equipment and dilapidated buildings, hedges and ditches. Most families relied on the farm wages of thirty shillings a week and prayed that their employment would continue. The farmers themselves, George Dunn among them, were grey-faced and morose, except when they were drowning their sorrows at The Plough (they had run out of credit at the Fox and Hare.) Without exception, they had all borrowed money from the bank and then borrowed more money to keep up with the interest payments on their loans. Three farmers had already been forced to sell but with land going for as little as £5 per acre, the rest were grimly hanging on.

At Willow Farm, Norah was forced to listen to constant complaints from her stepmother and sister about the lack of decent society in Great Chalkham. Chalkham Hall had recently been sold and Adele was disappointed that its new owners, Cyril and Edith Brooke, did not appear to entertain a great deal. She and Hope had visited shortly after their arrival in the village and found Mrs Brooke to be 'rather plain and dull.' Apparently, according to the village grapevine, Mr Brooke was 'something in trade' but Adele had yet to meet him. She had suggested to George that they have a small dinner party to which they could invite the Brookes and other worthy guests but George had dismissed the notion out of hand.

'He has become so ill-tempered recently,' she berated Norah, as if it were her fault.

'I think he's just got a lot on his mind,' Norah replied evenly. 'You'll just have to be patient. He's not normally so down.'

Truthfully, she was becoming increasingly concerned about her father. When at home, he spent most of his time in his study where, Norah suspected although she could not be sure, he kept a bottle of whisky. At mealtimes, he was typically taciturn and would answer in monosyllables. Occasionally, Norah thought, his speech was slightly slurred and then he would react angrily to his wife's admonishments.

Norah no longer attended the village school and instead she and Hope were instructed in needlecraft, music and household management by a retired teacher called Mrs Beecham. She was a sour, humourless woman and Norah frequently found herself feeling like a prisoner in her own home. She would gaze longingly out of the window until she was inevitably scolded for her inattention. After every session, Mrs Beecham would please Adele by flattering her with the magnitude of Hope's accomplishments whilst criticising all of Norah's efforts. Norah, in turn, had begged her father to be excused from these 'lessons' but, on this matter, George had sided with Adele.

'I'm sorry, Nolly,' he smiled wanly at her, 'but you can't spend all day out on your horse and these are things you may well find useful in the future.'

Norah endured the sessions with as much patience as she could muster and did her best to become, in the words of her stepmother, 'a proper young lady.' Meanwhile, she spent as much time as she could studying for the exams she would have to take to be admitted to St Hilda's.

Adele's habit of dispensing food to the poor ceased entirely when she found her household budget cut by a considerable margin. Despite her vociferous complaints, George insisted they get by on just thirty shillings a week. Poor Mrs Morris found herself reduced to buying cheaper cuts of meat to make ends meet and struggled to provide meals to Adele's exacting standards.

Norah was just thankful they had food on the table at all. She was recently made painfully aware of the poverty in the village. Her buxom friend Sybil, still just fifteen, had been married last week to a much older wealthy widower from the nearby village of Copton. When Norah had naively asked her how she could bear to marry such an old man, Sybil had shrugged her shoulders.

'It's better than starving,' she answered bluntly, 'and it means I'll be able to take care of Ma and Pa and all the little 'uns. It's all right for you, Norah. You don't know what it's like to go to bed hungry every night.'

Sybil's words had struck home and Norah had since secretly begged scraps from the kitchen to take to those with the most need. She was shocked to see how thin many of the children were and how grateful their mothers were for small pieces of cheese and crusts of bread. It made her resolve to do more and, without Adele's knowledge, she asked her father to sell Trojan. He initially refused.

'Is this because of your stepmother?' he demanded angrily. 'I've already said that we are not selling your horse. How dare she keep interfering!'

'No, no, she doesn't know anything about it,' Norah replied quickly. 'This is my decision. I would like to use the money to help some of my friends in the village. I cannot bear to see them struggling.'

George shook his head sadly. 'When the money is gone, they'll still be struggling.'

'Yes but at least then I won't feel so guilty,' Norah persisted. 'You should see them Daddy. The Joneses are living on next to nothing since Albert got laid off by George Coombes six weeks ago. I just can't ride by on Trojan and ignore them. I have to do something, however small.'

Her father smiled and put his arm around her. 'I'm so proud of you, I hope you know that. Alright, I'll sell Trojan if that's what you wish. We can't expect to get much for him though. There's not much demand for riding horses at the moment.'

So, Trojan was duly sold and Norah dispensed food staples throughout that winter to the neediest families. When news of what she was doing got back to Adele, her stepmother was quick to take the credit.

'I'm delighted to see Norah following my example,' she confided to Mrs Rogers, the vicar's wife. 'The girl was quite wild when I first came to Willow Farm but I have taught her the importance of charity and it's most pleasing to see my influence bearing fruit.'

With her daily lessons with Mrs Beecham, her private studies and her regular food trips into the village, Norah saw little of Arthur that winter but he did take the opportunity, when it presented itself, to tell her how much he admired what she was doing. She was walking past the stables when she heard his voice calling her name and turned back. He was in the middle of feeding the farm horses and she immediately began filling hay nets. She had missed the smell of the stables and, she realised, she had missed Arthur's company.

He had grown taller and filled out over the years he'd worked on the farm and Norah could not help but notice how well-muscled he now was. He gave her a grin.

'Good to see you haven't forgotten how to do that, now you've become a young lady,' he teased and she reddened slightly.

'Don't be daft!' She finished filling the hay nets and deftly started hanging them up. 'There wasn't much point hanging around here with no horse to ride. I do miss Trojan. I hope he's settled well in his new home.'

'Let's hope they feed him well,' Arthur retorted. 'He was the greediest horse I ever knew! That was a fine thing you did,' he continued. 'Selling him like that. It couldn't have been easy.'

Norah turned away, feeling uncomfortable under the warmth of his praise. 'It was nothing,' she shrugged. 'I don't have much time for riding these days, not with all the embroidery Mrs Beecham is having me do. I'm constantly amazed at just how exciting my life has become!'

'Well I know a lot of folks who are very grateful to you. You have a good heart Norah.'

She looked up and felt flustered by the intensity of his gaze. His brown eyes were glowing with an emotion she struggled to identify and she swallowed hard.

'Right, best be off,' she said hurriedly retrieving the basket she'd put down. 'Things to do, people to see and all that.'

She was very aware of his eyes on her as she continued up the lane towards the village and it made her feel very self-conscious. It was a most strange sensation, she decided, and not one she had encountered before or one she liked. She subsequently found herself daydreaming about Arthur at odd moments of the day and wondered what it would be like to be kissed by him. It was fortunate that she would soon be leaving for Oxford. Study at St Hilda's would soon extinguish such girly, romantic fancies.

Snow fell in mid-December and continued for the rest of the month. On Christmas Day, a blizzard raged and Norah was thankful that she did not have to go out. She thought of those who would be feeding the cattle and horses and considered herself fortunate to sit beside the fire.

This was their first Christmas with Adele and Hope; Norah missed the comfortable days she had spent celebrating alone with her father. Traditionally, Mrs Morris and Elsie would spend the day with their own families and she and George would eat cold cuts and toast chestnuts on the fire. This year, though, Adele had insisted that she needed the servants to serve Christmas lunch, a small goose she decided, and that only once that had been cleared away were the servants free to do as they wished. The blizzard, however, made it impossible for them to leave and, as evening approached, Norah found them sitting in the kitchen.

'I've brought you both a glass of sherry,' she announced. 'You certainly deserve it. That was a delicious lunch, Mrs Morris. I'm so sorry you can't get home. Won't you both come and join us in the sitting room? Hope is playing Christmas carols on the piano so it's quite jolly.'

'No, no, I don't think Mrs Dunn would approve,' the cook said hastily and Elsie nodded her agreement. 'The sherry's a kind thought though and most welcome. A real Christmas treat.'

'Well alright, if you're sure you can't be persuaded,' Norah said and then smiled. 'I'll bring you a top up in a little while.'

She made her way back to the door of the sitting room and peered around. Hope was halfway through O Little Town of Bethlehem, Adele was sitting opposite and her father was nowhere to be seen. Norah felt a twinge of anxiety. Even for him, he had been uncommonly quiet throughout lunch and had then spent the next two hours reading yesterday's paper which Norah was sure he had already read. She decided he must have retreated to his study and resolved to do her best to entice him out of his gloom. She headed to the drinks cabinet to pour him a glass of his favourite malt but the bottle was gone. He'd obviously taken it with him.

George's study was a small room tucked away beyond the dining room. As Norah approached, she detected something which sounded like a low moaning noise. It was this which made her hesitate to knock on the door and she listened more intently. It sounded like sobbing. With a heavy heart, she quietly turned the handle and peered around the door. There was her father, sitting slumped at his desk, his head in his hands, and crying as if his heart was breaking.

Norah watched him for a few minutes, unsure what she should do, before silently turning away and closing the door. She knew that her father had been troubled for the past year but this was much worse than she'd thought. When the moment was right, she would have a chat with him and attempt to find out the exact extent of his worries.

Boxing Day dawned cold, crisp and clear and Norah felt considerably cheered as she hastily pulled on her clothes. After being cooped up all day yesterday, she could not wait to get outside.

Downstairs, Mrs Morris was busy in the kitchen and Norah called out a greeting before fastening her coat and pulling on her hat, gloves and boots. No one else was about and she took great delight in stamping her footprints in the fresh, glistening snow. It was like a magical world, eerily silent and still, and she tramped slowly across the lawn and towards the front of the house.

Another trail of larger footprints led from the front door and down the drive. Her father was already up and she decided to follow his path. Maybe, away from the house, they would be able to have a proper chat. It was always so difficult indoors with Adele, Hope and the servants ever present.

The footprints led past the stables and the farm buildings and down into the village where there were a few more signs of life. A small group of children, in brightly coloured hats and scarves, were busily building a snowman and Norah stopped to admire it. Then, around the corner, she met a young lad sprinting as if his life depended on it. The next second a snowball whizzed past her head.

'Oops, sorry Miss.' A small boy, bare-headed and rosy cheeked, gave her a rueful grin. 'I was trying to get Charlie Dawkins.'

The first boy emerged from behind her. 'Missed!' he yelled and plunged his hands back into the snow.

'Just hold fire boys until I get out of range,' Norah smiled.

The footprints continued past the church, the shops (which were all closed for the holiday) and on beyond the mill. There, they became muddled with other much smaller footprints and eventually they disappeared up the small slope which served the village children for sledging. They had stamped down on the snow to make it more slippery and there were already four makeshift sledges precariously sliding with varying degrees of success.

Norah stood and watched, remembering how her father used to pull her around on the wooden sledge he had made for her. It was heart-warming to see the sheer joy on the children's faces as they shot down the slope and the squeals of delight when they toppled over into the snow.

After a while, she circled around the mound, trying to spot where her father had headed next, but it was hopeless. Instead, she decided to walk back the other way along by the old chalk pits.

She had not ventured this way for a while and walked briskly, keeping well clear of the edge of the pits which were steep sided and very deep. There was something about them which had always given her the creeps when she'd been younger and even now, when she knew there was nothing to be afraid of, the sight of them, stark and menacing, gave her chills down her spine.

Shrugging off her foolishness, she marched on and, when she turned the corner, she could see, in the distance, Willow Farm, smoke billowing from its chimneys. Immediately, she thought of breakfast and realised she was starving. The fresh air had given her an appetite. In no time at all, she was back inside the warmth of the kitchen and chattering to Mrs Morris as she tucked into her eggs.

'Have you seen Father at all this morning?' she asked.

The cook shook her head. 'No. He was already up and out before I surfaced.'

'I expect he'll turn up shortly,' Norah continued. 'Now, you and Elsie need to take today off as you couldn't get home yesterday. I know where everything is and I can take care of things just for the day.'

'Ah, thank you, Norah. I was hoping to spend Boxing Day with them. Elsie's already headed home as it'll take her a while to walk.'

Elsie's family lived in Newham, five miles away, and she had her own room at Willow Farm whereas Mrs Morris did not live in. She usually walked the mile and a half from the house she shared with her husband and two sons in Little Chalkham.

'Right, I'll be off then. I'll see you tomorrow.'

'You have a lovely day, Mrs Morris. You deserve it.'

Norah finished her breakfast and began washing up her plate and cup. Adele and Hope were notoriously late risers and she knew it would be some time before they appeared. It would be an ideal time to talk to her father, if only he were to return.

However, George failed to put in an appearance throughout the morning and, by lunchtime, Norah was seriously worried.

'Did Father mention to you where he was headed this morning?' she asked Adele as they sat around the dining table eating soup which Mrs Morris had left for Norah to heat through.

'Of course not.' Adele's tone was sharp. 'He never tells me anything. I expect he's having lunch with one of his cronies ... or he's off gallivanting around the countryside somewhere.'

Her words gave Norah an idea.' I wonder if he's gone shooting,' she pondered aloud. 'It would be a fine, clear day for it. I'll see if he has taken his gun with him.'

She leapt from the table and walked through the house to her father's gun cabinet, which was kept in his study. Sure enough, his gun was gone. Relief flooded through her. At least now she knew what he was up to.

Norah decided to go out again in the afternoon rather than sit and make conversation with Adele and Hope. First, she headed back to the kitchen and surveyed the well-stocked pantry. She could take a few leftovers from yesterday's goose to the Partridge family, she thought. Bernard Partridge had been unable to find work since he had been laid off by George Coombes in the autumn and his family had been suffering more than most.

With a small paper bag in her hand, she headed out of the door once again. It was still bitterly cold and the sky had darkened after the bright morning sunshine. Norah shivered. The day no longer felt filled with promise.

Suddenly, she saw a figure running up the drive towards the farmhouse. She recognised Arthur immediately and smiled broadly in welcome. Then she wondered what had happened to cause him to run with such urgency. Was it one of the horses or maybe one of the cows? As he approached, there was something about his face and the way he refused to meet her eyes which filled her with dread. Something awful had happened. His pace slowed to a walk and then he stopped, staring at her helplessly. She stood rooted to the spot and waited. Already, she sensed the horror of what he was about to say.

'Norah, I'm so sorry. There's been a terrible accident ...'

CHAPTER 7

Jennifer - November 2016

Jennifer was used to walking a solitary path. As an only child, she became accustomed to her own company from an early age and spent many hours, growing up, in her bedroom alone, immersed in the fantasy worlds that books had provided. At school, she never lacked friends but she was one of the quiet ones, serious and studious, preferring to watch from the side-lines rather than taking centre stage. She was known as the class swot because lessons came to her so easily. She quickly learnt it was best to keep a low profile and adopt an air of self-deprecation. No one liked a know-it-all.

She was ambitious though. Her father was a doctor and he had nothing but the highest expectations for his only daughter. Unwilling to disappoint him, she worked hard through school and university and always achieved the highest levels. Stephen Thompson was a dour man, twenty-six years older than Elizabeth Bainbridge, Jennifer's mother, whom he'd married when she was barely sixteen. Elizabeth had told her daughter that she'd experienced a very strict upbringing by parents who had adopted her as a young child. She was desperate to escape. When Jennifer's father had proposed marriage, after a brief courtship, she was swept along by the romance of it all. She had considered herself fortunate to have attracted the regard of the tall, elegant doctor. Jennifer's arrival had followed just nine months after the wedding but complications during the birth meant she was unable to have any more children. The marriage deteriorated quickly after that but they had stayed together and Jennifer's childhood was coloured by bitter rows and cold silences between her two parents. Elizabeth had been a very pretty woman with red gold hair and brown eyes but years of disappointment in a loveless marriage prematurely aged her and she died of cancer when she was only thirty-nine.

At the age of twenty-one, Jennifer joined a large firm of accountants. She had always enjoyed the logic of numbers and, at the time, it had seemed an obvious choice of career. For the first few years, she had enjoyed the challenge of working her way through all the exams and gradually earning herself more responsibility. Once she was fully qualified, though, a sense of dissatisfaction crept in and she began to cast around for something more.

The turning point, when it came, was totally unexpected. Children from a local primary school were doing a project on women in business and she was asked to go in and answer questions about her job. Now aged twenty-six, she considered children an anathema and did not look forward to the experience. She wondered how she could make her job seem exciting and interesting to a group of ten-year-olds and spent some while preparing a talk.

The day came. With trepidation, she walked into the classroom and proceeded to have the time of her life. The children were polite and interested during her brief presentation and then bombarded her with questions.

'Do you enjoy your job?' asked one boy with piercing, blue eyes.

'Er ... of course,' Jennifer replied lamely.

'What do you enjoy most about it?' he persisted.

Jennifer thought quickly. What exactly did she most like about her work? 'The bit I like best,' she began, 'is .... the people ... the clients ... getting to know what their needs are and what solutions I can provide.'

'Do you spend much time doing that?' asked a small girl with frizzy, brown hair. 'You said you spend most of the time in your office working on your own.'

'Er ... well yes, that's true ... but I like that too.'

'If you like working with other people, why did you choose a job where you spend most of your time on your own?' asked the blue-eyed boy.

'That's a very good question,' Jennifer smiled at him ruefully. 'I suppose the truth is that, while I enjoy my job, I'm always looking for a new challenge. There's nothing to say I won't be doing something entirely different in a few years' time. That's why it's so important to work hard at school,' she rushed on, having intercepted a questioning glance from the class teacher, Miss Potter. 'Then you have lots of choices open to you. You can do whatever you want.'

'Could you be an astronaut?' asked a small boy sitting in the front row. 'That's what I want to be when I'm grown up.'

'That's great. I think I would need a lot of training to become an astronaut. I would probably have to start by going back to university and doing a different degree but there's no reason why I couldn't do that.'

'If you weren't an accountant, what would you most like to be?' This question came from a serious- looking girl with long, plaited, blonde hair and large, black framed glasses.

'I would have to think about that,' she answered truthfully. 'It's not something I've seriously considered.'

'You could be a hairdresser like my mum,' another girl chimed in helpfully.

'Or a stunt pilot,' exclaimed a boy from the back of the room.

'You could be a teacher. I think you'd be a good teacher. You could come and teach us,' the girl with plaits offered excitedly.

Jennifer snatched a look at the alarmed face of Miss Potter and smiled at the girl. 'That's very kind of you but you already have an excellent teacher and I would need lots of training. It's a very difficult job.'

'No, it isn't,' snorted the blue-eyed boy. 'It's us who have to do all the work!'

'That's enough, Kevin,' Miss Potter snapped with a steely glare. 'Now, are there any more questions for Miss Thompson before she leaves?'

'I like your shoes,' said another girl in the front row who had spent most of Jennifer's visit staring at her feet. 'Where did you get them from?'

'*Relevant* questions only,' Miss Potter interrupted before Jennifer could reply. 'Remember Angela, we talked about this. Just questions about Miss Thompson's job.' Her tone was becoming increasingly exasperated.

'Actually, I think I bought them from Debenhams.' The girl was now looking distinctly downcast and Jennifer gave her an encouraging smile.

'Hey, my mum works there. She probably sold them to you. She's their top saleswoman,' a boy with a snotty nose announced joyfully, following up with a loud sniff.

'Right. Well if there are no more questions, what do you all want to say to Miss Thompson for giving up her time for us this morning?' prompted Miss Potter.

'Thank you,' the class chorused dutifully.

'It's been a pleasure,' Jennifer beamed at the children. 'I thought you asked some excellent questions. Good luck to you all in whichever career you choose to pursue.'

As she was picking up her things and putting on her coat, she heard the girl with plaits whispering to her neighbour. 'She's really nice. I wish she was our teacher.' The comment gave her a warm glow and she drove back to her office with a broad smile on her face. Maybe she could become a teacher … If that class were anything to go by, it would certainly be entertaining.

The seed was planted but she didn't rush into it. Instead, she arranged to volunteer at another local school – one day a week for six weeks – which she took off work as holiday. Each time she went, she worked in a different class so she could experience the true flavour of life as a teacher and, each time, she thoroughly enjoyed the day. It made her accountancy work seem dull and unrewarding and she decided to bite the bullet. Without further delay, she applied for a place to study for a post graduate certificate of education and, having been successfully awarded a place, handed in her notice at work.

Her father had been furious. 'All that hard work ... the last five years ... totally wasted!' he raged. 'All that money spent on that fancy school thrown away on a dead-end job like teaching. You'll hardly make your fortune in a profession like that. The way you were going, you could have made partner in just a few more years.' After the bluster, he tried a more subtle approach. 'I would never have believed you were a quitter. I thought I'd brought you up with the determination to see things through.'

However, the decision had been made and Jennifer stood firm. She went through the training course, secured her first teaching job and so began her new career. There were many times, after a particularly difficult day, when she wondered what on earth she was doing but she never regretted her choice. Twelve years later, she was awarded her first headship; teaching had become her life. The traditional, 'husband and children' route was not for her. To do her job to the best of her ability and to make a difference to the lives on the children in her care overrode everything else. All her passion she poured into her work and, now that had come to an end, she needed something else.

It had felt so strange, almost surreal, leaving school that last time, handing over the keys to the caretaker, walking to her car, driving out the gate, no longer a part of that community. Her colleagues had taken her out for a quiet dinner, as a send-off, but there had been none of the fanfare she might have expected after a successful career spanning thirty years. She wouldn't have wanted it. It would have been inappropriate in the circumstances.

At least her new venture had kept her busy and given her a fresh purpose for the past few months. But now, she had to admit, as she sat alone in her cottage on a wet November afternoon, she was lonely. She missed the buzz of school life, the chat, the laughs, the constant demands made upon her by colleagues, pupils and parents. She missed being needed.

Having recognised the problem, Jennifer concentrated her efforts on thinking of solutions. It was not in her nature to sit about feeling sorry for herself. She decided that it was time to get involved in village life – maybe join a club or two, offer her services as a volunteer, meet new people. So far, she could count on one hand the villagers of Chalkham she could name.

She reached for the parish magazine and the telephone. The race night David Brewer had mentioned was tomorrow night. Maybe it wasn't too late to get a ticket. Remembering that the initial invitation had come from Jill Riddleston, the landlady from the popular village pub, The Fox and Hare, she found the telephone number and keyed the number into her mobile. She'd been in the pub a few times for lunch, when she had been visiting the cottage to see how the improvements were coming along, and for an evening meal when she had first moved in. Jill, she recalled, was a tall woman in her forties with cropped blonde hair and a wide smile. It had been good of her to think of inviting Jennifer to a village event. Hopefully, there would be tickets left.

'Oh lovey, I'm so glad you rang,' Jill exclaimed in her broad Suffolk accent after Jennifer had explained she was free to go to the race night after all. 'We're still one short on our table so that's perfect. Just come along to the community centre for seven o'clock and you can pay for your ticket on the night.'

'Wonderful. I'll see you then.'

Jennifer put her phone down with a sense of satisfaction. She'd made a start.

It was a dry night so Jennifer had decided to walk the mile down to the hub of the village where the community centre was situated. If David Brewer was on her table, she would probably need a glass of wine, she thought.

Jill was hovering near the doorway, looking out for her, and greeted her with a hug. 'I'm so pleased you could make it after all. This is my husband, Jeff.' She gestured towards a large, portly man with a bald head and twinkling grey eyes.

'Pleased to meet you,' Jennifer said formally, extending her hand.

Jeff ignored it and enveloped her instead in a generous hug, kissing her loudly on her right cheek. 'You don't stand on ceremony with me,' he grinned. 'Now, let me get you something to drink.'

He headed towards the crowded bar while Jill led her across the room to a round table where five other guests were already seated. One of them was David Brewer, smartened up for the evening in a brown jacket and white open-necked shirt which suited his dark colouring. He immediately leapt from his seat and also, rather disconcertingly, greeted her with a hug and a kiss.

'You didn't bring your friend then,' he said.

'No. She couldn't make it after all.' Jennifer surveyed the other people round the table who were introduced to her as Sheila and Mike Blake, Jeremy Willis and Pandora Pardew. She took her seat next to Jeremy who, she quickly discovered, was a retired bank manager in his early seventies whose wife had died six years ago. He liked talking about himself and completely monopolised her attention for the next half hour. Fortunately, at that point, food was served and he focused his attention on his lamb curry, leaving Jennifer able to speak to the others around the table.

Sheila and Mike were a grey-haired couple in their fifties wearing almost matching blue jumpers and black trousers. In response to her enquiry, they told her that they had run the village post office for the last thirty years and had two children, both married, and five grandchildren. They had a habit of finishing each other's sentences and then bickering good naturedly about what they were actually going to say.

Pandora was obviously David's date, judging by the proprietary hand she kept on his arm and the way she kept calling him 'darling' in cut glass tones. She was an attractive, expensively dressed brunette, probably in her late forties although she looked younger, with flawless skin and glossy, red lips, curved in a flirtatious pout. David was clearly enjoying her company, although perhaps, Jennifer thought cattily, the view down her low-cut, silk blouse had something to do with it.

'Do tell us about yourself, Jennifer,' Mike Blake prompted politely across the table.

'And what brings you to Great Chalkham?' his wife, Sheila added.

'I fell in love with Horseshoes Cottage and decided it was just what I was looking for. I'm planning on using the two spare bedrooms for bed and breakfast or holiday lets,' Jennifer replied.

'Oh. Have you always done that sort of thing?' Jeff Riddleston joined in the conversation.

'Not at all but it's always been a dream of mine. In my previous life, I was a primary headteacher in Norfolk.'

'Heavens, that's a bit of a career change! Well, I wish you luck with it,' Pandora said dismissively. 'Jeff, this lamb curry is divine. You must give me the recipe.'

'Jeff's the chef at the pub,' Jeremy explained to Jennifer, 'and they've provided the food for this evening.'

'Well, I have to say I agree with Pandora,' Jennifer said. 'It's absolutely delicious.'

Jeff beamed. 'That's good. I'm glad you're all enjoying it.'

'I really admire anyone who can teach young children.' Jill directed the conversation back to Jennifer. 'I know I wouldn't have the patience and nowadays it's such a tough job. There isn't the respect for teachers that there used to be and so many children behave so badly. We see lots in the pub, running around and annoying other customers, and their parents just seem to ignore them.'

'I bet they didn't misbehave in your school, did they Jen?' David winked at her. 'I bet you ran a tight ship and the kids didn't dare put a foot out of place.'

'They had their moments,' Jennifer replied drily. 'In any school, there will be difficult children but that's all part of the challenge. It's a very rewarding career and I loved my job.'

'So why the change?' Mike Blake asked. 'You seem much too young to retire to a quiet life in the country.'

Jennifer smiled warmly at him. 'Thank you. I'll take that as a compliment.' She shrugged her shoulders. 'In answer to your question, it just seemed the right time. I'd been in teaching for thirty years and I was ready for something new.'

'Wasn't it awful about that child that died! That was a school in Norfolk wasn't it?' Sheila Blake said suddenly.

Jennifer felt her blood go cold. She carried on eating although her food had lost all its flavour.

'Yes, it was terrible. Poor little devil! He fell, didn't he, when he and his class were on some trip?' Jill added. 'Shocking to think that something like that could happen this day and age, what with all the health and safety regulations there are now.'

There was a moment of silence in which Jennifer willed someone to change the conversation. Instead, Pandora laid down her knife and fork and, observing Jennifer's sudden pallor, said, 'Did you know the school, Jennifer? Did you know the people involved?'

'I did.' Jennifer laid down her own cutlery and rose, unsteadily to her feet. 'Please excuse me for a moment.'

She felt the blood returning to her face in a rush as she made her way to the ladies'. She should have expected it, she realised. After all, it had been on the national news and in all the papers at the time. The memory of it all still made her feel sick, over a year later. It had been a residential trip to an outdoor activity centre run by trained staff and led by her most experienced teacher. Nothing should have gone wrong. Yet it did and a child had died; a likeable, outgoing, cheeky boy named Jasper Jones. His face still haunted her dreams at night. She herself had not been there but, as the headteacher, she felt acutely that his death was her responsibility. An enquiry had exonerated her and her staff and blame instead had focused on the activity centre and some of their procedures but that made no difference. Ultimately, she knew she would have to live with the guilt for the rest of her life.

Remaining in her job became untenable. How could she face parents when something like that had happened? The following term she had written to the chair of governors, tendering her resignation, and had remained in post until her replacement had been found.

She stared at her reflection in the mirror. Her cheeks were flushed and, to compose herself, she splashed her face with cold water. She then took her time reapplying her make up while she considered what she might say in response to further questions. Should she tell them? That would certainly put a dampener on the evening! Well, she decided, she would not lie if asked a direct question but she would not offer information either. She would just have to play it by ear.

Fortunately, when she returned to her table, the preliminaries had started for the first race of the evening and she was able to join the queue to place her bets, unsuccessfully as it turned out. The rest of the evening passed in a blur as the races were shown in quick succession and the raffle was drawn. It was then announced that two thousand pounds had been raised for the Air Ambulance and thanks were given to all who had helped to make the evening a success.

Jennifer realised, as she fetched her coat, that she had thoroughly enjoyed the evening and the company of the people around the table. She would have to invite them all round to the cottage for a meal perhaps. When she returned to say her goodbyes, she discovered there had been some discussion, in her absence, about who should walk her home. She had to laugh. For years, she had locked up her school late at night and gone home alone, completely unmolested. She was unused to such old-fashioned chivalry.

'It makes no sense for you to walk Jen home,' David was saying to Jeremy. 'You live on the other side of the village. I live next door – I'll do it.'

'But I thought you were taking me home,' Pandora pouted.

'You brought your car, remember,' David replied, looking pointedly at her red high heels. 'You didn't want to ruin your shoes.'

'Yes, but I was going to drive you home. I thought we were going to have a nightcap at mine,' she wheedled, taking hold of his arm and stroking his bicep.

'Ok, as long as we take Jen home too. Do you fancy a nightcap, Jen?' he asked, gently extricating himself from Pandora's grasp. Pandora shot her a venomous look.

'I'm fine thanks. I could do with some fresh air and I'm very capable of walking home myself. Please don't change your plans on my account,' she said diplomatically.

'I could use some air too. Right that settles it. I'll walk with Jen. Sorry Pandora, can we take a rain check on the nightcap?'

Pandora hid her disappointment with a sultry smile and leaned forward to kiss David lingeringly on the lips. 'Of course, darling,' she said huskily. 'Just don't leave it too long.'

'You didn't need to do this,' Jennifer said as they were walking home. The indignation she felt at David's usual high-handedness was tempered by the fact that she felt unexpectedly, secretly pleased he had given her preference over the very glamorous Pandora Pardew.

'I know.'

'Pandora was obviously expecting you to go home with her. I feel bad for her.'

'No need. She'll get over it.'

'Have you been together long?' she asked politely.

'We're not *together*, as you put it. We're just friends.'

'Oh, I see.'

They settled into a companionable silence as they walked briskly along Chalkham High Street. Jennifer was feeling distinctly mellow after three glasses of wine and, she rationalised, this made David's presence more palatable. It was a cold, clear, starlit night and the cover of darkness made her feel much more comfortable with him.

'She's lonely,' he said suddenly. 'Pandora, that is, and she's also used to having her own way. That's a dangerous combination for a single man of a certain age.'

She could feel his smile. 'I can't imagine she's been on her own for long.'

'About two years. She moved into the old farmhouse with her husband about five years ago. I think she was his second wife and I don't think he was her first husband. Anyway, he worked in the city so she was left to her own devices quite a lot. I guess she was bored. Well, the upshot of the story is that she had a fling with the gardener, the husband found out, they split up and later got divorced. She got the house so we were stuck with her.'

'I see,' she said again. 'What about you? Have you always been single?'

'No, I was married. I've got two kids, both happily settled themselves. My wife died six years ago.'

'Oh, I'm so sorry.'

Instinctively, she reached for his arm and gave it a squeeze. They walked the remainder of the journey in silence and stopped outside Jennifer's cottage.

'Thank you for walking me home,' she said formally.'

'Thank you for letting me,' he replied.

There was a brief, awkward moment and then he reached forward to give her a clumsy hug. 'Bye then. See you soon.'

'Bye.' To Jennifer's surprise, she found herself smiling as she unlocked her front door. Overall, it had been a good night.

CHAPTER 8

Norah – October- December 1926

Norah laid out her most treasured possessions on her bed ready to pack in her case. There was her locket, which she'd managed to find in Hope's jewellery box, her scrapbook of photographs and the press clippings she'd collected, including one about Lydia Turner graduating from St Hilda's. Not much to show for sixteen years; not much to bear witness to the life she had lived at Willow Farm.

Idly, she flicked through the first few pages of the scrapbook, reminiscing at the photographs from her twelfth birthday. How young she looked and how happy! She raised her head to view her reflection in the gilt framed mirror which hung on her wall. The face staring back at her was the same but thinner, paler and so much sadder. Her green eyes had worn the same haunted look for the past ten months, ever since that most terrible of events which had changed her life forever.

Her father was dead and her world had fallen apart. He had been killed in a shooting accident - at least, that was what she'd believed for the first two days after his death. It had only been then that the note was found, the note he must have written that evening on Christmas Day when she'd overheard him sobbing in his study. It was addressed to Norah and the words had filled her with horror.

My dearest Norah,
I am truly sorry but I cannot go on. My debts have grown and the bank is about to foreclose. Willow Farm is to be sold and I have lost everything – everything except you, my precious daughter.
Always know that I loved you and your mother dearly. My biggest regret is that I have not been the father you deserved these last few years.
Please forgive me, Nolly.
Your loving father.

She read the note over and over, unable to believe its meaning. Her father had taken his own life. How could he do that to her? Her grief had turned briefly to anger and she had raged against him. He'd left her alone in the world with no thought for her future. Obviously, he had not loved her enough or he could never had done such a thing. The tears flowed hotly down her cheeks as she struggled to come to terms with this new knowledge.

Eventually, though, her anger subsided and she was left again with the terrible grief of her father's loss and an overwhelming sense of guilt. If only she'd disturbed him that evening, this might never have happened. She had turned away from her father when he had needed her the most and this was the consequence. She could never ever forgive herself for that.

The next few weeks and months had passed in a haze of awfulness. Firstly, the funeral had taken place, with Hope crying noisily throughout and Adele adopting a martyred air. Norah had felt numb until the moment when the coffin had been lowered into the ground. Then the enormity of her bereavement had struck her afresh and she struggled to hold back the sob of despair burning her throat.

It was at that moment that Arthur had squeezed her arm. His quiet support had helped her through the rest of the ordeal and for that she would be forever grateful.

A visit from the bank manager had confirmed that Willow Farm was to be sold to cover George Dunn's debts. If it made a reasonable price, then Adele and Norah would be left with just a small amount each, certainly not enough to live on.

Adele had been livid. How dare her husband leave her in such straitened circumstances! He was a selfish, good-for-nothing coward who had betrayed her trust. Many in the village sympathised with her; she and Hope were frequently invited to tea at the vicarage or at Chalkham Hall. Norah was also invited but refused to go. It was hard enough listening to Adele berate her father's good name at home without having to listen to her badmouthing him to other people.

George's friends, though, from the farming community, had expressed their genuine condolences to Norah and spoken warmly of him as a good man.

'We're all in the same boat,' George Coombes had stated grimly. 'I can understand what George did. I'd consider doing the same if I lost Chapel Farm. This place was his life. How could he carry on?'

Norah had just nodded. She knew he meant well but it was impossible for her to agree with him and she wasn't ready to discuss her father with his friends. He, like the rest of those who had come to pay their respects, had awkwardly shaken her hand, lowered his head sadly and left her alone with her grief.

As arrangements were made for the sale of the farm, Adele swiftly made clear her own plans. She was still an attractive woman and lost no time in casting around for another husband. A candidate was found in the shape of Albert Johnson, an elderly widower who owned a successful printing business in Bury St Edmunds. Even before the farm had been sold, their betrothal had been announced and she and Hope were happily making wedding plans.

Adele informed Norah bluntly that she should be doing the same. 'You need to find yourself a husband or you'll be out on the streets. For goodness sake, stop looking like such a wet weekend and smarten yourself up a bit. No man is going to be interested in you when you look such a frump.'

She insisted Norah accompany her to a charity Spring ball held at Chalkham Hall and made sure that both she and Hope had new frocks for the occasion. 'We need to ensure you both look your best. You never know who might be there.'

Norah went to the ball in a green, silk gown which matched her eyes and was thoroughly miserable. She did receive a flattering amount of male attention but politely and firmly rebuffed all advances. She had no intention of getting married and giving up all her plans of university, although, she realized, these would now need to be postponed to some future date. Meanwhile, she was busy making schemes of her own. When a few friends, who had since moved away, wrote to her offering their condolences, she'd written back and asked if they knew of any suitable employment for her. She struck lucky when an old school friend, Amy Thompson, who had married the baker in the pretty village of Collingworth ten miles away, had sent her a reply. She'd heard of a vacancy for the position of nanny at Collingworth Hall and urged Norah to apply for the position. Lord and Lady Collingworth had three children under the age of eight and urgently needed someone to take over their care and schooling. Apparently, the last nanny had left under a bit of a cloud, Amy revealed in her letter. The word was that she'd behaved indiscreetly with Lord Collingworth and had been dismissed.

Norah considered her options, which were, at that point, limited to marriage or employment, and decided to apply. If successful, this would provide her with a chance of independence, live-in accommodation and a modest wage. At least she wouldn't be out on the streets and she could begin to save for her future. Certainly, it would be a come-down from what she was used to but, when she'd discussed it with her friend, Sybil, now six months pregnant with her first child, Sybil had just shrugged. 'Beggars can't be choosers.'

Seeing Sybil had only made Norah more determined to seek employment. Her friend's marriage was not happy; her husband, a large, coarse, much older man, was not averse to hitting her if she didn't complete all her wifely tasks to his satisfaction. Whilst he had provided for her extended family, this generosity was Sybil's only consolation as she found herself irrevocably committed to a man she detested and of whom she was afraid. Although pregnant, she had lost weight and her face was pale and drawn, with dark circles under her eyes.

Norah pitied her friend and was determined not to succumb to a similar situation. At least she had no other family to worry about and could make her decision for herself. She penned her letter of application carefully and waited for a reply.

Meanwhile, the farm had been sold for £5 per acre to Cyril Brooke of Chalkham Hall. This had come as something of a relief to the farmworkers who had all been retained to work on the land and to continue the dairy herd. Mr Brooke had promoted Arthur to the position of farm foreman and provided him with a larger cottage on the estate.

Arthur told Norah of his good fortune when he paid a visit to Willow Farm on a warm Sunday afternoon in October. Adele had taken Hope in the pony and trap over to Bury St Edmunds to spend some time with her fiancé in his house. She wished to make some alterations to the furnishings before she moved in and therefore wanted to instruct the servants to take some measurements.

Norah was alone in the garden reading when Elsie announced Arthur's arrival. She could not help the way her heart skipped a beat as he approached. He had become so tall and fine looking, with his thick, dark hair and intense brown eyes. She rose from her chair and greeted him warmly.

'Arthur, how nice of you to visit,' she said, taking his arm and steering him to the chair opposite. 'Would you like some tea?'

'That would be most appreciated, Miss Norah.'

Was it her imagination or had his voice deepened? She gave herself a mental shake and smiled at Elsie who was waiting for instruction.

'Two teas, please Elsie,' she said and then turned back to Arthur. 'It seems ages since I've seen you. How are things with you? Have you heard yet what is to happen to all the workers?'

He told her his news in his usual self-deprecating manner. 'To be sure, it's much more than I deserve but I'm grateful all the same. Mr Brooke seems a good man and a fair employer. I've been very lucky. But enough of me. How are you?'

He looked at her intently. She seemed very thin and frail, like a delicate flower. However, her auburn hair still shone like burnished gold and her green eyes, although filled with immeasurable sadness, were as beautiful as ever. She smiled bravely. 'I'm fine, thank you. I've just heard that I have secured a position at Collingworth Hall so I will be leaving Great Chalkham which will be sad but things could be worse.'

Arthur frowned. 'Collingworth Hall?' He shook his head. 'I'm sure I heard some gossip about Lord Collingworth some time ago but I can't quite remember what it was. I think perhaps it involved one of the servants.'

'No, it was actually the nanny and it was she who was at fault. She tried to ingratiate herself with him, apparently, but it didn't work. That's why they need a new nanny,' Norah assured him.

'No,' he mused thoughtfully. 'I don't think it was the nanny - it was one of the maids ... and it was some time ago ... but anyway,' he turned to her, suddenly serious, 'is this what you want? It will be very different from the life you're used to, always at someone's beck and call. You're used to giving orders, not taking them.'

'Beggars can't be choosers,' she recited Sybil's mantra. 'It's either that or find some old man to marry me and I know which option I prefer.'

'Are you so set against marriage then?' he asked carefully.

'Of course not but I will only marry for love. Do you remember how happy my parents were together before my mother died? It seems so long ago but I always knew I wanted that for myself.' She told him what had happened to Sybil. 'I think I would rather starve than marry such a man,' she said firmly. 'Besides, if I marry, I give up on my ambition to attend university at Oxford. At least I can save some money to support myself at a later date.'

'I understand what you're saying and I applaud your determination to be independent. It's admirable that you wish to pursue a university education and a career. The reality, however, is that a position of nanny is more likely to lead to a lifetime of servitude. Surely a husband would provide your best hope of fulfilling your dreams?'

'It sounds like you're trying to marry me off!' Norah smiled briefly.

Arthur shrugged and lowered his eyes. 'If you married me, I would support your decision to go to Oxford.'

Norah looked across at him sharply, unable to believe what she had just heard. 'Are you asking me to marry you, Arthur?' she asked. Her heart seemed to be doing a wild dance in her chest as she awaited his reply.

He nodded. 'Aye. Now I've got this promotion, I've a bigger cottage and I'm ready to take a wife. It seems to me it would make sense for us to get married. I'd be able to support you and you could get on with what you've always wanted.'

Norah swallowed hard as the frantic beating in her chest subsided. He was such a good man to want to protect her in this way but it was not enough. She was a romantic and only wanted a husband who would love her wholeheartedly and forever. There was no mention of love in this unexpected proposal.

'I'm honoured by your very generous offer,' she began carefully, 'but I cannot accept. As I said earlier, I will only marry for love or not at all.' Impulsively, she reached across and patted his hand. 'However, I do appreciate your kindness. You are a fine man to wish to forego your own happiness in order to look after me but I can look after myself.'

He stood abruptly. 'So be it,' he replied gruffly, refusing to meet her eyes. 'I hoped that in time you could grow to love me but perhaps I was just deluding myself. I'll bid you good day.'

He tipped his cap at her and strode off across the lawn, leaving Norah feeling bemused. What did he mean about her growing to love him? Did that actually mean that he had feelings for her?

'Arthur ... wait!' she called after him but he'd already left and she sat back down, feeling very confused. The speed of his exit would seem to suggest that her rejection had hurt his feelings but surely he understood it would be wrong for her to marry him just to secure her future? Perhaps she'd been clumsy in the way she'd handled the situation. He had definitely seemed upset. She would leave it a day or two and then pay him a visit before she left to make sure he understood. She hated to think they might part on bad terms.

However, she didn't get the chance to speak to Arthur again. When she called at his cottage two days later, she was told he had taken his annual leave to visit his family in Yorkshire and, the next day, she left Great Chalkham to begin her employment.

Collingworth Hall was an imposing, large, red-bricked, Georgian mansion with large sash windows and several chimneys. It was the most impressive building Norah had ever seen and she couldn't help feeling a little intimidated as she sat stiffly beside old Jake Withers in his pony driven trap. They stopped briefly by the wrought iron gates and stared up the lime tree lined avenue to the house beyond.

'That'd cost you a penny or two,' Jake commented unnecessarily. 'No shortage of money there, I'd say.'

He shook the reins and they continued round to the back driveway. The parkland in which the Hall was set looked stunningly beautiful in the autumn sunshine with its rolling, green meadows and mighty beech and oak trees, their leaves a myriad of russet and golden shades. Norah relaxed her shoulders and drank it all in. She would surely be happy living in such a lovely place. Memories of Willow Farm and the old, white farmhouse fluttered painfully at the edges of her brain but she pushed them away. She was making a fresh start and already things were looking good.

This optimism was soon muted when, having arrived at the rear entrance, they were greeted by a stern looking, grey-haired woman with thin lips pursed in a frown of disapproval.

'We were expecting you sooner,' she barked as Jake lifted Norah's bag off the cart.

'I'll be off then,' Jake mumbled. 'Good luck, Miss Norah.'

'Goodbye, Jake. Thank you,' she replied and watched as he heaved himself back up on to the cart.

'Come along. We haven't got all day. You're already late!' snapped the grey-haired woman. 'Follow me.'

She marched briskly into the house and Norah had no choice but to pick up her bag and follow her as she was whisked through a series of passageways and into a small room with a single bed and a tiny wooden wardrobe and dresser.

'This is your room,' said the woman. 'I'm the housekeeper, Mrs Clark. If you need anything or have any questions, you should come to me.'

'I'm pleased to meet you, Mrs Clark.' Norah wondered if she should proffer her hand in greeting but Mrs Clark had already turned away and was running her fingers along the dresser, checking for dust.

'Right. Leave your coat and your bag and I'll take you to meet the family. Poor Lady Collingworth has been waiting in the drawing room all afternoon with the children. I expect she'll be needing a rest.'

'I am sorry if you were expecting me sooner,' Norah apologised. 'The letter didn't specify a time - it just said to arrive in the afternoon.'

'Save your apologies for Lady Collingworth,' Mrs Clark said curtly and headed out of the room. She led Norah through another maze of passageways and Norah wondered how she would ever find her way back. She hoped someone might be on hand to guide her.

They arrived in what were obviously the main living quarters. There was a large hallway with a high ceiling and a curved, stone staircase. The walls were covered in dark red and gold wallpaper and a series of portraits of finely dressed men and women. Heavy, gold, brocade curtains framed the enormous windows and patterned rugs adorned the polished, wooden floor. The doors leading from the hallway were made of oak with brass handles and one of those doors suddenly opened, revealing a small girl with dark curls and a serious face which broke into a smile when she saw Norah.

'Oh goody, you've arrived. I said you'd be pretty.' She turned back into the room, announcing, 'She's here ... the nanny's here!'

Norah followed Mrs Clark into what was clearly the drawing room. 'Miss Dunn has arrived, my Lady.'

'Thank you, Mrs Clark. That will be all.' A very elegant woman dressed casually in a grey skirt and pale pink cardigan rose from the chaise longue on which she had been reclining. 'Welcome to Collingworth, Miss Dunn. We're most happy to have you here.' She held out a delicate hand and Norah took it gingerly, wondering whether she should curtsey. If only she'd asked Mrs Clark but she hadn't thought of it. In the end, she inclined her head and bobbed her knees briefly.

Lady Collingworth laughed, a tinkling silver sound which immediately alleviated Norah's trepidation. 'Oh, you don't need to stand on ceremony with me. When it's just us, you can call me Clarissa and I shall call you Norah. It is Norah, isn't it? I hope we'll be great friends. Now let me introduce you to my little monsters. You've already met Anne ...' She waved a hand at the dark-haired girl who was now sitting perched on an enormous sofa and looking at her with big eyes. 'She's my eldest. She's nearly eight.'

Norah smiled across at her. 'I'm very pleased to meet you, Anne.'

Sitting next to her and clutching a threadbare teddy was a smaller girl with long, dark hair tied up with ribbons.

'And this is Mary ... she never goes anywhere without Barclay ... she's six.'

'Hello Mary,' Norah smiled. 'Is Barclay your teddy?'

Mary nodded solemnly.

'She's the quietest one,' Lady Collingworth continued as an even smaller girl sidled up to her and attached herself to her leg. 'This is Margaret. She's four and is usually the noisiest but she's going through a shy stage at the moment. She'll be fine when she gets to know you.'

Norah bent down to her. 'Hello Margaret. I'm Miss Dunn and I'm going to be your nanny.'

Margaret peeked out from behind her mother and Norah saw that she too had dark curls and enormous, brown eyes. All the girls must take after their father, she thought, for Lady Collingworth was fair skinned with bright, blue eyes and golden hair shaped in a bob. She was much younger than Norah had expected and, with her smiling eyes, open face and obvious devotion to her children, Norah warmed to her immediately.

'Have you been a nanny before?' Anne asked.

'No. This is my first time but I can see you are all beautifully behaved so I'm sure we'll have lots of fun,' Norah replied.

'Oh definitely. I do think it's so important for children to have fun,' exclaimed Lady Collingworth. 'Our last nanny was lovely but very serious and extremely keen on formal lessons. Obviously, I expect them to have lessons in the morning but perhaps some more light-hearted activities in the afternoon and time for play. When I was young, my sister and I had a very strict governess who insisted that we only engage in pursuits she considered worthwhile. It was all terribly tedious and we used to spend all our time plotting our escape.' She smiled wistfully.

'I think all learning should be fun,' said Norah, 'because then it's so much easier. It's very difficult to take things in if you're bored. I remember dull lessons spent staring out of the window for entire afternoons when I was at school and thinking about riding my pony when I got home. I'm sure I didn't learn anything in those lessons. However, I do realise the importance of the three Rs,' she continued hastily, lest her employer began to consider her unfit for the job. 'Formal lessons every morning sounds like an excellent plan.'

'Marvellous. I'm sure you'll be perfect,' Lady Collingworth declared and then turned to the housekeeper who had re-entered the room. 'Yes, Mrs Clark?'

'Mrs Evans is ready to serve tea for the children in the nursery, my Lady. Would you like me to show Miss Dunn where it is?'

'That's alright, Mrs Clark. I'll show her myself and supervise teatime and bedtime proceedings today. Then I know I'll be able to leave things in Miss Dunn's capable hands. Perhaps you would be so kind to tell Mrs Evans to serve dinner at eight o'clock tonight so I have time to change.'

'Very good, my Lady.'

'I'm afraid Mrs Clark doesn't really approve of my modern ways,' Lady Collingworth confided to Norah as, with a child holding each of her hands, she led them upstairs to the brightly furnished nursery. 'She thinks children should be seen and not heard and she definitely doesn't approve of me spending time in here.'

'What a lovely room!' exclaimed Norah.

Three of the walls were covered in pale pink, embossed paper but the fourth was entirely covered by a large, brightly painted rainbow mural.

'It is fun, isn't it,' Lady Collingworth agreed. 'I had it done before Anne was born. The nursery in which I spent all my time was dark and dingy. It always felt like a prison. I wanted my children to have a beautiful room where they felt happy, at least while they're still so young.'

Norah watched as the girls all dutifully washed their hands in a porcelain bowl on a wooden table in the corner of the room and then sat expectantly at another table covered with a white linen cloth. Two maids dressed formally in uniform carried in trays laden with dainty sandwiches and cakes and set them down. After grace had been said, they politely helped themselves each to a sandwich. A fourth place had been set for Norah and, although she wasn't very hungry, she also helped herself to a cucumber sandwich with the crusts removed. Throughout the meal, Lady Collingworth chatted amiably with her daughters, occasionally reminding them of their manners but mostly discussing their normal routines. Norah realised that this was for her benefit and, by the time tea was finished, she felt she had a clearer understanding of her position in the household. Whilst everything felt very new and strange compared to the life she'd been used to, her spirits were high and she was looking forward to the challenges facing her.

The girls' bedtime routine reminded Norah of her own whilst her mother had been alive; they washed and changed into their nightdresses and then snuggled on the sofa in the nursery ready for their bedtime story. There was a large selection of books on the shelf and each of the girls took it in turns to choose the story she was to read. Tonight, it was Margaret's turn and she immediately pointed to a thick, hardbacked book of Grimms' Fairy Tales.

'Which one would you like me to read?' Norah asked.

Margaret remained silent, still unsure of her new nanny, but her sister answered for her.

'Rapunzel, except Margaret always calls it Wapunzel,' Anne said helpfully.

'She always chooses that one. It's her favourite,' chimed in Mary, still cuddling Barclay the teddy.

It was Norah's first time reading aloud a bedtime story and she began a little nervously. However, the children did not appear to notice and she soon relaxed, reading the characters' speech in different voices. They particularly enjoyed the witchy cackle she used for Rumplestiltskin and when the story was finished, there were immediate appeals for another.

'Not tonight,' Norah smiled. 'It's bedtime. Come on. I want you each to show me your bedrooms.'

They went to Margaret's room first. When she was beneath the covers, her mother kissed her forehead. 'Sleep tight, pumpkin,' she murmured and blew out the lamp by her bed. 'She doesn't always settle so quickly but it's late for her. She normally goes to bed at least an hour before the others,' Lady Collingworth whispered.

Soon the other girls were also tucked in for the night and Lady Collingworth directed one of the housemaids, a pretty but sullen looking girl by the name of Rose, to show Norah back to her room, which was, she soon realised, just along the corridor from where the girls were sleeping.

'So, you're on hand should the children need you in the night,' Rose explained.

'Is there anything else I should know?' Norah asked.

'You'll learn soon enough,' Rose replied cryptically as she headed for the door. Then she stopped and turned back with a sigh. 'They usually wake up around seven o'clock. It's your job to have them washed and dressed ready for breakfast in the dining room with Lord and Lady Collingworth at eight o'clock. They eat their other meals in the nursery.'

'Thank you, Rose. I wouldn't have wanted to be late on my first morning,' Norah smiled gratefully. 'Sleep well,' she called out to the maid's retreating back but received no response.

Norah returned to her room and started to unpack. It was the first time she'd ever slept in a room away from Willow Farm and it felt strange to be arranging her clothes in unfamiliar surroundings. However, as she laid out her nightdress on the bed and placed her framed photograph of her mother and father, taken on one of her mother's better days in the garden shortly after she had received her camera, on the dresser, she felt optimistic about the immediate future. The children and Lady

Collingworth could not have been more welcoming, she decided, and Collingworth Hall and its surroundings were truly beautiful. For the first time since the death of her father, she had people other than herself to look after and the challenge was a welcome distraction from the grief of the past months. Maybe things would turn out alright after all.

CHAPTER 9

Norah- January- June 1927

D ear Arthur,
  I cannot believe three months have already passed since I left Chalkham. The time has positively flown, probably because my days are so busy.

Firstly, let me reassure you that I am well and enjoying my life here in Collingworth. I have fallen on my feet because the children I look after are a complete delight. They are a family of three girls, aged eight, six and four, and lovelier children you couldn't wish to meet. All are sweet natured and well-behaved but the best thing is their enthusiasm. It doesn't matter what I plan for us to do, they are always interested and excited. I think they take after their mother. Lady Collingworth is so kind and always appreciative of my bumbling efforts. Often, she will join us in the afternoons when we may be painting or, on sunny days, out on a nature walk and she gives the children her wholehearted attention. No wonder they adore her.

They are less demonstrative with their father and, to tell you the truth, I think we are all a little bit afraid of him, even Lady Collingworth! He is a large, stout, dour man in his late forties and he does not appear to tolerate children very well. Indeed, it is most fortunate that his girls restrain their natural impulsiveness when we all have breakfast together as he does not like to be disturbed from his newspaper.

Let me tell you a little bit about the girls whom, I confess, I love already. The eldest is Anne. She is like a little mother to her two younger siblings and is a very sweet, caring girl. She is quite serious and loves to read. Mary comes next and, although she is the quietest, she has a real sense of mischief. She likes to tease her sisters but then, when they berate her, she passes the blame onto Barclay (her teddy whom she has to have with her at all times!) Margaret is the youngest and, I think, the cleverest. She doesn't like to miss out on anything so is always determined to do everything her big sisters do. This includes lessons, for which *she is showing remarkable early aptitude. She is already reading and, despite Lady Collingworth's praise, I deserve very little credit as I only need to show her something once and she remembers.*

Although I adore the children and Lady Collingworth, I miss all my friends in Chalkham, especially you. I feel we parted in somewhat difficult circumstances and I am very much afraid that I may have hurt your feelings. If I have, please accept my sincerest apologies. I would love it were you to write back with all your news. I do so miss your friendship.

Yours,

Norah.

Norah put down her pen and read through her letter. It had been difficult to write but she hoped it struck the right tone. She had been putting off writing to Arthur ever since she had been at Collingworth and felt relieved that she had finally done it. Possibly, he had not been missing her at all - certainly not if she were to believe everything that her friend Gertie Bassett had written in a recent letter. By all accounts, Arthur had become quite the eligible bachelor of Chalkham and had several ladies chasing after him. Apparently, he had been courting Gertie's older sister Agnes since Christmas and, Gertie reported, Agnes had informed her family that Arthur was quite smitten. Norah had frowned when she read that part. She remembered Agnes, a pretty girl with sultry, dark looks but also unscrupulous in getting what she wanted. If she wanted Arthur, the poor lad would stand no chance.

She sighed and looked out of her bedroom window. It was a crisp, clear January morning and she had the day to herself. Lady Collingworth and her daughters had piled into the Bentley earlier that morning to spend the day with her sister and her family in Norfolk and she was told she was not needed.

'Amelia has more than enough staff to look after us all and you certainly deserve a day off,' Lady Collingworth had declared. 'I know you love riding so feel free to go down to the stables and ask for my mare if you wish or perhaps you'd like to go back home. Ask James to drive you.'

Norah had toyed with the idea of returning to Chalkham but had decided against it. Arthur would be working and she had no one else she particularly wanted to visit. Also, the invitation to go out riding was not to be passed up. That was something she really missed.

As she headed out to the stables, she reflected on her life at Collingworth. Everything she had written in her letter to Arthur was true but she had omitted a couple of things. Firstly, she had been disappointed that, no matter how hard she tried, the other staff steered clear of her and had rebuffed her attempts at friendship. They were all polite but distant and she had decided that her privileged position as Lady Collingworth's nanny made her an outsider as far as the servants were concerned. This was a shame but she held her head high, continued to behave in as friendly way as possible towards the maids and waited for a thaw in their attitude towards her.

The other person who made her feel uncomfortable was Lord Collingworth himself. She usually only saw him at breakfast time when he was polite but taciturn. However, there was something about the way he looked at her when he thought she was not looking which made her feel distinctly uncomfortable. Indeed, she had seen the same kind of look when he watched the housemaids clearing plates or delivering eggs and bacon from the kitchen. It was a lascivious stare, as if he were undressing them with his eyes. The maids themselves were clearly aware of his attention and were nervous around him, keeping their eyes downcast and working as quietly and efficiently as they could. In fact, apart from the children, the only person who appeared completely unaware of his lustful glances was Lady Collingworth who chattered happily through mealtimes and generally ignored her husband. Norah found that she too had learnt the art of averting her gaze from the head of the table and trying to make herself invisible. Once, in the early days, she had briefly met his eyes and seen an unmistakeable intent burning there before he casually looked away. It made her shudder and the resolve to steer clear of him as much as possible was formed.

Joe in the stables saddled a small, grey mare for her to ride and helpfully suggested some routes she might try. Her horse was willing and Norah enjoyed some pleasant canters across the surrounding fields. She was heading back to Collingworth when she became aware of the sound of hooves behind her. Slowing to a walk, she turned around and her heart sank. It was Lord Collingworth himself on his beautiful, black stallion. He easily caught her up and walked his horse beside her.

'I see you're making the most of your day off,' he said pleasantly.

'Yes, thank you, sir,' she replied. 'It's most generous of Lady Collingworth to loan me her horse.'

'You're obviously a very competent rider. You should take her out more often. I would be delighted to accompany you and show you my favourite rides.'

'You're very kind, sir,' Norah demurred, 'but I am always busy with the children and would be unable to spare the time.'

'Very conscientious.' Lord Collingworth wore the smile of a crocodile. He continued, 'But I'm sure I could arrange some time for us both away from your duties. In fact, I will insist upon it.'

They had reached the stables and he dismounted, carelessly flinging his reins at the waiting Joe. 'Good day to you, Miss Dunn. I will most definitely look forward to our next encounter.'

'Good day, Lord Collingworth,' Norah responded. For the first time since her arrival, she felt a knot of fear in her stomach as she watched him stride towards the house. There was no mistaking his interest in her and she was suddenly aware how vulnerable she was in her current position. She had no one to protect her and she promised herself that she would do everything she could to avoid being alone with him again.

When she returned to the house, Norah was relieved to see that her charges had returned home earlier than expected. Apparently, Lady Collingworth had suffered a headache and had retired upstairs so it was left to Norah to listen to excited recounts of the day from three girls talking at once. It was only much later that she realised she had forgotten to post her letter to Arthur. If it was a dry day tomorrow, she would walk the girls down to the village post box. After all the time it had taken for her to write it, the least she could do was send it on its way.

Winter turned to spring and then to summer. The longer days and warmer weather meant much more time outside which Norah loved. The girls continued to thrive in her care and the bond between them deepened.

She had recently received a short letter from Arthur saying how pleased he was that things were going well for her in Collingworth. Firstly, he had apologised for his tardiness in replying to her letter and for the fact that he was not much of a letter writer. Then he reassured her that they would always be friends and that she could always count on him for support if she needed it. He mentioned nothing of his own life and Norah was left to wonder if he was still seeing Agnes Bassett. Gertie's latest letter, back in the spring, had hinted at wedding bells and Norah remembered Arthur saying he was ready to settle down with a wife. The thought gave her uncomfortable feelings in her chest which were difficult to dismiss. Truthfully, much as she loved her charges, she did feel quite isolated and lonely in her current position. The other servants were still wary around her and she often longed for someone of her own age to talk to. She would sometimes hear two of the maids giggling together when she went into the kitchen but they were instantly silent when she appeared. One of the maids, Rose, had left very suddenly and she had seen the others whispering together when Mrs Clark was not watching but Norah did not know why. Perhaps they were worried that she would tell tales of them to Lady Collingworth.

The threatened outing with Lord Collingworth had not materialised and Norah was intensely relieved. She had been on tenterhooks for the first weeks after their encounter but he had seemed otherwise preoccupied, for which Norah was very grateful. However, after Rose's departure, she felt his eyes upon her once more and he had started to find excuses to touch her hand or her arm at the breakfast table.

Otherwise, life at the hall continued with a comforting normality and sense of routine. The girls grumbled good naturedly when it was time for them to settle to lessons in the morning but continued to work hard and display a gratifying thirst for knowledge. They were quite competitive with each other, especially the two younger girls who both strived to match their older sister, so Norah's job was more pastoral than educational. She was constantly balancing encouragement to succeed and praise to enhance their self-esteem with lessons in modesty and respect for others' feelings. The girls had learnt that it was important to encourage each other and to be proud of their achievements rather than boastful.

One lunchtime in the middle of June, Lady Collingworth burst into the nursery in a flurry of excitement.

'Darlings!' she declared, 'I've had the most marvellous idea. I'm going to take you all to the Abbey gardens in Bury for a picnic. James is going to drive us and Mrs Ellis is packing up some treats for us. It'll be such fun!'

Margaret squealed and leapt from her seat to hug her mother and Anne exclaimed, 'Oh goody. I love going to the Abbey Gardens. Can we take some bread for the ducks?'

'Of course.'

'And can Barclay come?' Mary asked. 'And Miss Dunn?' she added as an afterthought.

'Of course, bring Barclay. It wouldn't be much of an outing without him, would it? But Miss Dunn deserves an afternoon off. Papa mentioned just this morning that we were working Miss Dunn too hard and that she rarely had some time to herself,' Lady Collingworth beamed at Norah.

'I don't mind, honestly,' Norah said quickly but her protest was waved away.

'I know you don't. That's why it's so easy to take advantage of you but it just *won't* do. You are owed time off and I insist you enjoy yourself this afternoon. You could go riding or do whatever you want. The girls and I will be fine, won't we?'

The children chorused their agreement and the matter was settled. Norah smiled and hid her disquiet. Normally, she would have looked forward to some time for herself but the fact that it had been instigated by Lord Collingworth put a different complexion on the situation. She immediately dismissed the notion of going riding and then she wondered if she was being a bit silly. Maybe she was reading too much into things. How arrogant to believe that Lord Collingworth had any interest in her! However, there was something about him which filled her with unease and she resolved instead to catch up on her letter writing. Locked away in her room, she would be safe from unwanted attention, should any be forthcoming.

It was much later when she was in the middle of a letter to Gertie that there was a knock on her door. Her heart leapt.

'Who is it?' she called.

'It's Mrs Clark,' came the reply.

Instantly relieved, Norah got to her feet and opened the door. The housekeeper was wearing her usual dour expression. 'What can I do for you, Mrs Clark?' she asked politely.

'His lordship wishes to see you in the drawing room ... immediately.'

Norah's heart plummeted once again. 'But why ... what's wrong?' she asked.

'It's not for me ... or you ... to question his lordship. Follow me,' the housekeeper ordered and Norah had no choice but to follow. Her mind was racing with possible reasons for her summons, none of them good, and she forced herself to breathe normally as she entered the drawing room.

Lord Collingworth was alone, an imposing figure dressed in black standing by the window.

'Ah good ... Miss Dunn. Thank you for joining me. That will be all, Mrs Clark.'

'Good afternoon, your lordship,' Norah said politely as the housekeeper left, closing the door behind her.

'You are probably wondering why I wished to speak with you so let me put you at ease. I only want to assure myself that you are comfortable here at Collingworth,' he said pleasantly, his face bland.

'Very much so, your lordship,' Norah said stiffly. 'Thank you for asking.'

'You are certainly doing a remarkable job with my daughters. Lady Collingworth is continually singing your praises.'

'You're very kind, your lordship.'

'Good. Well now that's settled, I'd like you to come with me. I wish to show you something.' He took hold of her arm and led her gently out of the drawing room. Without making a fuss, which could prove highly embarrassing, she had no choice but to accompany him as he walked her in silence through a part of the house she had never seen before. He stopped at a door, removed a key from his jacket pocket and unlocked it.

'This way.' He ushered her into the room and closed the door behind him.

Norah looked around fearfully. The room was minimally furnished with a bed and a simple wooden dresser adorned with two heavy, brass candle sticks.

'What is it you wish to show me, your lordship?' she asked nervously, her heart thudding painfully in her chest.

'Oh, my dear, all manner of things,' he smiled wolfishly at her and, with a flourish, he locked the door.

'What are you doing? I wish to leave. Please unlock the door.' Norah struggled to retain her composure as she walked to the door and tried the handle to no avail. She was trapped.

'It's high time we got to know each other better.' He moved behind her as she struggled to open the door, placed his hands on her shoulders and kissed the side of her neck.

'Let go of me!' Norah pushed him away and ran to the other side of the bed. 'I demand you release me this instant.'

Lord Collingworth shook his head as he removed his jacket, his dark eyes gleaming with anticipation. 'I'm afraid you're not in a position to make any demands.' He licked his lips. 'In fact, I believe it is I who will making the demands and you who will be obeying them.'

Norah looked around wildly for a means of escape. There was a small window she could squeeze her way through. She started to edge towards it. 'I'll scream,' she threatened.

'By all means, be my guest. Scream all you like. I can assure you it will increase my enjoyment enormously.' He rubbed his hands together, his eyes locked on hers. 'I'm afraid that window is also locked,' he observed as she reached a trembling hand towards it. 'I like to be prepared.'

'You won't get away with this,' Norah's eyes filled with tears at the hopelessness of her predicament and she could only watch, terrified, as Lord Collingworth unbuttoned his breeches.

'Oh, but I will,' he smiled. 'Feudal rights and all that ... or, failing that, your word against mine. I don't think anyone will believe you when I have to reveal, reluctantly of course, that you tried to seduce me in the hope of becoming my mistress.'

'You're a monster!' Norah sobbed.

'No, my sweet thing ... just a man. A man who is now in urgent need of your attentions. It's time for you to remove your clothes.'

'Never!' she cried, her arms crossed protectively in front of her chest.

'In that case, I'll have to remove them for you.' He strode suddenly across the room, grabbed her arms and flung her roughly on to the bed. Norah screamed and tried to free her arms but he was too powerful. He sat astride her and pinned her arms above her head with his left hand. Then, with his free hand, he looped her wrists with a piece of rope which was already tied to the iron rail at the head of the bed and pulled it tight. Norah cried out at the sudden pain and squirmed helplessly beneath him as he knotted the rope. For the first time, she recognised that she was completely at this man's mercy and she clamped her eyes shut, trying to blot out the horrors she was facing.

Roughly, he pulled open her cotton blouse sending the buttons flying and tugged her camisole top downwards, ripping the delicate straps. She felt him feeling for the fastenings on her brassiere and then, as it came loose, grasping and kneading her small breasts with his large hands. He lowered his head and took one of her breasts in his mouth and she shuddered involuntarily as he licked and bit at her nipple. Then his mouth was on hers, forcing her lips open and thrusting his tongue into her. She could feel the hardness of him as he writhed, groaning with pleasure, on top of her and then she felt him pulling up her skirt and rubbing himself against her stockinged thighs. He was panting now against her cheek, his breath fetid and smelling of fish. He squeezed her breasts and then slid his hands down to her knickers. Swiftly, he yanked them down and tossed them aside. He brutally gripped her thighs and tried to prise her legs apart. Norah clenched them together for as long as she could but it was no use. He was too strong and she gasped in pain as she felt him force himself into her. Gripping her buttocks, he thrust into her violently, again and again, panting and moaning. Then, at last, he shuddered his release and collapsed on top of her.

Norah remained silent and kept her eyes closed, holding back the tears stinging her eyelids. She loathed this man with every fibre of her being and her mind was already set upon revenge for what he had done to her. If she had a knife, she would have had no compunction about plunging it into his heart.

Eventually, he stirred and idly traced his fingers round her nipples. 'Now you are mine,' he smiled cruelly, 'and you will remain mine until I tire of you.' He heaved himself off the bed and pulled up his breeches.

Norah opened her eyes and glared at him with intense hatred.

'Now then – a few rules,' he said as he began to untie her wrists. 'You will remain at Collingworth Hall and you will speak of this to no one.'

'You expect me to stay here after what you've done!' Norah exclaimed. 'You are mad if you think I will subject myself to that again.'

Lord Collingworth laughed scornfully. 'The choice is yours, of course, but be assured that, if you leave here without my permission, I will see to it that your reputation is ruined. Certainly, you will be unable to work again with children and no man will wish to marry you after I have divulged your lewd and disgusting behaviour. Believe me when I tell you that I have the power to turn you into a social outcast. Or you stay here and enjoy the favour bestowed on you by Lady Collingworth and the devotion of my children. In return you will be my lover for as long as I wish it but that is such a small price to pay, especially as you are now soiled goods. It would not be for very long at any rate. I seem to tire of young girls so quickly these days.'

With her hands untied and her fingers trembling, Norah began to fasten her clothing while he sat with his back to her, putting on his shoes. Suddenly, a surge of anger propelled her off the bed. Without pausing to consider the consequences of her actions, she grabbed one of the heavy, brass candlesticks and brought it crashing down on his head. He fell heavily on to the floor, blood pouring from an ugly gash on the back of his head, and lay completely still.

She stared at him in horror. What had she done? Had she killed him? Quickly, she found his jacket and withdrew the key. Then she pulled on the rest of her clothes, clasping her blouse around her where the buttons were missing and furtively slipped out of the door, relocking it behind her. Luckily, she saw no one as she sped to her room and locked herself in, breathing heavily. What should she do?

Urgently, she pulled her case out from under the bed and filled it with her belongings. She put on her cloak, hat and boots and was about to flee when she had second thoughts. She could not leave without a word to Lady Collingworth and the girls. She reopened her case to find her writing set. What could she say? How could she explain what had happened? She had to try to explain her absence somehow so she wrote;

Dear Lady Collingworth, Anne, Mary and Margaret,

I am so sorry to leave you like this but I have received an urgent summons from a member of my family and need to leave at once.

Girls – I have loved being your nanny and I truly wish I could have stayed. Please don't think too badly of me.

My very best wishes to you all,

Miss Dunn.

Norah left the note on the dresser and, head down, slipped out of a side door. It was raining heavily as she grimly set off across the parkland. She only knew that she had to escape from Collingworth as quickly as possible. For the moment, she could not let herself think beyond that, for fear that she would fall apart. She just needed to get away ...

CHAPTER 10

Emily - November 16

A dam arrived home early that night carrying an enormous bunch of roses. He grinned at Emily and enveloped her in his arms.

'Happy anniversary, darling,' he said and kissed her warmly on the lips.

'You too,' Emily replied, taking the flowers from him. 'These are beautiful. Thank you.' She inhaled the scent of the roses and exclaimed, 'Oh, they smell gorgeous! I'll find a vase.'

Adam crossed over to the kitchen table where Alex was sitting eating his tea. 'Ah … dippy eggs. My favourite. Is there some left for me?'

'Here you are Daddy.' Alex turned a yolk-stained face towards his father and held out a finger of buttered toast.

Adam gave him a swift hug and kissed the top of his head. 'You are a good boy sharing with Daddy but that's ok. You eat it up. I can wait until later.'

'Auntie Annie's coming around later,' Alex beamed.

'I know. What have you got planned for her this time?'

The last time Annie had babysat Alex, the two of them had decided to bake chocolate cookies and Alex had managed to get the biscuit mixture everywhere. They left the biscuits baking and went upstairs for bath time. The trouble was that they spent so much time playing in the bath with a boat which squirted water and bubbles from its funnel that Annie only remembered the cookies when Alex was in his pyjamas. He had yawned and said, 'Can I have my milk and cookie now, please?' She'd gasped in horror and raced downstairs where she was confronted with the horrible smell of burning. The cookies were black and, because she had forgotten to use some baking paper, glued to the base of the tin. Luckily, she'd managed to locate a packet in the cupboard and Alex was none the wiser but Emily and Adam had returned to find her still in the kitchen trying to scrape the charred remains from the tin.

'Cookies,' Alex declared and Emily quickly interrupted.

'Not this time, darling. Auntie Annie said she wanted you to show her how to build something with the duplo.'

'A castle?' Alex asked obligingly.

His father nodded. 'That should be safe enough,' he agreed. 'Now, if you've finished tea, let's get you upstairs and bathed before Auntie Annie gets here. Then you'll have enough time to build your castle.'

Emily smiled as she watched them leave the room, her heart brimming with love for them both. She was so lucky, she knew that. Surely it didn't really matter if she never found her birth parents; it was her family now who were important. She glanced across at the scrapbook which she'd moved onto the worktop when Alex had demanded her attention earlier that day. Looking at it again, when she had been feeling a bit down, hadn't helped. There were no new clues which she'd somehow missed during earlier perusals. She resolved to put it away again and focus her attention on the present. Molly's reappearance had just been a blip, she told herself firmly, caused by her own self-indulgence. She needed to grow up and put her past behind her. As she went upstairs, she could hear lots of splashing and Alex's giggles coming from the bathroom. Adam was so good with him and never too busy to play. There would be plenty of time for her to relax and get ready for their evening out while the two of them were together. She was really looking forward to it.

The restaurant was warm and humming with conversation as Emily and Adam were shown to their table. She had a quick glance around the room in case there was anyone there whom they knew and was relieved to see only unfamiliar faces. It was a rare occasion, these days, to spend a romantic evening alone with her husband and, so often when they had organised special nights out, they'd inadvertently met up with old friends or acquaintances of Adam through his work. She settled into her seat and sighed happily as Adam ordered some drinks. He was looking rather gorgeous, she thought, in a dark shirt and casual jacket, and he'd already been suitably appreciative of her own appearance in a flame red, figure hugging dress and high heeled Manolo shoes.

'I've bought you a present,' he said, producing a small box wrapped in silver paper from his pocket. 'I was going to give it to you later when we were on our own but I can't wait.'

'Really. That's not like you,' Emily smiled. Adam was notoriously impatient and always wanted things to happen there and then. He, far more than she, had struggled with waiting a full nine months for the birth of his first child. 'Oh, it's beautiful. Thank you.' Inside the box was a silver ring. It had a ruby set with small diamonds and glittered in her hands. She slid it on to one of the fingers on her right hand and held it up to the light. 'I love it. I would say you shouldn't have but I know I'm worth it.'

'Too right. You're the best wife any man could wish for as well as the sexiest.' His eyes smouldered with promise and she felt a tingle of anticipation tickling her spine.

'Food first,' she said firmly, picking up the menu.

'So demanding!'

The waiter returned with drinks and they ordered their choices, along with a bottle of Malbec.

'To us,' Adam held up his glass and she chinked her own against it.

'To us,' she repeated.

'All the men in this room are so jealous of me right now.'

'I know. You are *that* good looking, I guess they all want to be you,' she chuckled, deliberately misunderstanding.

He smiled ruefully. 'You know what I mean. Seriously Em, I couldn't be happier being married to you.' He took her hand and squeezed it. 'No actually that's not true. I would be happier if I didn't have to leave you and Alex so often.'

'I know. Same here … but I always knew the business trips were part of the package. Even when you were still working for Hatfields, you were away a lot. At least now, you're doing it for yourself. And look how much new business those trips have generated. I'm so proud of you.'

He shrugged carelessly, a little embarrassed by her praise. 'Yeah, business is good – in fact so good we're expanding further. I'm afraid that means a long trip away in the new year.'

'Where to?'

'Australia and New Zealand. I'll probably be away for at least two weeks. I did wonder about you and Alex coming with me but it will be mostly travelling. Chris and I were finalising the details today.'

'Chris is going with you?' she asked. Chris Thompson was Adam's right-hand man and general manager.

He nodded and gave her hand another squeeze. 'I'm sorry. I know it's a long time to be away.'

'Don't be silly!' She gave him a bright smile. 'You've got to do what you have to do. Alex and I will be fine. We always are.'

'You won't miss me?'

Emily pondered the question. 'Well ... maybe ... just a little ... but you don't have to worry about us.'

'I know but I do worry. I've been working so hard I realise we haven't had a proper holiday this year but I will make it up to you next year. That's a promise.'

'Mm. I'm thinking somewhere warm and luxurious. I could use a bit of pampering.'

'Wherever you want. You choose and we'll get it booked up before next year's diary gets too busy.'

'Great. I'll start looking tomorrow. I'm thinking maybe Italy again ... or perhaps Portugal. Then the flights wouldn't be too long for Alex.'

He smiled. 'Anywhere where you spend most of the day in a bikini is fine with me. Actually, I've just had a thought. Why don't you and Alex book to go away somewhere while I'm in Australia? It would be a change of scene and give you a bit of a break. Perhaps Annie would go with you ... or Jenna.'

Emily mulled the idea over in her head. Jenna would not want to leave the children and, as they were now in school, they would not be able to go away in January. Annie was a possibility though. Perhaps they could get a cottage somewhere. 'Good idea,' she said as the waiter headed their way bearing ornate plates of food. 'I'll think about that too. Thank you,' she smiled at the waiter. 'That looks delicious.'

The food was beautifully presented and tasty, the wine gave them a rosy glow and, after the short taxi ride home and coffee with Annie who reported no major disasters, the evening ended with fantastic sex. She was incredibly lucky, Emily thought, as she lay cuddled in her husband's strong arms. She really did not need anything else.

Later that week, Emily was curled up on the sofa with her iPad while Alex watched his favourite TV programme. Outside, it was a bright, clear November day and the grass was laced with frost glistening in the sunlight. It was the kind of day which made you want to be outside and Emily had already been out for a walk with Alex down to the local park. She had toyed with idea of driving to the beach for a bracing day at the coast but had decided against it. The last time she'd done that, she'd been disappointed to find the beach shrouded in sea mist. Still, thoughts of the coast reminded her of her plans to hire a cottage for maybe a week in January to break up the time Adam was away. Alex loved splashing in the shallows in his wellies and building sand castles so she had decided to concentrate her search around the North Norfolk coast.

Molly sat beside her on the sofa, watching her glumly, but Emily resolutely ignored her. She was disappointed that Molly was still appearing on a regular basis, even though her depression had dissipated. Of course, she still thought of her as Molly even though her name was probably Norah. That first time when Emily had looked through the album, it had not taken her long to realise, when she had looked closely, that the young woman in the photographs was the same person as the cheerful girl on the pony. It had been an incredible shock to see that her imaginary friend had actually existed. However, it had also been exciting to discover that she was also in some way inextricably linked with her past. If only Molly would talk; if only she could share her secrets. How many times had she wished for that? With every disappointment she encountered in her search for her birth parents, it seemed that the mystery of her relationship with Molly moved tantalisingly further from her grasp.

With a sigh, Emily turned away from her iPad and reached for Norah's scrapbook, intending to put it out of sight and therefore, hopefully, out of mind. As her fingers brushed the leather cover and struggled to grasp it fully, she slipped and the book fell harmlessly onto the thick, beige carpet, open at a news clipping dated 1927. The report was about the appointment of Eva Greene as the first female mayor for Bury St Edmunds. Emily had always wondered if Eva Greene, like Lydia Turner, was perhaps a relative. If not, Norah must surely have known these women to wish to keep a record of their achievements. That link with the town of Bury St Edmunds was the main reason Emily had wanted to live there, although she'd never disclosed that fact to Adam.

She turned idly to the last page of photographs and frowned. These were the photographs which showed Molly/Norah standing outside a small cottage. In one she was smiling, holding a baby in her arms. In another, she was standing beside the same tall, young man in the picture of the stables. They had their arms around each other and were grinning broadly. Emily was certain that this man must be her husband, the father of her child. The final picture had been taken perhaps a couple of years later because the child was no longer a baby. He was now a young boy on his father's shoulders, gripping dad's curly hair in his tiny fists. Had Norah taken that last photograph? Why were there no more? What had happened to this young family and why did this pale, wraithlike woman now haunt her life with such persistence?

There was something else bothering Emily, though, as she examined the pictures yet again, something niggling the back of her mind like an unreachable itch. She looked up and was surprised to see Molly standing directly in front of her, staring at her with such painful intensity that she had to look away. It was something to do with the cottage. Where had she seen it recently? She turned back to the photograph. It was an unremarkable, small, single storey country cottage with a thatched roof. There was a narrow path leading up to the front door and the garden was planted with roses. The walls were covered in pale coloured plaster and the two windows either side of the front door were both quite small. Its only distinctive feature was a column of horseshoes hanging beside the door. She was sure she had seen the very same thing somewhere else.

Emily turned again to her iPad. She'd been looking at holiday cottages for the past hour. Perhaps one of those was the very same cottage. With a rush of excitement, she began trawling back through the country cottage websites. Most of the cottages she had looked at were set in a coastal location with a sea view and, however hard she looked at the photograph, she could only see fields around and behind that cottage but she was determined not to overlook anything.

An hour and several interruptions from Alex later, she set the iPad aside. Nothing. Not one of those cottages looked remotely the same. It must have been somewhere else. She shook her head at Molly and got to her feet. Maybe inspiration would strike when she was cooking tea or doing something else equally mundane. She would not allow herself to be disappointed, she decided. It was best to be philosophical about these things. Fate would determine when, where or even if she were to unearth any information about her past. She just needed to keep an open mind. However, it was to be a week later before her hopes were raised once again.

CHAPTER 11

Jennifer – December 2016

The article which featured Jennifer's cottage appeared in the Sunday Telegraph supplement in early December and her journalist friend had done a great job in promoting it. As well as two photographs showing the cottage to its best advantage, there was a chocolate box view of Great Chalkham High Street showing the quaint half-timbered cottages which made it so popular with tourists. Then there was a photograph of the idyllic Chalkham lake, once a chalk quarry and possibly how the village got its name, and another of the historic Church of St Paul where, legend had it, St Paul himself appeared to offer solace to the bereaved Lord and Lady Congleton after the death of their first-born child in 1788. In the article, it told the story of how he had apparently told them they would go on to have seven more healthy children who would all live to maturity – a fact borne out in later years.

Once upon a time, Jennifer would have dismissed such a thing as fanciful nonsense, a charming tale and nothing else. Her parents had been atheists and she had been brought up in the belief that everything in the world could be explained by science, even if the human mind did not yet have the capability of understanding that science. She didn't believe there was a God and considered revelatory visitations of saints and angels to be the stuff of fiction. Indeed, she had often told her more religious friends that, while she would like to believe there was something out there, some all-powerful, all-loving being protecting mankind from its worst excesses, she sadly did not have a mystical bone in her body.

However, since she'd been living in her cottage, some of those firmly held convictions had been shaken by the intermittent appearances of 'ghost girl', as she'd named her. She had googled 'the science of ghosts' and the evidence suggested that the belief in the supernatural was all in the mind, just as she had always argued.

However, it was difficult not to believe the evidence of her own eyes and, unless she was truly going mad, she found she could not dismiss her as a construct of her own imagining. There had to be a scientific explanation, she reasoned, something perhaps to do with the residual energy of a person being left behind after their death.

At least 'ghost girl' was not a threatening presence and she'd become used to seeing her drifting through a room, one moment there and the next gone again. Her only concern was what her potential bed and breakfast customers might make of her, if they could actually see her. If not, then perhaps she really *was* a creature of her own troubled mind.

She turned her attention back to the magazine article. There was also information about other places near Great Chalkham worth a visit and Jennifer thought, on reading it, that if she didn't already live here, she would definitely want to visit. Her friend really had done her proud and she resolved to send her some flowers as a thank you.

It was not long before the phone started ringing. Soon she had taken bookings for most of June, July and August the following year and also, unexpectedly, a booking for Christmas. She had been looking to her own Christmas getaway; she usually took herself off somewhere, often abroad, rather than spend the holiday alone. The enquiry was from a couple whose only son had recently emigrated with his wife and family to Australia. For the first time, they would be spending Christmas alone and they just couldn't face it in their own home.

'Of course, I can fit you in. That's no problem,' Jennifer had said, putting her own plans on hold. 'I'll make sure you have a wonderful time ... yes, I'll do all the catering ... yes, there will be turkey ... and a tree ... yes, yes, all the trimmings. It'll be a real home from home Christmas.'

She put the phone down flushed with excitement and mentally making instant plans. Her first thought was where she was going to get a tree - only a real one would do. David would probably know the best place to get one.

She hadn't seen him since the Race Night ten days earlier but otherwise her social life had definitely picked up. Jeremy had phoned the next day to invite her for dinner and he had taken her to a lovely restaurant in the nearby village of Little Chalkham. It had been a pleasant evening and the meal had been exquisite. Jeremy could talk the hind legs off a donkey but he was an interesting raconteur and made her laugh at his tales of his travels when he was a salesman. At the end of the meal, she had insisted on paying half and then, later, when she had chastely offered her cheek and he had instead kissed her with unexpected passion on the lips, had made it clear that she wasn't interested in anything beyond friendship. He had accepted that philosophically and, since then, they'd been out twice more, once to the cinema and once to a different restaurant.

She had also walked down to the Fox and Hare on a few occasions and had got to know a few more of the locals. It soon became clear that her outings with Jeremy had been noticed and much discussed on the village grapevine when she had to counter some good-natured teasing.

'Where's Jeremy this evening?' Jill had greeted her. 'I hear you two have become a bit of an item.'

Jennifer had raised an eyebrow. 'Not at all. We're just friends.'

A man sitting on a bar stool snorted derisively. 'That's not what I heard. I heard that the two of you were seen getting very cosy together outside your cottage.' He grinned, revealing a plethora of missing teeth. 'Good old boy! I didn't know he had it in him!'

'This is Harry Gardiner,' Jill introduced him to Jennifer. 'Our resident comedian.'

'Pleased to meet you, Harry.' She shook his work-roughened hand and smiled coolly. 'I'm afraid you've been misinformed.'

'Aye, well we'll see about that. Can I buy you a drink?' he offered.

'That's very kind but won't people talk?' she replied wryly.

He chuckled. 'I'll risk it if you will. What will you have?'

'A gin and slimline tonic, thank you.' She settled on the bar stool beside him. 'So, what do you do when you're not spying on people outside their homes?'

'I'm a groundsman. Work for the council. It'll be thirty years next spring.'

They chatted companionably for the next half hour, long enough to finish their drinks and for Jennifer to buy him another, and were joined at different times by other customers on their forays to the bar. Harry seemed to know most people and persisted in introducing her as Jeremy Willis' young lady, even though she scolded him for it. It seemed to amuse him hugely that she continued to correct him painstakingly every time. By the end of the evening, she felt she knew half the village.

One evening, there was a quiz night and she made up the numbers in a team comprising Sheila and Mike Blake and their friend, Maggie Freeman, a large, jolly woman in her fifties who had lived in Great Chalkham all her life. Jennifer immediately asked her about her cottage and the people who had lived there.

'Oh, all sorts,' said Maggie, screwing up her face in the effort to remember. 'When I was little, in the sixties, the Catchpoles lived there. They had two children and one of them, Martin, was in my class at school. Then I think it was the Spencers ... or, no, was it the Darbys? It was a bit run down in those days, a bit rough, if you know what I mean. Then an old lady lived there ... oh, what was her name?' She looked at the Blakes and tutted at herself. 'Of course, silly me, she would have died before you got here. Well, I can't remember her name but I know it was empty for a long time after that. It was in quite a state. That would have been some time in the nineties.' She shook her head ruefully. 'It's so hard to remember details these days ...

Anyway, eventually a developer got hold of it. It was modernised and sold to a couple in London who used it as a weekend retreat. After that, the Masons had it and, of course, you bought it from them.'

Jennifer listened carefully. There had been no mention of a young woman in her twenties who had perhaps died in tragic circumstances. 'What about before the sixties?' she asked. 'Do you remember any stories about the cottage which date back to earlier in the century? I'd love to know about its previous history and any information which gives the cottage some character would be good for business.'

Maggie shook her head. 'I don't remember anything.' She thought for a moment and then added, 'You ought to talk to Angela Carr. She's a bit of a pain, between you and me, but she's a history buff and I know she's been compiling an archive of information about the village. She's one of these typical newcomers to the village – here for five minutes and immediately an expert. Oh ...' She coloured slightly as she looked across at Jennifer. 'No offence ... I didn't mean you.'

'Of course not.' Jennifer gave her a reassuring smile. 'I'm not an expert on anything, as you'll soon find out when the quiz starts! A village archive sounds fascinating. Would you happen to have a number for Angela?'

''Fraid not. I try to avoid her, to be honest. But her number will probably be in the parish magazine. She seems to be on every committee going – a right busybody.'

'It's good to have people in the village who are prepared to go on to the committees or nothing would ever get done. At least she's prepared to give things a go,' Sheila said in a tone of mild rebuke.

'I know, but she doesn't need to take over. She's practically running the village now and some of her ideas are just ridiculous. Do you know that she proposed taking over some of the children's playing field as a village car park?'

'Yes, but you can't deny the village desperately needs another car park that end of the village. At least she is trying to do something about it,' said Mike, joining in the debate.

'Well, she's not my cup of tea.' Maggie was determined to have the last word on the subject.

Fortunately, the start of the quiz precluded further argument and the four of them turned their attention to answering the questions. They proved quite tricky and Jennifer was relieved that she did at least manage to come up with a few of the answers. Her team came a creditable third out of the six teams taking part and, by the end of the evening, she was surprised how much she'd enjoyed herself.

Things were going well, she thought, as she picked up the list she'd been making in preparation for her Christmas visitors. Top of the list was the tree and she grabbed her phone to ring David Brewer.

'Sure, I can help,' he said in response to her enquiry. 'Didn't think it would be long before you needed me for something.'

She felt the familiar prickle of irritation. 'Just trying to make you feel important,' she retorted briskly, 'so if you could just let me know the name of the best place to go ...'

'I can do better than that. I'm going there myself this afternoon so I can pick one up for you ... or you could come along yourself to choose your own.'

Once again, she felt unsettled at spending time alone with him. 'Er ... I had plans for this afternoon.' That, at least, was true. She had planned to go into town to buy some Christmas decorations. 'If you could pick one up, that would be very kind.'

'Oh, out with Jeremy again, are you? The whole village is talking about it,' he teased.

'None of your business. A six-foot tree would be fine, thank you.'

'Ok, I'll drop it off. I'll put it around the back if you're not home.'

'That would be very kind,' she said stiffly. 'Can I settle up when I see you?'

'No problem.'

'Right. Well, thank you.'

She put the phone down with a sense of relief. It irked her that he always managed to make her feel so discomfited. She thought back to the quiz night and wondered at how relaxed she had been walking home with him. It must have been the wine, she decided. She would have to have a glass or two before she spoke to him in future!

She was, however, decidedly sober when she pulled up outside her cottage later that afternoon to find his truck already parked in her driveway.

'Damn,' she thought to herself. 'What bad timing! Another few minutes and he would have been gone.'

As she got out of the car, he appeared from her back garden. 'Good, you're back. You can take a look at the tree and make sure it's what you want.'

She followed him round and was startled to see not only a bushy, perfectly symmetrical fir tree but also 'ghost girl' standing right beside it. She looked quickly at David to gauge his reaction but he had eyes only for her.

'What do you think? Is it ok?' he asked anxiously when she failed to comment.

'Oh, yes ... the tree ... it's perfect, thanks.'

'Are you alright, Jen? You look as white as a sheet.'

'Er yes, of course. I'm fine,' she smiled wanly.

Ghost girl was now slowly circling the tree, trailing her fingers lightly over the branches. Surely, he could see her?

'Right, I'll be off then.' David was looking at her strangely and she snapped herself out of her reverie.

'Oh, let me make you a cup of tea first.' Her innate good manners surfaced and the words were out of her mouth before she realised what she was saying. 'It's the least I can do after you've been so good as to fetch the tree for me. I'd have struggled in my little car.'

'Anytime,' he grinned at her. 'I'd love a cup of tea but I've got a five o'clock meeting with some clients. Tell you what … I'll pick you up tomorrow night and we'll go out for something to eat instead … unless you think Jeremy would be jealous?'

'Of course, he won't be jealous,' she snapped.

'Good, that's settled then.' He got into his truck and wound down the window. 'I'll pick you up at seven. Looking forward to it.' He was grinning broadly as he reversed his truck out of the drive.

How had that happened? How had she let herself be manoeuvred into going out with that man? She shook her head in disbelief as she dragged her bags from the boot of her car and unlocked her cottage. It was because she had been in shock – shock that he clearly could not see the girl standing beside the tree.

As she put the kettle on for a much-needed cup of tea, she rationalised that this was a good thing. The cottage was not haunted after all and she no longer needed to worry about guests being terrorised by a ghost. What was more troubling, though, was the fact that the girl was obviously a figment of her imagination. What did that say about her state of mind?

CHAPTER 12

Norah – June- August 1927

Dusk was throwing a gauzy film over the fields of Great Chalkham and the earlier rain had finally stopped when Arthur was awoken from his doze by the fireside. The knock came again – tentative, timid. With a sigh, he got to his feet and crossed to the door. Just lately, Clara the cook from the Chalkham Hall had been finding excuses to pay him a visit and he was already framing his excuses as he opened the door.

His heart skipped a beat. 'Norah,' he said, 'What are you doing here?'

Her face was pale in the gloom and she shuffled awkwardly beneath his gaze. He noticed her cloak and boots were caked with mud and that she was carrying a brown, leather case.

'I'm sorry for the imposition, Arthur,' she murmured, 'but I wondered if I might rest here a while?'

'Of course, of course. Come in.' He stepped to one side and allowed her to pass. 'You know it's not an imposition; we're friends. You can stay as long as you like. Go sit yourself down.'

'Thank you.'

She sat stiffly on one of the wooden chairs by the table and looked around. The cottage felt warm and comforting after her earlier ordeal and subsequent ten-mile walk. She longed to sink down in Arthur's battered, old, comfy chair by the crackling fire and chat with him as she had in the old days but things had changed. She had changed.

'I was just about to brew a pot,' said Arthur setting the kettle on the stove. 'Would you care for a cup?'

It was as if they were polite strangers, he thought. Surreptitiously he watched her as he busied himself with cups, sugar and milk and wondered what she was doing there. This was not a happy visit; he could see that much. Her eyes were troubled and he noticed her hands were twitching nervously as they rested on the table. Something had gone badly wrong at Collingworth Hall. His stomach clenched at the thought of it.

'This is very kind of you ...' she began.

'Don't be daft. You know you're always welcome here. We're mates, you and I. Mates look out for each other.'

Her eyes filled with tears. 'I know ... and I'm sorry about ... you know ... before. I wasn't perhaps as tactful as I should have been.'

'You said what you felt and I respected that. You can't help your feelings, I know that.'

He handed her his best china cup and saucer and sat down on the chair beside her. They sat in silence for a few moments while she sipped at her tea and avoided his gaze. How could she even begin to tell him what had happened? Earlier, she had not thought of anything but escape. It was only a few miles on that she had realised where she was heading. It was the only place she could go. She knew in her heart that Arthur would not turn her away. Now she was here, though, she realised she had not thought through how difficult things might be. She was going to have to tell him something but she burnt with shame at the thought of telling him exactly what had transpired at Collingworth Hall. Worse than that, he had cared for her, enough to propose marriage, and now she was damaged goods. She dreaded seeing the disappointment he would surely feel writ large on his face.

'Are you hungry?' Arthur's voice broke the silence. 'I have a bit of bread and cheese. I'm afraid I've eaten all the stew I had for tea.'

'No, please don't trouble yourself. I'm fine,' she replied.

'Well I can see you're not fine but I can also see you're falling down tired so perhaps we'll talk about it tomorrow when you've rested. I'm pretty bushed myself and I'll need to be up at five to milk the cows. You make yourself at home in my room and I'll take the chair. That way I won't disturb you when I get up.'

'No, no,' Norah leapt to her feet. 'I couldn't possibly deprive you of your bed. I'll sleep in the chair.'

'Sorry. Decision's made,' Arthur said firmly picking up her case and marching it through to his bedroom. 'Things will seem better when you've had a sleep. They always do.'

Mutely, Norah followed him and stood by the neatly made bed as he gathered up some of his clothes and a blanket.

'Give us a shout if you need anything. Sleep well.'

He closed the door behind him and settled down in the chair. Questions churned through his brain but patience was a virtue, his mother had always said. She would give him answers when she was ready. On the other side of the door, he could hear her moving around and he thought how lonely his life had been since she had left. Suddenly, he could not subdue the hope surging through him. Maybe he was being given a second chance with her – he did not want to blow it this time.

In the bedroom, Norah lay still, eyes wide open and her emotions in turmoil. When she undressed, she had suffered the fresh shock of seeing ugly bruises purpling the white skin of her inner thighs. She was very sore and had suffered some bleeding which she was anxious not to transfer to the sheets.

Beyond the door, she could hear the fire still crackling and, eventually, Arthur's gentle snores telling her he was asleep. He was such a good man. She should have married him when she had the chance; then none of this would have happened. Now it was too late and her life would not be the same again. Fearfully, she wondered what had happened when Lord Collingworth had regained consciousness. He would be furious and would want revenge. Doubtless he would send men to find her and bring her to account. She could be faced with an indictment for attempted murder should he decide to bring charges. However, she could not regret her actions and, truthfully, she wished she had hit the bastard harder. The memory of his hands pinching her breasts and her bottom as he thrust himself into her and his breath, his foul breath, as he panted and gasped his pleasure made her feel sick. How could she ever forget it? At last, the tears came and she sobbed herself to sleep.

When Norah awoke the next morning, it was just beginning to get light and the birds were singing. 'Birds are singing; all's right with the world.' Her mother's words came back to her with a jolt as she realised where she was. All definitely *wasn't* right. The memories came flooding back – sickening, horrible ... With a burst of determination, she pushed back the covers and gingerly got out of bed. She felt stiff and sore. It will pass, she told herself firmly.

The cottage was quiet and Arthur had left for work. She found a note he had left for her by the stove.

Make yourself at home. See you later. A.

At least that gave her time to think about what she might say to him. In the meantime, she might as well make herself useful.

Norah was busily setting knives and forks on the table when Arthur returned that evening. In truth, the table had been laid for an hour but she'd seen him coming down the lane and wanted to be doing something when he came in. He sniffed the air appreciatively and smiled broadly. 'Something smells good.'

Norah smiled back. 'I'm not much of a cook so don't get your hopes up. It's just cheese and potato pie with a bit of ham.'

'Sounds good. I'm starving. I'll just get washed up.'

Norah carefully served up the food and set the plates on the table. It did look pretty, she thought, with the wild flowers she had picked, arranged in a jam jar as a centrepiece.

'You've been busy.' Arthur had noticed the clothes hanging on the line earlier when he passed by the cottage on his way up to the farmhouse. He had wanted to call in and see how she was doing but he'd thought it might be awkward and decided to leave her be.

'Not very,' Norah replied. 'Not compared to the life of a nanny.' She stopped abruptly and bit her lip in annoyance at herself. The last thing she wanted to bring up was her time at Collingworth Hall.

Arthur studied her face carefully and decided to take the opening. 'About that,' he said as casually as he could muster, 'I take it you're not going back.'

'No.'

Norah pushed her food around her plate as if it demanded all her attention.

'That's fine with me.' Arthur took a deep breath, 'Look, you don't have to tell me what's happened. You can stay here with me. My previous offer still stands.'

Her eyes filled with tears and miserably she laid down her knife and fork. She couldn't meet his eyes and she stared down at the table as she spoke.

'You're such a good man, Arthur and any woman would be very proud to be your wife. But I can't accept your offer ... I'm sorry.'

Arthur swallowed hard. It was not easy being turned down twice by the same woman but he refused to let his pride get in the way of his heart. 'Look, just hear me out,' he said quietly. 'I know you don't love me ... at least, not in the way I love you ... but I don't mind that. You need somewhere to stay and I could use some female company. We've always been good friends, you and I. We get on well. Think of it as a practical solution.'

Norah forced herself to look at his face. It was such a kind, honest face. She knew she had to tell him the truth.

'It's not that. Lord Collingworth ... he ... he ...' She took a deep breath. 'He attacked me. I tried to push him away but he was too strong and then afterwards I hit him over the head with a candlestick. Knocked him out. I expect he'll press charges. I'll probably be going to jail.' Tears filled her eyes and shame reddened her cheeks but she managed to hold his gaze.

'Oh God, oh Norah ... the bastard. I'll kill him myself.' Arthur leapt from his chair and put his arm around her. 'My poor girl.' He squeezed her tightly against him. 'This isn't the first time he's done this you know. I now know of a few girls who went to work there and were ...' He struggled to find a word, '... abused by him. I found out recently from someone whose sister suffered terribly at his hands. I was about to write and warn you.'

She shrugged. 'What's done is done. I thought I could handle anything. How stupid I was! You're not to do anything though, Arthur. Promise me that. I don't want you to get yourself hanged for his murder – that's if he's not dead already.'

Arthur remained silent, inwardly seething with anger and frustration. Norah was right. There was a good chance she would be jailed for hitting him. It would be his word against hers and he had no illusions about the judge taking the side of a lowly nanny against a peer of the realm. He could not let that happen but how could it be avoided? Feeling fiercely protective, he gave her shoulders another squeeze and turned her to face him.

'I will promise you one thing, Norah. I won't let him hurt you anymore. That's certain.'

The next day dragged by in a haze of uncertainty and dread. Norah was sure she was about to be arrested and it was difficult to find something to distract herself. She longed to walk down to the stream or to go and say hello to the horses in the meadow opposite but she did not want anyone to see her. Her thinking was that she could not be arrested if no one knew where she was.

Arthur had ridden past on his horse earlier and she watched him as headed up the lane and around the corner, wondering where he was headed. His face had appeared grim and set, very unlike his usual, open countenance. She wondered if his mood was the result of her disclosure and felt a renewed sense of guilt. Her own life was ruined but she had no right to disrupt his life. Perhaps it had been a mistake to come here, she thought, but then where else could she have gone? Certainly not to the home of her ex-stepmother and her latest husband.

Now it was getting dark and Arthur still had not returned. Norah sat by the fire, watching the dancing flames. She could not help but wonder where he was. She feared he may have ridden out to Collingworth Hall to confront Lord Collingworth himself. Such a meeting would be fraught with difficulty and danger. She imagined Arthur angry and vengeful, threatening him, maybe even attacking him, being beaten off by the servants, being arrested. It would be her fault. Maybe she should not have come back here at all …

Just at that moment, she heard a horse's hooves trotting up the lane. Anxiously, she rushed to the window and peered out into the blackness. It was impossible to see who it was.

Then she heard Arthur's voice. 'Norah, I'll be back in about an hour. I just need to take Jock here back up to the stables, rub him down and feed him. I'll be as quick as I can.'

She pondered his tone of voice as she sat back down by the fire and decided she felt reassured. He had sounded normal. He had probably just been into town on business. Maybe he had met up with a friend and had a few pints at the Hare and Dog. She got up and walked over to the shelf where Arthur kept a few books. Most were books about crop or animal husbandry but there was also a copy of Treasure Island. She picked it up and read the inscription inside the front cover - Awarded to Arthur Fletcher, July 13th, 1910. First prize. She wondered what he had done to win first prize and realised how little she knew about Arthur's early life. In the past, he had always been there to listen to her highs and lows. He had shared her triumphs and comforted her when first her mother and then her father had died. 'I'm so selfish,' she thought to herself. 'I never really asked him much about his life; I never asked him how he was feeling.' She resolved to be a better friend, no matter what the future might bring.

At last she heard Arthur's footsteps and smiled as he came through the door. 'I wondered if the bogeyman had got you,' she said, reminding him of the day when she had refused to walk through the woods on her own because the bogeyman might get her. Eventually, he had walked with her and, after that, had taken to walking her home whenever she visited him in the stables.

He grinned. 'No, it was the other way around. I got the bogeyman, otherwise known as Henry Collingworth.'

Dread flooded through her. 'You didn't do anything stupid?' she asked anxiously.

'Let's put it this way; I didn't do what I was sorely tempted to do but I have stopped him from having you arrested for assault.'

'How on earth did you manage that?'

'This morning I went to see my old chum, Josh Hill. He's a lawyer now – works for a firm in Bury. He agreed to help me and came up with a great plan. I told you that this is not the first time Collingworth … er … has done what he did.'

She nodded.

'Well, Josh suggested we both ride over to Collingworth Hall and confront him with the threat of a court case should he decide to pursue prosecuting you. He would find it difficult to maintain his innocence against the word of at least six independent witnesses.'

'But surely those women would be most reluctant to testify in court?'

Arthur smiled broadly. 'You know that and I know that. Luckily Josh Hill was very convincing and said he already had six sworn affadavits in his possession. He told Collingworth that his good name and that of his lady wife would be dragged through the mud. The press would have a field day, he said. I wish you could have seen him. He was brilliant.'

'So, he's definitely agreed not to press charges?' She could hardly believe what he was saying.

'He definitely did. He was a snivelling wreck by the time Josh had finished with him. Kept pleading his innocence and saying he had no intention of pressing charges against you or any other servant girl. In fact, he said it was all a misunderstanding and he'd fallen and hit his head. Nothing to do with you at all. Oh, and by the way, he was sporting a magnificent black eye. You really gave him a belter!'

Norah shook her head. 'I can't believe it,' she murmured. 'I've been so worried.' She took the two steps needed and threw her arms around him. 'Thank you. And thank Josh too.'

Arthur hugged her close, savouring the moment. 'It was nothing. I'm just glad it worked out.'

The days drifted into weeks and fell into a comfortable pattern. When Arthur was at work, Norah would clean, tend the vegetable patch out back, fetch the shopping and cook. The villagers of Great Chalkham were delighted to see her back and then horrified to learn that she was staying in Arthur Fletcher's farm cottage.

'While he's living there as well! Living in sin!' the postmistress, Edna Barrow, confided eagerly to all who stepped over her threshold. 'Her mother would turn in her grave if she knew, God rest her soul.'

'Her father let her run wild after Iris died,' Mrs Isabel Batty uttered sagely. 'She was always hanging around those farmworkers. Might have guessed it would lead to this.'

'I always thought Arthur Fletcher was a decent sort.' Edna shook her head sorrowfully. 'You'd have thought he would make an honest woman of her ...'

Norah was not impervious to the stares and whispers. She guessed that her situation was much talked about but she held her head high as she walked through the village each day. She knew she could not continue to stay with Arthur but had yet to find a position. When she had asked at the post office if Mrs Barrow knew if anyone who required a home help or a nanny, she was greeted with pursed lips and a shake of the head. She was going to have to try further afield but was reluctant to leave the safety of Arthur's cottage.

Also, she could not deny that the more time she spent with Arthur, the more she liked him and the more she eagerly awaited his return every day. He was good humoured and easy company; she found herself entertained by his recount of his day's events. Every day, he would have something amusing saved up to tell her. By comparison, she felt dull and uninteresting. There was little exciting she could tell him about her day.

She was also painfully aware that his brown eyes made her heart flutter and she could not help but notice his lean, muscled torso. At odd times of the day, she found herself imagining him taking her in his strong arms and asking her to marry him again. This time, she realised, she would gladly give him a different answer.

However, he gave her no sign that he thought of her as anything but a friend. He was a perfect gentleman around her. That was just typical, she thought in frustration. Before, he had definitely hinted of his love for her but now he seemed to be completely indifferent to her charms. Sadly, she wondered if her disclosure had anything to do with it. Although he had gallantly come to her aid when she most needed it, any love he had felt for her must surely have dissolved at the thought that she had been another man's lover, however unwillingly that may have been.

The days continued to shorten and the annual corn harvest was just around the corner. Norah had been under the weather for several days and had been feeling queasy, particularly at mealtimes. Arthur had noticed her lack of appetite and asked after her health but she had insisted she was fine. It was just a bug and would soon pass, she thought. The sickness had continued, though, and she wondered if she should pay a visit to the village doctor, old Dr Bell. Certainly, Arthur had encouraged her to do so when he discovered she had been taking a bucket with her at bedtime in case she was sick in the night. Norah, who was hardly ever ill, continued to dismiss his concerns right up until the moment she was struck by a truly awful thought. The moment of revelation occurred as she noticed her old school friend, Elsie Thickthorn, waddling up the lane.

'Poor Elsie. She's put on a lot of weight,' thought Norah. Then Elsie drew level with the cottage and Norah could see that she was, in fact, heavily pregnant. Instantly, she realised her own terrible truth. She was expecting a baby!

Arthur returned that evening and found Norah quiet and morose. When he asked her what was wrong, she told him that she had to find employment as soon as possible.

'I really feel I am outstaying my welcome and people in the village are talking. You have been so kind letting me stay here as long as you have but I need to get on with my life.'

'You've never worried about people talking before,' he protested. 'Has something happened?'

'No, nothing,' she lied. 'I just feel I need to make a break from here, that's all.' She smiled ruefully, 'If I stay too much longer, I'll never leave.'

Arthur shrugged. 'What's wrong with that?' he asked. 'I've told you you're welcome to stay as long as you like.'

'I know. You've been far kinder than I deserved.' She laid a hand on his arm. 'Thank you for all you've done for me but I need my independence.'

'Very well.' He turned away from her and headed towards the door.

'Where are you going?'

'I've just remembered I've been invited for supper at Jack and Cissy Richards' house. Cissy has a big family, many of whom are in service. She may know of something that would suit you,' he replied coolly and he shut the door firmly behind him.

Norah was in bed when she heard Arthur return and he had left for work when she surfaced in the morning. She'd slept badly and felt terrible. Just when her life seemed to be getting back on an even keel, she had been dealt another cruel blow. The thought of carrying Lord Collingworth's child filled her with horror and she could think of no solution. She had heard gossip all her life about unmarried mothers and knew that she could no longer stay in Great Chalkham where everyone knew her. The shame would be too great to bear. It would be better to find a position where no one knew her and then perhaps, when the baby was born, she might be able to find someone who wanted to adopt a child.

Miserably, she poured herself a cup of tea and sat down at the table. She had never felt so helpless - so utterly alone - and she felt hot tears prickle down her cheeks.

Just at that moment, there was a knock at the door. Hastily wiping the tears from her eyes and taking a deep breath to pull herself together, Norah opened the door.

Standing in front of her was the prettiest girl she had ever seen. She was about Norah's age or a little older, with golden hair swept into a bun and enormous, cornflower blue eyes.

'Hello, Norah. I'm Cissy - Cissy Richards. Arthur was telling us all about you last night and I just know we're going to be friends so I had to come over and visit. I hope you don't mind.'

She was smiling warmly and Norah immediately felt at ease with her. 'Of course not. Please come in. It's a pleasure to meet you. Would you care for a cup of tea?'

'Absolutely. Two sugars if I may.' Cissy bustled in and sat herself down at the table. 'Arthur was saying you are presently looking for a position. I have a sister who works at Marchmont Manor in Lincolnshire and in her last letter she was telling me all about the problems Lord and Lady Marchmont have been having finding a nanny for their children. Between you and me, I suspect they may be holy terrors! If you're up for a challenge, I'm sure you would be suitable, being from a good family and all that.' Cissy paused for breath. 'As long as you have good references, I think they'll just be happy to find someone. At least that's the impression I got from Elsa- she's my sister. She works in the kitchen there so at least there would be a friendly face looking out for you.'

'References ...,' Norah stammered, 'might be a bit of a problem. You see I've only worked at Collingworth Hall for about nine months and then I had to leave ... well, rather suddenly. I don't think I could ask them for a reference.'

'No, no, you don't need to say anything about Collingworth. One of my other sisters, Anne, worked there for a time and she too left in difficult circumstances. Don't worry,' she continued, seeing the way Norah's face had paled. 'Arthur didn't say anything about what happened to you but if your situation is anything like Anne's, then of course you couldn't stay there. No, I was thinking about references from people like the vicar and maybe your old headmaster. You are a young lady from a good family who has fallen on hard times. I'm sure you'd be just what they are looking for. I have the address here written out for you.' She handed Norah a piece of paper from her pocket. It was written in an exuberant, flowing hand which matched perfectly with Cissy's bubbly personality.

'This is very kind of you. Thank you.'

'No trouble at all. I'm happy to help, although do you mind if I ask you something? Jack said I shouldn't because that would be interfering but I have to ask you and it's quite all right if you don't want to answer. Just tell me I'm a nosy busybody and it's none of my business.'

Norah smiled. She could not help but like Cissy's irrepressible manner. 'Go ahead,' she said, 'but I may not be able to give you an answer.'

'Oh, you are a good sport!' she exclaimed. 'Righty oh, here goes. Why are you looking for a job at all when you have a perfectly decent chap willing to marry you?

All the single women in the village are after Arthur Fletcher but, so Jack tells me, he's always only had eyes for you. Apparently, he was heartbroken when you left before and now here you are back again and even living with him in his cottage so you can't dislike him that much. I just don't understand it. Sorry ... I know I probably shouldn't have said anything. It's just, last night, Arthur seemed so down and he's just such a nice chap. Oh dear, I knew I shouldn't have said anything.'

Cissy reached across the table and took hold of Norah's hand as she saw her eyes filling with tears.

'You're right. I can't talk about it,' she murmured.

'That's fine. Oh, I am sorry, Norah. I didn't mean to upset you. Is there anything I can do?'

'No ... it's just that ... you're right. Arthur did want to marry me. He asked me before I left to work at Collingworth Hall but I didn't want to get married then. I had these fancy notions about being independent and saving up to go to university. Also, at that time, I could only think of us, Arthur and I, as friends. And he is ... a really good friend. That's why I turned to him when ... when I needed somewhere to stay. But now I feel I'm overstaying my welcome.'

'Nonsense,' Cissy said briskly. 'Arthur's upset that you're suddenly in such a rush to leave. He wants you to stay, I know it.'

'I can't stay.' Norah withdrew her hand and stood up. 'Another cup of tea?'

'No, no more tea for me thanks. But *why* can't you stay? You and I have only just got to know each other,' Cissy persisted. She sighed and shook her head. 'You don't exactly seem thrilled to be leaving. There must be something ... Has someone said something to you?'

'It's not that. I'm used to disapproving looks when I venture out.'

'Then something else has happened. Oh, I wish you'd confide in me. I might be able to help. I come from a family of ten so I'm familiar with plenty of relationship problems.'

Norah sighed and then clasped a hand to her face as a wave of nausea took her by surprise.

'Excuse me ... I've just got to go ...' She rushed outside and was promptly sick on the vegetable patch. After a few moments, she felt Cissy's arm go around her and together they walked back into the cottage.

'I'm so sorry,' Norah began. 'It must be something I've eaten.'

Cissy shook her head sadly. 'You poor, poor girl. That explains everything. You're pregnant.'

When Arthur returned that night, he immediately asked Norah to go and sit down. 'I've spoken to Cissy,' he said flatly.

She felt the colour flood her cheeks. 'I wish she hadn't told you,' she muttered, her eyes downcast. 'I begged her not to but she said she thought you had a right to know.'

'I'm glad she told me. There is a simple solution to this problem. We marry straight away and everyone thinks the baby is mine.'

Norah sighed. Arthur was such a good man and she knew now that she loved him dearly but she could not allow him to sacrifice his future in this way. The baby was her problem - not his.

'That's very gallant of you but not necessary. It would be very unfair of me to saddle you with another man's child. You deserve so much better than that.' She looked up at him and tried to smile. 'I've made such a mess of things but it's my mess and I need to sort it out.'

Arthur took a deep breath and clasped her hands in his. 'Look, Norah, I *want* to help you. I don't want you to have to face this on your own.'

'I know but I can't bear to be a burden to you and that's what I would be. The child is obviously Lord Collingworth's,' she continued bluntly. 'How could you bear to raise another man's child, especially when it's a man you detest?'

'The child is yours so I would love it as I love you,' he replied simply. There was a silence and Norah hardly dared breathe.

'God help me, I didn't think I'd be doing this again.' He got to his feet and then knelt on one knee before her. 'I love you,' he repeated. 'You are the only woman I will ever love. It would be an honour to marry you and live out my days with you. I will love your baby as my own and, hopefully, in time, we'll have more babies. Marrying you is all I've ever wanted. I'm not being gallant. This is what I want. Norah Dunn, will you please marry me?'

'Oh Arthur!' She pulled him to his feet and flung herself into his arms. 'I love you too. Yes!' She hugged him tightly as if she would never let him go. 'Yes, I will marry you, if you're sure?' She looked up into his deep brown eyes and saw his love for her shining there.

'I'm sure,' he grinned and then he kissed her.

CHAPTER 13

Emily - December 2016

D ecember had crept in on a tide of damp, gloomy weather and Emily had decided to get the Christmas decorations out. Now Alex was three, he was all too aware of what that meant. Despite his mum's best efforts, he had seen seasonal advertisements promoting the latest toys and games so he was already at a fever pitch of anticipation. That evening, Adam had promised to bring home a tree and they were all going to decorate it together.

A week had passed since she'd looked at the photographs in Norah's scrapbook and had that moment of recognition about the cottage but she was no further forward in her efforts to identify where she'd seen it. Probably another dead end, she thought dispiritedly. Perhaps it had just been a figment of her imagination. Once again, she felt unsettled and restless. All the time, answers seemed to dangle tantalisingly out of reach, as elusive as the end of a rainbow.

Molly had been almost constantly in attendance during the daytime while Adam was at work and the sight of her mournful face did not help Emily's mood. Instead of being the reassuring presence she had been during Emily's childhood, she had become the focal point for her frustration.

'For goodness sake, haven't you got someone else you can go and torment?' she snapped on one occasion when she had looked up from the newspaper to find Molly staring at her across the kitchen table.

Molly, of course, did not reply; she just continued to watch with baleful, green eyes and Emily felt full of reproach.

'I'm sorry, Molly. I know I'm being snappy and short-tempered. Just ignore me.'

Luckily, the anticipation of Christmas and the joy of her son's wonder at it all had provided a welcome distraction. Emily resolved to channel her energies into making the celebrations extra special. First though, the boring bit - she needed to declutter and do some serious tidying. She was no longer surprised at the havoc a three-year-old could wreak in a room in the space of a few hours and, whilst they did endeavour to tidy the worst of it together at the end of each day, inevitably the chaos spread throughout the house. Emily resolved to start with Alex's things and then move on to her own. Toys had to be put away; piles of mail needed to be sorted and either filed, actioned or thrown out; an ever-growing pile of newspapers and magazines had to be collected up and put in the recycle bin.

Initially, she decided to make it into a game to do with Alex. She gave him clues and, once he'd successfully identified the correct toy, they ceremoniously returned it to the toy box. After an hour though, very little had been achieved and Alex had tired of the game. She decided instead to let him watch his favourite DVD while she did the rest on her own.

It took until lunchtime to clear all the floors and other surfaces of Alex's paraphernalia. It was incredible the number of toys and games he had managed to accumulate in his short life and Emily resolved to have a bit of a clear out in the new year. She also made a mental note to hold back a little on the presents he received for Christmas. It was a constant source of anxiety to her that he should not be a spoilt child who took things for granted.

In the afternoon, while Alex was having his nap, she made a start on her own clutter. There were piles of newspapers, magazines and junk mail both in the kitchen and the sitting room. She grabbed an armful and headed for the back door, only to find Molly standing in the doorway, blocking her path and staring at her with a look of such intent that Emily felt quite alarmed.

'Come on, Molly. Move out of the way. I haven't got time for this.' She spoke sharply, struggling to maintain her hold on the shifting mound of paper but Molly stood firm. Emily sighed and put the pile of papers on the floor. Hands on hips, she glared at Molly.

'What is it? Why won't you move?'

She knew she could just keep going. After all, Molly had no substance, no skin, bone or muscle to stop her. How many times, as a child, had she reached out for her, only to have her dissolve around her fingers and disappear? Still, something gave her pause.

'What is it? What's wrong?' she demanded. 'Oh, this is ridiculous!' Huffily, she picked up the pile again and set it on the worktop next to the door. 'Ok, you win. I won't go out there. Happy now?'

Molly continued to stand in the doorway as Emily collected the rest of the newspapers and magazines and deposited them along with the first pile.

'I get it. You don't trust me. You really don't want me to go out there ... but why?'

'Mummy, who are you talking to?' A sleepy Alex appeared in the doorway.

'Oh, hallo darling. You're awake! Just to myself as usual! Now, I expect you'd like a drink after your nap and then perhaps we could go out for a walk and get some fresh air.'

'Christmas tree,' Alex reminded her.

'Later darling. When Daddy gets home. He's bringing it with him. Remember?'

'When will he be home?'

'Not long. After our walk.'

The afternoon passed uneventfully with a visit to the park nearby and a long session of pushing Alex on a swing. By the time they got home, Adam was already in the process of manhandling a large tree out of his Mercedes estate.

'Wow! Fab tree!' Emily exclaimed.

Alex's face crumpled when he saw it. 'Where are the sparkles?' he wailed. 'I want tree with sparkles.'

'Me too,' Emily replied. 'That's why we're going to decorate it - so it sparkles.'

'Let's get it in through the front door first.' Adam hefted it, with some difficulty, on to his shoulder and carried it into the house. 'It weighs a ton.'

With Emily directing operations, the tree was established in its position in the corner of the living room and Adam lit the fire while Alex began putting baubles on the lower branches. There was something truly special about dressing the tree as a family, Emily decided. It was like a signal that the magic of Christmas had begun. When they had finished, they switched on the lights and received a rapturous reception from Alex.

'Pretty lights!' he exclaimed. He reached out chubby fingers to touch them.

'Yes, they are pretty but you need to leave them alone, Alex, or they might break,' said Adam.

'Presents?' Alex asked hopefully.

'We have to wait for Christmas for presents,' Emily answered. 'Father Christmas won't be coming until Christmas Eve and that's as long as you're a good boy. Now it's time for tea. Daddy will take you to wash your hands while I get it out of the oven.'

After they had eaten and Alex was bathed and in bed, they decided to watch an episode of Game of Thrones with a cup of coffee and Adam went into the kitchen to make it. While he was waiting for the kettle to boil, he noticed the piles of newspapers and magazines on the worktop in the utility room.

'What do you want doing with all this rubbish?' he called through to Emily. 'Shall I bin it?'

'What rubbish?' Emily walked through to the kitchen. 'I tidied up today, remember?'

'All this paper.' Adam signalled the offending heaps. 'Looks like you didn't really tidy the mess - you just moved it out of sight!'

'Oh yes, I was going to put that out earlier. Then Alex woke up.'

'Ok, I'll do it.' As Adam grabbed an armful of paper, Emily noticed Molly once again standing in front of the back door. Her face looked panic stricken and her eyes were beseeching Emily to do something.

'Er … no. Leave it. I just wanted to go through it one more time - just in case I'd thrown out something important. You know what I'm like.'

'Only too well,' Adam smiled ruefully. They were both remembering the time when, about to leave for a holiday in France, Emily couldn't find her passport which she distinctly remembered putting safely in her bag. After twenty minutes of desperate searching, Adam discovered it in the bin, along with the detritus Emily had decided to empty out of her handbag before they left.

Adam returned to the kitchen to make the coffees while Emily continued to watch Molly. The panic had left her face and Emily would have sworn that she looked relieved. She wandered over to the papers and began to flick through them. Could there really be something of significance in amongst all this rubbish?

'Your coffee's waiting for you,' Adam called through from the living room.

If there was something important there, it would have to wait until tomorrow. With a final glance at Molly, she switched out the light and went to join Adam.

It was the afternoon of the following day before Emily once again retrieved the piles of paper and dumped them on the kitchen table. Molly stood beside her, watching her intently, and Emily felt a frisson of excitement. Was she about to discover something important?

'Don't be silly. You're being ridiculous,' Emily said aloud and gave herself a mental shake. She was looking through a pile of old newspapers and magazines after all - not opening the lid of a suddenly discovered box of antiquities. Picking up the first paper, an edition of the East Anglian Daily Times, she started turning the pages, her eyes quickly scanning the headlines. Nothing. She set it to one side and picked up the next one. Again nothing. She sighed. This was going to take forever!

'Can't you give me a clue what I'm looking for?' she demanded but Molly just continued to watch her with the same intensity. 'Thought not.' She picked up the next one. This time it was a magazine, a copy of Ideal Home. Nothing. She continued to look through every newspaper and magazine for the next hour without finding anything of interest. Simmering with frustration, she pushed the current pile to one side and got to her feet. She needed a break.

As she pushed her stool away from the table, her elbow caught one of the remaining piles and around half of them fell heavily to the floor.

'Brilliant!' Emily exclaimed

Sighing, she bent to retrieve them when some wording on the front of a Sunday supplement caught her eye; 'Country retreats on a budget.' She remembered the article. It featured a number of properties in East Anglia offering bed and breakfast accommodation. A jolt of realisation shot through her and she began fumbling quickly through the pages to find it. There were several glossy photographs of different cottages, taken from different aspects and, then, there it was; a recently renovated, thatched cottage with whitewashed walls, small, leaded windows and a column of horseshoes hanging beside the door.

She stared transfixed at the photograph. The cottage definitely looked the same but there was only one way to find out. She scurried upstairs to her bedroom and retrieved Norah's scrapbook from her bedside table. Heart pounding, she took it downstairs and opened it at the final page of photographs. Then she placed the two pages side by side. Although the cottage in the magazine looked considerably larger and had obviously had some additional building work done, there could be no mistake. At last, she had found the cottage where Norah had lived with her husband and child.

CHAPTER 14

Jennifer – December, 2016

Jennifer spent a considerable amount of time getting ready for her evening out with David. She wanted to look her best – any woman would, she rationalised – but she also did not want to look as if she had made a real effort. It was a tricky thing to balance and she finally settled on a plain navy, long sleeved, fitted dress which she embellished with some chunky jewellery and high heeled, navy shoes. Looking critically at herself in her bedroom mirror, she decided the overall effect was attractive but business-like. It was not an outfit to give a man any ideas.

She had no idea what to expect in any case. 'Something to eat' could turn out to be an informal gathering of friends down the pub. She was hoping that might be the case. The prospect of spending an entire evening alone with him made her feel curiously anxious and she couldn't understand why. She'd never felt like this about any other man. Over the course of the day, she wondered what it was about him that made her feel nervous and had eventually acknowledged to herself that she hated not feeling in control. He was so arrogant and high-handed that she found his company akin to being hit by a steamroller. As someone who was used to being in command of most situations, she resented the way he managed to outmanoeuvre her. She needed to up her game, she decided, if she were to get the better of him.

When he arrived, promptly at seven, she couldn't help the giddy skip of excitement tingling her spine at the sight of him. He really was very good looking for a man in his late fifties and Jennifer was suddenly all too aware of it. His brown eyes, crinkled in a smile, were framed by extraordinarily long lashes and yet his face was very masculine, lean and strong-jawed. He was dressed smartly but informally in dark brown jacket and trousers and a green, checked shirt and Jennifer mentally ticked her own choice of attire as she picked up her wrap and bag and locked her door behind them.

He took hold of her arm solicitously as they walked to his car, a silver Audi. 'Watch your step! It's pretty icy already.'

Jennifer shivered in response. 'Yes, the forecast said it could well be minus five tonight.'

As they drove, David asked her about her tree. 'All sorted,' she replied. 'It looks lovely in the corner of the sitting room, in that little alcove. It was a perfect fit. Thank you again for getting it for me. I'll pay you for it when we get to .... where are we going?'

'Gino's,' David answered. 'It's a little Italian restaurant in Bury. I overheard you saying at the race night that you loved Italian food.'

Jennifer felt a warm glow at his effort to please her. 'That's very thoughtful of you,' she said and then added politely, 'I'm looking forward to it.'

'Me too. I'm starving.'

When they got to the restaurant, the proprietor, presumably Gino, greeted David warmly and kissed Jennifer effusively on each cheek. 'Lovely to see you again,' he said. 'But ... this beautiful lady ... I know we have not met. I would remember.'

After David had introduced her, Gino led them to a table set for two in a quiet corner of the restaurant. It was reasonably busy for a midweek night in December and humming with conversation. Jennifer looked around, absorbing her surroundings and feeling relaxed. The place had a charming, rustic feel, with a wooden floor, tables covered with checked tablecloths and casual arrangements of fresh flowers. It was the sort of restaurant she loved, comfortable and friendly.

'Oh, how much do I owe you for the tree?' she said, retrieving her purse from her navy clutch bag. He told her the amount and she counted out the cash. Seeing the couple on a nearby table watching her curiously, she stifled a giggle and leaned across the table to whisper to David. 'They probably think you're my escort and I'm paying you for your services!' she said, nodding towards the couple who looked quickly away.

He laughed. 'I'm willing to provide any services, as you put it, free of charge,' he said with a wink.

Jennifer blushed. 'I'm sure you are,' she said drily and cast around quickly for a change of subject. She really should do better at keeping her guard up. Picking up the menu, she asked David what he would recommend.

He shrugged. 'I'm not a great pasta lover myself so I usually have a steak - the Filleto Rossini,' he said, struggling a little with the pronunciation, 'and maybe some bruschetta or the seafood to start.'

She nodded. 'Well, it all looks good. How about if we share some bruschetta to start and then, perhaps, I'll have the pappardelle ragu d'anatra?'

'What's that?' he asked, peering at his menu.

'Pasta with a ragu of duck in a garlic, tomato, red wine and thyme sauce with parmesan shavings and truffle oil,' she read aloud. 'It sounds delicious.'

'If you say so. I'll take your word for it.'

A waiter appeared to take their order and then swiftly reappeared with a bottle of the house red wine and a large orange juice for David.

'Do you come here often?' Jennifer asked. 'The staff seem to very keen to please you.'

He shook his head. 'Not very often. The kids like to come here when they visit me. I think that's the best thing about Italian restaurants – the service. Italians seem to be very good at the personal touch. I know Gino makes a point of remembering the faces of his customers.'

The food, when it arrived, was exceptional and, by the end of it, Jennifer was feeling comfortably full and distinctly mellow. The conversation had flowed easily and David had been a charming companion, frequently making her laugh with his observations about some of the characters who lived in Chalkham, some of whom she had met on her evenings at the Fox and Hare.

She had reciprocated with some of her own funny anecdotes about her time in schools.

'I was doing some phonics with a class who weren't the brightest. We were working on different ways of making the ay sound. I'd made it into a game. I gave them clues and they'd have to guess the word with the ay sound. Anyway, it was going well until they got stuck on a particular word. The clue was that it's something Santa rides on. They were all looking puzzled when this young lad, his name was Jay, shot up his hand. 'What do you think, Jay?' I asked encouragingly. He was a boy who found spelling particularly difficult. He screwed up his face. 'I know what it is but I can't think what it's called.' 'Remember it rhymes with ay, like Jay – that should help,' I said. He shook his head despondently and then, suddenly, his eyes lit up. 'I've got it,' he shouted triumphantly, 'It's a don-kay!' My teaching assistant had to go out of the room, she was laughing so much.'

David chuckled. 'It must have been difficult to keep a straight face.' He paused. 'You obviously loved your job.'

'I did. I don't miss all the hassle and the endless meetings and the ridiculous amount of paperwork but I do miss the children and moments like that. There was always something to laugh at.'

'So ... why did you retire so early? Look, I couldn't help but notice your reaction when there was talk of that poor lad who died when we were at the quiz night. It's fine for you to tell me it's none of my business ... I was just wondering, that's all.'

Jennifer blanched and stiffened as he spoke and he reached across to take hold of her hand.

'Sorry. Forget I mentioned it.' He could have kicked himself for bringing it up. The evening had been going so well and she had seemed so relaxed.

Jennifer took a deep breath. She had nothing to be ashamed of but it was incredibly difficult to talk about it. All of those constantly suppressed feelings of grief and guilt rose to the surface and her eyes filled with tears. Perhaps it would help to talk about it. Maybe then she would stop seeing things that were not there.

'He was a pupil at my school,' she began, her eyes turned away from him. 'His name was Jasper Jones and he was a lovely lad. He hadn't been with us long; he'd come from somewhere in Wales. Anyway, he was on a year six residential trip at one of those outdoor activity centres and there was a terrible accident. Somehow, his safety equipment came loose and he fell when he was on a rope course. He died instantly.'

She felt his fingers tighten around hers and shook her head. 'I still can't believe it happened. That poor boy ... and his family. I can't think of anything worse than to lose a child. The whole thing was just terrible.'

'It must have been awful for the other children and his teacher too,' he said softly.

She nodded. 'It was. The whole community was devastated and, quite rightly, wanted someone to blame.'

'Surely they didn't blame you? Were you even there?' he asked.

She looked up and saw the concern in his eyes. 'No, I wasn't there and no, they didn't blame me, at least not directly. There were some pretty horrible things said on social media sites about the staff who had been on the trip and, well, it was all a nightmare really ...' Her voice tailed off as she remembered the inquiry that followed and the angry faces of the parents in the playground. 'All the school staff were completely exonerated by the police and the venue was closed down following an inquiry. Apparently, the webbing on his harness had snapped so it must have been in poor condition. People were meant to check these things but they obviously hadn't done so.'

'What happened after that?'

She sighed. 'We all tried to carry on as before but it was hopeless. How do you recover from something like that? A child in our care had died; we all felt responsible. I had booked the trip myself. We'd often taken children there over the years and they'd always had a great time. But the fact remains that if I hadn't organised it, he would still be alive today.'

'You can't think like that. It wasn't your fault. You couldn't have known,' he argued. His heart constricted with pity for her as she shrugged.

'I was the headteacher and, as such, I was in charge. I *have* to take some responsibility for what happened.' She sighed again. 'The teacher who had led the trip decided to leave the profession and I took early retirement. It was just too painful to stay on; the reminders were there every day.' She gave him a watery smile. 'Sorry … that's well and truly put a dampener on the evening. It was a lovely meal. Thank you, and thank you for listening too.'

He squeezed her hand once more and then let it go. It was strange how adrift she suddenly felt without it to hold on to.

'You're welcome,' he said. 'I feel honoured that you trust me enough to tell me your story.' His dark brown eyes were brimming with sincerity. 'And I honestly believe you really should not blame yourself. You should try to focus on all the good things that happened in your teaching career; all those children you helped; all those lives where you have made a difference.'

She smiled. 'I know. It's just easier said than done.' She pushed back her chair. 'Shall we make a move?'

David insisted upon paying the bill, even though she argued about paying her share. 'I invited you. You're my guest. Sorry but I'm old-fashioned about that kind of thing,' he said with an air of finality and, for once, she withdrew her objections.

'Thank you,' she said simply and they walked in silence out to the car.

On the way home, he told her about a project he was working on in Little Chalkham. 'It's hopeless,' he said. 'At the rate it's going, we'll be working on it for the next ten years! The clients are lovely people but they keep changing their minds. No sooner have we finished something than they decide it wasn't what they wanted and we have to do something different. Dave and Will are tearing their hair out!'

She grinned. Dave and Will were the builders who had worked on her cottage. 'I can imagine!' she said.

'That was what was so great about working with you – you always knew exactly what you wanted.'

She was glad of the darkness concealing the blushes brought on by his tone of approval and said nothing until they pulled up outside her cottage. 'Thank you again. It was a lovely evening … oh, don't bother about getting out!'

He had already undone his seatbelt and was halfway out of the car. 'I've already told you – I'm old-fashioned about these things. I'll see you to your door.'

There was no arguing with him. He came around to her side of the car, helped her to her feet and held her arm as they walked up her path.

'I feel like someone's granny!' she chuckled at his solicitousness.

'Well, you certainly don't *look* like someone's granny!' he murmured huskily. He turned her to face him and brushed his lips gently against hers. 'I've really enjoyed your company. I hope you'll let me take you out again … soon,' he added. 'Night. Sleep well.'

She fumbled her key into the lock. 'Goodnight.'

Without looking back, she stepped into her cottage and closed the door behind her. Her heart was racing. It had been such a chaste kiss but it had sent a charge of current through her entire body. In her whole life, no man had ever made her feel like this, like a giddy teenager. She had to admit it; she was very attracted to him and, judging by the smouldering look he'd just given her, he felt the same about her. How could that have happened? How could she have gone so quickly from antagonism to a schoolgirl crush? More to the point, what was she going to do about it?

For the first time in a very long while, that night she slept peacefully, dreaming of something other than the tragedy which had blighted her life.

The next morning, she was reluctant to get out of bed. It had been a good dream and she lay under the covers, trying to recall the details. There had been a man with her; he had been *such* a good lover ... She tingled as she remembered. God, it had been a long time since she had had good sex ... or *any* sex, come to that! She luxuriated in the sensations for a few moments more. The man lifted his head from her breast ... his face swam into her consciousness ... oh God, it was David Brewer! The realisation was like being doused in cold water. For goodness sake, get a grip, she admonished herself as she swung out of bed. One kiss and she was having fantasies about him!

Her landline started ringing and she grabbed her dressing gown as she rushed to answer it. 'Good morning,' she said smoothly, as if she had been up for hours. 'Jennifer Thompson speaking.'

'Hello.' It was a young woman's voice. 'I'm ringing to enquire about your rooms. I saw an article about your cottage in a magazine and I would love to book to stay for a week in January if that was possible.'

'Let me just check my diary,' said Jennifer, knowing full well that she had no bookings that month but needing time to retrieve a pen and some paper. 'What week were you thinking?'

'The week starting January 7th,' came the reply. 'It's a Saturday. If possible, I'd like a twin room for myself and my son. He's three. You do accept children?' The last question came out in a bit of a rush, as if the speaker had suddenly realised that could be a problem.

'Of course,' Jennifer replied calmly, already mentally listing the childproofing measures which would need to be taken. 'Let me take down your details and, as your booking is less than one month away, I'm afraid the full amount will be payable straight away.'

She spent another five minutes organising the booking and put the phone down with an air of satisfaction. Another customer! She could not believe how well the business was taking off. Now it would just be up to her to ensure that all her customers had a wonderful stay and a lot of that was in the planning. Adrenalin coursing through her body, she picked up her 'To do' list and started adding more items. Her Christmas guests would be arriving in less than one week and she had more than enough to keep her busy. It was all in the planning; as long as she had everything organised, nothing could go wrong.

CHAPTER 15

Norah – April 1928.

Norah kept her eyes squeezed shut and willed the noise to stop but it did not. She was so tired; she just wanted to sleep for a little bit longer. The noise persisted, louder now, insistent. Something was crying. A baby. She snapped her eyes open in a rush of consciousness.

At the same moment, the weight shifted in the narrow bed and she felt Arthur's hand on her shoulder. 'You stay there in the warm,' he murmured. 'I'll fetch him.'

It was still dark but the moonlight illuminated his pale back and buttocks as he headed across the room. She felt a rush of desire, immediately dampened by the sound of his voice crooning to the wailing infant, and with a sigh, sat up in bed. The crying continued until the baby was latched on to her left breast, sucking furiously and Norah felt her shawl being draped around her shoulders.

'You'll get cold.' Arthur yawned as he got back into bed.

'Thank you,' she said quietly but there was no response and she could tell from his steady, rhythmic breathing that he was already asleep.

This was the worst time, she thought, sitting alone in the night, tired to the point of exhaustion but unable to let her body drift back to slumber. This was the time when those feelings of resentment crept in, dark and insidious. Her baby, James Arthur Fletcher, had been born a month ago after a long and difficult labour and since then her life had not been her own.

Up until that point, she'd been happy, very content in her new role of wife. She and Arthur had married seven months ago and life had been good in so many ways. To start with, he was a wonderful homemaker. With two of his friends, he had built another room on to the back of the cottage for a nursery, ready for when the baby was older and then had built a beautiful crib. He could not have done more to show his love for her and his complete acceptance of another man's child.

The thought of being intimate with another man had secretly filled her with terror but Arthur had been sensitive to her feelings and hadn't rushed her. He had kissed, stroked and caressed her until she relaxed and then she had surprised herself with the strength of her passion for him. Throughout her pregnancy, they could not seem to get enough of each other but that had stopped with the birth of the baby. Initially, her body had been too sore and damaged after her delivery. The baby had been large and her hips were narrow so the birth had been traumatic. She'd needed time to recover and Arthur had cosseted her tenderly, for which she was grateful. Now though, she missed his touch and wondered why he was reluctant to have sex with her. Two nights ago, while baby Jimmy was sleeping, she'd reached out for him, running her fingers down his chest, his stomach and then, as she went lower, she'd felt his hand grasp hers firmly and lift it away from him. He had kissed her chastely and apologised that he was feeling tired. The rejection had left her feeling shattered and also jealous. His adoration of the baby had been instant, from the moment he took him in his arms and rocked him gently against his chest. Norah had worried, despite his protestations to the contrary, that he may not be able to love him as his own, but that was clearly not the case. All his love seemed to have been transferred to the baby after his arrival and Norah wondered if his desire for her would ever be rekindled.

Her own feelings about Jimmy were complicated. She had expected to feel a strong surge of motherly love for her son the first time she held him but it just hadn't happened, nor at any time subsequently. He was a fine-looking baby, with bright blue eyes and a head of curly black hair but she had been unprepared for the exhaustion she would feel in meeting his physical needs. She would feed him, change his nappy and put him down for a sleep and, within an hour, he would be crying, ready for another feed. Her nipples were cracked and sore and there was no let up. She had talked to Cissy Richards, with whom she had become close friends, about her lack of maternal instinct when she had visited.

'It's hardly surprising after all you've been though,' Cissy declared, giving her a hug. 'Just give it time.'

'But what about you? How did you feel when your two were born?'

'Honestly, I felt too tired to think about my feelings at all. Obviously, I love them both dearly but I don't recall how or when that happened. Listen, Norah, you've been through a lot and now you have a big, strong baby who is taking his toll on your reserves. No wonder you're feeling a bit down about things!'

'But what if I can never love him because ... well, because of his father?' Norah wailed. The tears which she had been holding back now streamed down her cheeks.

'Oh Norah!' Cissy handed her a handkerchief and took her in her arms. 'You must try not to worry about such things. Just take one day at a time. There now ...' She patted her back soothingly. 'Try not to upset yourself with foolish notions. You have a beautiful son and a hardworking husband who adores you. You have lots to be thankful for.'

'I know.' Norah blew her nose and wiped her tears away. 'I'm just being silly.'

'Never that.' Her friend gave her a final squeeze and stood up. 'What you're feeling at the moment is perfectly normal for new mothers. It will pass, you'll see.'

That had been a week ago and her attitude towards her child had remained the same. She sighed again and transferred Jimmy to her other breast, wincing with pain as he continued to suckle greedily. It was at times like these that she pondered how differently her life had turned out from her childhood dreams. Her ambition to study at Oxford and to become a doctor had faltered at the death of her father but was out of the question now she had a child to care for. She felt imprisoned by motherhood and another wave of resentment surged through her.

At last, she realised that the baby had stopped sucking and had fallen asleep at her breast. Gently, she carried him back to his crib at the foot of the bed and crept back under the covers, relieved to be able to close her eyes once more.

Arthur had left for work by the time Norah woke to the sound of the baby crying. When he returned at six o'clock in the evening, he found the baby hot and fractious in his crib and Norah only just starting preparing their supper.

'He's been like this all day,' she wailed as he walked through the door. 'Crying for no reason. He doesn't want feeding or changing, I've cuddled and rocked him for hours but nothing seems to work. I don't know what to do!'

Arthur picked him up carefully and began to croon gently. 'There now. Hush little man. What's the matter?' To Norah he added, 'This parenting lark will be much easier when he can tell us what's wrong. He's very hot. Perhaps we should get the doctor to take a look at him?'

She shook her head. 'I think he's just hot because of all the crying. He's worked himself into a proper state. There you go ... you've got the magic touch.' Jimmy's cries had reduced to whimpers as he snuggled into Arthur's shoulder. 'I could have done with you here sooner,' she added tartly. 'I've got virtually nothing done all day and supper will be at least another half hour.'

'Don't fret yourself so.' He gave her an encouraging smile. 'No one said babies were easy. We'll get through it.'

Norah remained silent as she finished vigorously chopping the carrots. It was all very well for him, she thought to herself. He could escape during the day. She was the one trapped in the situation.

'I think he has got a bit of a cold, poor little mite,' Arthur observed. 'His nose is a bit runny and he sounds a bit wheezy. My ma always used to say a bit of fresh air was the best thing for a cold. Maybe tomorrow you could take him for a walk in the pram. Some fresh air would probably do you the world of good too.'

She shot him a venomous look but his attention was totally focused on the baby. Did he not think she would have taken him out had she enough time? He had no idea what her days were like! And what did he mean by saying she would benefit from fresh air? Was he suggesting that she was growing cranky? That thought gave her pause ... well, maybe she was a bit grumpy but that was because she was so tired. Suddenly she felt like bursting into tears.

'Are you all right, Norah?' Arthur was looking at her now, concern etched on his face. When she did not reply, he stood up and placed a comforting hand on her shoulder. 'Look, I can see you're beat. Why don't you go and have a nap? I can finish getting supper ready.'

The thought of sleep was so appealing but her pride would not allow her to accept his offer. 'I'm fine,' she said gruffly. 'We'll have tea, I'll feed Jimmy and then, if you don't mind settling him, I'll go straight to bed.'

'Fair enough.'

The cloud of tension hanging over her made for an uncomfortable evening meal. Arthur did his best to entertain her with a steady stream of conversation but her replies were monosyllabic and eventually he lapsed into silence. Her depression since the birth of the baby seemed to be growing and he had no idea how to deal with it. He had sought advice from his friend Jack Richards but he could offer no advice.

'The missus just seemed to get on with it when our two were born,' he had shrugged. 'Sorry mate, I can't help you. I'll have a word with Cissy though. She might have an idea.'

Cissy had told him that he needed to be supportive and ignore his wife's moods. 'It's a big change for her,' she had said, 'And the poor thing's exhausted. Things will soon settle down, you'll see.'

Arthur had nodded solemnly. April was a busy time on the farm, sowing spring crops, or he would have asked for a bit of time off. He would just have to do as much as he could to help her when he was at home, he decided.

He watched her now, struggling to keep her eyes open as she fed Jimmy, and felt his heart melt with love for them both. Whatever it took, he thought fiercely, he would make sure they got back to the way things were. Things could only get better.

The next morning Jimmy was clearly unwell. They had all endured another difficult night; he had struggled to feed and then been unwilling to settle. Arthur had spent many hours in the darkness, rocking him gently and murmuring words of comfort while Norah slept fitfully in between attempts to feed him. Now, Arthur had gone to work and Norah stood by the sink, retrieving nappies from the hot, soapy water in which they had been soaking and squeezing and rubbing them against the ridged surface of her washboard. She could hear the baby snuffling listlessly in his crib and tried to block out the sound. First, she needed to get the washing finished, put through the mangle and out on the line. It was a fine drying day and she knew she had to make the most of it. Tiredly, she rubbed her forehead with the back of a hand cracked and raw from the endless washing. She already felt condemned to a life of drudgery and the baby was only one month old.

By the time the washing was safely pegged on the line, Jimmy was beginning to whimper. She would feed him and then take him out for a walk, she decided. Arthur was right; it would do them both good. Certainly, his airways needed clearing, she realised, as she tried to find a comfortable position for him to feed. As usual he latched greedily on to her nipple and sucked fiercely but then, after a few seconds, he released her as he struggled to breathe through his blocked nose. Poor little thing, she thought in a moment of tenderness; none of this was his fault.

She wrapped him securely in his shawl and lay him down beneath a blanket in the pram she had borrowed from Cissy. Then she combed her hair, put on her coat and stepped out into the April morning sunshine. Her spirits lifted almost immediately. It felt good to be outside and to have a break from the chores awaiting her. She walked briskly up the lane, past the old barn and paused for a moment beside the driveway leading to Willow Farm. It was no longer a farmhouse, as such, because the original farm was still owned by Cyril Brooke who lived at Chalkham Hall. Now, it was owned by a family called the Catchpoles. There was a stir when they'd first arrived in the village as they had their own automobile – a black MG. Since then, the Brookes had also purchased a motor vehicle but this was not often seen on Chalkham's roads. Rumour had it that Cyril was afraid to drive it.

She headed down the hill towards the village. On the way, she met old Mrs Cardew, the retired schoolteacher, carrying a bag of groceries.

'Why if it isn't Norah Dunn!' the old woman exclaimed, peering into the pram. 'And who have we got here?'

'It's Norah Fletcher now and this is James Arthur Fletcher,' she replied.

'My, he's a fine-looking chap. Looks just like his daddy with that dark colouring.'

'Yes ... yes, he does,' Norah said firmly. She was aware that there had been a certain amount of gossip about her surprising return to Chalkham, marriage and delivery of a son in quick succession and she was determined to quash any rumours. 'He is the very image of Arthur. Lovely to see you Mrs Cardew.'

She walked on and reached Chalkham High Street where her appearance created a buzz of interest. Mrs Allen was nattering to Mrs Nobbs outside the butcher's shop but immediately stopped and watched Norah's approach with undisguised curiosity.

'How are you, my dear? I understand it was touch and go for a while but there … we all have to go through it. Let's have a look at the bairn.' Mrs Allen pulled back the covers to get a better look. 'My, he's a bonny chap and a good size too, by the look of him.' She cast a sly glance at Mrs Nobbs. 'Considering he was born so early …'

Mrs Nobbs returned her look with one of reproach and smiled warmly at Norah. 'It's good to see you out and about. We were all most concerned when we heard what a difficult time you had. But what a beautiful baby!' She reached out a gnarled finger to tickle him under his chin.

Norah felt a glow of pride. 'Thank you, Mrs Nobbs. How's Jack?'

'Ah, bless you for asking. He's doing a little bit of labouring for Mr Brooke which helps. We get by, same as everyone else. But we'll never forget how you came by to help us after Jack was laid off by your poor father. You were an angel, you were.'

Norah smiled, a little embarrassed by the praise. 'It was the least I could do.'

'Sounds like the bairn is a bit wheezy,' said Mrs Allen, once again peering into the pram. 'What did you name him by the way?'

'James Arthur. Jimmy for short. Yes, he's got a bit of a cold at the moment.'

'Ah, you named him for his father.' Another sly look at Mrs Nobbs. 'Well, you're doing the right thing in getting him outside. You don't want it settling on his little lungs. That was what happened to Blanche Crabtree's new-born … ouch!' she exclaimed as Mrs Nobbs poked her with a sharp elbow. 'You're right. Best not to talk of such things. Well, I'm glad we've seen you, young Norah. You and little Jimmy. You make sure you take good care of him.'

As the two women headed away from her, Norah felt a momentary pang of fear. Blanche Crabtree's baby had died of pneumonia after just a few weeks. She watched Jimmy anxiously as she continued on her way. Surely it was just a cold … nothing to worry about … and he did seem to be breathing more easily than he had in the confines of the cottage.

It took a while for Norah to negotiate Chalkham High Street as all the shopkeepers and their customers wanted a first look at the baby. Jimmy was much admired and she felt warmed by the plethora of compliments. Eventually, she managed to make her escape and turned up the lane which would take her, in a loop, past the chalk pits, round the back of Willow Farm and then back home. Jimmy was sleeping soundly by the time they returned and Norah felt quite pleased with herself. She would have to ask Arthur for some money so she could buy some meat and groceries if she went out again tomorrow. He had taken over shopping duties since the birth but it was time she became less dependent upon him. Already, she was looking forward to another walk the next day.

However, Norah was unable to leave the cottage that following morning. After that first excursion, Jimmy took a turn for the worse. He started coughing, huge wheezy coughs which wracked his whole body and then developed a fever. Arthur had brought home a small bottle containing a mixture of brandy and port wine which Cissy had said was good for such illnesses.

'Just give him a drop on a teaspoon,' she had advised. 'It will help him to settle.'

They had duly dispensed the mixture but it made no difference and the doctor was called. Dr Darkins had been Norah's doctor for as long as she could remember and he had safely delivered her baby. She had absolute faith in his judgement and she watched him now with anxious eyes as he solemnly examined Jimmy.

'I'm afraid he has developed a chest infection,' he declared finally, his eyes compassionate. 'Try to keep his fever down with cold compresses and make sure he drinks plenty of fluids. He may not want to feed so make sure he has water on a teaspoon. Also, keep him upright as much as possible and keep tapping him lightly on his back. It will help prevent the mucous from further congesting his lungs.'

Since that visit, Norah and Arthur had taken turns to hold him against their shoulders, patting his back gently as the doctor had directed. Arthur had stayed home from work, determined to do all he could to help his son and to support his wife who had become almost hysterical at the thought of losing her baby. Indeed, Norah had undergone a complete transformation since she'd realised that Jimmy's life was at risk. Her previous indifference towards her son had been replaced by sheer terror when the doctor had revealed the seriousness of his condition and a passionate resolve to do all she could to keep him alive. She sat for hours, desperately clutching Jimmy against her breast and reluctant to allow Arthur to take him from her. The rush of love she now felt for him was overwhelming and she wondered how she could have been so self-centred before.

'Please God, spare my baby,' she murmured as she stroked Jimmy's head. 'I'll do anything if you let him live.'

Another night passed, tense and nerve jangling. Norah and Arthur sat together, listening to their child's fast, shallow breathing. His skin had taken on the pallor and sheen of death and they could do nothing more to help him other than pray.

'I can't bear it,' Norah whispered. 'Surely this is a test of faith no mother should endure?'

Arthur took her hand and gripped it firmly. 'We're going to get through this. We have to stay strong, for Jimmy's sake.'

'But what if we lose him?' Tears rolled unheeded down her cheeks.

'We won't lose him.' Arthur spoke with a confidence he did not feel. 'We're not going to let it happen.'

The doctor visited again in the morning and pronounced no change which, he told them, was good news. 'These next few hours will be crucial. If he makes it through another night, then I would expect him to recover. At least, he seems to be a fighter, a good, strong, little chap.' He patted Norah on the shoulder, shook Arthur's hand and took his leave.

Jimmy's condition remained critical throughout the afternoon and his parents were near collapse with fear and exhaustion. They were still taking turns to hold him, patting his tiny back and cooling his feverish brow. Norah had been trying to feed him but he had no interest. She could almost feel him growing weaker in her arms and felt herself sinking deeper into a pit of despair.

As evening fell, she clutched him once again to her breast and squeezed a little milk from her nipple to tempt him. 'Come on, Jimmy,' she pleaded. 'Just try a little. Please Jimmy.' She closed her eyes. It was hopeless.

Then, suddenly, she felt his lips around her nipple, sucking weakly. She held her breath, not daring to call to Arthur. 'There's a good boy,' she whispered. 'Just a little more … that's it.' Gently, she caressed his head. His skin was no longer clammy to the touch; his fever had broken.

Arthur appeared at her side. 'It's a miracle,' he breathed. 'Oh, thank God.'

From that point, Jimmy made a swift recovery and Dr Darkins shook his head in amazement when he visited the next morning. 'The little lad obviously has a very strong constitution,' he said. 'I've not seen another infant get over such a serious chest infection so speedily.' He beamed at Norah. 'I'm very happy to say his lungs are completely clear. This is good news indeed.'

'It certainly is. Thank you, Dr Darkins.' Norah gave him a broad smile in return. 'Don't take this the wrong way but I hope we don't have to see you any time soon.'

She watched him shut the door behind him and threw herself into Arthur's arms. 'I'm so happy I could sing!' she declared.

'Please no! Anything but that!' he replied, hugging her tightly. Norah's tuneless singing was a standing joke between them.

She giggled into his chest. 'Well, if I'm not allowed to sing, what am I allowed to do?'

His grip tightened and he kissed her hair. 'I can think of something …'

She took a step back and looked into his eyes. 'Mr Fletcher, are you suggesting what I think you're suggesting?' Heat rushed through her body.

'Why not? Jimmy's sound asleep and we are married after all.'

'Oh, I'm so relieved!' She threw herself back into his arms and kissed him. 'I thought you had gone off me!'

'What on earth made you think that?' he asked, his hands sliding down to her hips.

'Well let's face it, you *have* proved more than indifferent to my charms ever since Jimmy was born. What was I supposed to think?'

His lips found hers. 'You can blame Dr Darkins for that. He told me in no uncertain terms that there should be no marital relations, as he put it, for at least a month to give your body time to recover from the birth. I've been a saint but now, I think you'll find, Mrs Fletcher, your time is up!' he grinned at her and then swept her into his arms. 'I hope you're ready to do your duty.'

'More than ready,' she sighed blissfully as he carried her to the bed.

CHAPTER 16

Emily – January, 2017

Emily drove slowly through the village of Great Chalkham, listening to the instructions on her satnav. Her first impressions were very positive. It was a picturesque village, resplendent with quaint thatched buildings and wooden beams, very much as it had been described in the magazine article. She wondered why she had never been here before; after all, it was so close to her own home. She turned past the old mill and into the main street which was lined with cars on either side. There were a number of shops and cafes all the way along but she kept her eyes on the road. She was glad she was driving her mini and not Adam's 4 x 4 as it was a tight squeeze through the stationary vehicles. At the end of the street, she turned left, as directed, up a narrow lane. She checked the sign – 'Chalkpit Lane' – and smiled. 'This is right. Alex, we're nearly there,' she said.

She followed the road for almost half a mile, passing just two houses until she saw the cottage on the left, set back a little way from the road behind a hedge. She stopped the car and stared. The recognition was instant, like a jolt in her chest, and anticipation thrummed though her veins. It looked utterly charming with its whitewashed walls, thatched roof and leaded windows – just as it had in the photograph. The extensions, which had been added to the right and rear of the property, had been sympathetic to the original building and the overall impression was one of simple, rustic beauty. Even if this proved to be another dead end, like so many times before, Emily was sure she would enjoy her stay.

It had not been a difficult decision, once she'd identified the cottage in Norah's scrapbook, to make it the destination of the short January break she'd been planning. Adam had laughed when she had told him where she was going. 'I know you didn't want to go too far afield,' he said, 'but that's ridiculous! You could easily do that as a day trip.'

She had then shown him the two photographs she had of the cottage, side by side, and he'd exclaimed in shock. He took hold of her hand. When they'd got engaged, she'd told him of her adoption and her quest to find her real mother. She did not want there to be any secrets between them or, at least, any *big* secrets. Her imaginary friend, Molly, had been part of her own, private history for so long that she just could not bring herself to tell him. She could not bear to see that look of scepticism or, even worse, doubts about her mental stability, appear on his face. Anyway, after they were married, Molly seemed to have disappeared from her life ... until just a few months ago.

'Why don't we go and have a look together?' Adam had said. 'I've got to work on Saturday but we could go on Sunday, have a day out.'

She shook her head. 'I'd thought of that but my plan will give me the chance to stay in the very place where Norah lived with her husband and baby. I can take my time to explore the village – maybe find the house where she lived as a child. There may be someone in the village who remembers her, who knows what happened to her and why there are no more photos after that last one ...' Her voice tailed off and she waited for his response.

'Try not to get your hopes up, Emily. It's very unlikely anyone who knew the family will still be alive. Even if they were, would they still be able to remember? They'd have to be in their nineties.' He gave her a hug. 'I'm not saying it's impossible – just that it's unlikely. I don't want you to be disappointed and especially not when I'm unable to support you. I still think you should wait. Maybe I can take some time off in February.' He frowned. 'Well, maybe not February. I've already got a number of short trips away booked up. Maybe March.'

'Or maybe I just take Alex and go in January,' she said, giving him a smile. 'Honestly, Adam, I'll be fine. I know I'm unlikely to find out any more but this cottage is somehow linked to my past. It's the first bit of concrete evidence I've found since I discovered the names of my birth parents. I want to go and stay there and I don't want to wait until March, or April, or May. Please understand.'

He kissed the top of her head. 'Ok, if that's what you want. I do understand; I just worry about you, that's all. What if you find out something really upsetting and I'm not there with you?'

She sighed. 'It's not knowing which is the hardest to live with. It's like a constant pain inside, nagging and gnawing away at me, the thought that I might have family out there somewhere, people who are my own flesh and blood, people who belong to me and I belong to them. I need to find them if I can.'

He squeezed her against him. 'We're your family, Alex and I, and my parents and my sister Kate and her family and your two dotty aunts. We're here for you. We're your here and now.'

'I know that and I love you all. It's just that I have a past, a heritage that's missing and I can't help feeling lost without it. It's a part of me and I have to try to discover it ... oh, it's so difficult to explain.'

'You don't have to explain,' he had said. 'I understand.'

Now she was actually here- just she and Alex. She'd decided against asking Annie to come with her. That way she was free to do as she pleased without having the distraction of another person to worry about. Taking a deep breath, she got out of the car and helped Alex out of his car seat. The front door of the cottage opened and a slim, blonde-haired woman with a broad smile walked down the path to greet them.

'Hi. You must be Emily and Alex. I'm Jennifer. Welcome to Horseshoes Cottage. I'll give you a hand with your luggage.'

'There's quite a lot of it, I'm afraid.' Emily smiled ruefully as they unloaded her three matching blue suitcases while she held on tightly to Alex's hand. 'You'll think we're planning on staying for a month rather than a week! I can never decide what to pack so I end up taking pretty much everything.'

'I'm the same,' Jennifer nodded. 'Better too much than too little, I say.'

They manoeuvred the cases through the front door. 'I'll show you to your room first and let you get settled. Then I'll show you round the cottage. It won't take long as we're very small and cosy! Just come along to the kitchen,' Jennifer gestured to the room on her right, 'as soon as you're ready. I'll put the kettle on.'

They walked through the tiled hallway and along to what was clearly a newer part of the cottage where their room was situated.

'Oh, this is lovely!' Emily exclaimed.

The room was bright and sunny with a large window overlooking a frosted field of wheat still in its infancy. It had been decorated in neutral tones but there were lots of vibrant touches, like the brightly coloured patchwork throws covering each of the two single beds and three small landscapes on the far wall.

'What a fabulous room!' she continued as she gazed around her, soaking up the details. 'I love those paintings.'

'They're wonderful, aren't they,' Jennifer said, very pleased by Emily's reaction. 'They're all views of Great Chalkham painted by a local artist. 'You'll be able to see those places for yourself this week and more of the artist's work, if you're interested. He has a small shop just off the High Street.'

'Mummy, I'm hungry.' Alex tugged impatiently at Emily's arm. 'When's teatime?'

'Not for a while yet,' she replied, 'but we'll have a drink in a minute and maybe you can have a biscuit.'

'I'll leave you to it,' said Jennifer. 'You have tea and coffee etcetera on the tray over there but you are welcome to join me for a drink in the living room if you would like. I'm sure I can rustle up a biscuit or two.'

'That would be very nice. Thank you,' Emily smiled.

She unpacked swiftly, toys for Alex first to keep him entertained while she did so. He was such a good boy, she thought fondly as she placed piles of woolly jumpers on the shelf in the oak wardrobe. Mostly, he was quite content to sit building something or drawing a picture when she was busy. She stood for a moment at the window, staring out at the landscape before her. On the far edge of the field, she could see a small copse and, beyond that, she caught glimpses of water - a pond or a lake. How had it looked when Norah had stood watching out from her window over eighty years ago? She waited for a moment, half expecting to see Molly appear beside her (she still couldn't think of her as Norah) but there was no sign of her. 'We're here, Molly,' she whispered under her breath. 'What should I do now?'

The first thing would be to talk to Jennifer. She still hadn't decided how much of her background she might share with her, if any, but she had warmed to her immediately and, she thought, she might well prove to be a useful source of information, depending on how long she herself had lived there. She found her in the spotless, modern kitchen getting a tray of biscuits out of the oven.

'Have you just baked those while I've been unpacking?' Emily asked in astonishment. 'I can't have been much more than half an hour.'

Jennifer was a little flushed. 'Biscuits don't take long to make,' she said dismissively. 'I thought some home-baked ones would be nicer.' The truth was that she'd found, to her dismay, that she had no biscuits in the cupboard and, having promised some to young Alex, had flown around the kitchen to ensure some were provided.

'Wow, home-made biscuits! I think I'm going to love it here - we both are, aren't we Alex?'

Alex buried his face in his mum's jean-clad legs, suddenly shy.

'What would Alex like to drink?' Jennifer asked.

'Some squash, if you have it, or water's fine.'

Emily looked around the kitchen as Jennifer assembled a tray of drinks. It was small but modern and very functional - lots of cupboards and worktop space. There was a strong sense of order and everything gleamed with cleanliness.

'Was this room part of the original cottage?' she asked.

'It was - this and the living room, which is just through here.'

They walked out of the kitchen, across the narrow hallway and into the room opposite. This room was full of olde-worlde charm, with a large, oak beam running across the ceiling, a wood stove burning brightly in the hearth, thick, beige carpeting and uneven walls painted the colour of apricots.

'Oh, it's lovely!' Emily exclaimed. 'I love all these nooks and crannies in the walls. They give the room such character. You just don't get that with modern houses.'

Jennifer smiled. 'I think it was the sense of history which drew me here. This part of the cottage has been here since the seventeenth century. Probably this cupboard sized space around the corner here ...' She indicated a concealed alcove where a bookcase was standing, '... was where they kept the larder.'

Emily tried to picture it. What would this space have been like in the 1920s and 30s when Norah lived here? There would have been a sink and a stove, a table, maybe some comfortable chairs, maybe a rug near the fire ... Her thoughts began to drift. It would have been a hard life; was it a happy one?

She turned her attention back to Jennifer who had produced a box of toys from behind one of the sofas.

'Would you like to see if there is anything you would like to play with, Alex?' Jennifer said, giving him an encouraging smile.

He looked up at her and his blue eyes travelled across to the box but then he shook his head.

'He's just a bit shy at the moment,' Emily explained. 'That's very kind of you. I'm sure he'll want to have a look in a moment. Perhaps when he's finished his biscuit and then we'll maybe have a little walk around the village before it gets dark.'

'There's a children's playground near the village hall. I'm sure he'd like that,' said Jennifer, handing over a mug of tea.

'It's a lovely village,' Emily smiled politely. 'I noticed the play area when I drove in. It's just before the High Street, isn't it? The setting is beautiful too. Have you lived here long?'

Jennifer shook her head and briefly outlined her retirement from teaching, the renovation of the cottage and her decision to venture into the world of commerce. 'I'm afraid you're only my second proper customers.' she admitted. 'I didn't like to say that on the phone in case it put you off! May I ask what made you decide to choose Horseshoes Cottage?'

'I saw the article in the magazine supplement and I fell in love with it straight away. My husband Adam is away on business and, when I read the piece about the cottage and the village, I thought it would be an ideal opportunity to have a break myself.' A bland answer, Emily thought. Although Jennifer seemed very pleasant, she was reluctant to share anything too personal so soon, especially as Jennifer was a newcomer to the village herself. She would be unlikely to know much about the cottage's past. Still, it was worth a try.

'Do you know anything about the history of the cottage,' she asked, 'or anything about the people who lived here? I'm especially interested in that kind of thing.'

'Are you? Me too. Sorry. Since I moved in, I've been too busy to do any research but apparently, there's someone in the village who has been compiling an archive of local history. I'd love to know if she's found out anything about this place. It's on my 'to do' list.'

'Cool.' Emily felt a small frisson of excitement. 'Perhaps you could give me a number to contact them? While I'm staying, it would be great to get to know a bit about the place. I looked it up online before I came and all the stuff about the church and how the village has grown is fascinating but it's the people who really interest me.'

Jennifer frowned. 'I can't actually remember her name at the moment. I'm sure it will come to me, perhaps by the time you come back from your walk.'

'Right. Well, thank you for the tea and biscuits. They were delicious. We should get going. By the time I get Alex all togged up and the buggy out of the car, the best part of the afternoon will already be over.'

Ten minutes later, they made their way down the narrow lane back towards the village. It was a grey, blustery afternoon, with a chill nip in the air, and Emily was glad of her soft, red leather gloves and bright, red scarf – Christmas presents from Adam. She wheeled the buggy into the main street and negotiated a path along the slightly uneven pavement past the shops and cafes. There were a few antique shops and some selling bric-a-brac and local produce, as well as a number of charity shops. The Plough also sat on the High Street, right in the centre of the village, advertising great food and real ales. She passed a road on her right which led to the church, standing tall and proud on the crest of an incline, and another on her left which was signposted School Road.

At this point, the historic character of the village gave way to more modern, residential lanes and cul de sacs, smart, detached houses jostling for space with featureless terraces and squat bungalows. After a further five minutes walking, having passed another pub, The Fox and Hare, Emily reached the children's play area and she glanced briefly at her watch so she would know how long to allow for the return journey. Twenty minutes in total. There were four other children, all older than Alex, already there and two mums were busy engaged in conversation, sitting nearby on a bench. Emily directed a smile their way as she helped Alex out of his buggy but they appeared not to notice her.

Alex had become animated as soon as he had seen the swings and headed straight for them as fast as his chubby, little legs would allow. 'Swing, mummy. Push me!' he demanded and she hefted him into the bright, blue swing seat. 'More. Make me go higher!' he giggled, as he swung back and forth.

'Ok, superman,' she said. 'Let me know when you've had enough.'

While she was on pushing duty, Emily took stock of this part of the village. The play area had been recently renovated; all the equipment was bright and shiny and secured in a base of rubber matting. Beyond it was a large field with a football pitch marked out and to the south was a car park and a sprawling, brick building which comprised the main village hall as well as a separate bar and changing rooms, all signposted. On the drive in, Emily had noticed that this end of the village was the most densely populated. She had passed three, newish-looking estates and another which was a work in progress. The village was a real mix of old and new yet both kept separate from each other.

It was some while before Alex would consent to being lifted out of the swing and then there was just time for a brief sit on a multi-coloured merry go round before they had to leave. The gloom of dusk was already darkening the sky and Emily did not want to be pushing a buggy along a road where motorists might struggle to see her.

When they arrived back at the cottage, Emily could see Jennifer busy in the kitchen and gave her a friendly wave. She let herself in with the key she had been given and poked her head around the kitchen door.

'We're just going up for a bath. I forgot to ask what time you are serving dinner.' She had thought it easier with Alex to book the dinner, bed and breakfast option Jennifer offered.

'Any time you like. I was aiming for about six as I thought, with Alex, you'd want to eat quite early but it's entirely up to you.'

'Six sounds fine,' said Emily.

They returned to their room and she set the water running in the bath in their ensuite bathroom. Alex always enjoyed bath time and Jennifer had thoughtfully provided some bath toys for him to play with. He particular liked the little boat which created bubbles as he pushed it through the water.

It was about five minutes to six when they returned to the living room. Alex immediately dived into the box of toys still sitting in the middle of the floor and Emily wandered over to the door on the right-hand wall. It was a typical cottage door with a black, metal latch. She opened it and peered into the room beyond – the dining room, obviously, with a table set for two. Feeling a little like she was prying, she closed the door quietly and returned to Alex, just as Jennifer appeared.

'Let me show you to your seats,' she announced and headed for the door Emily had just opened. She stood back to allow her guests to go through, Alex still clutching a robot he had been playing with. 'You get yourselves settled and I'll be along shortly with your food.'

The dining room was quite small and sparsely furnished with cream, painted walls, a wooden floor and a small window, covered by some pretty cream curtains with a terracotta floral print. The table was covered with a crisp, white linen tablecloth, a basket of crusty rolls and a vase of pink alstroemeria. It felt warm and welcoming.

Jennifer placed a small tureen of soup in the middle of the table. 'It's homemade leek and potato,' she said. 'I wasn't sure what Alex would eat or how much so I thought it would be easier for you to serve yourselves.'

'That's great. Thank you,' Emily replied. Alex was a reasonably good eater but she was impressed by the care and thought Jennifer had put into their stay.

The soup was delicious, as was the rest of the meal. Jennifer served a cottage pie with vegetables and extra gravy and a chocolate tart with cream. At Emily's request, they had water to drink.

'That was amazing,' Emily told her as she cleared the plates. 'If I eat like that all week, I'll be the size of a house when I leave!'

Jennifer smiled. 'I'm so pleased you enjoyed it. Now feel free to treat the cottage as your own. I'll be in the kitchen or in my snug if you need me. The snug is the room opposite your room. Just give me a knock.'

Emily played with Alex for a while in the living room until he started to yawn when she took him back through to their room to get ready for bed. He was excited at the thought of sleeping in a bed next to his mummy and disappointed when she was not going to bed too.

'It's a bit early for me, poppet,' she said as he snuggled under the covers, 'but I'll just be down the hallway. I've switched the monitor on so, if you wake up, you just need to give me a call and I'll be right here – just like at home.'

She waited until his even breathing told her he was fast asleep and then returned to the living room with her phone. After a call to Adam, who had arrived safely in Australia, she turned on the television and flicked through the channels but there was nothing which caught her interest. It was still early, barely half past eight and a solitary evening in someone else's house held little appeal. In the excitement of her quest to find the cottage in Norah's scrapbook, she had not thought through what bringing an infant on her own to a rural part of Suffolk in early January might mean. Bit of an error, she thought ruefully. She should have asked Annie to accompany her after all.

Then she thought of Jennifer. Perhaps she would like to join her. Without thinking about it too hard, she leapt to her feet and made her way back down the hallway. Silently, she opened the door to her room and peered in. Alex was still sleeping peacefully. Like an angel, she thought, with his fair hair a halo around his head. She crossed to the door opposite and knocked quietly. Jennifer appeared almost at once, her face creased with concern.

'Hello Emily. Is everything ok? Can I get you anything?'

'No, no, everything's fine,' Emily quickly reassured her. 'I was just wondering if you'd like to join me in the living room ... only if you're not doing anything else. Please say if you are.'

Jennifer beamed at her. 'Of course; I'd love to. I wasn't really doing anything at all. I'm still getting used to having company in the cottage and I suppose I've been on tenterhooks, just a little, listening in case there was anything you needed.'

'You shouldn't worry. It's all wonderful. You seem to have thought of everything. Alex loved the bath toys, by the way.' She had another thought. 'Perhaps we could have a glass of wine together, if you have some – just add it to my bill.'

'Great idea. Let's go to the kitchen and you can choose what you would like.'

Wine chosen, Jennifer poured them each a glass and they settled down on opposite sofas in front of the wood stove. A polite exchange of background information about themselves and their lives followed, becoming more relaxed as the evening wore on. By the time they were on their second glass of wine, Jennifer had embarked on one of her funny school stories.

'There was a knock at the door and this year five lad was standing there looking red in the face. "Can you come, Miss Thompson? Ivor's got his foot stuck in the toilet!"

"Whereabouts?" I asked, meaning, which block of toilets?

"In the toilet. It's stuck right in."

I gave up and asked him to show me and sure enough, there was Ivor, standing on the toilet seat with his left foot and his right foot wedged in the bowl, right down in the u bend. It was hilarious. I sent the other lad to fetch help from the staffroom, not because I needed help necessarily but because I knew they'd want to see this. Ivor was the sort of boy who was always up to mischief. Obviously, he'd been standing on the toilet, up to no good, giving other boys a fright over the top of the cubicle no doubt, when he must have slipped. Once we had a good crowd of teachers assembled, we tried to lift him out but it was no use – his foot was completely stuck. We were reluctant to pull too hard in case we caused him injury.'

'So, what happened?' Emily asked.

'We had to phone the fire brigade ... and inform his parents. He had a great deal of explaining to do and it did at least put an end to that particular trick ...' She paused to take a sip of wine. 'But I haven't told you the best bit. His name ... he was called Ivor Plumber!'

Emily burst out laughing. 'You've made that up!' she declared.

'No, honestly, that was his name. Ivor Plumber ... I wonder what he's up to now.'

'I wonder what his parents were thinking when they called him Ivor. It's the same as a girl I was at school with. Her name was Henrietta – Henrietta Pye!'

Chuckling, Jennifer put down her glass and stood up to put another log in the wood stove. As she did so, Emily became aware of Molly's presence, even before she could see her. She turned to see her sitting on a chair in the corner of the room, next to an occasional table piled with assorted magazines. Although she had been expecting her – this was the cottage where she had lived, after all – her appearance was a little unsettling and she lapsed into silence. 'What should I do next, Molly?' The unspoken entreaty echoed in her brain as Molly stared into the fire, the corners of her mouth twitching in a secret smile.

Jennifer turned back from the fire and Emily intercepted a fleeting look of panic on her face before it was quickly extinguished. She was looking directly towards Molly. Weird. Did she sense something? Emily wondered. She was so used to being the only person who could see her that it didn't occur to her that Jennifer could see her too – at least, not at first. They carried on their conversation, had lots more laughs, continued to bond, but Jennifer seemed distracted and kept glancing nervously towards the corner of the room.

'Is anything the matter?' Emily asked. 'You keep looking round. Am I keeping you from something?'

'No, no, nothing at all.' Jennifer smiled but she could not help herself from taking another quick look.

Emily stared at Molly who had now focused her attention on her, a silent plea in her sad, green eyes. She decided to take the plunge, to say something – after all, she would probably never see Jennifer again beyond this week. 'You're going to think I'm mad,' she began slowly, 'but can you see her, a young woman dressed in black?'

Jennifer looked at her in astonishment and then swallowed. 'She has long, red-gold hair and green eyes,' she said quietly. 'I thought I was going mad but you can see her too.' She spoke with certainty.

Emily nodded. 'Yes, all my life but, before today, I've never met anyone else who could see her.

The two women stared at each other as, before their eyes, the ghost disappeared once more.

CHAPTER 17

Jennifer – January 2017

I t had been the strangest day, Jennifer thought as, much later she lay in bed, still buzzing from her conversation with Emily. She had spent the morning filled with anxiety and wondering if she had made a seriously bad decision about her latest choice of career. Her Christmas guests, Elspeth and John Carter, had, at first sight, seemed placid and unassuming, but they had thoroughly taxed Jennifer's patience during their short stay. Nothing had been right for them.

It had started with the room. On their booking form, they'd indicated they would like a double bed. Actually, they wanted two singles. Then, when she'd served breakfast the following morning, Elspeth had reminded her that she required a dairy free diet. Jennifer, who had been completely unaware of that fact until then, had to apologise and make a rushed trip to the supermarket to restock. That was Christmas Eve and the shop was packed to the rafters with last minute shoppers. It took her over three hours to get what she needed. By the time she returned, the Carters were waiting impatiently to complain about the shower in their ensuite which was not working. They were quite tetchy and Jennifer's heart sunk. She knew she would find it difficult to get a plumber, today of all days. Again apologising, she put down the shopping and went to investigate, only to find that the shower worked perfectly. It turned out that they'd been trying to press the dial, rather than turn it, as that was what they did at home. This set the tone for the duration of their stay. Nothing was good enough or, rather, nothing was the same as it was at home. When they moaned that there were no Yorkshire puddings with their Christmas lunch and it just was not the same without them, Jennifer felt like throwing the turkey at them.

The only good thing that happened over Christmas was that they obviously couldn't see ghost girl who had wafted through the living room at different times on

Christmas Day. If the cottage was haunted, other people seemed to be unaware of it - reassuring for the business, if not for her state of mind.

After the Carters, Jennifer had been especially anxious about the arrival of a young mum and her three-year-old son. She had gone to great lengths to childproof the cottage and had scoured charity shops looking for a selection of toys for him to play with. Great Chalkham was not the sort of place which would usually attract a young woman alone with a child in January and Jennifer wondered at their choice and how they might wish to spend their time. When her car had pulled up, she had actually felt butterflies in her stomach as she prepared herself for the worst. She need not have worried. Emily was charming, polite and eager to shower her with compliments and her son Alex, so shy and serious for a three-year-old, was adorable. After the biscuit fiasco, she found herself relaxing and enjoying looking after them. There was something about Emily, so slender and wistful looking, which made Jennifer feel protective of her. She had jumped to the conclusion that Emily had parted from Alex's father and had needed to get away from painful memories in the marital home and it was only later, when Emily had spoken about Adam, with such warmth in her voice, that Jennifer had been forced to re-evaluate. Even as they'd chatted and laughed so amicably together throughout the evening, she was still thinking that something did not quite add up. There was some kind of mystery attached to Emily's visit here, she was certain of it.

Then ghost girl had appeared and all her previous thoughts had been blown out of the water. Emily could see her too. What's more, she'd been able to see her all her life. Once this had been established, Emily had fetched a leather-bound scrapbook and proceeded to tell her story. They had sat long into the night, poring over the photographs and debating theories. By the time they said goodnight, they'd come up with a plan. Firstly, they would telephone Angela Carr, the Chalkham resident who had been compiling information about the village's past, and, if possible, pay her a visit. They would then have a pub lunch at the Fox and Hare and ask Jill Riddleston if she knew any older villagers who might be able to help. Jeremy Willis and the Blakes, whom she had met at the quiz night and who had run the post office for thirty years, were other candidates who might be able to provide some information.

From the moment she had found out about Emily's quest, Jennifer had been determined to help. The fact that she owned a haunted cottage and had seen proof that the ghost had once been a real person, with a husband and son, was enough incentive but she was also hooked by Emily's story and, indeed, by Emily herself. The young woman was striking to look at – a heart-shaped face, lovely smile, gorgeous, curly, strawberry blonde hair – but there was something about her eyes which was quite compelling. They were an unusual colour, almost green, and fringed with long lashes, extremely beautiful, sparkling with good humour and yet there was something else, a sense of yearning hidden in their depths. Now she thought about it, the ghost girl, Molly, had the same eyes, except hers held the infinite sadness of a tragic life. Their colouring and build was similar too, she realised, although Emily was taller and her hair was a much lighter shade. It was definitely a possibility that the two could be related.

With that thought, she closed her eyes but found that her brain was still whirring. There was something else niggling her, something about Emily's mannerisms which struck a chord but which she was unable to pin down, something that felt familiar and somehow comforting. Maybe that was why she felt so drawn to her and why already she felt like she had known her for years. If only she could think what it was ...

By ten o'clock the next morning, Emily, Jennifer and Alex were heading down School Road on their way to visit Angela Carr. When Jennifer had phoned her earlier, she'd been thrilled by their interest and very keen to show them what she had. Even better, she was free that very morning. Jennifer could not help but feel optimistic and, judging from the barely concealed excitement in Emily's face, she felt the same.

Angela Carr lived in a detached cottage not dissimilar to Jennifer's except that it was larger, with two storeys and had lots of modern details. It was in pristine condition, with an immaculate, thatched roof and pink, painted walls but it also boasted aluminium-framed windows, a glossy, white front door and an expensive security system which were clearly twenty first century.

Angela herself was a large, square-jawed woman with short, iron grey hair and a bulbous nose. She was dressed in a baggy, beige, woollen jumper and a tweed skirt. Her voice had the loud, booming quality of a woman who was used to giving orders and getting things done.

'Come in, come in,' she bellowed. 'Leave the child's pushchair there. It will be quite safe, I'm sure. No, don't take your shoes off. Follow me. I've got all the photographs in the study. This way. That's it. Take a seat. Have a look through these while I get some refreshments. Will tea be alright for you? What about the young man? I've probably got some squash in the cupboard somewhere.'

She handed Jennifer a small folder of papers and bustled out of the door without waiting for a response. Emily moved to sit beside her on a small, green sofa covered in cushions and lifted Alex onto her knee.

'You need to be a good boy while Mummy looks through this lady's things,' she told him. 'If you sit here quietly for a little while, we will go back to the park after this.'

Alex nodded solemnly. 'Swings,' he said.

Emily smiled and gave him a hug. 'Absolutely.'

Jennifer was already lifting a brown envelope marked 'Amos' from the folder. Inside was a collection of photographs and together they went through them carefully. They depicted various aspects of the village at different times throughout the twentieth century. Some had dates written on the back but most were unmarked. There were lots of the High Street and the church and some of the village school. There were also photographs of the different pubs in the village – Jennifer counted six in total. They were all fascinating in showing how the village had changed and developed through the years but there were none of her cottage or any of Chalkham's inhabitants.

The door banged open and Angela clattered through carrying a tray laden with cups and saucers, a teapot, matching milk jug and sugar bowl and a blue plastic mug.

'There we go.' She put the tray down on the desk in the corner of the room and handed Alex the mug. 'It's orange squash,' she beamed.

Alex stared at her with wide eyes.

'What do you say, Alex?' Emily prompted.

'Thank you,' Alex said dutifully and took a sip before handing it to Emily.

'Don't you want any more?' she asked.

He shook his head emphatically. 'Tastes funny.'

Fortunately, Angela was blissfully unaware of the exchange as she was busily pouring tea. 'I assume you both take milk. I won't add sugar. You can help yourselves if you want some. Now, I'll leave you to it. I'll be back in a little while if you have any questions and if you need anything, just shout. I'll not be far away.'

'Thank you,' Emily and Jennifer chorused to her departing back.

Jennifer smiled. 'She reminds me of the first headteacher I ever worked for. I was terrified of her!' she said quietly.

Emily nodded conspiratorially. 'I can picture her running the local pony club – brilliant with the animals and scaring all the children!'

Jennifer returned the first set of photographs to their envelope and pulled out a second envelope marked 'Baldwin.' This contained only two photographs, both black and white and dated 1910, showing the mill. One of them had a horse and cart in the foreground and a young lad in a waistcoat and peaked cap loading a tray onto the cart.

The next envelope was thicker and marked 'Chapman'. Inside were a number of photos showing scenes from a street party. Long, trestle tables were laden with food and lined with smiling people of all ages. Bunting hung from the buildings and many of the men were in soldiers' uniforms. The pictures were undated but clearly were taken after the war in 1945.

'It's remarkable how little the fabric of the buildings in the High Street has changed,' Jennifer observed.

The photos were fascinating but ultimately unhelpful so, after taking care to ensure everything was returned in the correct order, they turned their attention to the next envelope. This one was named 'Evans' and contained images of a much larger, three storey house. One was a shot of the front of the building, an imposing, eighteenth century house constructed in the Palladian style, but the rest were shots of the rear of the building. Some had groups of servants; some were pictures of stables and other outbuildings.

'That's Chalkham Hall,' Jennifer said. 'I can see the chimneys from my back garden. It's just across the fields from me. I would imagine these were taken in the 1920s or 30s, judging by the clothes the servants are wearing.'

'What a stunning building.' Emily turned the first photo over but there was nothing written on the back. 'No date. Do you know who lives there now?'

'It's owned by Aidan Armstrong, you know, the lead singer of Fresh, but I don't think he's there very much.'

Emily gasped. 'I love Fresh! I went to see them last year at Wembley with my best friend, Annie. Gosh, I wonder if he's staying there at the moment. That's so cool – I'll have to text her later.'

The next three envelopes all contained glossy, coloured snaps from much more recent times which they quickly skimmed through. Alex was growing restless and Jennifer started to sift through the remaining envelopes to speed things up.

'This one looks a bit more promising,' she said, passing Emily a chunkier package labelled 'Stanhope'. 'At least, some of the photos are from the right time frame.'

This envelope held a thick wedge of photographs and they rapidly sorted them into two piles, black and white shots and those in colour. The older pictures were mostly of the same family and Emily started to order them chronologically. They were not dated but the earliest depicted a young, good-looking couple with a baby. The man was tall with slicked back hair and a broad grin. By contrast, the woman was tiny but very pretty with hair swept up in a bun and sparkling eyes. She was looking to one side at the baby in a pram beside her, lips curved in a smile, her fingers holding the small hand which was just visible. Subsequent photos chronicled the growth of the family until there were eight children in total, five boys and three girls. In some, they were in their garden and the church was visible in the background. One showed them at the beach in their bathing costumes, sitting on a blanket sharing a picnic. There was something about those relaxed family group shots that reawakened an old, long forgotten ache in Jennifer. She would have loved a large family like this, lots of siblings to play with, argue with, tease and grow old with. This was the kind of family to which she would have liked to have belonged.

She passed them in turn to Emily who carefully perused each one, showing it also to Alex before setting it aside. 'What a lovely family!' she sighed. 'They look so happy together.'

Some of the photos also contained other people. There was an older couple, possibly grandparents and also various other adults and children, good humouredly smiling at the photographer. One of these made Jennifer pause.

'I'm not sure,' she said, passing it to Emily, 'but the dark-haired man on the right looks like an older version of the man in your album.'

Emily stared at it intently for at least ten seconds before exhaling in a rush. She looked up at Jennifer, eyes bright with recognition. 'I can't believe it. It *is* him. Let's look at the others. There may be one of Norah or their little boy.'

Excitedly, they scanned the rest of the photographs but the man did not reappear and there were none of Norah herself. They returned to the first picture and looked again. In this, the father was missing and only four of the children framed there belonged to the family group. Another child, a little girl with dark curls was sitting on the grass. One of her shoes had been discarded and it looked as if she was trying to pull of the other one, her face screwed up in a grimace.

'I wonder who she is,' Emily said, pointing at her. 'Her curly hair looks like Norah's husband's. She could be their daughter.'

Jennifer nodded. 'Perhaps the son is actually taking the photo, or maybe Norah is.' She reached across and squeezed Emily's hand. 'This is so exciting. It's a real lead.'

At that moment, Angela poked her head around the door. 'How are you getting on? Are you ready for another cup of tea? Oh, I forgot the biscuits! I'll just go and fetch some ...'

'Actually,' Emily interrupted, 'could you just take a look at this photograph for me? One of the people in it is the same as a man in an album I had handed down to me. I've never been able to trace him.'

Angela took a pair of wire rimmed glasses out of her pocket and peered at the picture. 'Oh, how fascinating. Golly, that's an old photo. Now I wrote the surname of the person who gave them to me on each envelope.' She picked it up. 'Ah, Stanhope,' she read. 'That'll be Daisy Stanhope. She's in her late eighties now but still as sharp as a tack. These are her photographs. I'm planning to make copies of them all and then put the most interesting on display in the village hall,' she explained. 'I'm also hoping to write a book so I'm currently making notes on all the things I've been given and then I'm going to interview the people who gave them to me. She's top of my list but I just haven't got around to it.'

'Does she still live in the village?' Jennifer asked.

'Yes, she does. All on her own. Looks after herself. Amazing woman. Did you want to ask her about the photo?'

'That would be brilliant.'

Angela beamed at them. 'Oh, I'm *so* pleased that you've found something useful. Do you think this man could be one of your ancestors? How thrilling! I feel just like one of those people on *Who do you think you are?* I love that programme. Well, you carry on looking through the photos. I've got a whole stack of newspaper clippings about the village too, if you're interested. Is this the period you're particularly interested in? I could have a look through them if you like. I'm afraid I haven't managed to sort them yet and they're all in a bit of a jumble.'

'That would be great. Would it be possible for us to come back, maybe tomorrow, and have a look at them then, and the rest of the photos? I think we're reaching the limit of Alex's patience,' Emily said, smiling ruefully at the child squirming on her lap. 'And, in the meantime, we'll pay a visit to Daisy Stanhope. Perhaps we could phone her first, if you have her number?'

'I'll give her a ring if you like,' Angela replied. 'Might be better if I ring her first, you know, to explain. Daisy is rather suspicious of strangers now, ever since that wicked man ... oh, what was his name ... Edward something ... horrible chap ... smooth as you like ... anyway, he tried to con her out of a fortune to repair her roof. Told her she needed to pay up front, so he could buy the materials and so on. Almost got away with it too. She had the cheque written waiting for him to turn up when I just happened to call round. Thank goodness I did! I soon sent him packing with a flea in his ear. Some people think nothing of taking advantage of older folk. That nice builder, David Brewer, repaired her roof at a fraction of the cost.'

'That would be very kind,' Emily said politely, responding to Angela's original statement. 'May we take this photo with us do you think? So, we can show her.'

'I'm sure that will be fine. I'll ask her when I ring. If she's agreeable, shall I suggest half two this afternoon?' Angela headed towards the door.

'Great. Thank you.' Emily gave up the struggle of keeping Alex still and let him, slide to the floor, still holding his hand.

As they packed away the photographs back into the folder, having made a note of the names on the three envelopes still to look at, they could hear Angela's voice bellowing down the phone. Every word she spoke was clearly audible so they were already aware of the outcome by the time she rejoined them. They were putting their coats back on as she burst in.

'All sorted. I've written down her address for you.' She handed Jennifer a slip of paper. 'She's really looking forward to meeting you. There's nothing Daisy likes better than chatting about the old days.' Still talking, she led them back to the front door. 'And I'll look forward to seeing you tomorrow. Shall we say the same time? I'll try to remember the biscuits!'

'Please don't go to any trouble on our account,' Jennifer said. 'You've been very kind.'

'No trouble, none at all.' Angela waved them off and they walked briskly, feeling the chill after the almost cloying warmth of her cottage.

Back in the High Street, they parted company. Jennifer wanted to pick up a few groceries and Emily, as promised, headed off towards the play area. They agreed to meet for lunch at the Fox and Hare at half past twelve.

Jennifer stood for a moment and smiled as she watched Emily wheeling Alex's buggy expertly along the pavement. She was buzzing from the morning's success so she could imagine the excitement Emily must be feeling. Hopefully, Daisy Stanhope would be able to tell her all about the family in the photo and know something about the mystery man and child. A thrill of anticipation tingled down her spine. She could not wait!

As she turned to enter the grocery store, she spotted David Brewer's silver Audi heading towards her down the street. She stiffened her spine and schooled her features into a smile while, subconsciously, her right hand reached up to smooth her hair into place. Despite the success of their evening out together, she hadn't seen him since and, whilst she told herself that a casual friendship was fine by her, she couldn't help but feel disappointed and a little hurt. The kiss he'd given her was imprinted on her memory, seared on her brain like a brand, and had led her to believe that there was definitely a connection between them. He had phoned on Christmas Eve to wish her a happy Christmas and good luck with the Carters' stay and she had told him she had more customers booked in January but there was no getting away from it. She had expected him to call after Christmas to suggest another outing and felt very let down that he hadn't done so.

As the car approached, she realised he was not alone. A woman was sat in the passenger seat – sleek brown hair, bright red lips, Pandora Pardew. His head was turned slightly towards her and he was laughing at something she was saying. At the last moment, he glanced her way and gave her a grin and a belated wave as he continued along the street and out of sight.

Jennifer was not the type of person who ordinarily jumped to conclusions but she frowned nonetheless. No wonder she had heard nothing from him, she thought crossly. He was obviously otherwise engaged. The man was clearly nothing but a flirt and she resolved to steer well clear of him in future.

CHAPTER 18

Norah – August 1930

N orah sank into the comfort of the soft, threadbare chair, thankful to escape the oppressive heatwave which mid-August had brought to Great Chalkham. She would rest for just a few minutes, she told herself, her hands lightly stroking her swollen belly. The baby was due in October – still six weeks away – and she felt incredibly tired, hot and bothered. Being heavily pregnant in mid-summer was definitely a bad idea. She would have to plan the next one a little better. Of course, it didn't help that she also had an energetic, two-and-a-half-year-old son to cope with at the same time. He was outside, under the shade of a beech tree, playing with some toy soldiers given him by Agnes Catchpole whose sons had outgrown them.

Earlier that afternoon, they had been out in the fields where Arthur was working, watching the corn harvester at work. Norah made this trip every day at dinner time to take Arthur a hot meal in a billy can. Today, it had been stew and dumplings. They had sat with him while he ate, beads of perspiration gleaming on his forehead and covered in wheat dust. Then Jimmy had found himself a stick, like many of the older village children who waited at the end of the field, hoping to catch themselves a rabbit or two as they fled through the standing crop. They were trying to get away from the horse drawn binder which was busy cutting the corn and tying it into bundles called shoafs. The shoafs were then put into 'shocks', each shock made from twelve shoafs arranged in an inverted V-shape. Norah had watched Jimmy running unsteadily, short, sturdy legs pumping, falling often and flailing his little stick as the rabbits darted round him. He had stuck at it for a long while, determined to be like the other children, until Norah had thought he had been out in the sun long enough. He cried that he hadn't caught anything.

'Maybe you will next year when you're a bit bigger,' Norah consoled him.

They walked the half mile back to the cottage, keeping as much as possible within the shade of the hedgerows, and drank a much-needed cup of water. It would not be long until four o'clock, when Arthur would be expecting his tea, or 'farses' as the men called it. Harvest time was hard work for everyone, even those not directly involved in it. They were all thankful for this spell of hot, dry weather to get the crop safely gathered in but it made for long, back-aching, sweat-ridden days.

Norah felt a sudden lurch in her stomach as the baby shifted inside her. She, the baby, was moving less frequently now as the birth drew closer. From the onset of this pregnancy, Norah had thought of the baby as a 'she', a little girl. Everything about this pregnancy had felt different from the first time around and she was convinced she was going to have a daughter. She had even been thinking of names, although Arthur had told her this was bad luck. Her favourite was Iris, her mother's name. Iris Fletcher – the name sounded right for the baby she was carrying, pretty but strong and determined, a woman to be reckoned with. Already she had dreams for Iris, a glittering future mapped out, well away from the drear and toil of working class, country life. She could picture her too – a slender, feminine version of Arthur, with long, curly, black hair and soulful, brown eyes which crinkled with wit and humour. Or maybe her eyes would be green, like her own. That would be nice, if she had her eyes.

One thing was for sure, though - she would be a girl with spirit. Norah often felt these days that her own spirit had somehow ebbed away, erased bit by bit, dream by dream. It was if each harsh event, each choice she had been forced into making, had taken its toll on her and shaped her into someone who only existed as a wife and mother, completely unrecognisable from the ambitious, carefree, privileged girl she had once been.

She was content though. She loved Arthur dearly and he had proved an excellent husband in all the ways that mattered. He had spent recent weeks extending the cottage yet again to make room for the new baby and worked tirelessly to provide for her and Jimmy in these difficult times. Many other women in the village, she knew, were not so fortunate. As for her son, she adored him with a passion and a fierceness which proved there *was* still fire burning inside her. It was just that it had been redirected somehow, away from herself, all for her family, in the constant, daily struggle to care for them.

Her thoughts continued to drift and her eyelids grew heavy. Her mind absorbed the sounds from the garden, bees humming in the lavender by the front door, birds chirping and calling from the safety of the beech tree, the distant murmur of voices in the fields ...

She awoke with a start and her first thought was the time. She still had Arthur's farses to prepare and she hated to be late. A glance at the clock on the mantel told her it was half past three and she instantly relaxed. She had only been sleeping for ten minutes or so. If she hurried, she could still make it down to the field by four o'clock, when Arthur would be expecting her.

She struggled uncomfortably to her feet and crossed to the larder to fetch some bread and cheese. The loaf was almost finished and she had not yet made the dough for the next, she thought guiltily. Usually this was something she did early every morning but today she had felt so heavy and slow, so drained by the heat, and everything seemed to have taken three times as long as normal. Now it meant that when she returned from the fields for the final time that day, she would still have several chores to complete before she could go to bed.

Wearily, she trudged to the drawer where she kept the bread knife. As she did so, she glanced out of the window and frowned. Jimmy was no longer visible beneath the beech tree. Craning her neck for a better view, she could see the soldiers discarded under the tree but of her son there was no sign. Sighing, she detoured to the door which was open to let any breeze through and called his name. There was no response. He was not anywhere to be seen in the front garden; he must have gone around the back.

However, when she looked, he was not there either. She searched the privy in the corner of their small yard and then back into the cottage, all the time calling, 'Jimmy, come here this minute. We need to go back to the harvest field to take Daddy his tea. Jimmy!'

Shielding her eyes from the sun, she scanned the fields to the rear of the cottage but could see no small figure, dressed in white short-sleeved shirt and grey shorts. Refusing to panic, Norah made her way back to the front garden to look up and down their lane and to check the field opposite. Still no sign – just Agnes Fowler walking back from the shops.

'Agnes, have you seen Jimmy?' Agnes shook her head. 'He was playing right here, under the tree, but now he's disappeared.'

Agnes set down her shopping and put her hands on her hips. With a frown, she asked, 'How long as he been missing?'

'I'm not sure but probably no more than ten or fifteen minutes.'

'Well, he can't have gone far, not with his little legs.' Agnes turned to gaze across the field and shook her head. 'Can't see him but then my eyes aren't too good these days. Do you want me to help you look?'

'No, no, that's kind but I'm sure you're right. He won't be far away. I wonder,' she mused, 'if he's headed back to the corn field. He was having fun chasing the rabbits and he wasn't best pleased when I brought him home.'

'Aye, I expect that's it,' Agnes nodded sagely. 'I'll keep my eyes peeled and bring him back if I find him.'

Norah hurried back inside to grab Arthur's bread and cheese and set off towards the fields as fast as her bulky frame would allow. She was breathing heavily, her whole body clammy with heat and the fear now broiling inside her. 'Jimmy! Jimmy!' Her cries were shrill, increasingly urgent.

'He'll be down the field with his Dad.' She spoke the words aloud, over and over like a mantra, between her shouts. 'He'll be down the field. Stop fretting, Norah.' They helped to calm her, to dampen her rising terror, as she arrived, breathless and panting, at the entrance to the field. She paused and stood for a moment, eyes scanning the furthermost corner where the men were working. There were children out there too, smaller figures, some dressed in white. She could hear their shouts above the noise of the corn binder. From this distance, she could not tell if one of them was small enough to be Jimmy.

She strode across the stubble. No point calling now. If he was there, he would not hear her above the other noise. 'Please let him be there!' she murmured. 'Please God, let him be safe with his Dad!'

She drew closer, eyes desperately searching for a sign that her son was amongst the throng. She could see Arthur now and the figures became identifiable. She could not see Jimmy.

Arthur's welcoming smile turned to a look of puzzlement as he looked at his wife's face, now streaked with tears. 'What's up, love? What have you done with the little 'un?'

Norah clung to his arm for support. 'He's gone missing!' she cried brokenly. 'Oh Arthur, I'd thought maybe ... he'd gone down the field ... on his own. You know how he likes to be independent ... But he's not here!' She finished on a wail, crying openly.

Arthur hugged her to him. 'Try not to worry. He'll not have gone far. We'll soon find him. He's probably round at Cissy's or down by the stables. I'll come and help you look.'

'But the harvest ...?' Nothing was allowed to come before harvest, she knew.

'They'll manage without me for a few minutes. Try not to fret so, love. If he's wandered off on his own, someone will have found him and brought him home. He's probably back there already. Let's go and look.'

Norah took his arm and together they set off at a brisk pace. 'Did I tell you about the time I ran off?' Arthur's voice was cheerful, comforting. 'I was about Jimmy's age. Ma had left the back door open and I wandered out. I didn't mean to go far, just a bit of exploring. You know what boys are like. Anyway, I was out in the street when I saw this cat. I can still picture it now. It was a great, big ginger cat with a long, bushy tail. I just wanted to stroke it but, before I could reach it, it shot off down the street. I followed it ... it must have been for some while. Never got close to it. Eventually it disappeared and I thought I'd better go home. That's when I realised I didn't know where I was. I started to cry, I remember, and this nice lady found me. I couldn't tell her where I lived but I told her my name and she managed to find out and take me home. My Ma was beside herself with worry and I got a good hiding from my Da when he came home that night. I bet our Jimmy has done the same – got himself lost.'

Norah said nothing. She was already blaming herself; she should not have left him alone outside; she should not have fallen asleep.

There was no one standing outside the cottage when they reached it. No one standing there, smiling, holding Jimmy's hand.

'You wait here. You need to rest. I'll go and find him.' Arthur patted her hand but his voice was suddenly serious, its tone urgent.

'I'll go and look too,' Norah said immediately.

'No. Someone needs to stay here in case someone brings him back. I'll go around the houses first and maybe anyone who's not out in the fields harvesting will come and help me.' He gave her shoulders a quick squeeze and headed down the lane towards the village. As she watched him, struggling to suppress the panic rising inside her, he turned and called back to her. 'Don't worry. I'll find him. I'll bring him home.'

She could not rest. How could she? Instead she again searched the immediate vicinity of the cottage, always keeping it in sight, and calling Jimmy's name until her voice was hoarse. She then walked up to Willow Farm, her old home. When the Brooks had bought the farm, they had sold the house separately to a family called the Catchpoles, the same people who had given Jimmy the toy soldiers. Douglas Catchpole had just returned home from work and immediately headed off to join the search in his MG motor car. Ellen, his wife, offered Norah a cup of tea but she refused. She needed to get back, she said.

After that, she was forced to sit and wait - long, agonising minutes which stretched into hours. Every time she heard a voice outside, she leapt to her feet ... but it was not him. As the shadows lengthened and the skies darkened, she could not help herself from imagining the worst. Something had happened to him, she knew it; all her nerve endings tingled with the certainty of it.

Still she waited, sitting in the chair, stiff and alert, as night fell. The harvest moon cast a ghostly glow across the fields and she could still hear voices calling for her son, somewhere out there, in the distance. Norah stood, walked slowly outside and stared up at the star-laden sky, looking for a sign that all would be well. Nothing. The stars winked coldly, dispassionately, and, deep down inside the core of her, she felt her hopes unravelling. Then, she sank to her knees, closed her eyes and prayed.

CHAPTER 19

Emily – January 2017

Daisy Stanhope lived in a sandy coloured, brick bungalow just off the High Street. In front of it, a small, overgrown garden rambled across a narrow path and the building itself looked sad and worn. The brickwork was flaked and chipped and the wooden window frames creaked of neglect.

Emily parked Alex's buggy round the path to the left of the house as Jennifer, clutching a gift of biscuits and chocolates, rang the front door bell. The yellowing net curtains twitched in one of the windows and they stood waiting patiently for the door to open.

After the promising start this morning, Emily was still buoyed up with optimism, even though their plans had stalled at lunchtime. The food at the Fox and Hare had been delicious but Jill hadn't been there so Jennifer had been unable to ask her anything. Someone called Harry, whom Jennifer seemed anxious to avoid, was sitting on a stool by the bar but otherwise the pub was deserted.

Emily was once again whispering to Alex, exhorting him to be on his best behaviour, when Daisy finally appeared. She was a tiny, shrunken woman, shrivelled as if she had been in the bath too long. Wispy, white hair hung wildly round a thin, wizened face. She moved slowly as she stood aside to allow them entrance and her voice was frail and reedy as she greeted them and directed them through to her sitting room.

They sat down on a paisley print sofa in a room stuffed with memories. Photographs cluttered every surface and Emily's eyes were drawn to them, searching the older, black and white portraits for a face she recognised.

'Thank you so much for agreeing to see us,' Jennifer was saying.

'It's nice to have visitors and thank you so much for these. It's very kind of you.' Daisy held up the gifts she was still clasping with gnarled, misshapen fingers. 'Would you like a cup of tea? I could open the biscuits.'

'Please don't go to any trouble. Tea would be lovely but why don't you let me make it?' Jennifer said politely. 'If you could just show me where everything is …'

Daisy nodded and hobbled painfully out of the room with Jennifer following. Emily got her iPad out of her large, brown, leather bag and clicked on Alex's favourite app, something called Monkey Mayhem. He held out his hands impatiently. 'Me, Mummy,' he demanded.

'Just be careful with it. You'll need to keep still. Stay sitting down, there's a good boy.'

She would have liked to wander around the room, taking a closer look at the photographs, but she thought she'd better stay where she was, keeping Alex under strict supervision. There were so many things for him to knock over. In addition to the countless frames, there were ornaments everywhere – vases, figurines, old perfume bottles – all covered in a layer of dust. She could hear Jennifer's voice clearly, coming from the kitchen, but the older woman's responses were more mumbled, indistinct. Angela Carr had implied that Daisy was still sharp mentally but Emily's first impressions were of a woman struggling to cope physically. Her heart went out to her. Poor woman. All alone with just her memories to keep her company and clearly enduring the pain of arthritis.

Daisy shuffled back into the room and sank carefully into a worn armchair. She smiled at Emily. 'I'm very slow these days - can't get about like I used to.' She turned her attention to Alex. 'What's your name, young man?'

Alex was too absorbed in his game to hear her and Emily gave him a nudge. 'This is Alex. Say hello to Mrs Stanhope, Alex.'

In the way of all young children told to do something by their parents in front of a stranger, Alex remained stubbornly silent and Emily's cheeks reddened slightly. 'He's a bit shy,' she explained apologetically. She changed the subject. 'You have lots of wonderful photographs. Are they all of your family?'

Daisy nodded. 'More or less. Some are pictures of my godchildren. I have four, you know.'

At this point, Jennifer appeared carrying a tray. She set it down carefully on the coffee table, nudging a china ballerina aside to make some room, and began efficiently pouring the tea. 'I know Emily doesn't take sugar. How about you Daisy?'

'Just three for me. I'm cutting back!' She chuckled to herself. 'Got to think of my figure!' Her laugh was infectious, a joyous, cackling sound, and the other two women laughed with her. 'Now I'm sure you are very busy – everyone is busy these days – and Angela mentioned something about one of my photographs, one of the older ones. She said you were interested in it and thought one of the people could be one of your ancestors. Is that right?'

'Spot on.' Emily was already fumbling in her bag for the picture and leaned across to show it to Daisy. The old woman's face creased into a smile as she stared at it for some time. She smelt of peppermints, Emily thought. It was a nice smell – the scent of childhood, journeys in the car.

Daisy looked up at her with sudden intensity, her watery, blue eyes sharpening with interest. 'This takes me back,' she said. 'It must have been some time around nineteen thirty-six or seven because I was only about six years old in that photograph.'

Emily gasped and pointed to an elfin-faced girl, grinning at the camera, hands on her hips, her head tilted at a jaunty angle. 'That's you!' she said.

Jennifer stood and came around to look over her shoulder. 'My word, Daisy,' she teased. 'Looks like you were a right handful.'

Daisy beamed, eyes glowing. 'I was that all right. Used to tease my brother, Tom, something rotten. That's him there.' She indicated a serious looking boy of about ten years with his hair slicked back like a matinee idol. 'My Ma was always on at me to leave him be. That's her.' She pointed at the pretty woman with the upswept hair. 'And that's Bert and that's little Freddy. He must have been about three then.'

'You had a large family,' Jennifer commented.

'We did indeed. There were eight of us children altogether. We're not all in the photo. I was the third youngest and probably the most trouble.'

'Can you tell us anything about this man in the photo?' Emily asked. 'He's not your father, is he?'

'No, no. My Da was taking the picture. I can remember it clearly because I kept sticking my tongue out - just for a laugh, you know – every time he told us to smile. In the end, he told me if I did it again, I wouldn't be in it. That put an end to my fun and games. My Da always followed through on his threats so I didn't dare risk it any more. That man ...,' she paused, thinking hard, stabbing a bent finger at the face Emily had recognised. 'Mr Fletcher, Iris' dad. That's Iris there.' She pointed at the girl with a shoe missing. 'Now what was his name ... I think it began with A ... Albert ... No, that isn't right. It'll come to me in a minute. He was a good friend of my parents and Iris was my best friend growing up. She was the same age as me and we got up to some mischief together, I can tell you. I remember, one time, we decided to do some gardening and we dug up all my Ma's prize chrysanthemums. My backside stung for a week after that one. Arthur!' she exclaimed triumphantly. 'That was his name. Arthur Fletcher. I knew it would come to me.'

Emily's eyes were shining. 'Arthur Fletcher,' she repeated, 'and his daughter, Iris. I *thought* there was a family resemblance between them.'

'You can't see in the picture obviously, because colour photography wasn't about those days, but she had the most amazing, green eyes.' Daisy looked up at Emily with a jolt of recognition. 'Like yours.'

Emily swallowed, hardly daring to breathe in case the moment slipped away. This really could be it, she thought - the family she had never known. She stared at the photo in silence as the future revealed itself to her in a series of still frames; meeting Iris, who would be an old woman now, like Daisy; learning about Iris' children and grandchildren; being told the story of her birth; then finally, being reunited with her mother.

The silence stretched and Emily wrenched herself back to the present. 'Are you still in touch with Iris? Do you have an address for her?' Her voice was husky with emotion.

Daisy shook her head sadly. 'We kept in touch for a while but the years passed and we both had families to keep us busy. She moved away from the village during the war, I seem to remember. It was all a bit sudden and there were a few rumours flying around at the time but I never believed the gossip. Then she wrote to me out of the blue a few years later to tell me she was getting married. She was going to live in Norfolk, in a village near Swaffham. I got married shortly after that and my Bert and I moved to Cambridge where his work was. I sent Iris my new address and we exchanged letters for a while but eventually the communication dried up. I don't know why. I can't even remember which one of us failed to write. Probably me – I had three children in quick succession and they kept me pretty busy. I was never the best letter writer either. Shame really, especially as we'd once been so close. I wish I knew where she is now or even if she's still alive. It would be good to see her again and talk about old times.'

The disappointment was instant but Emily refused to let it cloud the excitement she was feeling. 'Can you remember what happened when she moved away?' she persisted.

'I can. It was all very sad. Iris had a young man, Billy Talbot. He was about four years older than her and she'd have only been about fourteen or fifteen at the time but they were in love. Course it was during the war and he was serving in one of the Suffolk regiments.' She paused and took an unsteady sip of tea, the cup shuddering as it settled back in the saucer. 'Poor lad was killed. Right near the end of the war it was. Well, Iris was beside herself with grief, of course, and then, out of the blue, she came around to tell me that she and her Da were moving away. Too many memories in Chalkham, she said. She didn't want me to write to her, she said, so she wouldn't tell me where she was going. Well, I remember being a bit hurt by that – we were best friends after all. Lots of women in the village had lost loved ones; she wasn't the only one. It was all a bit odd. Then, after they'd gone, I heard a rumour that she'd gotten pregnant, just like her Ma before her. It was old Mrs Gooding, who ran the village shop; she was the one saying things. When I found out, I went around there and gave her a piece of my mind; a horrible woman she was. It might well have been true. Billy and Iris had been courting pretty strong, if you know what I mean, but it was none of her business and I told her so.'

'Good for you, Daisy,' Jennifer said. 'Let me take your cup.' It was balancing precariously on the edge of the saucer and she deposited it safely back on to the tray.

'I don't suppose you still have an address for where she was staying in Norfolk?' Emily asked.

Daisy thought for a moment and then shook her head. 'I remember it was in my red address book. I had that book for years but eventually it fell apart and my daughter bought me a new one. It wasn't as nice as my old one but I didn't tell her that. Anyway, by this time, I hadn't heard from Iris for years so I didn't bother transferring her address. She'd probably moved anyway.'

Another dead end. Emily sat back, feeling a little deflated. The photograph still sat on Daisy's lap and she picked it up again. 'I don't know what happened to Arthur, her dad, either. Lot of use, I am, she added dolefully.

'No, no, you've been very helpful.' Jennifer was quick to contradict her. 'We now know the names of the people in the photo and that's a very good start.' She smiled encouragingly across at Emily. 'Do you know what happened to Iris' mother and, possibly, her brother?'

Again, Daisy shook her head slowly. 'I don't know anything about her mother. I always assumed she'd died. She never spoke of her ... oh ...' Her eyes suddenly lit up as she recalled something. 'Yes, she did. She always said that her Ma had wanted her to have a good education ... wanted her to go to university. She was certainly clever enough and she worked hard. Then the war came along and I suppose things just didn't work out for her. It was difficult for women in those days, not like today, when having a career seems to be the priority rather than caring for the family.'

'What about a brother?' Emily asked.

'Iris didn't have a brother. She was an only child. I suppose she sort of adopted all my brothers and sisters as siblings. She was always round our house and she could squabble with the others as well as I could. What made you think she had a brother?'

Emily delved into her capacious, brown bag and pulled out Norah's scrapbook. She turned to the page with the photograph of the family outside Horseshoes Cottage and showed it to Daisy who peered at it intently.

'You're right,' Daisy said finally. 'That's definitely Arthur and the child looks like a boy. It certainly isn't Iris, although he does look a bit like her. How did you come by this?'

Once again, Emily told her story and, having done so, she handed Daisy the album for her to look through.

'Oh, my word,' Daisy gasped as she turned to the first page. 'This Norah is the spit of Iris. Just the hair is different. She has to be her mother. Oh ... and that's Willow Farm.' She pointed to the picture of the frail woman in the garden. 'I don't know the woman but that's definitely Willow Farm. When I was little, we used to go around the back there to buy eggs. Of course, it isn't called Willow Farm anymore. After they flooded the old chalk pits, someone decided to call it Lakeview. That awful woman, Pandora Pardew, lives there now but she hasn't been there very long.' She continued turning the pages. 'Is this all you have?'

'Yes.' Emily took back the album and returned it to her bag. 'There was just a silver locket with it, inscribed with the initials ND, just like the front of the scrapbook.'

'Well, this is a proper mystery,' Daisy said with a certain amount of relish. 'I wish there was someone I could ask about all this but they're all dead and gone. Apart from me, all my brothers and sisters have passed on. Bessie Fowler would have known Iris but she's in a home now and is away with the fairies most of the time. She's got that disease where you can't remember things. What's it called?'

'Alzheimer's,' Jennifer supplied. 'That's sad.'

'It is,' Daisy agreed. 'I may be old and crippled with arthritis but at least I've still got my marbles.' She tapped the side of her forehead. 'If only I could remember where I've put them!' She cackled with laughter, delighted with her own joke.

'Can I leave you my phone number?' Emily asked. 'In case you think of something else. Anything at all.'

'Good idea. I'll have a look through my own albums. You never know – there may well be more pictures of Iris, if you'd like to see them,' Daisy replied.

'Oh, I would!' Emily exclaimed. 'That's so kind of you.'

'Nonsense. It'll give me something to do ... and it's nice to have some company.'

'You mentioned three children,' Jennifer said quietly. 'Do they live nearby?'

Daisy shook her head sadly. 'My two sons both moved to Scotland. I hardly ever see them. My daughter lives in Milton Keynes. She's a granny herself now and looks after two of the youngest grandchildren while their mother goes out to work so it's difficult for her to get over to see me. A while back, she tried to persuade me to sell up and move nearer to her but I didn't want to. Bert and I moved back here when he retired and he's buried in the churchyard here. I wouldn't know anyone except my daughter and her family in Milton Keynes and I don't want to be a burden to them. I'm better off here.'

'Do you have anyone help you, you know, to fetch groceries and that kind of thing?' Jennifer asked. 'It must be difficult for you living here alone with your arthritis.'

'Ah, bless you for your concern, my dear, but I manage. The Williamsons, who run the village shop, are really good and deliver my groceries to me. So does Fred

Lightfoot, the butcher, although I don't buy from him so much anymore. I don't seem to have the appetite for meat these days, unless it's a bit of ham or pork pie, which I don't have to cook.'

'I'm sure there's help available for someone like you. There must be things you can't manage so well any more – things like cleaning and doing the garden. Would you like me to investigate on your behalf?'

Daisy's face frosted over. 'I don't want any charity. Leave that to the people who really need it,' she said firmly.

Jennifer patted her hand gently. 'I'm sorry, Daisy. I didn't mean to offend you. I'm not suggesting charity – just a bit of help so you can carry on living here as long as possible. There's no harm in seeing what is available. You can always say no if you don't feel comfortable with it.'

Daisy sighed. 'My daughter's been on about me getting a cleaner. She said the house was a disgrace when she last came but I don't think it's too bad. I suppose I'm a bit stubborn about these things. We had a bit of a falling out over it, to be honest with you.'

'Well, why don't you let me find out what services are available?' Jennifer persisted. 'As I said before, you can always say no.'

'Alright, if you're sure you don't mind. I know the garden's got a bit out of hand. I used to love getting out in my garden,' Daisy admitted wistfully.

'There you go. Maybe we could get that sorted for you ready for the Spring. I've recently taken up a bit of gardening myself and know how lovely it is to see everything looking tidy. No, don't get up.' Jennifer laid a hand on her shoulder. 'I'll just sort these tea things and we'll be on our way.'

'She's a right, old bossy-boots, isn't she,' Daisy muttered as Jennifer swept out of the room, carrying the tray of empty cups.

Emily smiled. 'I think she's used to being in charge. She's just retired from being a headteacher so we have to make allowances for her.'

'What about you? Do you work?'

'Not since I've had Alex. I keep thinking I should get a job – maybe later this year...'

'Well, personally I think it's good that you're looking after your own child. I don't hold with all this going out to work and leaving the baby with strangers all the time. It wasn't like that in my day.'

'No, times have changed. Nowadays, most women don't really have a choice. They have to work to pay the bills. I'm very lucky we can afford for me to stay at home.'

'I suppose you're right. The world has changed and not necessarily for the better, if you ask me. You're a sweet girl.' Daisy reached for Emily's hand and gripped it tightly. 'It's been lovely talking to you. You do remind me so much of Iris. I hope you find her. It would be so lovely to see her again.' She leaned back in her chair and closed her eyes, lost in a reverie of times gone by.

Gently, Emily disentangled her hand and lifted Alex off the sofa as Jennifer returned.

'We'll be off now, Daisy. Thank you for your help.' She wrote her name and mobile number on a piece of paper which she left on the table. 'That's my number should you find, or remember, anything else.'

Daisy's eyes snapped open. 'I have just thought of something,' she declared. 'It's about Willow Farm. I think David Brewer used to live there when he was a boy. Do you know him? He's a builder – still lives in the village. He might know something.'

'I don't think ...' Emily began when Jennifer interrupted. 'I know him,' she said flatly. She paused briefly before continuing. 'Thank you so much for allowing us into your home today, Daisy. It's been a pleasure meeting you. I'll be in touch when I've found out about some help for you.'

'Goodbye, my dears, and good luck with your search.'

Daisy's eyes were already closing again as her visitors departed, Alex complaining loudly about having to give up the iPad.

'Oh, look at that beautiful cat!' Jennifer exclaimed, pointing at a small, black bundle of fur with glittering, green eyes, sitting on the wall opposite Daisy's bungalow. She knelt beside Alex and pointed.

'Cat!' he repeated, iPad immediately forgotten, as he toddled excitedly towards it. Lazily, the cat stood and stretched, leaping out of harm's way at the last moment and disappearing around the corner.

'Did you see it had green eyes, just like your mummy?' Jennifer commented.

'Like Molly, or I should say Norah, and Iris too.' Now she was outside, Emily's voice fizzed with renewed excitement. She clutched Jennifer's arm. 'I really feel we're getting closer. The photos are becoming real people now I know who they were and have spoken to someone who knew them.'

'I'm so pleased for you. I only hope that we can find Iris – that she's still alive.'

'She will be. I can feel it. I can feel Molly beside me urging me on. We must be getting close.' Laughter bubbled as she picked Alex up and swung him dizzily around. 'We're going to find our family, Alex. What do you think about that?'

Her son giggled in response. 'More!' he demanded, lifting up his chubby arms as she deposited him back on the ground.

'Later,' she replied firmly. To Jennifer, she said, 'Shall we head back to the cottage? I feel I need to absorb everything I've learnt so I can plan what to do next.'

'Good idea.'

That evening, David Brewer joined them for dinner. Upon their return to Horseshoes Cottage, Jennifer had phoned to invite him.

'I expect he'll be busy,' she said dismissively as she waited for him to answer her call but it turned out that he was free and delighted to accept her invitation.

'There's someone I'd like you to meet,' she said, a sharp edge to her tone as she made it clear they would not be a cosy twosome.

'I'm intrigued. See you at seven then.'

Jennifer ended the call and smiled brightly at Emily. 'All sorted. I'll organise something for Alex so you can feed him and get him into bed before he gets here.'

'You're so kind.' Impulsively, Emily gave her a hug. 'I can't believe you're doing all this for me. You barely know me.'

'Maybe but I'd like to know you better. I felt there was an affinity between us as soon as we met. I'm almost as excited about learning your family history as you are.'

David had arrived promptly at seven dressed casually in a maroon, chunky-knit sweater and beige trousers. He handed Jennifer a bunch of yellow roses and a bottle of wine before leaning in and kissing her lingeringly on the cheek.

'Mm, you smell good. I love that perfume you wear,' he murmured huskily. 'Oh, hello.' He stepped back as he noticed Emily standing in the doorway and grinned. 'You must be the mystery person Jen mentioned.'

Jennifer performed the introductions and then disappeared back into the kitchen. 'I'll leave you two to get to know each other,' she said.

David raised his eyebrows and waited while Emily busied herself moving cushions to get comfortable on the sofa opposite him. Molly, she noticed, had joined them and was sitting primly on the third sofa, opposite the wood burner, waiting to listen to what David had to say. Meanwhile, her own first impressions were positive. He seems like a nice guy, she thought, watching as he stretched his long legs out and relaxed back into the furnishings. He was clearly waiting for her to initiate conversation and she pondered how best to start.

'I understand you've always lived in the village?' She made it into a question and he nodded a response.

'More or less. I was brought up here but then went off to college and moved around for a bit after that. Then I moved back here with my wife about thirty years ago.'

'Oh, you're married.' Emily could not quite keep the surprise out of her voice. She had noticed the warmth of his greeting to Jennifer.

'A widower. My wife died in 2005.'

'Oh,' Emily said again. 'I'm so sorry.'

He shrugged and smiled at her. 'Thank you. It was a while ago but I still miss her.'

She nodded her understanding and silence stretched between them. Emily fiddled with the cushion she was leaning against, as if tracing the pattern embroidered there would show her the way forward.

David watched her with interest. She was a striking young woman and there was something about her that echoed a chord, a soft ringing, in his memory. Where had he seen those eyes before?

'So, what brings someone like you to Chalkham at this time of year?' he asked eventually.

She pondered the question. 'I'm looking for some answers,' she said slowly. 'I have reason to believe that my family may have lived here a long while ago and I'm trying to trace them. My biological family that is – I was adopted when I was a baby.'

'What have you found out so far?'

She told him about her visits to Angela Carr and Daisy Stanhope and what she had discovered. As she was showing him Norah's scrapbook, Jennifer appeared with three glasses and a bottle of wine. She glanced sharply at Molly still sitting on the sofa and then at David who was poring over the photographs. She looked across at Emily who shook her head slightly, attuned to the silent question.

'How are you doing?' Jennifer asked brightly as she handed round the glasses of wine.

David looked up and frowned. 'I'm afraid I don't recognise anyone here,' he said, 'but I *do* recognise the house in this photo.' He tapped the picture of the frail looking woman in the garden. 'That's Willow Farm. I used to live there.'

'That's what Daisy said,' Emily exclaimed. 'Of course, this picture would have been taken in the nineteen twenties.' She gave him a mischievous glance. 'I don't suppose you're that old!'

'Cheeky!' David smiled back at her. 'I was born in 1958 and my family moved back here in the mid-sixties. My mother had lived in Chalkham when she was a child, I remember, and she was so happy to return here. My dad's business was doing well and he bought Willow Farm.'

'Is your mother still alive?' Jennifer asked.

David nodded. 'She is. She's eighty-seven and still going strong. She lives with my sister, Caroline, and her husband.'

'Does she live locally? Do you think she'd agree to talk to me?' Emily asked eagerly. 'She might remember what happened my family.'

'I'm sure she would. She likes nothing better than talking about the past. She would love this.' He tapped the album. 'She lives in Copden, only a few miles away. I'll phone her tomorrow and see if she's available to see you then. I presume you'd like to go as soon as possible?'

'That would be fantastic! Thank you so much.'

'Do *you* know the names of these people in the photographs? If you know their names, then they will have been recorded in a census and it may well be that they appear in the parish records.'

Emily turned back to the beginning of the album where Norah's name was inscribed on the flyleaf. 'I'm assuming that the girl is Norah and that her maiden name began with D because of the initials stamped on the front cover. Daisy was able to tell me that the man was called Arthur Fletcher and that *he* had a daughter called Iris. I'm assuming that Norah was married to Arthur so she would have become Norah Fletcher but we don't know anything about the little boy in this photo here. Daisy was friends with Iris and said that she thought her mother had died but she had no knowledge of a brother.'

'Iris Fletcher ...' David pondered the name. 'I remember my mother had a friend called Iris but *her* surname wasn't Fletcher. I'm trying to think what it was ... it began with M ... Miller, I think. Iris Miller. She might have been someone else entirely.'

'I can't wait to meet her. If her friend is my Iris, she might be able to tell me where she is now, if she's still alive, of course.'

'Just one thing – my mum has been a bit poorly. In fact, she was in hospital all over Christmas and gave us a bit of a scare. She's recovered now but she's still quite frail. If she's up to a visit, we may have to keep it short. I wouldn't want to overtire her.' He looked across at Jennifer. 'That's the reason I haven't been in contact, if you had been wondering.'

Jennifer took a sip of wine and avoided his gaze. 'I really hadn't given it any thought,' she lied. 'I'm glad your mum's on the mend. Right.' She put her glass down and stood up. 'I'll fetch our dinner through, if you two would like to make your way to the dining room.' She sailed out of the room like the Queen Mary and David winked at Emily.

'She's mad about me really,' he grinned. 'She just doesn't know it yet.'

Much later that night, Emily kissed Alex softly on the top of his head and slid under the bedcovers. She had just had a long, hushed phone conversation with Adam, filling him in on all that had happened. Once again, he had sounded a note of caution in the face of her unfettered optimism but had agreed that it all seemed very promising. He was currently in Tasmania and was heading for his appointment with a major winegrower in the region. His trip was going well, he told her, but he missed her and Alex desperately.

'Me too,' she'd whispered. 'I love you. Take care. See you soon.'

She had put the phone down and sat for a while in the darkness, staring out at the stars as she often did. The vastness of the sky never failed to take her breath away but she also found comfort in the permanence of the constellations, each star in its place as it spun through the galaxy millions of miles away, each brilliant in its own right but each a part of one amazing, awe-inspiring, starry pattern. She liked to pick out a single star and name it Emily and then name the stars around it - Adam, Alex, Norma and Frank, her adoptive parents. Recently, she had included Norah. Tonight, she also named one for Arthur and one for Iris.

CHAPTER 20

Norah – August/September 1930

It was morning when they found his body at the bottom of the chalk quarry.

Norah sat in the chair by the window, looking out, watching, waiting all night, and leapt up immediately at the first sight of the figures on the horizon. She flung open the door and raced towards them as fast as her ungainly body would allow.

When she reached the first field of stubble, she stopped, panting hard, as a searing, agonising spasm shot through her stomach. Shielding her eyes from the morning sun, she ignored the pain and gazed at the human forms moving towards her. That was when she knew ... although she would not allow herself to believe it. She could see the tall shape of Arthur and the smaller shape he was carrying in his arms and, for a split second, she was drenched in the ecstasy of relief. They had found him. Arthur was bringing him home.

Then she saw the slump of his shoulders, the despair in his lowered head. Another man, she could not yet see who it was, had his arm around Arthur; the other men had their eyes cast down. They moved like a funeral procession across the empty field towards her.

She could not move for the heaviness of the weight in her chest, squeezing her heart like a vice, crushing the breath from her. Instead, once again, she waited, praying for a sign, just a tiny movement, anything, to come from that small, limp body in her husband's arms. As the men grew closer, she became aware of a low, rumbling, choking sound. Then she saw the tears coursing down Arthur's face and she realised he was sobbing uncontrollably.

She exhaled in a splutter, unaware until that point that she'd been holding her breath. Now she was confronted with the certainty of her son's death, with that final extinguishing of hope, she felt strangely calm, like this was happening to someone else. Once again, she headed towards the men, walking slowly this time but without fear.

'I'm so sorry, Norah. He was dead when we found him. There was nothing I could do.' His voice was raw with pain, with terror for her.

She held out her arms. 'Let me take him.'

He lay there, gently cradled, his features composed as if in sleep, as she carried him home. His skin was cold and white but unblemished like a marble statue. Chalk dust shrouded his hair and clothes and puffed in tiny clouds as she walked heavily, step by step, one foot in front of the other. The birds were silent, their chorus sung; the morning breeze held its breath; no one spoke.

They reached the cottage and she walked inside, oblivious to the mumbled condolences of the men who had helped with the search. By the window was the chair where she had spent the night's vigil and once again she lowered herself into the faded cushions. The morning sunlight was already warm as it shafted through the glass and she adjusted her son's position so he could feel its rays on his icy skin. She watched the dust spirals, caught in the sunbeam, drift aimlessly, specks of nothingness. Tenderly, she stroked Jimmy's head and she could hear someone singing a lullaby, the same one she had crooned when he was a baby fighting sleep. The notes were pure and clear; over and over the tune was repeated.

Arthur stood by helplessly, watching his wife trying to sing her son back to life, and wept.

Norah's calm lasted for five days, even while they prised his body from her arms and took him off in the undertaker's cart, even while they buried him. Dr Darkins gave her sleeping draughts and told her she needed to rest for the sake of her unborn baby. Friends brought food while Arthur returned to the harvest field. She accepted their offerings and their tears with impassivity; she was numb to it all.

Life was cruel, she agreed. No mother should have to endure such pain as the loss of a child. Yes, she would carry on because she had to, because another was dependent on her. Yes, her husband and her friends had provided her with wonderful support – she was lucky to have them.

This had always been her way, she realised in a moment of insight. She was a carer; she always sought to reassure and comfort others; their needs always came first. Arthur had clung to her that first night, unable to contain his grief, and she had held him, hushed his tears, told him that as long as they had each other, they would get through this. She was the strong one. She had to be – it was her penance. Her failure as a mother, her moment of weakness, of self-indulgence, had caused the death of her son. She would never forgive herself.

When they buried his body in Great Chalkham graveyard, she watched stony-faced whilst others shed tears. Never again, she vowed to herself, would she allow harm to befall one of her family. Whatever it took, she would give her life in a heartbeat. She did not deserve to live and it was her punishment to endure.

The weather had broken and thunder rumbled through the village. The torrential rain meant no work in the fields and almost the entire population of Chalkham assembled at the church to pay their respects to the bereaved family. Norah had always been a favourite in the village, many remembering her previous kindnesses, and the congregation looked on, genuine compassion and sadness in their eyes for the heavily pregnant, red-haired figure in black and her tall, dark husband.

Afterwards, many trudged to the Fletchers' cottage, where Cissy, Sybil and Stella, her closest friends, had organised sandwiches, cake and copious cups of tea. They stood, shoulder to shoulder, packed in like sheep in a pen, dripping rain on to the floorboards and murmuring platitudes. Norah and Arthur shuffled their way through them, listening politely, expressing thanks, moving on until at last they were alone. Then, exhausted, they lay in bed, staring uncomprehendingly into the darkness, reliving the torture of the day, unable to sleep.

The next morning, after Arthur had gone to work, Norah dressed in the same black dress she had worn the day before, put on her sturdy, brown boots and went outside. The rain had stopped but it was still overcast, the sky heavy with slate grey clouds, and remnants of puddles rippled in the fresh breeze. She took the direct route across the fields, struggling a little to manoeuvre her bulk over the stile at the edge of Chalkham wood. The last time she had struggled so was when she was no older than three or four and she recalled the laughing eyes of her father as he helped her over. How many times had she walked this way? Too many to count. She had ridden this way too, jumping Rusty over the ditch at the edge of the field and then cutting back through the wood. Her memory edged to more recent times and Jimmy, fiercely independent, desperate to climb over himself although he was still too small and batting away her helping hand. She pictured him reaching the stile all alone, that last time, fearless, seeing no danger ahead, keen to return to the harvest field which lay to the south. What had happened then when he realised he could not manage it on his own? Had something distracted him? Probably. Something had made him veer off course and towards the chalk pits.

'You must never ever go near the edge, Jimmy. It's dangerous. Do you understand?' She had reminded him often and each time he had nodded solemnly, even though he was too young to understand the meaning of danger.

She walked there now, stopping as she reached the first gaping hole in the earth. The familiar prickles of fear tingled down her spine, just as they had when she had been a child. She had always hated the pits. Now she knew why.

She walked on, head down, one arm supporting the weight in her belly. Arthur had told her that they had found Jimmy in the furthest pit, his body obscured by the rotting trunk of an ash tree, uprooted in a storm many years before. That was why it had taken so long to find him. He had a broken neck, Dr Darkins had told them. Death would have been instant. He had not suffered.

It took her twenty minutes to find the spot. She stood at the edge and looked down. Ironically, the slope was not so steep there as in some places. You would think that anyone who slipped over the side might roll harmlessly – no more than a broken arm or leg at worst. The tree trunk was a long way down, at least one hundred feet. Mercilessly, she stared at its jagged edges, forcing herself to imagine what it might have been like, tumbling down, down, down and then the impact, the crack and snap of delicate bones. After that, nothing - only blackness, the tiny candle of his life stubbed brutally out. She felt suddenly dizzy and stumbled backwards, sinking to the damp ground. It was too much to bear; she was not strong enough; she could endure no longer.

Once she started screaming, she could not stop. Her fury at herself, at God, at the laws of nature, all of whom had failed to protect her child and keep him safe, was finally unleashed.

That night Norah lay in bed with Arthur snoring gently beside her. Sleep once again eluded her and she had refused to take any more sleeping draughts for fear of hurting the unborn baby. Taking care not to wake her husband, she peeled back the sheet and swung her legs around so her feet rested on the cool, wooden floor. She then pushed herself upright and padded over to the window. It was another starry night and she searched the sky, looking for that one special star. There it was – small but glowing more brightly than those surrounding it. She smiled.

'Goodnight my darling. Sleep tight.'

The star flickered and her heart skipped. It was a sign, she knew it. He was not gone forever; he was there, a beautiful, shining star. She opened the window and leant out, letting the breeze cool her face and neck, letting the velvet night caress and soothe her, her eyes all the while fixed on that one tiny star. Her hand, almost of its own volition, crept upwards and reached, stretching out towards it like a lightning rod, waiting for the fizzle of a connection. If she willed it hard enough, she would feel it. She stood like that for some time until the hairs on her arm were prickling with the chill.

How she wished she could believe it! But some small part of her, a stubborn kernel of doubt, held her back and now the moment was lost. She pulled back her arm and scanned the sky once more but, however hard she looked, that star was no longer calling out to her. It had been absorbed by the others and she could not distinguish it.

Her shoulders slumped; she shut the window and turned away, still feeling unbearably restless. There was no point returning to bed where she would only disturb her husband, sleeping blessedly soundly after a long day at work. Instead she padded through to the sink, poured herself a glass of water and fetched her knitting. She had been making a matinee jacket for the baby and this was a chance to do a bit more. Settling herself in the chair, she picked up where she had left off, letting the rhythmic click of the needles fill her consciousness.

Her knitting had grown by two inches when she set it aside, rubbed her eyes and stretched her back. She just did not feel comfortable in the chair. Listlessly, she began to heave herself upright when a sudden pain clutched her stomach. It clawed and pinched for a few seconds and then eased off. She had experienced similar, mild contractions at odd times over the past week but she had ignored them. Her baby was not due for another five weeks at least.

'Be patient, little one,' she murmured, rubbing her bump. 'It's not time yet.'

Over the next half hour, she suffered four more, increasingly intense contractions and she could deny it no longer. The baby was coming early. She shook Arthur's arm urgently.

'Arthur, wake up. You need to fetch Dr Darkins. I'm having contractions and .... oh!' She gasped as another wave of pain hit her.

Arthur sat up, eyes wide in shock. 'But it's too soon. The doctor said another five weeks.'

'Tell that to Iris,' Norah replied wryly. 'I think you'd better hurry.'

He shot out of bed and began dressing, wildly grabbing trousers, socks and a shirt. 'Will you be alright on your own? I'll be as quick as I can.'

'Yes. Hurry!' Norah sat down on the bed as he sped out of the door. Alone once again, she nestled back into the pillows and waited.

CHAPTER 21

Jennifer – January 2017

J ennifer awoke the next morning with an eager sense of anticipation. She had immersed herself entirely in Emily's quest and could not wait for the next chapter to unfold. Her feelings also had something to do with David Brewer and the clear intention in his brown eyes whenever he had looked her way. It was ridiculous at her age to indulge in such giddiness, she told herself, especially as, just a few short weeks ago, she'd found his domineering personality so irritating. She had to admit, though, that she'd been grumpy about his lack of attention since they'd last been out together. Now she knew that was because of his mother's illness, she felt much happier. He could have sent a text or phoned her to explain the situation but she was prepared to overlook that. After all, one date hardly constituted a relationship. It also didn't explain what he was doing with Pandora Pardew two days earlier but, she rationalised, that could have been for any number of reasons. He'd promised to call this morning once he had spoken to his mother and she was allowing herself to look forward to it.

Her thoughts turned once more to Emily and her determination to track down her real family. It reminded her of the television programme, *Long Lost Family*. Previously she had watched and dismissed it as sentimental nonsense when people described how, all their lives, they had felt like a part of them was missing without a particular family member. Jennifer had loved her mother but, when she had died, her relationship with her father was one of duty and responsibility. Yes, she *had* loved him because that was what was expected but now she questioned the depth of that love. Certainly, it was nothing like Emily described when talking about her adoptive parents and her desperation to find her birth parents. After her mother's death, her father had retreated even more into a cocoon of disapproval as far as she was concerned. She hadn't minded. It had made her focus entirely on her career and that had been immensely rewarding. She'd had a good life ... except now she couldn't help but wonder if perhaps something was missing. Perhaps she *was* a homemaker after all. The cool, analytical part of her brain pondered the question. She loved nurturing others, taking care of them; that was why she had decided to go into the teaching profession in the first place and now why she had chosen to create space in her home for paying guests. Was her whole career path a substitute, an attempt to compensate for the lack of a real family?

She thought about her grandparents, people she remembered more from photographs than real memories of times spent with them. Her maternal grandfather was in the army and she had been terrified of him. He showed her his war medals and told her in gruesome detail how he had carried a friend whose leg had been blown clean off to safety. She remembered her grandmother, a small, timid woman, commenting that such a young girl did not need to know such things.

'Nonsense,' he had bellowed. 'Life is harsh and cruel. The sooner she realises that the better!'

They had both died within three months of each other when she was still small, maybe six or seven, and all she had felt was a sense of relief. Her other grandparents, her father's parents, were also strict, like Victorian school teachers. They were fiercely religious and preached hell and damnation after every small sin she had committed. They insisted the whole family went to church every Sunday morning and that Jennifer should also attend Sunday School in the afternoon. She remembered listening to sermons telling her that the Lord God was a loving God and wondering why her grandparents never preached this to her. Instead they held God over her as an instrument of retribution and punishment. No wonder she herself had grown up an atheist. Her grandfather had died when she was about ten and her grandmother had lived another six bitter years before she too passed on. Jennifer had shed no tears for them.

Emily's story had reawakened old, long suppressed emotions, those feelings she had as a child when she spent time with her friends' families, when she saw how they laughed, joked and even argued together. There was warmth there, a security blanket of love and support, which contrasted starkly with the cold, distant veneer of politeness which ruled her own home. There were glimpses of it from her mother who always kissed her goodnight and briefly comforted her when she cried until her father ordered her to 'stop mollycoddling the child'; but then her mother had died and even those small comforts disappeared. There *had* been love in her life - friends, lovers, people with whom she shared parts of herself – but she had never actually been a part of a real family unit and all which that entailed. Still, it had always been that way and she needed to get on with it. Too late now to mourn the fact that she was childless.

A glance at her alarm clock told her it was five minutes past seven, fifteen minutes since the ringing had woken her. Time to get up and prepare breakfast. Emily had requested an eight o'clock start but Jennifer also wanted to get some cleaning done while the cottage was quiet.

She was downstairs unloading the dishwasher when her mobile phone rang. The caller ID told her it was Angela Carr.

'Morning Angela. How are you?'

'Very well thank you. Sorry to disturb you so early but last night I was looking through the press cuttings people had given me about events in Chalkham and I came across something which Emily may well want to see.' Angela's voice was slightly breathless. 'Can you still come around as we agreed this morning?'

'I'm sure we can. I'll have to check first with Emily and get back to you if there's a problem. What have you found?'

'I think you need to read it, see it for yourselves,' Angela said mysteriously, clearly relishing her own involvement. 'I *do* hope you can come this morning as I have a dentist appointment this afternoon and then I'm visiting my sister in Norwich for a few days.'

'Ok, we'll do our best.'

Jennifer ended the call and was speculating what kind of news the clipping might contain when Emily and Alex appeared.

'Morning Jen. Mm, are you making pancakes? Fab. We love pancakes, don't we Alex?'

Jennifer frowned slightly at the abbreviation of her name. Emily had obviously picked it up from David. She decided to let it go – what was the harm, after all? 'That's good. Coming right up.' She then told her about Angela's phone call.

Emily glowed. 'Oh, how exciting! I can't believe how well things are going. Definitely I'd like to see the news cutting this morning. We can go by ourselves if you're busy.'

'No chance. I want to see it too, if you don't mind.'

'Course not. It's great to have you along, like a big sister looking after me.' Emily picked up plates to carry through to the dining room. 'Come on, Alex. Let's go and sit down for breakfast.'

Jennifer smiled after her. A big sister. She did feel a bit like that where Emily was concerned. Just several years too old, she thought ruefully.

It was another cold, bright day, with clouds scudding swiftly across a blue sky so they wrapped up warmly and walked to Angela's house. She was waiting for them, excitement, tinged with something else, written on her face.

'Come in, come in, my dears. Now can I get you anything? Tea? Coffee?' Her effusiveness was even more pronounced than when she had welcomed them yesterday.

'Nothing for me, thank you,' Emily said as she unravelled Alex from his outer layers. 'Jen said you'd found something. You're so kind to take all this trouble.'

'Oh, no trouble at all,' Angela declared. 'Let's get you sitting down then and I'll show you what I discovered yesterday. Lily Baker had kept press cuttings which she found when her grandmother died. Do you know Lily? Lovely girl. Well, I say girl. I suppose she's got to be in her fifties.' She paused briefly, contemplating the accuracy of her information and then nodded. 'Yes, at least fifty. Anyway, *her* grandmother, who was called Doris Allen, made a point of keeping anything about Great Chalkham when it appeared in the newspapers. I had a proper look through them for the first time yesterday evening. Fascinating, they were. Did you know that the Queen herself visited the village in 1978? No? *I've* met the Queen. My husband and I – sadly he's no longer with us – were invited to a garden party at Buckingham Palace in 2010. It was wonderful. The Queen was *so* gracious, such an *incredible* woman.' There was another brief pause while Angela beamed at her guests, affording them the opportunity to reflect upon the importance of such a meeting. 'Of course, while my husband was alive, I met all sorts of amazing people.' She lowered her tone confidentially. 'He worked for the Foreign Office, you know. Anyway, I digress. These newspaper cuttings.... there was one from 1930. August, I believe, and I remembered that you were particularly interested in that period. Oh, by the way, how did you get on with Daisy? Isn't she marvellous? I hope I'm as sharp as her when I'm that age. Such a shame she suffers so with arthritis.'

They waited patiently for Angela to draw breath when Emily swiftly leapt in. 'Yes, it is and we got on really well, thank you. Daisy remembered the man and the young girl in the photograph I showed you. He was called Arthur Fletcher and the girl was his daughter, Iris.'

At the mention of the names, Angela paled and sat heavily down on a chair.

'Are you alright, Angela?' Jennifer asked, concerned by her sudden pallor. 'Would you like me to fetch you a glass of water?'

'No, no, I'm fine. It was just a shock hearing that name, Fletcher ...' Her voice tailed off and she looked directly at Emily. 'Oh, my dear, I'm so sorry. It's just that it's such sad news and now I know that ... well, the story may be about one of your relatives ... oh, I am sorry. I should have handled this better.'

'Angela, perhaps you should just show us what you found,' Jennifer inserted gently. 'There's no need for apologies. You're only trying to help.'

'Right,' Angela nodded. She walked over to a dresser and picked up a plastic wallet. 'It's just here. I put it with the rest of the photos you wanted to look at.'

Jennifer stood up and took hold of Alex's hand. 'Let's go look out of the window to see what we can spot,' she said. 'Oh look, Alex. There's a robin- see his red breast. Look how he's bossing those sparrows away from the bird feeder.' He stood obediently beside her, listening and pointing, repeating unfamiliar words, while she distracted his attention away from Emily. Jennifer could feel the heaviness of the silence behind her, the weight of a tragedy unfolding.

'That's so sad.' Emily's voice, when it finally came, was small and slightly husky.

Jennifer turned and regarded her anxiously. Her face was composed but her eyes were beginning to film with tears. 'Here.' Emily stood and handed her a tiny slip of yellowed parchment covered in small newsprint. 'You read it. Right Alex, tell mummy what you've seen in the garden.'

Jennifer read the stark headline. **Boy killed in Quarry**. She took a deep breath and read on.

A two-year-old boy, James Arthur Fletcher, was killed on Tuesday when he fell into one of the chalk quarries in the village of Great Chalkham in Suffolk.
The boy went missing at approximately 3pm and his body was discovered by his father, Arthur Fletcher, a farmworker on Wednesday morning. He died from a broken neck.
This is the second incident regarding the quarry. Three years ago, two teenage boys also slipped and fell, sustaining injuries to their arms and legs.
Villagers are now calling for the chalk pits to be fenced off.

The words, so plain and stark, were filled with such terrible import. In her mind, she pictured the young family in the photograph, smiling serenely at the camera, unaware of the fate yet to befall them. She turned over the paper where another news story, parts missing where the scissors had cut, had a date written across it in flowing black ink. **August 25th, 1930**. Drawing a shuddering breath, she squeezed Emily's shoulders as she showed it to her. 'It is, it's terribly sad. Poor Norah and Arthur. No wonder Iris never spoke of it to Daisy. I wonder if she even knew she once had a brother.'

'There are two other articles concerning the chalk pits.' Angela's voice interrupted their thoughts. 'Apparently, they were finally closed in 1954 and then in 1990 there was an environmental scheme to turn the area into a wildlife haven. The pits were flooded and now, of course, we have the lake. I can find them up for you if you're interested.'

'That's ok.' Emily gave her a watery smile. 'Perhaps we could just take a quick look at those other photographs and then we'll be out of your hair.'

'Yes, yes, they're right here.' She handed Emily the plastic wallet containing three more brown envelopes, each meticulously named. 'I've had a look myself and I'm not sure there's anything there of interest to you but, well, I'll leave you to have a look.'

The first envelope was labelled Turner and contained numerous, recently taken artistic views of the village. Emily sifted through them quickly and set them to one side. The next, marked Watson, held numerous black and white and also colour photographs of events such as fetes, Remembrance Day marches and, as Angela had said, pictures of the Queen's visit.

'That must have been such a wonderful occasion,' said Angela, craning her neck to see the images from across the room.

The final envelope, Williamson, looked more promising. There was a thick bundle of black and white pictures and Emily scoured each one avidly, handing it in turn to Jennifer when she had finished with it. There were some of wartime, young men dressed in uniform, smoking cigarettes, saying goodbye to loved ones, returning home and Emily paid these photographs particular attention. Was Iris one of those young women? Was one of these young soldiers the man whom Iris had loved and who had been so tragically killed? She could not tell. With a sigh, she handed the final photograph to Jennifer and smiled once again at Angela.

'Would you mind if, at some point in the future when I've maybe discovered a bit more about my family, I came and looked at all the photos, and the news clippings again? There could well be pictures of my relatives but I just don't know it yet.'

Angela rubbed her hands in delight. 'Of course, my dear. Obviously, I will need to return all these originals to their owners but I will certainly keep copies of everything. Maybe your search could form part of my book!' she exclaimed.

Emily frowned slightly. 'I'm not too sure about that ...'

'No, no,' Angela interrupted hurriedly. 'It was just a thought. Of course, I will respect your privacy. Silly me. What *was* I thinking?' She was still berating herself under her breath as her visitors departed, promising to keep in touch.

'Poor Angela. I'm sure she means well,' Jennifer said as they headed back down the lane.

'I think I'll walk Alex down to the play park.' Emily turned the buggy towards the High Street when they reached the junction. 'I'll see you back at the cottage in time for lunch. Hopefully you might have heard something from David by then.'

Jennifer stood and watched Emily's retreating back, dressed in a navy, woollen coat and jaunty, red scarf, her long hair scrunched into a ponytail, swinging as she walked. She felt a ripple of protectiveness and, for the first time since she had learned of her search, a genuine fear that she could well be hurt. The hunt for

Emily's birth parents could just as easily end in tears; there were no guarantees of a happy ending.

By lunchtime there had still been no word from David and, despite Jennifer's best efforts at conversation, the meal was a sombre affair. Both women were all too aware of Molly standing by the window, her shoulders tense, watching, waiting. It was painful to look at her. It felt like being witnesses to the tragedy, reliving it, like watching a film which you know is going to have a sad ending.

Alex was uncharacteristically fractious and Emily felt his forehead anxiously. He was certainly hot but she did not know if that was from temper or fever.

'I wish I'd remembered to bring my thermometer,' she said, her face creased with worry. 'I hope he's not going down with anything.'

'The chemist in the village is very good.' Jennifer spoke soothingly. 'I'm sure, if necessary, we can get anything you need ...and we can always phone the doctor.'

'Thanks. I *do* know that. It's just I worry about him and especially after... well, you know.'

Jennifer nodded. 'Why don't you put him down for a nap? Maybe he's just a bit over tired.'

'Good idea.'

While Jennifer was clearing the dishes, her phone pinged. It was a brief text from David.

Haven't forgotten. Waiting to hear back from my sister. Speak soon xx

She'd hoped they would be able to visit his mother that afternoon but that was looking increasingly less likely as time went on. Perhaps, if Alex was a bit under the weather, it was for the best. Her gaze lingered on the two kisses at the end of the message. Were they a promise of things to come? Personally, she always signed off texts to friends, female and male, with kisses but David did not strike her the type to use them lightly, carelessly, as she did. With a snort of self-derision, she put the phone down and opened the dishwasher. Honestly, was she really mooning over a couple of xx like a lovesick teenager? 'Get a grip, Thompson!' she muttered under her breath. 'Surely you've got more important things to think about!'

When Emily returned a few moments later, she seemed more relaxed.

'He's asleep,' she said. 'I expect you were right and he was tired. He does still need an afternoon nap every now and again.'

Jennifer told her about David's text and asked what she planned to do next if they were not able to visit his mother.

'I've been wondering about visiting the churchyard,' Emily replied. 'I know that's a bit gruesome but, now we know their names, there's a chance we might find their gravestones if they were buried here.'

Jennifer smiled at her serious face. 'I don't think it's gruesome at all. In fact, I find it fascinating looking at gravestones, thinking about the people who have gone before us. When I went to Paris, I spent a whole morning going around the cemetery there, the Père Lachaise, looking for the graves of Jim Morrison, Chopin, Maria Callas and a few other famous people I've now forgotten. The cemetery was really busy. Apparently, it's a real tourist attraction. I would definitely want to see the graveyard where my ancestors may be buried. Not weird at all.'

'Ok.' Emily returned her smile. 'We'll see how Alex is when he wakes up.'

Fortunately, he was back to his placid, easy going self when he reappeared with his mum an hour later and allowed himself to be strapped once more into his buggy.

'You were right. He must have just got himself hot and bothered. You must think I'm a right old worryguts,' said Emily.

'Don't be daft. I'm sure I would have been just the same.' Having responsibility for a child, Jennifer knew, meant so much worry and heartache. She thought briefly of Jasper Jones, the poor lad who had died on the school trip, and succumbed once again to a fierce pang of regret. Losing a child was the worst thing anyone could endure. Poor Norah. How could she ever have recovered from such a terrible tragedy? Her eyes strayed to Molly, still gazing morosely out of the window. Was her son's accident the reason she could not rest, why she still drifted through time and space as a troubled spirit? Did she blame herself? What had happened to the family afterwards?

'If only you could tell us,' she murmured but the sad figure paid her no heed and, with a heavy heart, she left her to her vigil.

Once again, they strode along the High Street and turned right down Church Lane. It already felt late although it was barely three o'clock in the afternoon. The clouds had darkened the sky to grey and, with the chill wind, it was now feeling very cold. The church was an imposing, flint construction with a square, early English tower. As they walked towards it, their eyes were drawn to the monument which stood, in the shape of a cross, outside the gate. It read 'In grateful memory to the men of Great Chalkham who gave their lives for their country in the Great War 1914-1918.' Underneath were two columns of names inscribed in the stone. No one with the name Fletcher was listed there. Beneath that, the words 'Also in memory to those who gave their lives so bravely in the Second World War 1939-1945.' Again, there were two columns of names but no one with the surname of Fletcher.

'I wish we knew the name of Iris' soldier. His name is probably up there but we wouldn't know,' Jennifer said quietly.

They stood for a few more, sombre moments before entering the churchyard itself. It was well kept and spacious, dotted with large beech trees, branches still bare.

'Shall we split up?' Jennifer suggested. 'I'll go this way and skirt round the outside of the graveyard. You start at the graves here and where the grass is shortest. That will be easier with the buggy. I'll give you a call if I find anything.'

'Same here.'

Jennifer was glad of her sturdy walking boots as she steered a path around the rougher edges of the burial ground, checking each stone she passed for the Fletcher name. It was easy to read the more recent inscriptions but many were very old and covered in moss so it was difficult to make out the words. Those graves made her feel sad; the memories of those entombed there lost forever. Worse though was reading the memorials for children who had died so young. One was very recent; just last year parents in Chalkham had lost their darling daughter, a nine-year-old called Amy Marie. The words brought a lump to her throat as she recalled the last time she had stood by a grave. It was at the interment of the ill-fated Jasper Jones, and she would never be able to forget the image of his parents and family, overwhelmed with grief. She thought also of Norah and Arthur. How had they ever been able to go on after the tragic death of their two-year-old son?

She continued to pick her way through the mounds. Emily was now heading behind the church and she watched as her long, navy, woollen coat and brightly coloured scarf and hat disappeared out of view. Immediately she felt that strange sense of being entirely alone with only the dead for company. The wind had dropped and it was eerily quiet. Shivering slightly, she walked on, chiding herself for her fancifulness and there it was … a tombstone bearing the name Arthur Fletcher. Quickly she scanned the words, wanting to make sure before she called Emily. It read;

Born May 7, 1906. Died January 9, 1947.

Today's date, seventy years ago! Could it be coincidence that brought them here today, or something else? She read on;

Beloved father and grandfather.
Rest in peace.

'Emily,' she called. Her voice came out in a croaky rasp. 'Emily,' she shouted again, much louder this time. 'I've found Arthur.'

CHAPTER 22

Norah – September 1930

Norah had been in labour for several hours and could feel her strength sapping away. She had not minded the pain at first; in fact, she had welcomed it. She knew her baby would not be born without it. Her labour when Jimmy was born had also been protracted so she had expected the same again. She had been told that her slim, boyish shape was not ideal in these situations.

'It's your own fault for being so slender,' Cissy had joked with her at the time. 'What you need is childbearing hips like mine!' She had wiggled her own ample bottom.

That morning, Arthur had returned within an hour with Dr Darkins and had then gone out again to fetch Cissy. He had suggested, tentatively, that he wanted to stay with Norah during the birth but everyone had looked at him with such horror that he had immediately backed down.

'Childbirth is no place for fathers,' Dr Darkins had declared. 'Go off to work, Arthur. We'll look after Norah and the baby. Someone will fetch you when it's born.'

'She!' Norah had interrupted. 'When *she's* born.'

Reluctantly, Arthur had kissed his wife and done as he was told. Norah had given him a wan smile. 'I have a feeling Iris is going to give me a bit of trouble,' she had said. 'Best you're out of the way until it's all over.' She squeezed his hand and then gripped it harder as another contraction seized her body. 'Go on, go,' she insisted when it was over. 'Let me get on with it. I'll see you later.'

At work, he had waited all day for the news - a safe delivery; mother and baby doing well - but it never came. Fear was growing in his gut like a cancer by the time he eventually returned to the cottage, unable to stay away any longer.

The bedroom door was closed and he could hear the low murmur of voices, the deep timbre of Dr Darkins and the soothing tones of Cissy, but he could not hear

Norah. No moans, no cries. He found himself listening for the sound of her breathing, a reassurance that she was still alive. Swallowing hard, he knocked at the door.

It was opened by Cissy. Her hair was damp with sweat and she looked exhausted. He remembered that she too was pregnant, due to give birth in just three months' time.

'Hello Arthur,' she said and stepped into the room with him, closing the door behind her.

'How is she?' he demanded. 'I want to see her.'

She nodded. 'In a minute. You need to know that this isn't a straightforward delivery. Dr Darkins is concerned that it's a breach birth – that's when the baby wants to be born feet first. Norah's been doing well but she's getting very tired.'

'Is her life in danger?' His brown eyes bored into hers. She could see the panic brimming.

'No, not at the moment.' She tried to reassure him but she also knew she had to tell him the truth. 'However, it could be if the baby isn't born soon.'

'Oh God!' Arthur covered his face momentarily with his hands. 'I need to see her,' he insisted again.

'Of course. I'm sure seeing you will give her a bit of a boost. Try not to worry.'

He followed her quietly into the bedroom. Norah was lying on the bed, her modesty protected by a white, cotton sheet. Her eyes were closed and her face had a sickly sheen. He crossed to her bedside and gently took her hand.

'Norah,' he whispered. She opened her eyes and Arthur could see the pain she was suffering.

'Arthur.' She breathed his name and squeezed her eyes shut as another contraction shuddered through her. After agony-filled seconds stretched into minutes and he stood by watching helplessly, she spoke again. 'I'm glad you're here,' she said at last. 'I need to speak to you ... alone.' She looked pointedly at the other occupants in the room.

'Of course,' Cissy said at once. 'I'll go and put the kettle on. I think we could all use a cuppa. Come on Doctor.'

As they were leaving, Arthur picked up the sponge which lay beside her on the pillow and tenderly wiped her brow. 'My darling girl ...' he whispered.

'No, listen to me. Arthur, you need to listen.' She raised her head slightly, her voice low and urgent, and her fingers gripped his with sudden ferocity. 'I want you to make me a promise.'

'Of course. Anything. You know I would promise you anything you asked, if it was in my power to give it.'

'Good.' Her head slumped back on to the pillow and she was silent for a few moments, mentally composing the words she was to say next. She sighed heavily and began speaking, slowly, deliberately, willing him to understand. 'I want you to speak to Dr Darkins. I want you to tell him that, should it come down to a choice between me and the baby, you want him to save the child.'

'But ...'

'No.' She reached up and placed her finger on his lips. 'Let me finish. When Jimmy ... after he ...' She could not bring herself to say the words and tears filled her eyes. 'After what happened, I made a vow, a vow to protect my children and my children's children. I promised to give my own life if necessary for the sake of their future. Iris *has* to live and if that means I have to die, so be it.'

Arthur listened with growing horror. 'Don't ask me to make that choice,' he pleaded, his own eyes welling with grief. 'You are everything to me. I can't live without you.'

She gritted her teeth as wave upon wave of pain seared through her body. 'You have to promise, Arthur. I've already spoken to Dr Darkins and he refused. In the end, I asked him to speak to you, to act upon your wishes and he did agree to that. I mean it, Arthur. I would never be able to forgive myself, or you, if Iris died whilst I lived.'

She took another deep breath and bravely tried to smile. 'Hark at me, all doom and gloom! Chances are we'll all get through this. I just want you to know what I want, you know, in case ...'

They sat in silence for several minutes. Arthur continued to bathe her face, wiping away the beads of sweat and easing back the tendrils of red gold hair clinging damply to her head. He could not bring himself to speak. What could he say to her? If he did as she asked, these may very well be the last moments he would spend with her. He choked back the sobs building in his throat. How could he bear to lose her ...? But how could he bear to deny her request? He cast his mind back to the first moment he had seen her, grinning cheekily at him as she quizzed him about his background shortly after he had arrived at Willow Farm. She had charmed him then and the affection he'd instantly felt for her had slowly deepened into love, an overwhelming desire to hold and keep her close forever.

There was a knock at the door. 'Arthur, we really need to come back in.' Dr Darkins' imperious tone brooked no resistance.

'Just a moment.' Arthur leaned over Norah and clasped her desperately against his chest. 'I love you,' he whispered in her ear. 'I have always loved you and I always will, no matter what.' Tears rolled unheeded down his cheeks. 'I will do as you ask, even though it will tear out my heart to do so.'

They clung together. 'Thank you.' Norah whispered against his shoulder. 'I love you. I always will. And I will always be there for you and my daughter, remember that. Even in death, I promise I will not leave you.'

'Arthur ...' Dr Darkins knocked again.

'You can come in.' Gently, Arthur let her body rest back on the sheet and stood up. 'I'll be just outside if you need me.'

He stumbled out of the room, closed the door and wept.

The nightmare went on and on. Norah could hear anxious voices discussing the fact that her contractions were becoming weaker while she drifted in and out of consciousness. At one point she was floating mid-air, watching her own body writhing on the bed, listening to the doctor exhorting her to push. Up here she was free from pain, blissfully light and unencumbered, like a butterfly who has just struggled out of the confines of its cocoon. It was so tempting to leave it all behind.

She could not do it; she could not willingly leave her husband and child. Her body was once again wracked by a contraction and summoning all of what was left of her strength, she seized upon it, using it to push once again.

'Good, Norah. That's it. Good girl.' She could hear Cissy's voice, still calm and encouraging and then, suddenly, excited. 'Doctor, I think she's doing it. Norah, the baby's coming! You're almost there.'

'Next contraction, Norah.' Even Dr Darkins was sounding more animated. 'I want you to push as hard as you can.'

Norah lay back against the pillows panting hard, waiting. What did he think she had been doing? She was aware of the overwhelming irritation she felt for the middle-aged man who had been present throughout. Why was he there and Arthur was not?

'Arthur ... I want him here with me.' Her voice was thin and reedy.

'I really don't think ...' Dr Darkins began but Cissy leapt up immediately.

'I'll fetch him.'

She found him sitting outside, shoulders slumped, his head in his hands, and called his name.

'What is it?' He sprang to his feet and strode inside the cottage. 'What's happened?' His face was ashen, his eyes pools of fear.

She grabbed his hand. 'Come quickly. Hopefully, the baby is about to be born.'

As he entered the room, Norah screamed for the first time, a raw, primal sound of sheer will and effort. Arthur rushed to her side and grabbed her hand, just as her tiny, baby girl was delivered.

She was gorgeous, Arthur thought as he cradled her, wrapped in a thin blanket, in his arms. Although she had been born early and was very small, she was perfectly formed and he marvelled at her delicate, pink fingers and toes. She looked up at him now, so trusting and innocent, and he felt consumed by love for her. He could understand why Norah had been prepared to give her life for her; he would do the same in a heartbeat.

'Isn't she a darling?' Cissy was smiling at him. 'Look at all that lovely black hair, just like her daddy's.'

He stroked it gently, afraid he might hurt her with his work-roughened hands. 'How's Norah doing? Can we go back in and see her yet?'

'I'll go and see.'

After the birth, Dr Darkins had checked the baby over and pronounced her healthy before handing her to her mother. Pale and exhausted, Norah had clung to her daughter.

'Hello Iris,' she had crooned. 'Oh, she's so beautiful. Our daughter.' Her eyes gleamed with triumph as she looked across at Arthur.

He had shaken Dr Darkins warmly by the hand, almost overcome with emotion. 'I can't thank you enough for what you've done. You too Cissy.' He gave her a hug.

'We're not out of the woods yet.' The doctor's voice held a note of warning but Arthur was oblivious as Iris was lifted from her mother's arms and given to him. 'Take the baby through to the living room for a moment. I'll give you a call when you can come back in.'

He had carried her awkwardly over to the chair, unsure how best to hold such a fragile form, and sat down. Outside, it was still dark but the dawn was beginning to creep in. He'd had no sleep for twenty-eight hours and endured a roller coaster of emotions but now he'd never felt more alive or more at peace with the world. Jimmy's death had torn him apart but, sitting there, rocking his daughter, he had hope - hope of redemption, hope of a new beginning, hope for the future.

He felt Cissy's hand on his shoulder. 'The doctor said to stay here. At the moment, Norah's still bleeding. You're not to worry.' She saw the flash of concern in his face. 'That's often the case after a difficult delivery. I'm sure he'll call us soon. Meanwhile, I don't know about you but I could do with another cuppa.'

They sat together, chatting amiably, for some time. The sky lightened to a lilac hue, Iris slept peacefully and they waited.

In the other room, Dr Darkins did all he could but Norah continued to bleed. It was something he had seen too often before and he cursed his helplessness as he called Arthur and Cissy to rejoin him.

Once again, Norah felt herself weightless, looking down on the scene unfolding. Her friend Cissy was crying as she held her precious daughter.

'Don't cry, Cissy,' she wanted to tell her. 'Look how perfect she is. It was all worth it to see her born safely.'

Her husband, her darling husband, was holding the white-faced woman on the bed, his body shuddering with sobs.

The doctor was standing to one side, busying himself with tidying his instruments, sadness etched in the lines and pallor of his face.

How she wanted to return. How she wanted to hold her daughter, nurse her, see her grow, fall in love, have her own children. But she knew she could not. All she could do was to keep her promise to watch over her, to protect her and keep her from harm.

Not long now. She could feel death's shadow creeping ever closer, slowly engulfing her. With a sigh, she exhaled just one more time. It was her final breath.

CHAPTER 23

Emily - January 2017

he day ended in frustration. After finding Arthur's final resting place, Emily and Jennifer had searched the immediate area for Norah or James but to no avail. If they were buried in the churchyard, it was not near him. Then it had started to rain – fat, icy drops which rapidly became a downpour. They had returned speedily to the cottage but not before they became soaked through. Emily was especially concerned about Alex and insisted he have a bath to warm him. Alex himself was not so keen and threw a rare tantrum. By the time they had eaten supper, a chicken chasseur Jennifer had left in the slow cooker that morning, and he was peacefully asleep in bed, she felt completely frazzled.

Meanwhile, David had phoned but it was not good news. His mother had taken a turn for the worse and would be unable to see them today.

'We'll see how she is in the morning. She does particularly want to see you but obviously, we don't want her going downhill. I'll be in touch,' he had told Jennifer, who had relayed the news to Emily. Apparently, when David had phoned his mother that morning, she'd said that she would be only too happy to help if she could. Then, suddenly, she'd become agitated and breathless, rambling something about a letter and how could she have forgotten. David had been concerned and insisted his sister come to the phone. Between them, they had decided the doctor should be called and he would wait to hear what he had to say. She was calm and lucid by late afternoon when the doctor finally arrived but her blood pressure was high and he had prescribed rest; she was not allowed to have any excitement.

Emily and Jennifer sat quietly in the living room discussing the day's events.

'Arthur was only forty-one when he died,' Emily mused, 'and that was in 1947. I wonder if he was perhaps injured in the war. He might have sustained a shrapnel wound which ultimately caused his death. I'm sure I read somewhere that many men, who survived the war, died much later from infections brought on by their injuries.'

'It's possible,' Jennifer agreed, 'but we have to remember that anything could have killed him. People generally died much younger then than they do today. Hopefully, we'll find out in the fullness of time.'

'I do hope David's mother is feeling better tomorrow. This talk of a letter sounds promising.'

'Yes.' Jennifer paused for a moment before adding, 'But it could also be completely unrelated. She is an old woman after all. Try not to get your hopes up too much.'

'You sound like Adam!' Emily smiled. She glanced at her watch. 'He'll be expecting me to call about now. Then I might call it a night.' She stood up and crossed to where Jennifer was sitting to give her a hug. 'Thanks for all your help and support. You're a star.'

Jennifer hugged her back. 'You're welcome. Fingers crossed for a good day tomorrow.'

Emily nodded. 'Night.' She walked to the door and turned to give a small wave. 'Night Molly.'

Molly was standing in her usual spot by the window, an ethereal, waiflike figure dressed in black, still waiting. She always appeared to be waiting for something, all alone in her own silent world. The sight of her was an ache in Emily's chest.

Before, it had always seemed to Emily that Molly was there for her, a guardian angel. Now, for the first time, she wondered if she had got things the wrong way around. Maybe Molly was waiting for Emily to help *her*, to enable *her*, somehow, to find peace at last.

The next morning dawned dull and grey but Emily awoke filled with optimism. Already, in just a few days, she'd learned such a lot about the family in her scrapbook; today she could discover more; life was good.

Things continued to look up when, as they were just finishing breakfast, Jennifer's mobile rang. It was David so she put it onto speakerphone.

'Apparently, my mother is absolutely insisting upon seeing you,' he said, his tone one of exasperation. 'Caroline, that's my sister, said that the thought of you *not* visiting her is making her more distressed. Are you free this morning?'

'Yes, that would be great,' Emily exclaimed.

'In that case, I'll pick you up at ten. I just need to sort a few things first.'

'Oh,' Jennifer chimed in, 'we didn't expect ... that is, we don't want to put you to any trouble. If you give us the address, we can drive ourselves there.'

'No problem,' David said smoothly. 'I'd like to be there.'

He rang off abruptly and the two women stared at each other, glowing with excitement.

'Now I'd say that is *definitely* promising.' Emily clapped her hands together gleefully.

Jennifer nodded thoughtfully. 'I agree but, as I said before, just don't set your sights too high. Remember it could be another dead end. Listen, I was thinking, do you want to go on your own this morning? I could stay here and amuse Alex if you like.'

'That's really sweet.' Emily's face gleamed with gratitude. 'But, selfishly, I'd really like you there with me, if you're up for it. I don't know what it is, perhaps it's superstition, but I just feel, deep down, that it's important you are there too. Besides,' she added with a cheeky grin, 'think how disappointed David would be if *you* weren't there!'

Copden was another pretty village, Emily mused, as they drove slowly though the main street in David's silver Audi, Jennifer in the front and she and Alex in the back. It was not unlike Great Chalkham, characterised by beams, pink walls and thatched houses.

'What a lovely place!' Jennifer's voice echoed her thoughts.

David shrugged. 'Most of the villages around here are of a similar character.'

'In that case, aren't we lucky to live here?' Jennifer retorted sharply.

Emily smiled to herself. There was definitely a vibe going on between those two. She wondered when they were going to acknowledge the sexual tension between them, rather than using their frustration to snipe at each other. They would certainly make a striking couple, she decided, if they ever resolved their differences and got together. She was just wondering what she could do to smooth that relationship when David pulled into a driveway and stopped the car outside a large, detached, brick house, set back from the road, in a rambling, slightly untidy garden.

'We're here,' he said shortly and switched off the engine.

A stocky woman with short, iron grey hair and sporting a voluminous, long white shirt covered in smears of clay appeared from the side of the house.

'I'm just in the studio,' she called. 'Sorry I'm in such a state.' As they approached, she smiled in welcome. 'You must be Jen and Emily. Sorry but I won't offer to shake your hand.' Ruefully, she held up her own hands, caked in wet clay. 'And who is this handsome, little chap?'

David stepped forward with a grin. 'I'm David,' he joked and they all laughed.

'This is Alex,' Emily said proudly. 'He's only three and I'm afraid he's a bit shy.'

'He won't be shy for long with me. Would you like to see my studio, Alex? Would you like to help Caroline make a pot for Mummy?'

To Emily's amazement, Alex nodded.

'Right, why don't you come with me? In fact, why don't you all pop into the studio for a minute? I'll need to wash up first if I'm looking after a little one.'

They followed her into a separate, small brick building with large windows.

'Wow!' Jennifer gasped, staring at the stunning collection of earthenware on display all along one side of the studio. 'Is this all your work? It's amazing.'

There were masses of pots, bowls, mugs and plates of all different shapes, sizes and colours. Some were delicately painted with flowers – poppies, roses, forget-me-nots, daffodils – and other pieces were plainer, chunkier, in striking colours and patterns.

'How kind of you to say so!' Caroline beamed as she lathered her hands and arms in a large sink. 'It's for sale if you want to buy some. No obligation, of course.' She turned her attention to David. 'Mum is desperate to see these lovely ladies but she won't tell me why. She says they need to hear it first. I've managed to find the letter, thankfully, that she was going on about yesterday and she became much calmer when she had it by her. Still, I'd suggest that you don't stay too long. We don't want her overdoing it. She's still very frail.'

David nodded. 'I'll keep an eye on her. Don't worry.'

'I know.' Caroline looked at him affectionately. To Emily, she said, 'Now, are you happy to leave this young man with me?' She had produced a child-sized apron and was already expertly slipping it over his head. 'I've got six grandchildren so I know what I'm doing! We'll be fine, won't we Alex?'

'Are you sure, Alex?' Emily asked anxiously.

Again, Alex nodded. 'Make a pot,' he said, his blue eyes serious. 'Like that one.' He pointed a chubby finger at the largest piece, a dark red vase standing a metre tall.

'A man of ambition, I see.' Caroline gently took him by the hand and led him over to her potter's wheel. 'Let's see how big we can make it.'

With a final glance behind her and reassured that her son seemed perfectly happy, Emily followed David out of the studio and through the back door into the house. Her first impression was that this was a happy, comfortable family home. In the back porch, wellies in assorted sizes stood on a rack under a tumble of outdoor clothing, carelessly hung on pegs. They insisted on taking off their own shoes there before moving on to the kitchen, slightly cluttered, warm and decorated with children's artwork, pinned by magnets to the fridge and secured on large pin boards on the walls. The smell of bacon made Emily's stomach rumble.

David led them upstairs and knocked on one of the doors leading off the landing.

'It's me, Mum. I've brought some visitors to see you. Are you decent?'

They all heard the throaty chuckle followed by a rasping cough. He opened the door and peered around first before throwing it open and allowing the two women entrance.

'I'm Emily.' She crossed to the bed and gingerly squeezed the thin, gnarled hand of the silver haired woman lying there. 'It's so kind of you to agree to see us when you're not well.'

The hand snatched at Emily's fingers with surprising strength, pulling her closer. Brown eyes studied her face, absorbing every detail, before she finally nodded approval and released her hand. 'Emily ...' Her voice quavered like leaves in a breeze. 'Your eyes ... your face ... you have the look of Iris.'

Such simple words, but for Emily the world seemed to stop; everything was condensed into that single moment; it was the first time she truly believed she would find her family.

She was aware of her heart still beating, of Jennifer stepping forward and introducing herself, of David leaning over to kiss his mother's shrunken cheek but she could barely breathe as she waited for what would happen next.

'Come, sit by me.' The old woman patted the duvet next to her and Emily did as she was bid, taking the wrinkled hand once more in hers.

'My mother and Iris' mother had been childhood friends,' she began. Her voice was barely a whisper and Emily could hear the wheeziness, the breathlessness making every word a struggle. 'Sybil and Norah. I never knew Norah. I was just a baby when she died.'

'How did she die?' Emily heard her own voice, equally breathless.

'Giving birth to Iris, my Ma said. Women died in childbirth quite a lot in those days. Anyway, when my Ma married my father, she moved away from Chalkham but returned when he died. I was fifteen, I think. Iris was a year younger. I got to know her a little but we weren't close friends then. About a year after that, her young man was killed in the war, like so many young men. Then she moved away with her father. At the time, I didn't know why.'

She paused and closed her eyes. The only sound in the room was the rattle of her breathing.

'I got married in 1950 and we lived in Norfolk, in a village called Heverton. We'd only been there for a few days when I was in the village shop and I heard this voice calling my name. It was Iris. She had moved to Heverton a year earlier when she married her husband, a lovely man called Charles Miller. He was a carpenter; my husband, Henry, was a builder so the two of them got on like a house on fire. We all became very good friends. Then we moved back to Chalkham in the mid-sixties. I was happy to come back but I did miss Iris. We kept in touch – letters, Christmas cards - and we did visit each other every now and then. Iris loved Willow Farm. Of course, it held a special place in her heart because her mother was raised there. Sadly, those visits became less frequent and I didn't see her again for twenty years. Then, out of the blue, I had a phone call from her asking if she could come and see me. She arrived in a taxi the next day. I could see straight away that she was ill. Apparently, doctors had given her less than six months to live. She had bone cancer. Poor Iris, she was only sixty-one and her husband Charles had died a few years before. I did feel so sorry for her.' The brown eyes filled with tears and Emily could feel her own emotions building in her chest as the history unfolded. 'When she came, she told me something she had never told anyone, not even her husband. The reason she had left Chalkham in 1945 was because she was pregnant. She had a daughter, she told me, whom she loved with all her heart but had to give up for adoption. She had always hoped her daughter may one day come looking for her but that had never happened and now, she knew, it would be too late for her. She decided to write a letter and she asked me to look after it for her, just in case anyone ever came looking. I've kept that letter for twenty-six years. I'd completely forgotten about it, to tell you the truth, and then David phoned ... told me you were asking about Iris.'

Emily sat completely still, trying to absorb all the details of Iris' story. There was so much to take in; she felt completely overwhelmed. She realised that David's mother was speaking again.

'David, the letter's in the top drawer of the dressing table. Can you fetch it for me please?'

He passed her a white envelope with the name 'Elizabeth' written across it in spidery, black ink. She turned once more to Emily.

'Maybe Elizabeth is your mother's name, or grandmother's?'

'Not my mother – she was called Grace, Grace Smith. I don't know about my grandmother.'

'Well, I think you should have this. Read it and see what the connection between you and Iris is. Believe me, I know from looking at you that there is one. No, don't open it now!' she said, as Emily started to tear at the envelope. 'Later ... when you can be private. If it's good news, then I'd be very pleased if you came back to tell me.'

'Yes, yes, of course.' Emily squeezed the frail hand once more and rose from the bed. She gave Jennifer a shaky smile. 'I guess we'd better go and see what Alex has been up to.'

'Thank you so much, Mrs Brewer. I know how much this means to Emily,' Jennifer said warmly.

'My dear, you can call me Hannah. I'm sure I'll be seeing a lot more of you. I'm looking forward to ...'

'Mother, you need to rest!' David interrupted quickly. 'I'll pop back and check on you later. No more overdoing things, you hear.'

He ushered the two women from the room and they headed out to Caroline's studio, where they found Alex happily covered in clay.

'Made pots!' he declared, pointing proudly at his efforts.

'Wow, aren't you clever! I especially like this one.' Emily indicated a fat, lopsided bowl, 'but I think they're all fantastic.'

'I'll fire them for you,' Caroline beamed at her. 'He's been such a good boy and tried really hard. I'm very impressed.'

'You're very kind. Thank you so much.'

'How did your meeting with Mother go?'

'Very well thank you,' Emily said politely. She could not say any more; the information was too raw and fresh for her to spill carelessly to another.

Caroline nodded in understanding. 'I'm glad,' she said simply. 'When the pots are ready, I'll get David to run them over to you but feel free to pop in any time.'

Alex chattered happily all the way home about the sticky, wet clay and how it kept falling off the wheel while Emily gripped the envelope tightly in her right hand, all too conscious of its weight. Memories of holding another letter, the one from her mother, came flooding back. Would this one hold the answers she'd been seeking?

When David dropped them off and drove away, Jennifer took charge. She gave Alex a drink, found a DVD for him to watch and poured two glasses of wine.

'I think you could use one when you read your letter,' she said, 'and it would be rude for me to let you drink alone!'

Emily wandered into the living room where Alex was already engrossed in his film. Molly was there, her face serene, waiting patiently on one of the sofas. She sat down beside her and twisted the envelope between her hands. All she needed to do was to tear it open and read it but, now that moment had arrived, she felt the enormity of it and wished Adam was with her. Molly continued to watch her with her sad, green eyes; it felt right that she was there but still someone was missing. Those eyes were telling her so. Then, suddenly, she knew who it was.

She returned to the kitchen where Jennifer was chopping onions. 'Jen, I would like you to sit beside me, to read the letter with me.'

'But it's private. It was given to you. It's nothing to do with me,' Jennifer insisted. 'Obviously, I'm curious but I think you should read it first.'

'No. I'm not sure why or how I know but you need to read it with me. We're in this together, you and I, linked by the spirit of poor Norah. She's in the living room waiting for us, by the way.'

Without another word, the three of them sat together on a sofa, Emily opened the letter - there were four pages of it - with trembling fingers and they began to read.

CHAPTER 24

Iris – March 1991

I ris Miller picked up her best writing pen and stared at the blank piece of paper in front of her. How do you start a letter to a daughter you have not seen for forty-four years? Carefully, she wrote the date and the first line, *Dear Elizabeth.* That sounded a bit formal. She pondered starting again, changing it to *My darling Elizabeth* but decided that sounded too gushing, a little false when she was writing to a woman she had given to other people and had allowed to be adopted.

March 21ˢᵗ, 1991

Dear Elizabeth,
If you are reading this, then it means you have come looking for me and for that I am truly grateful.

She set her pen down. Truthfully, she did not believe this letter would ever be read and writing it was going to be painful. With so little time left, did she really want to be dredging up the most difficult decision she had ever had to face and one she had always regretted? She felt her mother's eyes on her, intense, determined, and, with a sigh, she picked up the pen once more.

When she was young and people had said, in that blithe, careless manner they often use with children, that it must be hard for her not having a mummy, she'd always wondered what they were talking about. In those early years, her mother was an intangible presence, her very own magic trick, watching over her, helping her face the things that made her heart beat faster. Her father knew, of course. It was a constant sadness to him that he could not see her.

'I can feel her though,' he had said. 'I feel her touch in the warmth of the summer wind, her voice in the lark's song.'

He was such a romantic, her dad. When he had died all those years ago, she'd hoped he would find his beloved wife once more, that together they would be at peace. She had insisted that he be buried in the graveyard in Great Chalkham, although he no longer lived there, so that his final resting place would be near his wife and son, even if it was not in the same plot. He had been her rock throughout her childhood and teenage years and especially when she fell apart after Billy's death. For her and her unborn child, he had given up his job, his life, in Great Chalkham and moved to a village in Norfolk where no one knew them, where she could bear the stigma of giving birth to an illegitimate child. He had never complained; she never doubted that his love for her and, later, his granddaughter, transcended all else.

She reread the sentence she had written. The rest of the page, blank, untouched, seemed to mock her. This was too hard, like trying to paint an appealing self-portrait when your face is covered in warts. How could she win her daughter's forgiveness with sentences in a letter? She needed to hold her, let her feel the love and the regret pulsating through her.

Just tell her your story. The words rang out so clear and true that she actually looked round to see who had spoken them but she was all alone, except for the ghost hovering at her shoulder. Just tell your story. She could do that; it was fairly unremarkable after all. The weight of the pen in her hand slid towards the page and she continued from where she had left off.

I have been told I have just a few months to live and that it's time to put my affairs in order. My affairs are not important to me – you are. I only regret one thing in my life but it is a huge regret, one that has weighed heavily on me, and that is my decision to give you up. Let me explain what happened.

For the first fifteen years of my life I lived in Great Chalkham with my father, Arthur after my mother, Norah, died giving birth to me. It was a happy life although times were very hard. When my dad was at work, I spent my time with the Mayhews who were like a second family to me. I worked hard at school and had ambitions to go to university. My dad always said that my mother had set her heart on going to St Hilda's in Oxford so that was my college of preference. However, then war broke out and life changed. My dad joined the Suffolk Regiment and thankfully came through the war unscathed. Others were not so lucky. One of those was a lad called Billy Talbot, your father, who was only nineteen when he died. Everyone loved Billy; he was that kind of person – funny, kind, generous, loyal to his friends. With his fair hair, blue eyes and cheeky grin, he was popular with the girls too but he never took any of them too seriously and then he and I became an item. We had always been friends, although he was four years older than me. He was frequently at the Mayhews too, larking about with the boys but he always had time for me, even when we were kids. Then war came and that was like a hothouse for romance. You had to take love when you could; who knew, when your young man went off, if he would ever return.

I was heartbroken when the terrible news came. Billy had been serving in the North-West Europe Campaign right near the end of the war and had been fatally injured.

It was about a month later when I realised I was pregnant. My dad was still away and I told no one. My heart was raw from my loss but, even then, my first feelings were of gratitude. Billy had gone but a piece of him was growing inside me.

The war ended and Dad returned home. It was his decision that we should move away. He said it was a good time for a fresh start. I know he did not want me to bear the shame of everyone knowing the truth but he never said so. At that time, I was indifferent to the idea and let him make all the arrangements. I didn't even tell anyone I was going. We just left, like thieves in the night.

We ended up in Norfolk in the tiny village of Hopeham. Dad found a job on a farm and I gave birth to you. You were a beautiful baby, with gorgeous red gold curls. I fell in love with you straight away and we were happy. For two wonderful years, we were happy.

Then my wonderful Dad, the Grandpa you adored, died of a heart attack. He was only forty-one. I have to admit that I fell apart after that. First Billy and now my Dad. I suppose, looking back on it, I had a bit of a breakdown once his funeral was over. On top of that we had been living in tied farm accommodation and were given notice to leave. I remember feeling completely desperate, no money, nowhere to live and somehow, I had to support you too. I couldn't cope. That was when I received a visit from the vicar, a man called Father Richard. It was all a bit hazy to be honest with you. I remember breaking down completely and you were crying and I told him I couldn't go on looking after you when I couldn't look after myself. He just listened - didn't say much at all. The next day he returned with a well-dressed couple in their late thirties, I would guess. They were leaving for India – I think he was in the army – the next day and offered to take you with them, give you a secure home and a future I would not be able to provide for you. They were childless and the wife was desperate. I remember screaming at them. How dare they try to take my child! They were very persuasive though. They asked me how I could bear to put myself before my child and why I was being so selfish. Then they talked about your future – a good school, everything that money could buy – and I was so tired, so weary of life. Perhaps they were right. Perhaps I was being selfish to deny you this chance. After all, I could offer you nothing but my love and that was not going to keep you from going hungry.

It all happened so quickly after that. I signed something which said I would not seek to claim you back or make contact with you and they took you away with them that day. They gave me money and I have been forever ashamed that I took it. When you had gone, I realised what I had done but it was too late. The money they had left sickened me. It felt like I had sold my own daughter. Then I tried to take my own life. The doctor had given me some pills so I took the whole lot and lay down ready to die. If it had not been for my mother, I am sure I *would not have survived. That might seem peculiar to you but the spirit of my mother, Norah, was always with me, watching over me. At the time, I was renting a room in a boarding house. I clearly remember locking the door before I took the pills but, when I was found, the door was wide open. Without that, I would not have been found in time, would not have been writing to you now. I can think of no explanation other than my mother's intervention- far-fetched as it may seem to you.*

Anyway, now I am grateful for I have had a good life. Less than two years later, I met another wonderful man, Charles Miller, who became my husband. We bought a home in the village of Heverton and, shortly afterwards, I gave birth to another daughter, your sister Susan so, you see, no matter how bad things are, life has a way of righting itself in the end.

As I said before, my only regret is you but I have always hoped that the decision I took was right for you. I never saw you again but I woke up every single morning after that fateful day thinking about you and reliving the pain of losing you. The only person whom I ever told the whole of this story is my good friend, Hannah Brewer and I leave this letter in her safe keeping. I am a coward, I know, but I never told Charles when he was alive (he died a few years ago) and I cannot bring myself to tell Susan now. I should have told her years ago but somehow the time was never right and I cannot bear to spend my final weeks on this earth enduring recriminations and heartache.

The only other people to know that you were born Elizabeth Fletcher, not Bainbridge, are Louisa and Thomas Bainbridge themselves. I truly hope and pray that you had a happy life with them and that they provided you with all the opportunities that you deserved.

Please know that I have always loved you,
Your mum Iris x

Exhausted, she laid the pen down. There – it was done. Would Elizabeth ever read it? She had to believe she would. It was hard to face dying with the thought that her daughter may believe she had been unwanted.

She had kept her promise to the Bainbridges and made no attempt to find her daughter. Always, deep down in the secret part of her, she had hoped that Elizabeth would one day find her. She still did.

CHAPTER 25

Jennifer – January 2017

The letter read, Emily and Jennifer sat silently side by side holding hands. Somehow that had happened whilst they were reading and now neither wanted to be the first to let go. Jennifer felt as if the world had shifted and she was falling through time and space. Nothing would ever be the same again.

Alex was still watching the DVD and cartoon images sprung garishly across the screen, chasing each other to the accompaniment of an orchestral soundtrack. The four pages of the letter lay still in Emily's lap.

They sat like that for a long time. Finally, Emily picked up the pages and began reading again, trying to absorb every detail, every nuance. With a sigh, she set the letter aside once more.

'Poor Iris,' she said sadly, eyes down, idly pulling at a loose thread on the jade green jumper she was wearing. She looked across at Jennifer for the first time. 'Jen, are you alright?'

Jennifer's face was drained of all colour and she was gazing at nothing, her thoughts a wild tumble of confusion. Emily's voice seemed to come from a long way off, tugging her back.

'I ... I ... don't know exactly.' She stared at Emily helplessly.

'What's happened?'

Jennifer shook her head. How could she put this into words? It was all too new, too much of a shock. Saying the words aloud would make it real and she was not ready.

'I'll fetch you some water.' Emily sprang to her feet and disappeared into the kitchen. She returned a few moments later and handed Jennifer the drink.

Jennifer took a sip and then another while Emily waited, watching her face anxiously. 'Was it something in the letter?'

A single nod. 'Yes.'

'Do you know her? Do you know Elizabeth?'

'Yes.' Jennifer took a deep breath. 'She was my mother.'

Stunned silence. Jennifer could see the shock in Emily's face.

'But ... I don't understand ...'

'I know. Me neither. Here we are looking for *your* family and I find mine. It's hard to believe.'

'But how do you know? What makes you so sure?'

'It was the names, Louisa and Thomas Bainbridge. They were my grandparents, Gramps and Granny. Gramps was a military man through and through, an ex-army Major General. I always knew that they had adopted my mum and she had spent most of her childhood in India.' She sighed. 'It's tragic, really. Iris would have been so upset to learn the truth; it's best she never knew. My mum did *not* have a happy childhood. Gramps was incredibly strict and tended to treat her like one of his recruits. Granny was scared of him and only knew how to obey. It was a life of hard work, regimental discipline and loneliness. She was fourteen or fifteen when they returned to England and settled in a village near Cambridge. Up until then, my mum had always toed the line. She knew nothing else. Then, at her English boarding school, she met girls of her age who were used to a lot more freedom. She started to rebel, get into trouble. Apparently, she got caught when she was out with another girl and a couple of the village lads after dark. She was expelled from the school and returned home in disgrace. Gramps was furious. By now she was sixteen and he decided he'd had enough of looking after her. She needed a husband to keep her in order. Suitable candidates were found and invited to tea. My mum was furious and refused to play ball but he wore her down in the end. She was introduced to a local doctor, a tall, handsome man called Stephen Thompson. He was quite a bit older than she was, twenty-six years older, I think, and he swept her off her feet. I think she thought that she was in love at the time and marriage to him meant a way out. She fell pregnant almost immediately and had me but there were complications with the birth which meant she could have no more children. My poor mum. It was a case of out of the frying pan and into the fire. My father was another who liked to control those around him and it was my mum's lot to make his life comfortable. He ground her down in so many ways, so many unkindnesses, and eventually the shine went out of her. Before that though, there were lots of arguments and lots of cold silences. She always looked out for me, stood up for me when he treated me unkindly. He wanted to send me away to boarding school when I was eight but she wouldn't let him. I remember they had the most terrible row but she insisted she wouldn't be parted from me.' She smiled briefly. 'I can still recall his face – so red with rage I thought his head might explode! Sadly though, all the battles took its toll on her health and she died of cancer when she was only thirty-nine. That was over thirty years ago.'

'Poor Elizabeth and poor you too!' Emily was immediately full of sympathy.

Jennifer shrugged. 'It was a long while ago. I never think of it, or hardly ever, and then I read your letter. It just seems so absurd. We were meant to be searching for your history, not mine! And what does all this mean for you?'

'Who knows? Hey, I've just thought. It means we could be *related*!'

Jennifer smiled and gave her a hug. '*That* would be the best news of all. I can't think of anyone I'd rather be related to!'

'Just imagine!' Emily's eyes were shining. 'Tell me more about Elizabeth. What was she like?'

'As a mum, she was quite strict. She wouldn't let me get away with any nonsense but I always knew she loved me by the way she fought my corner. She wasn't very demonstrative – I don't suppose she'd had much experience of hugs and cuddles herself – and she really didn't have much happiness in her life. By the end, she had grown quite bitter and had a tendency to complain. When she was younger though, she was incredibly beautiful, like an angel.' Her voice had grown wistful. 'Her hair was long and curly and the colour of autumn leaves. I remember longing for curls when I was little but my hair was always dead straight. Actually, I have some photos of her if you're interested?'

'Of course.'

Jennifer crossed over to one side of the room and pulled a blue covered album out of one of the cupboards in a solid, oak sideboard. 'These were from a stack of family photos she had accumulated. When she died, I went through them and picked out the best ones.' She handed the album to Emily who eagerly turned to the first page.

'Gosh, she looks so young!' she gasped. 'And *so* like you, Molly!' Emily looked across at the silent wraith sitting beside her.

'And you.' Jennifer nodded in reply. 'Seeing these pictures again...I suppose it's obvious. I just wasn't looking.'

'Isn't that often the way? Life has a knack of throwing up things which you don't know are missing whilst the things you really want to find remain elusive.' Her voice was laced with irony.

'Oh Emily, you *will* find what you're looking for, I just know it.' Jennifer squeezed her hand. 'I feel bad that I'm the one who has found a forgotten family, not you.'

'It was meant to be.' Emily gave her a reassuring smile. 'That's why I'm here, isn't that right, Molly?' she said firmly. 'And it's why you decided to buy this cottage. It's all part of Molly's plan to bring us together.'

'That sounds a bit far-fetched,' Jennifer frowned. 'Surely it's just a coincidence?'

Emily shook her head. 'You can believe what you like but I know what I believe. The ghost of Norah wanted us to find each other. I know it; I can feel it; I can feel it now.'

She turned her attention back to the photographs. The first pages were all black and white family portraits. There were several of a young Elizabeth holding her baby and some of the complete family group, Jennifer's father standing tall and stern in the background. One showed a close up of Elizabeth's face, smiling shyly as she looked down at her daughter. With her long hair hanging loose around her shoulders, her smooth skin and delicate features, she looked like the subject of a pre-Raphaelite painting. In later colour pictures, her hair was pinned back and her face had a tired, jaded quality, even when she was smiling at the camera. By the end of the album, she would still have been in her thirties, Emily realised, but she looked at least ten years older, her skin lined and sallow, her brown eyes hooded with pain.

'She was diagnosed with cancer when she was thirty-seven and lasted just two more years. My poor mum, I know she suffered terribly and she knew she was dying. She worried about me and told me that she did not think accountancy was the career for me. Turns out she was right but I didn't know it at the time.'

Emily turned back to the beginning and studied the photographs again, exclaiming over pictures of a young Jennifer, pudgy and round with short, thick, corn-coloured hair, her face screwed up in her attempts at a smile. Later pictures showed a slimmer, taller girl with long hair, a heavy fringe and serious grey eyes. 'You look very studious,' she mused.

'I was. Both my parents wanted me to excel at school and I didn't want to disappoint them.'

'I was the same. We may not look very similar but we definitely have a lot in common.' She placed the album on the table and smiled at Jennifer who was looking again at Iris' letter.

'I still can't quite believe it,' Jennifer murmured. 'Iris was my birth grandmother which makes Norah and Arthur Fletcher my great grandparents. I can't help wishing my mum had looked for Iris. She always knew she was adopted but I suppose she never really had the opportunity. Still ... I can't help wishing I had met Iris. If she died sometime in 1991, I would have been thirty-one. I was teaching at a school near Cambridge then, not very far away.'

'I know. It's heart-breaking, isn't it? But you do have an aunt, Susan. We have to find her!'

Jennifer swallowed back a lump in her throat. 'It's hard to take in. When I was little, as an only child, I longed for brothers and sisters. Then, when they failed to arrive, I would have loved a cousin, aunts, uncles, any extended family but it was always just the grandparents, mum, dad and me. Since they died, I've got used to being a family of one, I suppose ... except I'm not. I have an aunt, Susan. I wonder what she's like.'

'We've *got* to find her,' Emily said again.

Jennifer nodded. 'For you too. If you are descended from Iris, and you must be, then she must be the link. I know my mum only had the one child ... at least, that's what I always thought. Maybe she too had a child out of wedlock. Maybe that's why Gramps gave her such a hard time.' She thought for a moment and frowned. 'She would have been very young though. She was only sixteen when I was born.'

'It's possible though.' Emily sat back and ran her fingers through her hair. 'But I agree Susan is our best bet. How are we going to find her?'

Jennifer thought for a moment. 'Hannah Brewer might know something. After all, she saw Iris in 1991. They must have talked about Susan then.'

'Good idea. We need to speak to David, ask him if his mother is up to another visit.'

'I'll give him a call.'

At just after one o'clock when Jennifer, Emily and Alex were sitting down to lunch at the breakfast bar, the doorbell rang. Alex was tucking into his home-made tomato soup and already had orange smears all round his mouth and chin; the two women were idly toying with their spoons. Neither felt very hungry.

Jennifer was not expecting, when she opened the door, to see David standing there, looking rugged and masculine in jeans and a scruffy, navy sweater. She'd not long spoken to him on the phone when she'd briefly explained the contents of Iris' letter. There was a stunned silence on the end of the line so she ploughed on, asking if it would be possible to have another conversation with his mother concerning Susan's whereabouts. She'd heard him whistle his amazement.

'That's just incredible, Jen. Are you ok with all of this?' There was concern in his voice which she found touching.

'I'm fine. It's just been a bit ... unexpected ...' She struggled to find words to sum up how she was feeling.

'I guess so. Look, I'll speak to my mum but I don't think she'll be up to another visit just yet. I'm sorry.'

'That's fine. I understand.'

She had ended the call and relayed his comments to Emily. Over lunch they had been discussing other possible means of finding her. A search on Google had revealed a number of sites claiming success with finding long lost relatives and they had decided to give those a try when the doorbell sounded.

David's face was serious and he gave her a searching look. 'Are you sure you're ok? This must all have been a hell of a shock. Can I come in?'

'Yes, of course ... please.' She opened the door wider and waited while he took off his brown, leather work boots. 'It's David,' she called through to Emily. He followed her into the kitchen. 'Would you like some soup?' she offered.

'Actually, that would be great. I haven't had time for lunch but I wanted to come over straight away. I have some news which you may want to hear.'

'Really?' Jennifer spooned more soup into a bowl. 'What's that?'

'I know where Susan lives,' he answered. He watched Jennifer's reaction closely. Both women stared at him open mouthed. 'You're joking!' Emily exclaimed.

He shook his head. 'I wouldn't joke about something like this. It's true. I have her address. After you called, I went back to check on my mum. She wanted to know if the letter had been helpful and so I told her what you had found out and the answers you still needed. It turns out that Susan had contacted her to inform her that Iris had passed away. They met up again at the funeral and, since then, they have exchanged Christmas cards every year. She said Susan had two children but she couldn't remember their names. '

'Where does she live?' Emily's voice was slightly tremulous.

'Still in Norfolk, near Swaffham. It's about an hour and a half's drive from here.'

'We could drive there this afternoon.' Emily bounced off her stool and began clearing dishes. 'What do you think, Jen?'

'I ... yes ... I suppose so. Do we have a telephone number for her?' Jennifer looked across at David. Suddenly, she felt like she was on a rollercoaster, plunging into the unknown and not in control.

'No. Just the address.' He handed Jennifer a slip of paper. 'I've written it down for you. I need to get back on site or I would have driven you.'

'No need. I can drive us.' Emily threw her arms around David and hugged him excitedly. 'Thank you so much for all you've done. You've been brilliant.'

'No problem. Good luck this afternoon.'

'Yes, thank you, David. It's been very kind of you to put yourself out like this,' Jennifer said, her voice, even to her own ears, sounding stiff and formal compared with Emily's unfettered enthusiasm.

David escaped from Emily's embrace and, unexpectedly, wrapped his arms around Jennifer. 'Promise me you're feeling alright about all of this?' His breath was warm against her ear and she felt her body leaning into his. 'Your life has been turned upside down. You might need a bit of time to come to terms with it all.'

'I'm fine.' At least, I will be when you let go of me, she thought. She took a step back and he reluctantly released her.

'Right. I'll be off then. I'll phone you later.' He stepped through the door and Jennifer felt her tension dissipate. She smiled at Emily who was busily scrubbing at Alex's face with a wipe. 'Good news then. At least we know that Susan is still alive. How she'll feel, though, about me being her niece is anyone's guess.'

'First things first. Let's drive over there and see if she's in for a start. We can work out what to say on the way.'

Jennifer's face was pensive with doubt. 'It'll come as a dreadful shock, though,' she argued.

'Not dreadful – exciting.' Emily gave Jennifer's arm a reassuring pat. 'Come on. I want to get going.'

The address David had given them was for a village in West Norfolk called Corriton. They passed a rather garish village sign and the satnav instructed Emily to turn right and then right again. Jennifer had fallen silent as they drove down a narrow lane lined with moderately sized, modern brick houses, all squashed in beside each other with little space for gardens.

'You have reached your destination,' declared the monotone of the satnav and Emily parked along the edge of the lane, careful not to block anyone's driveway.

'It's number 16.' Jennifer craned her neck to peer at the numbers on display. 'I can't see it at the moment. I'll get out and see which one it is.'

Her stomach roiled nervously as she headed down the lane. There it was, number 16, a red bricked house with a white front door and a large brick weave driveway. A slightly grubby, black fiesta was parked in front of the garage door. She beckoned to Emily and waited while she unstrapped Alex from his car seat.

'This is it,' she said as they joined her. 'There's a car there so she might be at home.' She glanced at her watch. 'Quarter to four.'

Emily shot her an amused glance. 'Thanks for the time check!' She took hold of Jennifer's arm and started to steer her towards the drive. 'Come on. Let's do this.'

Assorted plant pots were vying for space in the porchway and the green shoots of spring bulbs were already visible. As they waited by the door, having rung the bell, Jennifer wondered if Susan was a keen gardener. What would she learn about this aunt she never knew she had? The thought was slightly overwhelming. Seconds ticked by and no one came. Already she felt her nerves being squeezed by strangling disappointment. Susan was not there. Shaking her head, she turned away.

'Hang on a sec.' Firmly, Emily rang the doorbell once more. 'Give her a chance. She might have just got out of the shower or something.'

Again, they waited. Already the sky was beginning to darken as dusk approached and Jennifer shivered. She was regretting leaving her coat in the car, unlike Emily and Alex who were both wrapped up warmly.

Then, suddenly, the door burst open and a small, dark-haired boy of about six or seven years of age stood there.

'Ryan, I've told you before not to open the door.' A small, slim woman in her mid-sixties with short grey hair and green eyes bustled up behind him. 'I must remember to put the catch up.' She turned her attention to the women on her doorstep. 'Yes? Can I help you?'

Jennifer cleared her throat with a cough. 'We're looking for Susan Miller. I don't know if you ....' Her voice tailed off.

The woman was eying them suspiciously now. 'Who are you?' she asked bluntly. 'I'm busy and whatever it is you're selling, I'm not buying.'

'I've reason to believe,' Jennifer leapt in quickly before the door was shut in their faces, 'that Susan Miller may be my aunt.' She had talked it over with Emily and together they had decided that a forthright approach would be best.

The woman shook her head firmly. 'That's not possible. I was an only child. I don't have any nieces or nephews, except by marriage. My husband had three sisters and they all have children.'

So, *you* are Susan,' Jennifer said quietly, although she had known it from the moment the woman had opened the door. 'Look, can we come in? This might take a bit of explaining.'

The woman hesitated, her face creased with anxiety.

'Please.' Jennifer persisted.

Susan sighed and took a step back. 'Alright, but you had best be quick. I need to give my grandchildren their tea before their mum picks them up at six.'

They took their shoes off at the door, watched by an audience of two identical boys with tousled, red hair and an older girl with long, brown plaited hair.

'My grandchildren.' Susan introduced them. 'Sasha's ten and the twins are Harry and Ryan. They're seven.'

'Pleased to meet you all. I'm Emily and this is Jen.' Emily flashed them a friendly smile as she removed her hat and coat. 'And this is my son, Alex. He's only three.' She pushed him forward but he clung shyly, as usual, to her right leg.

'Hey Alex, do you want to see our den? It's really good. We built it in Grandad's study under his desk yesterday and Gran let us leave it up so we could play in there today. Come on.' One of the twins seized Alex's hand and, much to Emily's surprise, he allowed himself to be led away.

Emily glanced anxiously at Susan. 'Is that ok? Will he be alright with them?'

201

Susan stood staring at her, trance-like. She seemed transfixed by Emily's face and hair.

Emily cleared her throat, feeling slightly uncomfortable under the intense scrutiny. 'Is that ok?' she repeated.

'He'll be fine.' Susan snapped out of her reverie and ushered them into a large living room with bold, patterned wallpaper and old fashioned, blue fabric sofas. 'I know they're my grandchildren and I'm biased but they're good kids, even if they wear me out.'

'Do you look after them every day?' Jennifer asked politely.

'Yes, just for a couple of hours after school. I work mornings at the garden centre just down the road and then pick the children up from school at quarter past three. No wonder I feel so old.' There was a pause. 'So ...?' she said expectantly.

'I'm really sorry to turn up out of the blue like this,' Jennifer began, 'but just this morning I learnt that Iris Fletcher was my grandmother.'

Susan frowned. 'My mum's maiden name was Fletcher but then she married my dad, Charles Miller. What makes you think they are the same person? There must be lots of Iris Fletchers out there.'

Emily reached into her bag and took out the letter. 'I think perhaps you ought to read this.' She handed it to Susan, her eyes full of concern. 'I'm sorry. It may well be a bit of a shock.'

Susan unfolded the pages with trembling fingers. 'This *is* my mum's writing,' she said, her face crumpling as she looked across at Jennifer. 'I'd know it anywhere, even after all this time.' She let the pages fall back onto her lap. 'I'm not sure I want to read this. Who's Elizabeth?'

'She was my mother ... and your half-sister,' Jennifer said quietly, her heart aching for Susan. Perhaps they had been wrong to confront her like this. 'She was born in 1945 and was given up for adoption when she was two years old.'

Susan was shaking her head in disbelief. 'That can't be right. My mum was born in 1930 so that would mean she was only fifteen.'

'I know.'

Somewhere, in the distance, the occasional high-pitched shrieks of children's voices filtered through the air.

'My turn!'

'Harry, let him have a go!'

'Moron!'

Emily twitched nervously. 'Do you mind if I just go and check on Alex?'

Susan did not look up but waved her hand distractedly. 'Go ahead,' she murmured.

Jennifer sat perched on the edge of the sofa, stiff with discomfort. There were no easy words to smooth the way forward; she waited and said nothing. A marble clock ticked ponderously on the mantelpiece above the fireplace; traffic hummed on the nearby A47. Susan stared with distrust at the pieces of paper in front of her. They were alien to her life, bringing a message from the past that she may not want to hear.

'Why have you come here?' She looked up, suddenly angry. 'Telling me lies about my mum!'

Jennifer shook her head sadly. 'They're not lies. I'm sorry if I've upset you. You don't have to read the letter.'

Susan snorted, her nostrils flaring. 'But that's the problem!' she snapped. 'I *do* have to read it. I have no choice.' Her eyes filled with tears. 'Can you give me a moment?'

'Of course.' Jennifer left the room without looking back.

She followed the voices and found the children and Emily all squashed under a large mahogany desk covered in sheets.

'That looks like fun,' she smiled as she peered round a pink cotton wall.

'Do you want to come in?' the girl, Sasha, asked excitedly. 'There's room!'

'Tell you what ... I'll just sit in this lovely annex here,' she indicated another space formed from sheets draped over sturdy mahogany chairs with bean bags on the floor. 'This looks very comfy.'

'It's our bedroom,' one of the twins informed her,' but you can sit there if you like.'

With as much dignity as she could muster, Jennifer sank down gingerly on a superman beanbag and the children disappeared back into their den. She closed her eyes, letting their chatter wash over her, wondering how the woman in the other room was faring. It was bound to be a shock. How would any woman feel upon discovering that her mother had lied to her, albeit by omission, all her life? Her mind drifted back to her own childhood; she remembered the moment she learned that her mum had been adopted as a young child. They had been reading a book together at bedtime about a fairy called Twinkle who grew up to be a star. It was one of her favourites. In the story, Twinkle's parents had died when she was a baby and she had been adopted by a witch who treated her cruelly.

'What's adopted?' she could hear her six-year-old voice asking.

Her mum had not answered straight away and she had been distracted by the story, turning the page to find out what happened to Twinkle. Luckily, the unfortunate fairy had been rescued by a fairy godmother who helped her become the brightest fairy in the land, so bright that she became a star. She remembered looking out of the window with her mum then, staring out at the sparkling canvas, trying to decide which was the brightest star, which one was Twinkle.

'What does adopted mean?' she asked again. She had searched Elizabeth's face, looking for answers, wondering at the pain she saw momentarily in hooded eyes.

'It means you live with a mummy and daddy who are not your real mummy and daddy.'

'Why would you do that?'

Elizabeth had hugged her then, one of those rare moments when she had felt truly loved. 'Sometimes your real mummy can't look after you anymore. That happened to me when I was very small. My daddy had died before I was born and my mummy had to find another home for me. As soon as I was old enough to understand, probably about your age, Gramps and Grandma sat me down and told me that they had adopted me.'

'But what happened to your real mummy?'

'I don't know.' Her tone was suddenly dismissive.

'But wasn't she really sad?' the young Jennifer had persisted.

'I don't know. Enough of the questions!' She had swept her up into her arms and carried her to the bed. 'It all turned out for the best, I expect. Night night.' A quick kiss on her cheek, the light was turned off, the lingering floral scent of Elizabeth's perfume and lots of unanswered questions tumbling through a child's brain.

Those questions surfaced regularly over the next few years but her mum's responses were flimsy, incomplete and increasingly impatient.

'I don't want to talk about it anymore.' That had been the last time. She knew her mum was fragile; she did not want to upset her.

The air shifted and Jennifer opened her eyes. Susan was standing by the door, still gripping the pages of the letter in her right hand, silent tears threading their way down pale cheeks. Jennifer struggled to her feet and crossed the room, folding the other woman in her embrace. Silently, still clinging to each other, they walked back to the sitting room.

'I'm so sorry ...' Jennifer began.

'No!' Susan raised her hand abruptly. 'Don't be sorry. You did the right thing. I needed to know. I just wish I knew sooner; I wish she'd told me. I feel so sad for her. I can't imagine what that must have been like, losing your child like that. She must have been completely desperate.'

'I know.' Jennifer nodded sympathetically. 'It's a tragic story.'

'And was she happy? Elizabeth? What happened to her? Is she still alive?'

Jennifer took a deep breath and skimmed through the pages of Elizabeth's life, recounting all the happier moments and leaving out many of the low points, the disappointments, the agony of her final days.

'So, the two of them never saw each other again. That's so terribly sad!' Susan croaked through her tears, her voice muffled by the tissue clamped to her face. 'And I never got to meet my half-sister.'

'I should have brought a picture of her. I didn't think.'

Susan nodded. 'I'd love to see a photo of her.' She looked across at Jennifer, studying her face. 'This means you are my niece. I have a whole family I knew nothing about.'

'Just me, I'm afraid. I was an only child and I've never married.' She paused as the two boys galloped into the room, followed at a short distance by Sasha, Emily and Alex.

'I'm hungry, Grandma. What's for tea? Why are you crying?'

Susan quickly wiped her face and shoved the soggy tissue in my pocket. 'It's just my contact lenses playing up.' She turned apologetically to Jennifer. 'I'm sorry but I really need to get their tea. Maybe we can catch up tomorrow. It's my day off.'

Jennifer glanced quickly at Emily who gave her a nod. 'Good idea. We'll be round at about ten o'clock. Do you have a phone number I can contact you on should there be any problems?'

They exchanged numbers and hugged a brief farewell.

'I *am* really pleased you came.' Susan smiled tremulously at Jennifer. 'I'm looking forward to getting to know you better.'

She turned to Emily and enveloped her in a hug, suddenly fierce in its intensity. 'And you too, Emily,' she whispered. 'We'll talk more tomorrow.'

CHAPTER 26

Susan – January 2017

Much later, when her daughter in law, Lucy, had bustled the children out of the house, after she and George had eaten their supper, Susan sat alone in the living room staring unseeing at the television and chewing her bottom lip. She had said nothing to George about her visitors or Iris' letter. It was all too new and she felt too raw and exposed, like layers of her, the solid, comfortable, safe layers of her unremarkable history, had been peeled away.

Secrets. Did all families have their secrets, buried and hidden beneath bluff exteriors, then surfacing when they were least expected? Her own secret was safe for now but for how much longer? It was the one thing she had kept from George, her solid, dependable, stubborn husband, for the last almost thirty years of their marriage. Then again, it was not her secret to tell and she had promised she would tell no one.

Her mind drifted back to memories of her mother, the forthright, sometimes brutally honest, straightforward, 'call a spade a spade' Iris. Who would have thought that someone like her could have kept such a painful secret for so long? Then again, the same could be said for her. Maybe she was more like Iris than she thought. Physically, they had not looked alike, apart from the green eyes. Her mother had been tall and willowy with dark, tumbling waves whilst she herself had always been short and inclined to chubbiness, like her dad and she had his fair colouring too, pale and freckled. He was bald by the time she knew him but in earlier photographs he had sandy coloured hair, always cut short. Her own hair was dead straight – how she had envied her mum's curls – and had an auburn tint which she hated. She hadn't even minded going grey – at least it was not ginger!

Her dad, Charlie Miller, had been a carpenter. He was a loud, gregarious man, quick witted and ready to laugh. People had always made comments about her parents being a mismatched couple but that was because they were always quick to assess their marriage on the basis of looks – a stunningly beautiful, tall woman could surely have done better for herself than a short, plump, bald man. It was not as if he had any wealth to speak of either although he made a decent living from his business. Susan knew better though. Her parents were very well suited and happy together. Quite simply, he made her laugh but there was more to it than that. He was such a gentle, caring man who always put his family before himself.

'You two are the world to me,' he would say, enveloping her and Iris in his beefy arms. 'I'm the luckiest man alive to have you.'

Iris would smile and kiss him tenderly on the cheek. 'We're lucky to have each other,' she would say.

That was the thing looking back – Iris always seemed utterly content with her lot. There never felt like something was missing. Yet she had given birth to another child, a daughter whom she had loved dearly and never forgotten. Why had she kept it a secret? Why had she not told the family who loved her? Susan sighed heavily. She wished now that *she* had known sooner, that she had been able to meet her sister but maybe, looking back, Iris had been worried that such a revelation would tear apart their tight, family cocoon.

She remembered asking her mum once, when she did not have long to live, if she had any regrets. Iris had not replied at once. Her lips had tightened slightly and there had been a flash of something in her eyes. For just a brief moment, Susan had thought she saw pain there. Then her mother had smiled wryly and patted her hand. 'I've had a good life and I've got no complaints. In my youth I was ambitious for myself and I would have said that I regretted being unable to go to university but, if I had, I might never have met your dad, might never have had you, so I'm glad things turned out as they did. You have made me so proud ... always.'

Susan had fought back the lump in her throat and put her arm around Iris, now very thin and frail. 'That's why you were so keen for me to go to uni ... so that I could have some of the opportunities you missed out on ... and I messed up. That's something *I* regret. Dropping out of uni and getting married at nineteen wasn't my best decision. Look at me now! Here I am, doing two dead end, part time jobs. Not much to be proud of there!'

'You're entitled to make mistakes. We all have. At the end of the day though, Susan, you always put your family first. That's the best thing that can be said of any mum. Nowadays, so many women focus on their careers and have no time for their children. That's not right either, not in my book.'

'Bless you, mum, but I'm hardly mother of the year. I have a daughter living in London whom I hardly ever see and a teenage son who barely ever speaks to me and treats his home like a hotel.'

'Tom is just going through a phase, you'll see. He'll grow out of it. He's a fine lad underneath all that hair. As for your daughter ... well, she's stubborn like her mum ... and proud. Her dad has got a lot to answer for, giving her an ultimatum like that. No wonder she's been reluctant to come home.'

'I know but I miss her.'

It had broken her heart when her daughter had left home at just sixteen to live in London with her boyfriend, John, but George had been plain furious.

'Don't think you can just come back here for us to pick up the pieces!' he had bellowed, his cheeks red with rage. 'If you choose to throw away your future, then you'll have to deal with it. I want nothing more to do with you.'

'George, you don't mean that!' Susan had exclaimed, fearful of her daughter's set face.

'Yes, I do. She needs to know the consequences of this choice she's making.'

He had slammed out of the door; Susan had cried and pleaded but her daughter had gone anyway, not returning to Corriton until 1991, for Iris' funeral. Although Susan had met up with her infrequently on excursions to London and kept in contact with her throughout, via letter and the odd phone call, Iris had never seen her granddaughter again and had never forgiven George. Susan had tried to act as peacemaker between them but Iris was adamant.

'It was the worst thing he could have said and he was in the wrong but he still won't admit it. Effectively, he banished that child from her home and family. That was unforgiveable.'

Now, especially in the light of her recent discovery, Susan could understand her rage. Iris had endured the anguish of giving her own child away; of course, she would be incensed that such a stupid thing as stubborn pride would keep a father from his daughter and a grandmother from her grandchild.

At the time, it had taken a long while for her own marriage to recover. In her anguish, she had been quick to blame and unwilling to forgive. Eventually though, the strain of being perpetually angry proved too much and, she decided, she loved her husband too much to lose him too. Instead, she settled into the role of the go-between and became the glue trying to hold the family together. Over the years, the father/daughter relationship had progressed to an uneasy truce and George had, at last, apologised for his impulsive ultimatum.

Her thoughts turned back to her visitors, Jennifer, Emily and her adorable, little boy Alex. She had liked Jennifer instantly; she had a dry, forthright way about her that reminded her so much of Iris but she was also clearly warm and empathetic. Her niece – it would take a little getting used to but, if you could choose your family, she could not have chosen better. Of course, it was still early days. Time would tell if she was right.

And what of Emily? She was clearly an anxious mum, judging by the way she fussed around her son, but there had not really been an opportunity to get to know her. That would come tomorrow.

Meanwhile, she knew she would have to phone her daughter and tell her what had happened. She had to tell Grace.

CHAPTER 27

Grace- May/June 1987

I t was uncomfortably warm behind the bar of The Golden Fleece and Grace's feet were swollen and throbbing. This was her last shift and, at eight and a half months pregnant, it would be a relief not to have to make the trek across London every day. She would miss the people though, the assorted characters who crossed her path and, drawn to her angelic face and warm nature, told her their life stories. More than that though, she would miss the money. Her wages, until recently, had been all they had to buy food.

Today the bar was quiet and she had time to reflect on the terrible mess her life had become. She had followed John Smith to London, a naïve, young singer chasing her dreams, and lived with him in a tiny bedsit in Dulwich. At first it had seemed like such an adventure. They had busked on the streets and in bars, wherever they could, waiting for their big break. 'Unusual' and 'quirky' was how they were described. John wrote haunting melodies which suited her husky voice and they received good press but they were not commercial enough to get a record deal. Their type of music was branded as a bit outdated in an era of pulsing, electronic pop and rejection after rejection followed.

It was hard to stay positive in the face of constant disappointment and their relationship had certainly suffered. In the early days, they had been so close, so in tune with each other; it had seemed the right thing to get married, on their own, no friends or family. They needed no one else. Then John had hooked up with some musicians living in a squat on the Heygate estate. Grace was worried by this turn of events and told him so.

'They're bad news, babe. We'd be better off staying on our own.'

John refused to listen and, suddenly, they had moved into the squat where drugs were readily available and privacy was non-existent. There were two other men there who always seemed to be high on something and the stench of weed, vomit and smoke clung like a fug. She had hated it - the squalor, the noise, the smell but, above all, the lack of her own, personal space. They slept on a mattress with only a blanket hanging from the ceiling separating them from the four other men living in the squat. When John wanted sex, he made no effort to stay quiet, to keep it private between the two of them. Instead, he would take vicarious delight in making a lot of noise, calling out what he was doing to her, loudly vocalising his pleasure. She felt like his trophy, a possession to be used as a means of impressing his new mates. It was as if he was saying, 'Hey guys. I've got a hot wife and we have great sex every night.' Meanwhile, she learned to ignore the sexist comments and leering looks from his two cronies. When John was too busy jamming with the guys to go gigging with her, she got a job in a bar.

Then she found out she was pregnant. After the initial shock, she glowed with the joy of it. It would mean a fresh start for them both. Maybe they would have to postpone their pop ambitions for a while and John would have to get a proper job but they would make it work. For a few days, she hugged the secret to herself, wondering how best to tell him. She needed somewhere quiet, away from everyone else. Eventually she decided on a picnic for just the two of them and lured him out with the promise of cans of beer which she had bought specially. It was a beautiful, warm September day and they sat together on a park bench. When he was mellow from the food and the alcohol and had his arm round her shoulders, she told him her news.

He reacted with cold fury. 'How did that happen? You said you were on the pill.' He withdrew his arm and moved away from her.

'I was. It must have been after I had that sickness bug. Do you remember I told you we needed to use a condom too after that but you wouldn't listen? You said it wouldn't matter.' She was defensive, trying to placate him.

'Well, you'll have to get rid of it. How do you expect to get a record deal if you're up the duff?'

It was at that moment she realised their relationship was over, although it actually took a few more months to unravel. 'How do you expect to get a record deal when you spend your days hanging about with those so-called mates and smoking dope?' She was angry too now.

'Ah, here we go again. Nag, nag, nag – that's all you do these days. I don't need this.' He leapt to his feet and strode away.

'That's right, you run away. Oh, go to hell!' she shouted at his departing back.

Much later, when she had returned to the flat having cried out all her frustration and unhappiness, he had ignored her and she had lain alone on her mattress, listening to the usual cacophony of life on Heygate estate – babies crying, men shouting, people arguing and, beyond the blanket, her husband getting stoned with his friends.

Things had only got worse after that. Sometimes John would nuzzle up to her, ask after her health, sigh that he was a moron and that he would do better. Then, when her defences were lowered, he would begin cajoling her.

'It's really not a good time to have a baby, Grace. Hell, I'm only twenty and you're barely seventeen. Let's get settled first.'

'You want me to have an abortion,' she said flatly.

'It would be best, babe. Surely you can see that.'

'I'm not doing it. I want this baby.'

Then, once again, his anger would erupt. 'Well, I'm not looking after it. You want a baby, you're on your own.'

'Fine.'

This would be followed by a stony silence which lasted for a few days until the whole cycle began again.

When she was six months pregnant, he told her that he and two of his mates were leaving, heading off on a six-month tour. While she had been working in the bar, they had been doing gigs as a three-piece band and now they had been signed up as a backing act for a new band called Jargon who had been getting rave reviews. She never saw him again.

Meanwhile, she stayed at the squat with the other two men, Wayne and Jacko; she had nowhere else to go. Jacko, with his long, greasy hair and unwashed clothes, was harmless enough and when John had abandoned her, Wayne had been genuinely kind. He had steered clear of her when John had been around but, since then, had become a much needed, if unlikely, friend. He told her he had been thrown out by his stepfather when he was sixteen and had slept rough for a while until he'd hooked up with Jacko, who was already living in the squat. Since then, he had managed to get the occasional labouring job but had lost it, just as quickly, when he failed to turn up for work after a late-night session.

'I know I need to get myself straightened out,' he had told Grace, 'but then I really need a drink or a smoke, you know, just to take the edge off, and, before I know it, I'm completely out of it.'

They had supported each other and Wayne had now been working for two, whole weeks without mishap. Jacko had moved on, bored now he had no one to get stoned with so it had become just the two of them.

Grace's pregnancy had meant the involvement of health officials who, in turn, contacted social services. A sharp featured woman called Linda Galloway visited the squat unexpectedly when Jacko was still there and the pungent scent of dope hung in the air. She told her in no uncertain terms that she couldn't expect to bring up a baby living as she did and that she should get help for her drug addiction before she harmed the baby.

'But I don't do drugs!' Grace had wailed. Linda Galloway did not believe her. The next time she visited, she brought with her officials from the adoption agency, a man and a woman. They were kinder but insistent that adoption would be the best option for the baby. She began to wonder if she was being selfish, wanting to keep the baby; after all, what could she offer, apart from her love? Wayne agreed with the social worker and added his voice to the argument. In the end, they wore her down – it was as simple as that. It would be a struggle to bring up a baby and not fair to the child. The paperwork was filled in and, after a few, last, agonising moments of doubt, completed with her signature.

Once the decision was made, Grace felt content. She was doing the right thing.

Her baby was born on June 1st, a beautiful girl weighing 7lbs 8oz. Exhausted but ecstatic, Grace cradled her baby in her arms. No one had told her she would feel like this, that she would immediately fall in love with her daughter. She was so perfect in every way.

Wayne had called into the hospital to see her. 'She's a real looker. Thank God she takes after her mum and not her dad!'

'Have you held your baby yet?' one of the nurses asked him in passing. 'Go on, she won't bite.'

'Oh, I'm not the ...' He grinned at her mistake but she had already moved on. 'When are the ... you know?' He looked searchingly at Grace.

She shook her head. 'I don't know. It'll be soon, they said. I've got a small bag of things to go with her and I've written her a letter, for when she's old enough to read it.' Her eyes filled with tears. 'Oh Wayne, I don't know if I can bear to let her go!'

'You must,' he said gently. 'It's for the best. Anyway, you've signed all the papers so there's no going back now.'

Later, she did not know how she got through it, how she was able to give her daughter one final kiss and hand her over to a middle-aged woman with pink framed glasses and short, spiky, bright red hair. 'She's called Emily,' she had fretted. 'She's just had a feed. Don't forget the bag of things to go with her.'

'We'll take good care of her until she goes to her new home. We have some lovely people lined up. You're doing the right thing.'

Why did people keep saying that when suddenly it all seemed wrong?

'Can I just ...?' She reached out tentatively.

'No, sorry. We need to get going. The traffic's terrible at this time of the day.' With a final apologetic look, the woman carried her baby off the ward and Grace learnt truly what it meant to have a broken heart.

CHAPTER 28

Emily – January 2017

Emily turned her mini once more into the village of Corriton eager with anticipation. She had so many questions buzzing through her brain. Yesterday had been tricky. Once they had established that this Susan was Iris' daughter, there had been no real opportunity to probe further and, whilst Jennifer now had some answers, she had left feeling slightly empty, still wondering and hoping.

However, she had a feeling of momentousness about this journey this morning, a strong sense that something was going to happen. Everything was finally going to fall into place and maybe, just maybe, she would find a way to meet her real mum. The yearning had become a constant ache in her chest.

She and Jennifer had talked long into the night, reflecting on the day's events, still reeling from the revelations contained within Iris' letter. It had been such a shock for Jennifer to discover blood relatives of whom she had no knowledge. For such a long time, since the deaths of her mother and later her father, she had been cut adrift from family ties and had learnt to be totally self-contained and self-reliant. Her friends had always been her family, she told Emily.

'Now I'm not really sure what to feel,' she admitted. 'I'm not sure I want to be part of a family I don't know. My life was fine as it was.' Then she had smiled ruefully. 'Actually, that's not true. Ever since giving up teaching, I've been searching for something but I didn't know what it was. I thought a fresh challenge would be the answer. Doing up the cottage and setting up a business have been rewarding but they haven't stopped me from feeling lonely. Maybe that's what I've always wanted all along – family.' She shrugged her shoulders. 'So why am I feeling so ...' She struggled to find the right word, '... strange about it all?'

'I think you'll just have to take things one step at a time,' Emily had said. 'I know what you mean. After all, you can choose your friends but you can't choose your family. You'll just have to wait and see how things between you develop. It may be that you become close but equally, you might both decide you would prefer to keep a distance between you. Who knows? It is exciting though, isn't it? And Susan did seem lovely, although we didn't really get to talk to her. Poor woman. It must have been a terrible shock to find out that her mother had another child.'

Jennifer had nodded slowly. 'You're right. I think I need a bit of time to get used to all this and she must feel the same.'

Molly had drifted in and out of the living room throughout the early part of the evening, a serene smile on her pale face. It was another sign that she was getting close, Emily thought. So often, Molly mooched around or sat looking so despairing that Emily could feel her sadness as a tangible thing, heavy and oppressive. It weighed on her as guilt that she had not done more to trace her past and discover the root of Molly's angst. She had said as much to Jennifer.

'Perhaps after tomorrow, if we can finally find out about your mother and maybe even reunite you, she will be free to leave us for good. It is sad to see her trapped in limbo like this, especially now we know more of her personal tragedy and it would be nice to think that she could eventually find peace,' Jennifer had replied solemnly. Then she had grinned at Emily. 'I cannot believe those words just came out of my mouth! I would never have thought that one day I would fret over the fate of a ghost or use such terrible clichés!'

David had arrived then and Emily had left them alone while she went to update Adam with all her news. She had returned some time later to find them in each other's arms, kissing like teenagers. About time, she thought to herself. She spun around, detoured to the kitchen and began filling the kettle as noisily as she could.

'Anyone for coffee?' she had called.

There had been a slight pause and Jennifer had appeared in the doorway, looking dishevelled and bemused in equal measures. 'Emily, you're a guest. I should be making the coffee!'

Emily raised her eyebrows and could not help smirking a little. 'That's ok. I ... er ... thought you might be busy.'

Jennifer flushed and turned away. 'I'll get the mugs. David has two sugars and I have mine black. Just milk for you?'

They had returned to the living room and told David of their plans for the following morning.

'That reminds me,' he had said. 'Caroline has fired Alex's pots and also wanted me to ask you if you'd like to take him to a session she's running tomorrow for mums and tots. She said, if you had other plans, Emily, and wanted to drop Alex off, that would be fine too. She said he would be no trouble. My niece, Anna, her daughter helps her run these sessions and so she could keep an eye on him.'

'That's so kind of Caroline,' Emily exclaimed. 'Alex had been asking about his pots and I know he'd love it, if she's sure she can manage. With all that's been happening, this hasn't been the most exciting week for him.'

'Good. I'll let her know to expect you at nine. Right, I'll be off then.' He had stood and kissed Emily lightly on the cheek.

'I'll see you out,' said Jennifer, heading towards the front door.

'Well I'll say goodnight now then.' Emily leapt forward to intercept Jennifer and envelope her in a quick hug. 'I'll see you in the morning. Night David.'

She strode down the hallway to her bedroom and shut the door behind her, smiling to herself. It was some considerable time later, as she was lying in bed trying to get to sleep, when she heard the front door slam shut and the jangling of keys as Jennifer locked up for the night.

This morning, they had dropped an excited Alex off at Caroline's and driven once more to Corriton. Both women had been quiet during the journey and Emily had turned on her music, humming along to her favourite tracks.

'You've got a great voice,' Jennifer remarked as Emily belted out the chorus of a Beyoncé song. 'Have you ever thought of singing professionally?'

'Don't be daft!'

'No, I mean it. There's a fantastic tone to your voice, sort of Adele meets Leona Lewis, and you definitely have the right looks.'

'Thank you. I'm flattered but I think you're biased and anyway I can't see myself ever wanting to take to the stage. I used to have ambitions but I never wanted to be famous.'

'What was it you wanted to do?' Jennifer asked.

'Oh, when I was at uni I really wanted to be a journalist but then my parents died and I had a bit of a breakdown – never finished the course. Later on, I met Adam and the rest is history. I have been wondering though, just recently, about finishing my degree and getting a proper job, something so I don't feel a complete waste of space.'

'Now you're being daft! There's nothing wrong with staying at home to look after your son.' Jennifer gave her a reassuring smile. 'But soon Alex will be going off to nursery and then school so that would be a great time for you to consider your options.'

'I know.' Emily was silent for a few moments and then added, 'Ever since I found out I was adopted and was given the album with photos of Molly, I've felt that this was something I needed to resolve before I could move on. Does that make sense?'

'Perfectly.' Jennifer patted her arm affectionately. 'Let's hope today is the day we find the final pieces of the puzzle.'

It was quarter past ten when they pulled up outside Susan's house.

'Here we go.' Jennifer gave Emily's hand a squeeze. 'Are you ready?'

'Yep. Let's do it!'

They slid out of the car and headed towards Susan's front door. It opened before they reached it and Susan stood there, smiling shyly at them. Today, she had obviously spent time on her appearance and was wearing a plain, navy shift dress with a floral scarf. Her hair had been styled and she was wearing makeup. She was an attractive woman, Emily thought.

'Hello again.' Susan reached forward to give both Jennifer and Emily a slightly awkward hug. 'Come in. It's a bit calmer here today without the children. I'm sorry about yesterday. I ... well ... you took me completely by surprise and the letter knocked me for six.'

'Please, don't apologise,' Jennifer said quickly. 'We felt really bad for upsetting you like that. There was just no easy way to tell you.'

'No, but I'm glad you did. Shall we sit in the kitchen and I'll get us some coffee, or tea if you prefer.'

They followed her into a spacious, homely room with a tiled floor and pine cabinets. A cafetiere of coffee, a milk jug, a sugar bowl, three mugs and a plate of biscuits sat on a large wooden table in the centre of the kitchen. Susan poured the coffee into the mugs and they sat around the table, watching each other with a degree of wariness and trepidation. Jennifer reached into the large brown, leather bag she was carrying and pulled out her photograph album. 'I've brought some photos of my mum, Elizabeth,' she said, sliding the book across the table. 'I thought you might like to see them.'

Susan turned the pages with trembling fingers. 'Oh,' she sighed. 'Oh, my word, she looks just like Iris. Wait a second. I have some pictures too.' She crossed the kitchen and picked up a pile of old Truprint envelopes. 'I keep meaning to put these in an album but I've never got around to it.'

She handed the pile to Jennifer and she and Emily pored over them while Susan looked at the album.

'There's certainly an unmistakeable resemblance between them and me too,' Susan murmured. 'Look at this.' She pointed to a photo of a teenage Elizabeth grimacing at the camera. 'I have a picture of me at a similar age wearing just that look! Oh, I wish I could have known her! Tell me,' she turned to Jennifer, 'What was she like?'

Jennifer smiled warmly. 'She was a lovely mum,' she said simply. 'She used to stick up for me when my dad was angry and then she could be quite feisty. Her parents were incredibly strict and she was quite rebellious as a teenager, that was how she ended up marrying my dad and having me when she was just sixteen. Sadly, though, my dad was quite overbearing and never really trusted her. She was very beautiful and always drew men's eyes when she walked into a room. They used to argue about it. He would accuse her of flirting when she had done no such thing. I have to say she did have quite a sad life and then she died of cancer when she was only thirty-eight.'

'That must have been awful for you.' Compassion shone in Susan's eyes. 'What did you do?'

Jennifer shrugged. 'Threw myself into work, became an accountant and then retrained as a teacher. Eventually, I ended up as a headteacher in Norfolk, believe it or not, and now I'm retired and running a bed and breakfast cottage in Great Chalkham in Suffolk. That's how I met Emily.'

'Oh,' Susan looked surprised, 'so you're not related? I thought ...' Her voice tailed off.

'No,' Emily chimed in. 'I booked to stay in Jen's cottage because I recognised it in a photograph I was given so I went to Great Chalkham to find some answers and we've ended up here.'

'Oh,' Susan said again. 'I'm afraid I don't understand.' She gave Emily a searching look.

'Sorry. I guess I need to start at the beginning. That might help!' Emily reached for her own capacious, cherry red bag and pulled out Norah's album, the box containing the locket and the letter from her real mother. 'My parents died in a car accident in 2007. That's when I discovered they had adopted me at birth; they had never told me. The solicitor passed on these which had been left with me by my real mum.' She looked up. 'Are you alright, Susan?'

Susan's face was chalk white and she was staring at the brown, leather album initialled N.D.

'This,' she said, reaching forward to stroke the soft cover, 'and this.' She indicated the jewellery box. Slowly shaking her head, she met Emily's eyes. 'I never thought I would see them again. My grandfather gave them to my mum, Iris and she gave them to me when I was just a small child. I remember the moment so clearly. It was when I first saw the woman, dressed in old fashioned, black clothes, sitting at the foot of my bed. I was a little bit frightened but mum explained that it was just my grandma, Norah, watching over me. I couldn't understand that because this woman was young and grandparents, I knew, were older so mum told me that Norah had died after giving birth to her. She said that Norah had made a promise that she would always look after her daughter and that, now I was born, she would watch over me too. Then she showed me the album and the locket. The initials stand for Norah Dunn – that was her maiden name.'

Emily stared at her, open-mouthed. 'Molly,' she breathed and then, 'I can see her too – I have done since I was little but I never knew who she was. I thought she was a figment of my imagination ... and then I was given the album and I realised she was a real person but, until now, I didn't know what the initials stood for. That's why I always called her Molly – I still do – because I never knew her name.'

'Oh, my goodness!' Susan's knuckles were white as she gripped the album. 'That means ...' Her voice tailed off and she continued to stare at Emily, drinking in every detail of her face.

'What does it mean?' Emily asked. 'How come the album ended up with me?'

Susan took a deep breath. 'That's a secret I swore I would never tell another living soul. It's not my secret to tell.' She glanced at the kitchen clock. 'Hopefully, you won't have to wait much longer for the answer to your question.'

'What do you mean?'

Susan shook her head. 'I'm sorry, Emily but ...'

At that moment, there was the rattle of keys in the door. Jennifer and Emily looked expectantly at Susan but she remained sitting at the table, her eyes fixed on the kitchen door.

'Mum?' The voice calling was husky with emotion.

'We're in the kitchen,' Susan called back.

The door burst open and a woman stood framed in the opening. The first thing Emily noticed was her hair – long, wavy and dyed purple. The next was her multi-coloured dress, leggings and black biker boots. Finally, she zoned in on her eyes, green like hers, searching her out across the room and that was when she knew. She was half rising from her chair when the woman took a step into the room.

'Oh, my God!' she exclaimed softly. 'It really is you! Oh, my darling, I never thought I'd see you again.'

They moved towards each other, carefully at first, unsure, hesitant. Then, with a sudden rush, Emily flung herself into her mother's arms.

CHAPTER 29

Jennifer - January 2017

Jennifer watched the scene unfolding before her with a lump in her throat. The two women clung to each other as if they would never let go, the older one murmuring over and over, 'I'm sorry, I'm so sorry,' while she stroked the younger woman's hair.

At last, they pulled apart a little, still holding each other by the arms.

'You really are my mum. I can't believe it. Look!' She reached for the note written all those years before. 'I still have your letter.'

'Grace, come and sit down,' Susan urged gently. 'We've all got a lot of catching up to do.'

Reluctantly, Grace released Emily from her grasp and sat down at the kitchen table. 'Mum phoned me last night. She said that looking at Emily was just like looking at me at that age, although I think I'd already started dyeing my hair by then! She was convinced that you were my daughter, turned up out of the blue so I've been in turmoil ever since. I dropped everything and drove up from London this morning. I *had* to see if she was right.'

'I'm so glad you did.' Emily reached across the table and held Grace's ringless left hand. 'Can you tell me about my dad? Is he still alive? Are you in contact with him? Would he be prepared to see me, do you think?'

Grace sighed heavily. 'I wish I could say yes to all those questions but the truth is that he died of a drug overdose more than twenty years ago. He was a talented guitarist but he fell in with the wrong sort of people. He and I had split up before you were born and I never saw him again.'

No one spoke for a few moments. The mood had changed as everyone waited to see how Emily would react to such tragic news. Eventually, she smiled tremulously. 'That's really sad but I never really felt a connection to him like I did to you. From the first, it was you I was looking for. Can you talk about what happened, you know, with the adoption? You don't have to explain if you'd rather not.'

'Of course. You need to know but first, tell me. What were your adoptive parents like? I always prayed that you were happy with them.'

'I was. They were wonderful and I loved them very much. I was devastated when they were killed in a car crash when I was nineteen. They never told me that I was adopted so it came as a huge shock to receive the album, the locket and your letter. That's when Molly started to make sense to me.'

At Grace's puzzled expression, she then went on to describe how Molly had appeared at different times in her life.

'But that was Norah!' Grace exclaimed. 'She did the same for me - at least she did until I had you. That's when she disappeared for good. I always thought she'd abandoned me but obviously, she was busy watching over you. I'm glad.' She squeezed Emily's hand and then went on to explain the circumstances which led her to give her baby up for adoption. 'After that, I was a mess for a long while. I felt I couldn't come home so I stayed in London. For a while, I lived with a guy called Wayne. He was a good chap and looked after me when you were born but it didn't really work out and we went our separate ways. I was just working in a bar for a while, just struggling to make ends meet. Then I saw an ad asking for volunteers to help a charity called COTS, Children on the Streets. I started helping out on my days off and my life changed. I loved the work so, eventually, I trained to become a social worker and here I am now. I never married again and I always thought of you, wondering how you were. Now, tell me all about you. I see you're married.'

Then it was Emily's turn to provide the highlights of her life. When she mentioned Alex, Grace squealed with delight and sat beside Emily as she scrolled through the hundreds of pictures on her phone.

'So where is the darling boy?' Grace asked. 'With his dad?'

'No, Adam's in Australia on a business trip. He has his own wine importing company,' she added proudly. 'Alex is at a pottery class this morning. He's already showing a great deal of artistic talent.'

'Wow. What a family! I'm so proud of you, Emily.' Grace threw her arms around her daughter once more, hugging her fiercely. 'We have so much lost time to make up.' She leaned back and scanned Emily's face, suddenly anxious. 'That's if you want to ...?'

'More than anything!' Emily's eyes filled with tears. 'I'm so happy to have found you at last ... and a granny too.' She smiled at Susan over Grace's shoulder.

'There's a whole extended family for you to meet. Grace has a brother, Tom, and his wife is called Lucy. Of course, you met their three scallywags yesterday - your cousins. You may well regret all this when you get to know them better!' Susan joked.

'It all feels a bit surreal at the moment. It's difficult to take it all in,' Emily mused and then she had a sudden thought. 'Hey Jen, this means we're related too!'

'Yes.' Jennifer pondered for a moment. 'Your granny is my aunt. Does that make us second cousins or something like that?'

'No idea,' Emily said. 'It's just all fantastic ... amazing ... incredible. I'm *so* happy right now.'

'Me too and I can't wait to meet my grandson,' Grace began flicking through the pictures on the phone once more. 'He looks completely adorable.'

'Why don't you come back to Chalkham with us?' Emily said excitedly. 'Jen has another room at the cottage you could use ... if that's ok with you, Jen?' she added belatedly. Jennifer nodded. 'Then you could spend a few days getting to know us both. Oh, that would be so cool! Please say you will.'

'Oh Emily, there's nothing I'd like more. I could do today and tomorrow but I need to be back in London for a case conference on Friday. Would that suit you?'

'That would be just great and, when Adam is back, we'll come down to London to see you. Oh, this is all just so exciting!'

Jennifer took a moment to observe the happy faces around her. Emily was almost bouncing with joy, in that endearing, puppy-like way she had; Susan had the air of someone from whom a great weight had been lifted, her features lightened with relief; Grace's face was luminous with love. She could not tear her eyes away from Emily as if that visual contact was keeping them together and the merest blink might cause her to vanish. Jennifer felt the emotion of the moment raw in her throat. These women were all connected to her, part of her life's tapestry and her future would be inextricably woven with their threads. It was an overwhelming thought but one, Jennifer realised, that made her incredibly happy. Now she was a part of a family she did not know existed and she knew she wanted to embrace it fully.

They drove back to Chalkham in convoy, Grace's old, green Peugeot following Emily's mini. Susan had stayed behind as she had to pick up her grandchildren from school later that afternoon. On the journey, Emily chattered non-stop, making plans, changing them and, most of all, talking about Grace. Jennifer listened tolerantly, still basking in the warmth that had enveloped her in Susan's kitchen.

Then David called her, wanting to know how the visit had gone.

'That's just fantastic!' he exclaimed when Jennifer had given him all the details. 'Tell you what, why don't I take you out tonight and we leave the new mum and daughter alone to get to know each other better?'

Jennifer thought for a moment. 'That could be a good plan. I'll check with Emily and call you back.'

Emily grinned knowingly when the last part of the conversation was relayed to her but kept her voice neutral as she said, 'That would be very kind of you and David. I can't deny that it would be good to spend this first evening alone with her. Are you sure you don't mind?'

'I expect I'll live,' Jennifer replied drily.

'Excellent,' David's voice was filled with satisfaction when she returned his call. He lowered his voice seductively. 'I have to admit I haven't been able to think of much else this morning other than kissing you again. I'll cook for you at my house. Then we can be alone.'

Jennifer felt the heat in her cheeks at his words and glanced surreptitiously at Emily who was studiously focused on the road ahead. 'That would be lovely, thank you. Shall we say seven o'clock? That will give me time to prepare something for Emily, Grace and Alex first.'

As she returned her phone to her bag, Emily began to argue. 'You don't need to cook us anything. We could get a takeaway or fish and chips. You just concentrate on enjoying your evening out. You deserve a treat. You've been amazing this week.'

'Absolutely not,' Jennifer insisted. 'You're my guests and it's no trouble to cook for you before I go out. Now I know you're family, it's even more important and I *do* think your first meal with your mum should be a bit more special than fish and chips.'

Emily sighed. Already she knew Jennifer well enough to know it was pointless to argue further. 'Ok then, as long as you let me help with the preparations.'

By the time they arrived at Caroline's house, the other parents and children had already left and Alex was sitting at her kitchen table eating some marmite fingers. Grace had waited outside in her car, wanting her first meeting with her grandson to take place in a more private setting.

'Look, my pots, mummy!' he shouted excitedly, spraying toast crumbs everywhere and wriggling off his chair. 'Look!' He toddled across the kitchen to where his previously fired and glazed, rather misshapen pots sat on a worktop.

'Wow! Don't they look good. Those were the ones you made last time. What have you made today?'

'We've been making some sculptures today with some self-drying clay. Alex chose to make cats.' Caroline indicated four shapes, all with long, curly appendages, alongside the pots.

'Ah, so I see. He loves cats.' She smiled at Caroline, grateful that she had identified the strange looking objects. 'Well done, darling. I can see you've given them some lovely tails.'

'And whiskers. Look mummy!'

Emily peered closer. Sure enough, there were some rather thick lines drawn on each head. 'Oh yes, I can see them now. You have done well. Now, we need to get back to the cottage. I have a surprise for you when we get there.'

Caroline raised her eyebrows. 'Did today go well then?' she asked, as she wrapped Alex's creations carefully in bubble wrap and placed them in a small box.

'It went completely brilliantly!' Emily replied happily. 'Thank you so much for looking after Alex this morning. What do I owe you?'

'Oh, first session's always free – like a taster session. I'll charge you next time.'

Emily gave her a swift hug. ''You're so kind. What do you say to Caroline, Alex?'

'Thank you,' he said obediently.

'Good boy. It's been a pleasure.' Caroline handed over the box and they headed back to Horseshoes Cottage.

Alex's first meeting with his grandmother did not go well. Sadly, Alex had anticipated that the promised surprise would be something rather more exciting than a strange woman with purple hair and he immediately burst into tears.

'I expect he's a little bit tired,' Emily murmured apologetically. 'I *am* sorry.'

Grace put her arm around her crestfallen daughter. 'No worries. He'll get used to me. It was a bit much to expect he'd want to cuddle someone he doesn't know just because she's his grandmother. It will take a bit of time. I'm just thankful that I didn't get the same reaction from *you* when I made my dramatic appearance!'

'Why don't you put Alex down for a nap while we have lunch – a very late one?' Jennifer suggested as she glanced at her watch. 'Then maybe we could go back to the graveyard later this afternoon. Iris' letter did suggest that Norah and her son were buried there when she wrote that she had returned to Chalkham to bury him in the churchyard. I feel we still need to find their final resting place to bring the search full circle, back to its beginning.'

Emily nodded solemnly. 'Good idea.' Then she looked across at Alex, still having a tantrum on the living room floor and ignoring Grace's efforts to engage him in a Lego building session. 'But I'm not sure Alex will succumb quietly to being put to bed!'

It was a dark, overcast afternoon when they arrived once more at the church. Alex, dressed warmly in woollen hat and padded jacket skipped along happily beside them, his mood much improved for a short sleep. As Emily had predicted, he did not settle willingly but she and Grace had combined forces and sung lullabies until he had finally closed his eyes.

'You have a wonderful voice,' Emily had whispered as they tiptoed out of the bedroom. 'I'm not surprised you were a professional singer.'

'Thank you but not a very successful one. I've never regretted becoming a social worker though. In the beginning, it felt a bit like reparation for losing you, trying to help other families having troubles. It was a way of coming to terms with myself and what I'd done.'

'You shouldn't feel guilty for doing what you thought was best at the time.'

'I know but anyone who has given a child up for adoption must feel like a part of them is missing. Iris obviously felt exactly the same.'

Grace had read Iris' letter with tears in her eyes. 'History really does repeat itself,' she'd said quietly, 'except that my story has had a happier ending. That, too, is thanks to Iris. Without her letter, we may never have found each other.'

Emily had reached forward to squeeze her hand. 'I would never have given up until I found you,' she muttered, her voice husky with emotion.

They stood silently beside Arthur's grave. 'My great, great grandfather,' Emily said solemnly, 'and husband of Norah, where it all started.'

My great grandfather and yours too.' Grace smiled at Jennifer. 'I'm sure he must have been a wonderful man.'

'Definitely if his ancestors are anything to go by!' she answered. 'I'll head this way to look for Norah and her son, James.'

They split up and headed in three different directions, carefully scanning every headstone they passed. Many were so old it was difficult to read the names engraved there and Jennifer was beginning to wonder if they would ever find them when she saw Molly, standing patiently at the furthest edge of the graveyard. She smiled and her shoulders relaxed. Of course, Molly would help them find her resting place. She should not have expected anything else. She picked her way between the stones and made a beeline for the silent figure in black. By the time she got there, Molly had disappeared but she was right. The worn headstone bore the legend:

In loving memory
James Arthur Fletcher (Jimmy).
Born 7 April, 1928. Died 22 August, 1930.
Our angel.

Also, Norah Grace Fletcher.
Born June 1, 1910. Died September 15, 1930.
Beloved wife and mother.
Rest in peace.'

Somehow, it seemed wrong to shout across a burial ground so Jennifer walked briskly to where the other women were still searching and led them solemnly to the grave.

'Molly, or Norah, was standing right there,' she said quietly after they had spent a period of silent contemplation. 'She's still with us, still watching. I wonder if she always will be.'

'Poor Norah. She was only twenty when she died,' Grace murmured, her eyes downcast.

'And poor Arthur. He'd lost his son and then his wife. It's heart-breaking.' Emily laid a small bouquet of flowers against the weather-beaten stone. She'd called in at the florist's shop on the high street as they made their pilgrimage back to the church.

The sombre mood lasted as they stood, united, three descendants around the grave. Then Jennifer forced a smile. 'It *was* tragic,' she agreed, 'but today is not a day for feeling sad. The spirit of Norah has brought us all together at last and I'm sure she wouldn't want us to spend that time moping by her headstone. We owe it to her to make the absolute most of every moment we spend together. It was her gift to us. We mustn't waste it.'

'You're right.' Emily took a step back from the grave and grasped Alex by the hand as he made a bid for escape. 'Life goes on. It's time to leave.'

The three women and the small child made their way slowly back to the path and out of the churchyard unaware of the slight, ephemeral figure in black, still watching anxiously.

It was a quarter to seven when the doorbell rang. Jennifer had just put on her coat ready to leave and when she opened the door, she found David standing there, tall and broad shouldered, in a dark overcoat.

'Oh hi.' Jennifer immediately felt flustered. 'I was just about to walk up the road to yours. Has there been a change of plan?'

'No change.' His deep, gravelly voice made her heart skip erratically. 'I've come to escort you.'

'Don't be daft. It's only a few hundred yards and I'm a big girl. I'm more than capable of walking myself.' The old irritation at the way he undermined her independence threatened to surface but melted away when she saw the warmth in his brown eyes, crinkled in a smile.

'I know that.' He leaned forward to brush his lips against her cheek. They felt cool and firm against her flushed skin. 'You'll just have to indulge me. I'm old fashioned about things like this. I don't want my woman walking up a dark lane on her own.'

His proprietary tone would, just a few short months ago, have pricked an indignant response but now she felt a glow building inside her at the words 'my woman'. Goodness, she admonished herself, she would soon be heading back to the dark ages and allowing him to drag her back to his cave by her hair if she carried on like this! She dismissed the thought, took his proffered arm and stepped out into the cold, night air. It felt good, leaning into his strong frame, walking companionably, side-by-side. They chatted about the day's revelations and he asked how the relationship between Emily and Grace was going.

'Love at first sight,' she said, smiling at the thought. 'They can't get enough of each other. I suspect it will always be like that for them.'

There was a pause as she waited for David to respond. He cleared his throat. 'I can't ignore an opening like that. I was going to wait until we were inside but, I have to admit, it's easier out here, in the dark.' He stopped walking and turned to face her. 'That's how I feel about you, Jen ... love at first sight, I mean ... I can't get enough of you ... all that stuff. When my wife died, I never thought I'd feel like this again, but I do and I don't want to waste any more time. After all, we're not getting any younger.' He coughed again while she listened, hardly daring to breathe. 'So, what I'm trying to say, in this hopeless, tongue-tied, schoolboy fashion, is that I love you and, when you've got used to the idea, I'd like to spend the rest of my life with you.'

He continued walking and she fell once more into step beside him, still reeling at his words. The lights from his house were much nearer now but she was glad of the darkness concealing the torrent of confused emotions, heating her skin and scrambling her brain. His declaration had stunned her into silence and her defences were already leaping to the fore, just as they always had when men had wanted more from her than she was willing to give.

The silence stretched and, without warning, David stopped walking once more. 'Can you say something, please? I realise that this has come as a bit of a shock but the suspense is killing me.'

She stood still, composing her words carefully. It was too soon; she was used to her independence; she valued him as friend. The trite words, her customary responses, floated through her brain and she grasped at them thankfully.

'Please, Jen. Just tell me what you're thinking.'

It was the vulnerability she heard in his voice which got to her, which cracked through the self-imposed walls she'd built around herself. He was being open and honest, putting his pride on the line. She owed it to him to do the same.

Taking a deep breath, she began, 'I'm not entirely sure how I feel ...' Immediately, she sensed a slump in his shoulders as he braced himself for her rejection. 'But ... it *could* be love. I know I haven't felt this out of control with anyone else. Is that what love is ... this dizzy, giggly feeling that seems to be over-riding my common sense?'

'Sounds good to me.' She could hear the smile in his voice as he began walking again, more briskly now. 'Let's get inside. I want to show you just how much I love you.'

Heat rushed through her body. She could not wait either. It seemed to take an age to get the door open as David first fumbled the lock and then dropped his key. Swearing under his breath, he swung his torch around until he located it and tried once more. At last, the door swung open and they stepped inside. Suddenly shy, Jennifer undid the buttons on her coat and slipped it off her shoulders while David yanked off his coat with a great deal more haste. Their eyes met for a moment, red-hot with passion, and they fell into each other's arms.

CHAPTER 30

Emily – January 2017

'I'm just so happy. The only thing that would make me happier is if you were back here with me.' Emily had spent the last twenty minutes on her mobile to Adam, updating him with the day's events. 'I can't wait for you to meet her and for her to meet you. She's amazing, Adam. We just bonded straight away. It's like I've known her all my life, except of course I haven't. We've got so much catching up to do. I feel I can finally move on with my life now. Everything is falling into place.'

'I'm so pleased for you, baby.' Adam's voice sounded slightly disembodied, like he was standing at the end of a long, empty corridor. 'I'm missing you terribly but the trip is going well and I should be home by the end of next week. Make sure you give Alex lots of kisses from me.'

'Will do. I'm missing you too. I probably ought to get back to Mum and Alex now. I've left them alone for the last twenty minutes and you can have too much of a good thing. I don't want to test their relationship too far when it's only just beginning. Bye, darling. Love you lots. Have a good day.'

'Will do. Love you too.'

Emily pocketed her phone and returned to the living room where she found her son and her mother stretched out on their backs on the floor, eyes closed.

'We're playing sleeping lions,' Grace explained, opening one eye, 'which means I've just lost! Well done, Alex. You've won. You've beaten Grandma.'

Emily grinned. 'Great choice of game,' she remarked. 'If it had continued much longer, I expect Alex might have been asleep for good!'

'Exactly. That was my cunning plan!'

After Alex was tucked up in bed, they sat drinking wine and talked long into the night, telling each other their life stories, completely engrossed in discovering all they had missed, good and bad. The only discordant note was struck by Molly who paced fretfully in and out of the room on a number of occasions.

'I thought she would be happy now we are altogether,' Emily mused, her frown creased in concern. 'I wonder what's bothering her.'

Grace shrugged her shoulders. 'It does seem odd. I really hoped, for her sake, that she could rest easy now, that maybe we would never see her again. Yet here she is. Maybe she can never escape.'

'Oh, that would be truly sad.' Emily watched as the troubled figure disappeared once more. 'I wish there was something we could do to help her.' She glanced at her watch and got to her feet. 'Hey, look at the time. It's almost one o'clock. Perhaps we'd better call it a night.'

Grace stood and smiled at her daughter. 'Today has been the best day of my life. I'm so happy you found me.'

'Me too!' They hugged each other tightly.

'Hey, you know what? I haven't heard Jen come in. I hope she's alright with that chap, David,' Grace murmured.

Emily grinned knowingly. 'Oh, I'm sure she's fine,' she replied.

Jennifer was busy cooking breakfast and singing along to the radio when Emily and Alex surfaced the following morning.

'Mm, someone's in a good mood,' Emily muttered under her breath.

'Morning,' Jennifer beamed. 'Did you sleep well?'

'Brilliant thanks. How about you?' she added mischievously.

'Oh, fine, thank you.' Jennifer coloured slightly. 'Isn't it a beautiful morning?'

'It really is.' Emily wandered over to the window as Alex began tucking into a bowl of cereal. Outside, the sun was already shining and the sky was a cloudless blue. 'Perhaps this morning we could do a walk all around the village. I know we've been up and down the High Street several times and to the play area but I would really love to get a proper look at Willow Farm and maybe wander down to the lake. From a distance, it looks really pretty. It's hard to imagine it was the site of such a terrible tragedy when the chalk pits were there.'

'That sounds like a plan. I'm up for it. Morning, Grace.'

Grace appeared dressed in black leggings and a baggy, purple sweater the same shade as her hair. She yawned theatrically and took a seat at the table. 'Morning. I'd offer to help but my brain is mush until I've had my first cup of coffee. That smells good.' She smiled at Alex. 'Got a healthy appetite, I see. How are you my darling boy? Too busy to talk? Fair enough.'

Emily relayed her suggestion for a walk and Grace responded with enthusiasm. 'I love walking. I just don't get enough time for it these days.' She patted her stomach ruefully. 'I could certainly do with the exercise. It's been a while since I was as slender as you.'

After they had finished breakfast, Jennifer had a few jobs to do so they agreed to go out at ten o'clock.

'That will give me time to get cleared up and organised for our meal tonight. David's coming around so we could all eat together, if that's ok with you both?' she asked.

'Sounds great,' Emily replied, looking across at Grace.

'Fine with me.'

While Jennifer and Grace cleared the dishes, Emily took Alex in the living room. A fat, tabby cat was stretched out on the wall opposite the cottage and Alex immediately rushed to the window.

'Cat! Want to stroke it, Mummy.'

'It's resting, darling. Let's not disturb it. Maybe we can get a closer look if it's still there when we go out later.'

Alex's chubby face creased in a frown but then he spotted the toy garage and cars he had discovered at the bottom of the toy box the day before and he darted across the room.

'Play with me, Mummy,' he demanded.

'Just for a little while. Then I'll need to go and get ready for our walk.'

For the next twenty minutes, Emily drove toy cars, on all fours, around the carpet. They had an exciting car chase until Emily, legs and back weary from crawling, suggested a new game, sorting the cars into a car park. She left Alex driving the cars, complete with sound effects, into wiggly rows and retired to their room to change into more presentable clothes than the joggers she'd pulled on that morning and put some make up on. Thoughtfully, she stared at her face in the mirror. Already, she looked different, happier, more relaxed, ready to move forward. For so long, she had been meshed in the mysteries of her history, ever since that fateful day when she'd discovered her parents were not who she thought they were. For a while, when she met Adam and then gave birth to Alex, she had felt she could be content without knowing, without unlocking the key to her past, but then Molly had reappeared. Was that because she was once more questioning her future? Was it because she felt unable to move forward without first taking a step back and having another attempt to discover Molly's real identity? Now, she and Jennifer together had unravelled the mystery of the photographs in the scrapbook and her link to them. There was still so much she didn't know but that was ok, she thought. She knew enough and had discovered her real mum; that was the most important thing of all.

She finished brushing her hair, added a touch of gloss to her lips and glanced at her watch. Ten minutes. It was time to prise Alex away from his cars and get him ready to go out. She remembered the cat and hoped it was still lying on the wall – if so, it could provide a useful incentive to get Alex to leave his game and go to the bathroom, something he was always reluctant to do.

When she entered the living room, her first glance was at the wall but the cat had gone. Damn. It would have to be plan B. A sweep of the room revealed that Alex was not there either and she frowned slightly, quashing her immediate tendency to panic. He must be with Grace. She had heard her voice earlier, talking to Alex.

'Mum,' she called as she knocked on the door. It felt strange, that word on her lips, but right.

Grace flung open the door. 'Just coming. My word!' Her green appraised Emily's brown, suede trousers, cashmere sweater and a scarf in autumn shades artfully arranged around her neck. 'Don't you look gorgeous! I still can't believe I have such a beautiful daughter!'

Emily was already looking over her shoulder. 'Is Alex with you?' she asked abruptly.

'No.' Grace was immediately concerned. 'He was still playing with that garage when I went out to my car about ten minutes ago.'

Emily's lips tightened. 'Don't worry,' she said, turning on her heel. 'He must be with Jen.'

'No,' Jennifer responded when Emily found her coming out of her sitting room. 'Isn't he still in the living room? Don't worry, Em. He won't be far away. He can't get out of the cottage. Perhaps, he's playing a game of hide and seek.'

'Alex,' Emily called. 'Where are you? Alex, it's time to leave.' Her voice was tight with suppressed panic.

'Alex!' All three women began calling but there was no response ... then they discovered that the front door was not completely closed.

'Oh no!' Grace wailed. 'I thought I had shut it when I came back in.'

'It's not your fault.' Jennifer laid a hand on her arm. 'It's mine. That door has been sticking for a week now. I should have got it fixed.'

Emily was not listening. She had already charged out of the door and into the lane. 'Alex!' she shouted, 'Alex! Oh my God!' Trembling, she ran up the lane and round the bend towards David Brewer's house but there was no sign of him and she sped back towards the cottage where Grace was waiting.

'Jen's round the back looking. Try not to worry; he'll not have gone far.'

Emily turned to her, wild-eyed, taut with anxiety. 'But he's not got a coat on and he's just in his slippers,' she wailed.

'We'll find him,' Grace said firmly. 'Now think. Where is he most likely headed?'

'I don't know … the play area, maybe … or he might have followed the cat … he could have gone anywhere.'

'He's not around the back,' Jennifer called as she reappeared from the right-hand side of the cottage. 'We need to split up and search in different directions.' She grasped Emily's arm. 'Grace, you go towards the village. Ask anyone you meet if they've seen him. He may already be sitting in someone's shop waiting for us to collect him. I'll head back up the hill. Emily, you take the track along the field which goes to the wood and, beyond that, the lake. We'll soon have him back, don't worry.'

Emily's face was ashen. 'The lake!' she gasped in horror.

'It's all fenced. He can't fall in and, anyway, he won't have gone that far. Right, let's get going. Have you got your phones with you so whoever finds him can call the rest?' They all nodded. 'We'll find him, Em.'

She headed briskly up the lane, calling Alex's name as she went. Grace set off in the opposite direction and Emily jogged along the track, criss-crossing so she could peer frenziedly into the ditches running either side of it. This could not be happening, she told herself. It had to be just a nightmare; she could not lose her son. At that thought, bile rose in her throat and she stopped to be sick, carelessly wiping her mouth with the back of her hand. Where could he be? Maybe, he had wandered outside and someone had snatched him. She had read books and real-life news stories with that scenario. Cold terror sliced through her body like a knife through butter as she plunged forward, desperately scanning the terrain around her. Everything, though, was just has it should be: fields green with wheat, a few centimetres high, trees with bare branches, ditches muddy with recent rain, the track itself, rough and uneven. Surely he had not come this way, not in his slippers. She should have insisted on going towards the village; that was the most likely route he would have taken.

Then, at the edge of the wood, she saw something … something pale … a face. 'Alex.' She gasped his name but it was not him. The figure was too tall and dressed in black. 'Molly,' she breathed and then, 'Norah.' Was this how it was for her when Jimmy had gone missing? Was this how she spent the empty hours, searching for the child she had lost? The fates were merging the present and the past in the most horrific way possible. Was history going to repeat itself?

She hurried towards the wood, towards the waiting figure. When she was close enough to see her eyes, yearning, reaching out to her, Molly turned and drifted into the wood, with Emily following her. Suddenly, she turned off the track and headed through a narrow gap between the trees. With blind faith, Emily followed, stumbling over brambles, unshed tears burning her eye sockets.

And then she saw him, curled up, wedged against the white bark of a silver birch tree. He was not moving; she was too late. Just like Norah, she had been unable to save her son.

'Alex!' she cried as she sped towards him. 'Alex!'

At the sound of her voice, he turned a tear-stained face towards her. 'I couldn't reach it,' he croaked as she flung herself beside him and gathered him into her arms.

'Oh, Alex, I was so worried. What are you doing out here?'

'I couldn't reach it,' he repeated, pointing up at the tree.

'What, darling? What couldn't you reach?'

'Cat.'

She looked up and there, peering suspiciously down at them from one of the lower branches, was the green-eyed tabby.

'Oh, Alex!' She hugged him tightly, breathless with the relief flooding through her. In a moment, she would call Grace and Jennifer but, for now, she held her son as if she would never let him go. 'Thank you,' she whispered, 'thank you.' Her eyes met Molly's and she saw the joy she was feeling mirrored there. Then it was gone, so fleeting she wondered if she had imagined it, and Molly was gone too. It was to be the last time she ever saw her.

Later, when they were all safely back at the cottage drinking tea, they unanimously agreed to stay in for the rest of the day. Instead, they sat together in the living room, taking turns to play with Alex, who was completely unfazed by his adventure, and discussing how, in the space of one short week, all their lives had changed.

Jennifer had spoken more of the pupil who had died and how that loss had had a profound effect on her. 'Up until that point, I thought I'd got my life all mapped out, just how I wanted it,' she said. 'Then a child in my care died and it made me realise that I was not the cool, self-contained person I thought I was. I was an emotional wreck for a while and I ended up having counselling. At those sessions, I talked a lot about my mother and the grief I'd kept bottled up inside since her death came flooding out. It made me realise that I needed a completely fresh start, something new to get my teeth into, and that's how I ended up here, with a bit of help from Molly, of course. This week, and meeting all of you, has made me realise how lonely I was. I've never admitted that before, not even to myself. Now, for the first time in a very long time, I have people I can call family. I can't tell you how special that makes me feel.'

'Aw.' Grace reached across to give her a hug. 'You're a very special person, Jen,' she said sincerely before adding, 'and a great cook. With those skills, you'd be welcome at any family dinner!'

'I'm thinking about going back to uni,' Emily announced suddenly. 'Alex will soon be starting nursery and it's time I started pulling my weight. I don't want to be the only underachiever in this family.'

'That's great, Emily,' Grace enthused. 'Any ideas about what you might do?'

'I'll need to check the courses at the local universities. I would want to live at home and commute but I'd really like to do a writing course. I'd love to base a novel around Norah's life, maybe.' She looked up and gave an embarrassed smile at the two women sitting with her. 'Just a thought. It probably won't come to anything. I'm not even sure I have the skills to write a book.'

'Darling, you're my wonderful, talented daughter. Of course, you could write a book. I think that's a great idea!' Grace exclaimed.

Jennifer smiled in agreement. 'Norah certainly deserves some kind of tribute. In person and in spirit, she was an amazing woman.'

That night, Emily read Alex one of his favourite stories and tucked him up in bed. She'd spoken earlier to Adam but hadn't mentioned the day's drama. It was still too painful to speak of it; she would tell him when he returned home on Friday, next week. The trip had gone really well, he told her and he'd agreed good terms with three new suppliers.

She was still trying to come to terms with what had happened herself and lots remained unexplained. She still couldn't understand how a three-year-old boy, wearing just his slippers on his feet, could have walked over a mile chasing a cat but all Alex would say was, 'I wanted to stroke it but it ran away.'

'Weren't you frightened?' she asked.

'No, don't be silly, Mummy.'

'I know. You're my brave boy but you *had* been crying when I found you,' she prompted.

He thought for a moment. 'I wanted to climb the tree to rescue the cat like the prince in Wa … Wa … Wapun..'

'Rapunzel,' Emily supplied. 'I see. Then, you were very brave.'

'But I couldn't. I was too little so I cried.'

Tenderly, she stroked his hair. 'Well I want you to promise me that you won't ever, ever run off again. Poor Mummy was really worried about you.'

'Sorry, Mummy,' he said solemnly, snuggling beneath the covers.

'That's alright. I just want to keep you safe, that's all.' She kissed his forehead and reached across to dim the light.

'Who was the lady, Mummy?' he asked sleepily.

Her hand stilled. 'What lady?'

He wrinkled his nose. 'The lady who kept trying to stop me. She kept getting in my way.'

'What lady, darling?' Emily asked again.

'Sad lady ... wearing a funny dress ...' He looked up at her with sudden inspiration. 'She looked like you.'

'Ah,' Emily smiled and reached once more for the light. 'That was Molly. She was looking after you, just like she had always looked after Mummy. She was my great, great grandmother, Norah but I always call her Molly.' Gently, she smoothed a blond curl from his face.

'Great ... grand ... lady.' Alex's voice had thickened drowsily.

'She was,' she nodded.

EPILOGUE

stand alone staring at the cold, starry sky. The night surrounds me and I can feel the silence humming, throbbing like a heartbeat. In this moment, I feel my smallness, my insignificance. I feel the world relentlessly spinning past as I watch.

I feel again my sense of otherness but it is no longer strange to me. Through unravelling my past, I have woven myself into my family tapestry. It is unique, rich with colour but its brightness is edged with dark places, the light and shade of my past and my future. I am no longer a loose thread, dangling alone. Now, I am bound and inextricably linked with other threads, other lives, joined in love.

My role in the tapestry is not yet finished. I am still weaving, alongside others, forming new patterns but, for the moment, at least, I have found my place.

I know where I belong.

ACKNOWLEDGEMENTS

It has long been my ambition to write a novel - there have been many failed and incomplete attempts along the way – and at long last, here it is. Thank you to anyone who has taken the trouble to read it. I do hope you enjoyed it!

Thank you particularly to my friends and family who have not only read it but have said nice things and encouraged me to self-publish.

A special thank you to my sister Sara, daughter Alex and husband Mark who took their roles as proof-readers seriously and spotted my mistakes. If there are any I have failed to rectify, I hope you will forgive me.

My son, Rob, took on the task of book cover designer. Thank you for doing such an amazing job.

Finally, I'd like to thank you, the reader, for choosing to read The Girl in the Scrapbook. If you enjoyed it, I would be very grateful if you could spare the time to post a review. This will help other readers to find it. You may also enjoy my second novel, Who to Trust.

I'd love to hear from you. My website is https://carolynrufflesauthor.com/

You'll also find me on Twitter, Facebook and Instagram.

Printed in Poland
by Amazon Fulfillment
Poland Sp. z o.o., Wrocław